Praise for *New York Times* bestselling author Cathy McDavid

"McDavid's characters are wonderful, and her story really showcases the hardships and love it takes to blend families."

—*RT Book Reviews* on *Cowboy for Keeps*

"McDavid does a fine job portraying a complex heroine dealing with immense guilt and self-doubt. This romantic story has some beautifully crafted, tender moments."

—*RT Book Reviews* on *Come Home, Cowboy*, Top Pick

"If you want a deep and emotional read, don't miss *More Than a Cowboy* by Cathy McDavid."

—*HarlequinJunkie.com*

Praise for *New York Times* bestselling author Lenora Worth

"The final installment in Worth's CHAIM series ends things with a bang. All the previous CHAIM agents are involved and the book closes with a satisfying finish."

—*RT Book Reviews* on *The Soldier's Mission*

"*Secret Agent Minister*, by Lenora Worth, is a fun and danger-filled treat, with love blossoming along the way."

—*RT Book Reviews*

"This second in the Texas Ranger Justice series solves one mystery as it skillfully advances the ongoing one."

—*RT Book Reviews* on the *New York Times* bestseller *Body of Evidence*

HOME ON THE RANCH:
UNBRANDED

New York Times **Bestselling Authors**
CATHY McDAVID
LENORA WORTH

HARLEQUIN® HOME ON THE RANCH

ISBN-13: 978-1-335-02040-6

First published as Last Chance Cowboy by Harlequin Books in 2011 and That Wild Cowboy by Harlequin Books in 2014.

Home on the Ranch: Unbranded
Copyright © 2017 by Harlequin Books S.A.

The publisher acknowledges the copyright holders of the individual works as follows:

Last Chance Cowboy
Copyright © 2011 by Cathy McDavid

That Wild Cowboy
Copyright © 2014 by Lenora H. Nazworth

Recycling programs for this product may not exist in your area.

Printed in U.S.A.

™ www.Harlequin.com

CONTENTS

Since 2006, *New York Times* bestselling author **Cathy McDavid** has been happily penning contemporary Westerns for Harlequin. Every day she gets to write about handsome cowboys riding the range or busting a bronc. It's a tough job, but she's willing to make the sacrifice. Cathy shares her Arizona home with her own real-life sweetheart and a trio of odd pets. Her grown twins have left to embark on lives of their own, and she couldn't be prouder of their accomplishments.

Books by Cathy McDavid

Harlequin Western Romance

Mustang Valley

Last Chance Cowboy
Her Cowboy's Christmas Wish
Baby's First Homecoming
Cowboy for Keeps
Her Holiday Rancher
Come Home, Cowboy
Having the Rancher's Baby
Rescuing the Cowboy

Harlequin American Romance

Reckless, Arizona

More Than a Cowboy
Her Rodeo Man
The Bull Rider's Son

Visit the Author Profile page at Harlequin.com for more titles.

LAST CHANCE
COWBOY

CATHY McDAVID

Chapter 1

The trail, narrow and steep, all but disappeared as it wrapped around the sheer mountain ledge. Good thing heights didn't bother him, Gavin Powell thought as his horse's hoof slipped and sent a shower of rocks tumbling to the ravine bottom forty feet below. He loosened his reins, giving the paint mare her head. She was small but sure-footed and carefully picked her way along the ledge with the concentration of a tightrope walker.

This wasn't a trail for novices—not one on which Gavin took the customers of his family's riding stable. He'd discovered the trail as a teenager over fifteen years ago and rode it every now and then when he craved peace and solitude.

Shaking his head, he chuckled dismally. Who'd have ever thought he'd need to retreat to this remote trail in order to find solitude? Not Gavin. Until a few years ago, their nearest neighbors had been fifteen miles down a single lane road that saw little traffic. Now, their nearest neighbors were at the end of the long drive leading from what little remained of Powell Ranch.

All nine hundred of them.

Gavin pushed away the thought. He'd come here to relax and unwind, not work himself into a sweat. Besides, if he was going to expend large amounts of mental and emotional energies, it would be on one of his many pressing personal problems, not something he was powerless to change.

The mare abruptly stopped, balancing on a precipice no wider than her shoulders. Gavin had to tuck his left arm close to his side or rub the sleeve of his denim jacket against the rugged rock face.

"Come on, Shasta." He nudged the mare gently. "Now's not the time to lose your courage."

She raised her head but remained rooted in place, her ears twitching slightly and her round eyes staring out across the ravine.

Rather than nudge her again, Gavin reached for the binoculars he carried in his saddlebags, only to realize he'd forgotten to bring them along. Pushing back the brim of his cowboy hat, he squinted against the glaring noonday sun, searching the peaks and gullies. The mare obviously sensed something, and he trusted her instincts more than he trusted his own.

All at once, she tensed and let out a shrill whinny, her sides quivering.

"What do you see, girl?"

Shasta snorted in reply.

Gavin continued scanning the rugged mountain terrain. Just as he was ready to call it quits, he spotted movement across the ravine. A black shape traveled down the steep slope, zigzagging between towering saguaro cacti and prickly cholla. Too dark for a mule deer, too large for a coyote and too fast for a human, the shape could be only one thing.

The wild mustang!

He reached again for his saddlebags, but he'd forgotten his camera, too. Dammit. Well, he really didn't need another picture. Especially one from such a far distance. He'd already taken dozens of the mustang, many of which he'd sent to the U.S. Bureau of Land Management when he'd first spotted the horse. All he'd received in response was a polite letter thanking him for the information and giving a weak assurance they would investigate the matter.

That was June. It was now October.

The BLM probably figured the horse was an escapee from one of the residents in Mustang Village, the community now occupying the land once belonging to Gavin's family. Or that the horse had crossed over from the Indian reservation on the other side of the McDowell Mountains. The last wild mustangs left this part of Arizona more than sixty years ago, or so the stories his grandfather used to tell him went. As a teenager, his grandfather had rounded up wild mustangs. No way could this horse be one of them.

But Gavin's heart told him different. Maybe, by some miracle, one descendant had survived.

Gavin was going to capture him. He'd made the decision two months ago when yet another phone call to the BLM yielded absolutely nothing. Even if the horse was simply an escapee, it was in danger from injuries, illness, ranchers not opposed to shooting a wild horse, and possibly predators, though mountain lions in this area were a rarity these days.

He told himself his intentions were selfless—he was thinking only of the horse's safety and well-being.

Truthfully, Gavin wanted the horse for himself. As a tribute. To his grandfather and to the cowboy way of life he loved, which was disappearing bit by bit every day. Then, he would breed the mustang to his mares, many of

which, like Shasta, had bloodlines going all the way back
to the wild mustangs of his grandfather's time.

He'd recently acquired a partner with deep pockets,
a man from Mustang Valley, and developed a business
plan. All he needed was the stud horse.

This weekend, he, his partner, his brother and their
two ranch hands would go out. By Monday, if all went
well, Gavin's family would have a new revenue stream,
and the years of barely making ends meet would be forever behind them.

All at once, the black spot vanished, swallowed by
the uneven terrain.

Gavin reached for his saddlebag a third time and
pulled out a map, marking the location and date. Later
tonight, he would add the information to the log he kept
tracking the mustang's travels.

"Let's go, girl."

With another lusty snort, Shasta continued along the
ledge as if nothing out of the ordinary had happened.
Her metal shoes clinked on the hard boulders beneath
her feet. In the sky above, a pair of redtail hawks rode
the wind currents as they searched for prey.

An hour later, Gavin and Shasta reached the main
trail that traversed the northern section of the McDowell
Sonoran Preserve. It was along here that Gavin and his
brother guided their customers. Most of the horse-owning
residents of Mustang Village favored the gently winding
trail, where four generations of Powells had driven their
cattle after spring and fall roundups.

Gavin hated thinking there wouldn't be a fifth generation.

As he neared his family's villa, with its large barn
and adjoining stables, his gaze automatically wandered

to the valley below, and he was struck with yet another pang of nostalgia. Not long ago, Powell cattle had roamed the open range, feeding on the lush vegetation that grew along a small branch of the Salt River.

These days, houses, apartments and commercial buildings took the place of open range, and the river had been dammed up to create an urban lake and surrounding park.

Gavin understood that progress couldn't be stopped. He just wished it hadn't come to Mustang Valley.

Dismounting, he waved to the adult students taking riding lessons in the main arena. Later, after the grade school let out for the day, the equestrian drill team would practice their routines there.

He'd given up hope that his twelve-year-old daughter, Cassie, would become a member. Not that she didn't like horses. Quite the opposite. She spent most of her free time in the stables, and for someone who'd never ridden until this past summer, she'd taken to it like a natural. Apparently there was something to be said for genes.

No, the reason his daughter wouldn't join the school equestrian team was the same reason she had few real friends and was struggling with her classes.

Slow to fit in, Principal Rodgers liked to say, despite scoring high on her placement tests. The move from Connecticut to Arizona was a big adjustment. As was switching from private school to public school. So was living full-time with her mom to living full-time with a dad she hardly knew.

The adjustments weren't easy for his sensitive and often emotional daughter.

Leading Shasta into the stables, he tethered her to a hitching rail outside the tack room, unsaddled her and proceeded to give her a good brushing. He heard a familiar whistling and glanced up to see Ethan approaching, his farrier chaps slung low on his hips. A casual observer might not notice the limp, which had improved considerably in the ten months since his discharge from the Marines.

Gavin noticed, however, and winced inwardly every time he thought of the injury that had permanently disabled his younger brother.

"You have a visitor," Ethan announced, coming to stand by Gavin and resting a forearm on the mare's hind quarters. "A lady visitor."

Gavin's stomach instantly tightened. "Not Principal Rodgers again?"

Ethan's eyes sparked with undisguised curiosity. "This gal's about thirty years younger than Principal Rodgers. And a lot better looking."

"Someone from town?" Though Mustang Village was technically a residential community, Gavin and his family always referred to it as a town.

"I don't think so. She doesn't have the look."

"An attorney?" He wouldn't put it past Cassie's mother to serve him with papers despite their recently revised joint-custody agreement.

"No. She's a cowgirl for sure. Pulled in with a truck and trailer."

Gavin knew he should quit stalling and just go meet the woman. But given the family's run of bad luck in recent years, he tended to anticipate the worst whenever visitors wouldn't identify themselves.

"Got a girlfriend on the side you haven't mentioned?" Ethan's mouth lifted in an amused grin.

"When's the last time you saw me on a date?"

"If you're considering it, you could do worse than this gal."

Gavin refused to acknowledge his brother's remark. "Where's she waiting?"

"In the living room. With Cassie."

He ground his teeth together. "Couldn't you have stayed with her and sent Cassie instead?"

"She'll be fine. Your daughter isn't half the trouble you think she is."

"Yeah, tell that to Principal Rodgers." Gavin pushed the brush he'd been using into his brother's hand. "Take care of Shasta for me, will you?"

Without waiting for an answer, he started down the stable aisle. As he entered the open area in front of the main arena, he dusted off his jeans, removed his hat and combed his fingers through his hair. Passing two of his adult students, he nodded and murmured, "Afternoon." He might not like people living in the valley once owned by his family and traipsing all over his property, but without their business, he and his family would lose their only source of income.

At the kitchen door, he kicked the toes of his boots against the threshold, dislodging any dust before entering the house. A tantalizing aroma greeted him, and he turned to see a pot of spaghetti sauce simmering on the old gas range. His father's doing. Since Gavin's mother died, cooking was the only chore on the ranch Wayne Powell did with any regularity.

The sound of voices carried from the other room, one of them Cassie's. Did she know this woman?

Gavin's anxiety increased. He disliked surprises.

His footsteps on the Saltillo tile floor must have alerted Cassie and the woman because they were both facing him when he entered the old house's spacious living room.

"Hi." He removed his hat and, after a brief second of indecision, set it on the coffee table. "I'm Gavin Powell."

The woman stepped and greeted him with a pleasant smile. "Sage Navarre."

He shook her extended hand, appreciating her firm grip. Ethan had been right. Ms. Navarre was definitely attractive, her Hispanic heritage evident in her brown eyes and darker brown hair, pulled back in a sleek ponytail. Her jeans were loose and faded, and her Western-cut shirt functional. Yet there was no disguising the feminine curves hiding beneath the clothing.

"What can I do for you?" he asked, noticing that Cassie observed him closely, her new puppy cradled in her arms. One of the ranch dogs had delivered a litter a few months ago, and Gavin had told her she could keep one. The pair had been inseparable ever since.

"I'm from the BLM," Ms. Navarre said, as if that alone explained everything.

A jolt shot through Gavin. "The BLM?"

"Bureau of Land Management." She held up the leather jacket she'd been carrying, showing him the badge pinned to the front, then handed him a business card. "Aren't you the person who contacted us about a feral horse in the area?"

"Yes." He glanced only briefly at the card, then spoke carefully. "I assumed from the lack of response, you folks weren't taking me seriously."

"Well, we are. I'm here to round up the horse and transport him to our facility in Show Low."

Cassie's expression brightened. "Cool."

"I'll need your cooperation, of course," Ms. Navarre

added. "And a stall to board my horse, if you have one available."

"I'm sorry, Ms. Navarre." Gavin returned her card to her. He had too much invested in the horse to forfeit ownership just because some woman from the BLM showed up out of the blue. And he sure as hell wasn't going to help her. "I'm afraid you've wasted your time coming here."

"I don't understand." Sage studied Gavin Powell, admittedly confused. "Is there a problem?"

"I've changed my mind."

"About?"

"The horse. *I'm* going to capture him and keep him."

She may have only just met him, but there was no mistaking the fierce set of his jaw and the steel in his voice. Here stood a man with a mission and the determination to carry it out.

Unfortunately, he was about to come up against a brick wall.

"You can't, Mr. Powell," she stated firmly.

"Why not?"

"It's against the law for anyone other than an employee of the BLM to capture a feral horse."

"The McDowell Sonoran Preserve isn't federal land."

"No. But it isn't private land, either." She bent and placed her business card on a hand-carved pine coffee table. "And besides, the law isn't restricted to federal land. If you capture the horse, you'd be in violation of the law and subject to fines and a possible jail sentence."

His jaw went from being set to working furiously.

Stubborn, she concluded. Or was he angry? Another glance at him confirmed the latter.

Sage's defenses rose. "I realize you had other plans for the horse, but you knew I was coming."

"No, I didn't."

"We called. Last week."

"I received no phone call."

"It's noted in the records. I don't have the name of the individual we spoke to offhand, but I can easily obtain it if you give me a minute."

He glanced at the girl—Cassie, wasn't it?—and his gaze narrowed.

"Don't look at me," she protested, a hint of defiance in the downward turn of her mouth.

Not that Sage was good at determining ages, but Gavin Powell didn't appear old enough to be Cassie's father. Sage guessed him to be around her own thirty-one years. Maybe older. Rugged and tanned complexions like his could be misleading.

Broad shoulders and well-muscled forearms also spoke of a life dedicated to hard physical labor and being outdoors. She'd always found that kind of man attractive. One who rode a horse or swung a hammer or chopped trees rather than earning his pay from behind a desk.

Gavin Powell exemplified that type, with the glaring addition of a very testy and confrontational personality. Something she *didn't* find attractive.

Sage stood straighter. She'd come to Powell Ranch on business, after all. Not to check out the available men.

"Is it possible someone else took the call and didn't tell you?" she asked.

"Not likely."

"Grandpa forgets to tell you stuff all the time," Cassie interjected.

"Go do your homework," Gavin told her.

"I hardly have any. I did most of it in class."

"Now."

"Dad!"

Her cajoling had no effect on him. At a stern "Cassie," she exited the room, another flash of defiance in her eyes.

So, the girl *was* his daughter. No sooner did Sage wonder how often those exchanges happened than she reminded herself it was none of her concern.

"Sorry about that," he mumbled when his daughter had gone.

For a tiny moment, he appeared human. And vulnerable.

"I have a daughter, too," she admitted, "though she's only six."

Why in the world had she told him that? She rarely discussed Isa when on the job. It was easier when dealing with obstinate or difficult individuals—an unfortunate and commonplace occurrence in her job—to keep the discussions impersonal.

She promptly brought the subject back around. "Look, Mr. Powell. I'm here to capture the horse, which can't be allowed to wander on state and city land. I'd like your help."

His scowl deepened. Heck, maybe it was permanent.

"To be honest," she said, making a civil plea, "I really need it. You know this area, I don't. And from the information you sent the BLM, you've clearly been tracking the horse."

"No." He shook his head. A lock of jet-black hair fell over his forehead. He pushed it back with an impatient swipe. "I want the mustang, Ms. Navarre. I won't help you."

"If you persist in capturing him yourself, I'll report you to the authorities."

"No kidding?" The challenge in his tone told her she would have to go that far, and perhaps further, to obtain his cooperation.

Sage released a frustrated sigh. Her tidy plan was unraveling at an alarming rate. A few days, a week at the most, was all the time she had to capture the horse. Then, as she and her boss had agreed, she'd spend her annual two weeks' vacation in nearby Scottsdale visiting her cousin. It was the main reason she'd asked to be assigned to this case—locating and confronting her errant ex with her attorney cousin-in-law at her side.

After four years, she'd finally gotten a reliable lead on her ex's whereabouts, and it had brought her to Mustang Village. The back child support he owed her—owed *Isa*—amounted to a considerable sum of money. Well worth two weeks of vacation and scrambling to rearrange both her and her daughter's schedules.

Much as she hated admitting it, she couldn't capture the horse without Gavin Powell's help and his resources. Not in one week. Probably not ever.

She could try for an order, but that would require time she didn't have. Besides, the task would go quicker and easier with his voluntary cooperation.

Sage thought fast. She was a field agent, her job was to safely capture wild horses and burros. Once in federal custody, the adoption of those horses and burros was handled by a different department. She knew a few people in that department and was confident she could pull a few strings.

"What if, in exchange for your help, I guaranteed you ownership of the horse?"

Gavin Powell studied her skeptically. "Can you do that?"

She lowered herself onto the couch, the well-worn leather cushions giving gently beneath her weight. She imagined, like the coffee table, the dated but well-constructed couch had been in the Powell family a long time.

"Can we sit a minute? I've had a long drive."

He joined her with obvious reluctance and, rather than recline, sat stiffly with a closed fist resting on his knee.

She'd almost rather face a pair of flailing front hooves—something she'd done more than once in the course of her job.

"The fact is, Mr. Powell, we have trouble finding enough homes for the animals we round up. Despite the novelty of owning a feral horse or burro, most people aren't interested in spending months and months domesticating them. Even then, some animals never truly adapt, and only a handful of the horses make decent and dependable riding stock."

"I wouldn't be using the horse for riding."

Though she was curious, she didn't ask about his intentions for the horse. "I think the BLM would be happy to have a home for the mustang and will likely just give him to you with a minimal amount of paperwork and processing."

He nodded contemplatively.

"You'd still have to pay a fee."

"How much?"

"I don't know for certain. I can find out if you want. Most of the horses are adopted for a few hundred dollars. My guess is it would be something in that range."

Another nod. Gavin Powell was clearly a man of few words.

"I have one week to round up the horse. After that, I'll be staying in Scottsdale with relatives until the end of the month. My daughter's there now, I dropped her off on the way." She paused, giving herself a mental shake. Why did she feel the need to rattle off personal information? "If you don't object, the horse can stay here with you on your ranch while I'm in Scottsdale. You'll have a chance to observe him, work with him, see if he…meets your needs."

She waited while he mulled over her proposition. He didn't take long to make his decision.

"Deal." He extended his hand.

"Good. Glad that's resolved."

Shaking his hand for the second time that afternoon, she tried to hide her relief. Like before, she noticed both strength and assurance in his callused fingers. Gavin Powell was *definitely* one of those men who didn't make his living sitting behind a desk.

"Would you like something in writing?" She asked. "I can have the office fax—"

"Not necessary. I was raised to take someone at their word. And not to give mine unless I intend to keep it."

She didn't doubt that. "Then we're in agreement."

"Yes, ma'am."

"Please, call me Sage. We're going to be working together, after all."

"Gavin."

She smiled.

So did he. And though reserved, it both transformed him and disarmed her. She hadn't noticed his vivid blue eyes or the pleasingly masculine lines of his face until now.

For a moment, Sage lost track of her thoughts. Standing, she promptly gathered them.

"About that stall for my mare."

"Sure." He also stood. "You can pull your truck around to the stables and unload her there."

"Any chance I can park my trailer here? My cousin's home-owners association won't allow me to leave it there."

"No problem."

They went through the back of the house rather than the front door where Sage had entered. She caught a whiff of something tantalizing when they entered the kitchen, reminding her that all she'd eaten since breakfast was a semistale leftover doughnut and a snack-size box of raisins Isa must have accidentally left in her purse.

A man stood at the stove, stirring a pot. He turned and before Gavin introduced the man, she recognized the resemblance.

"Dad, this is Sage Navarre. From the BLM. My dad, Wayne."

"The BLM?" Confusion clouded Wayne Powell's face, then abruptly cleared. "Oh. Yeah. I forgot. Someone called last week."

"That's what I heard."

To Gavin's credit, if he was annoyed at his father, he didn't let on. There was no point anyway; they'd reached an agreement about the horse.

"Nice to meet you, Ms. Navarre."

"Sage," she told Gavin's father.

"Will you be in Mustang Valley long?"

"A week at the most."

"We'd better tend to that mare of yours," Gavin said, inclining his head toward the door.

Sage got the hint. Gavin didn't wish to prolong the conversation with his father. "It was a pleasure, Mr. Powell."

"Enjoy your stay. I hope to see you again." He smiled, but it was mechanical and flat. Nothing like his son's.

"I'm counting on it," she answered cheerfully, and followed Gavin outside.

"I'll meet you in front of the stables," he told her.

They parted, and Sage headed toward her truck. As she drove the short distance to the stables, she caught sight of Cassie watching from the back porch, her form partially obscured by a thick wooden column.

Without thinking, Sage waved. Cassie ducked her head behind the column, then reappeared a second later, waving shyly in return.

An interesting family, Sage mused, though a little unusual. She supposed there was a lot more to them than met the eye.

Pulling up in front of the stables, she reminded herself why she was in Mustang Valley: capture the wild horse and collect four years' worth of back child support from her ex.

Any distractions, most especially those in the form of a good-looking cowboy, were counterproductive. Not to mention inviting trouble.

Chapter 2

Gavin waited as Sage unlatched the trailer door and swung it wide. He expected the horse to bolt backward as most did after a long ride. Not so this one. The mare lifted her left rear foot and placed it gingerly down, as if not quite believing solid ground awaited. Her right rear foot followed, then the rest of her compact and sturdy body emerged inch by inch. Once standing on all fours, she turned her head with the regality of a visiting dignitary and surveyed her new surroundings.

"She's a good-looking horse." In fact, Gavin had never seen one with that same charcoal-gray coloring.

"Her name's Avaro." Sage reached under the mare's impressively long mane to stroke her neck. "It's Spanish for *greedy*. And trust me, it fits. She attacks every meal like it's her last."

"A mustang?"

"She was brought in on a roundup about three years ago in the Four Corners area. I had another horse at the time, a good one. But as soon as I saw Avaro, I wanted her."

Gavin could appreciate that. He felt the same about his mustang.

"Not just because of her coat," Sage continued, "though it's pretty unusual."

"She'd make a nice broodmare." He was thinking of his own mares, the ones with mustang bloodlines.

Sage shrugged. "Maybe someday. Right now, I'm using her too much and too hard."

"How long did it take you to break her?"

"Six months." Sage laughed, her brown eyes filling with memories.

"That long?"

"It was weeks before she let me near her. Another month before I could put a halter on her."

Gavin considered the information. He'd been hoping to start breeding the mustang stallion right away. Might be difficult if he couldn't even get a halter on the horse. "Your perseverance paid off."

"I told you, owning a feral horse isn't easy."

"I'm up to the task."

She studied him with a critical eye. "I believe you are."

The compliment, if indeed it was one, pleased him.

They started toward the stables with Sage leading Avaro, who observed everything with large intelligent eyes. It was that intelligence that had enabled her to survive by her wits in what had been a harsh and dangerous world. It was a quality he hoped to produce in his foals.

At the entrance to the stables, they heard a familiar rhythmic clinking.

"Do you think your farrier could have a look at Avaro's right front hoof?" Sage asked. "Her shoe's a little loose, and I don't want any problems when we head out into the mountains."

"That's my brother, Ethan. As a rule, he only works on our horses, but I'm sure I could ask him to make an exception."

"If there's a local farrier—"

"It's all right. Our regular guy's usually booked several days out. We may not be able to get him here until after the weekend, and I know you don't want to wait that long."

"No, I don't," she agreed.

Gavin didn't explain the reasons his brother only shoed their own horses. Farrier work was physically demanding and hard on Ethan's prosthetic leg.

Fixing a single loose shoe, however, wasn't nearly as strenuous. And like Sage, Gavin didn't want to postpone capturing the wild mustang any longer than necessary. Business tended to slow down during the holidays. He wanted his stud and breeding operation well underway before then.

"You have a great setup," Sage said appreciatively.

"Thanks."

"How long has the ranch been here?"

At one time telling the history of his family's ranch had been a source of pride. No more. Not after the past ten years. But because she was being friendly, he answered her question.

"My great-grandfather Abe Powell built the original house and stables after he moved here from Texas. According to my grandfather, he was evading the law."

"Is it true?"

"I don't know. But it makes for a good story."

"When was that?"

"Right before the turn of the century. *Last* century. The house wasn't much more than a shack. The stable consisted of six standing stalls and one box stall."

"You've added on since then." She smiled.

It was, Gavin observed, a nice smile. Open and honest.

"For thirty years, we had the only cattle operation in

the area. Before he died, my great-grandfather was able to build the villa, the barn, the bunkhouse and expand the stables. We have thirty-two box stalls now. No standing stalls. And six pens out back along with three connecting two-acre pastures."

Gavin stopped at an empty stall not far from where his brother worked on a large gelding. He unlatched the stall door, and Sage led her mare inside.

"My office will reimburse you the cost of boarding Avaro."

"I'll draw up an invoice." He would have liked to tell her not to worry about it. But with six empty stalls, they could use the extra income.

They stood with forearms resting on the stall wall, watching Avaro acquaint herself with her new accommodations.

"With that much cattle, your family must own quite a bit of land."

"We used to. Six hundred acres. All of Mustang Valley, which is now Mustang Village."

"Wow!"

He swore he could see the wheels in her head spinning as she mentally calculated the huge chunk of change they must have received when they sold the land.

What she didn't know was that every dime had been spent on his mother's heart transplant and medical care. So much money. Sadly, it had bought her only another few months of life before her body rejected the replacement heart, and she died of severe infection. Even if there had been money for a second transplant, the doctors weren't able to save her.

"We kept about thirty acres."

"I'm surprised you didn't move," Sage said.

"Powell Ranch is my home. My family's lived here for four generations." He went to bed every night praying there would be a fifth. "And while most of the land is developed, the ranch is still the heart of this valley."

She looked at him. Really looked at him. Intently. As if she was trying to read what lay hidden beneath the surface.

Gavin turned away. He didn't want Sage, or anyone for that matter, seeing how deeply affected he was by his loss.

With Avaro settled and snacking hungrily on some grain, Gavin took Sage over to meet his brother. Two of the ranch's several dogs lay curled together by the tack room door, their heads resting on their paws and their wagging tails stirring up small dust clouds in the dirt.

Ethan slowly straightened, letting go of the gelding's hoof he'd had braced between his knees. "Hi, again." Setting his rasp on top of his toolbox, he removed his gloves and stuffed them in the waistband of his chaps.

"Ethan, this is Sage Navarre," Gavin said. "She's with the BLM."

"Really?" He wiped the back of his hand across his brow, which had risen in surprise. "Is this about the mustang?"

"Yes."

Ethan's glance cut to Gavin.

"Sage is here to capture the mustang, and we're going to help her."

"We are?"

"She says the BLM will allow me to purchase him and bypass the usual adoption process."

"That's great." Ethan's features relaxed into a grin. "Glad to hear it."

"Her mare has a loose shoe. Any chance you can check it out when you're done with Baldy here?"

"Happy to." Ethan stepped forward, his leg wobbling for a second before he steadied it.

"No rush," Gavin said.

Ethan responded to the concern in Gavin's voice. "I'll handle it." To Sage, he said, "How long you staying?"

They chatted amicably for a few minutes. Well, Sage and Ethan chatted amicably. Gavin mostly listened. And observed. While he'd struck a deal with Sage, he wasn't a hundred percent sure of her. Then again, to be honest, he was betting his future stud and breeding operation on his new partner, a man he didn't know a whole lot better than her.

Gavin wished he weren't so desperate. Normally, he proceeded far more cautiously.

"You ready to park your trailer?" he asked during a break in the conversation.

After a word of advice about Avaro's tendency to nip, Sage followed Gavin.

Outside the stables, she paused. "Which way?"

"I'll ride with you. It'll be easier than trying to give you directions."

The inside of her truck was messy. Crayons, coloring books, dolls, a stuffed cat and a collection of tiny farm animals occupied the passenger seat. A notebook, travel log, empty paper cup, a CD case and a partially folded map filled the middle. Unidentifiable trash littered the floor.

"Sorry about the mess," Sage said, sweeping her

daughter's toys into the pile of her things. "Isa gets bored on road trips. I'm sure you understand."

"Not really."

Her apologetic smile fell.

Ignoring the well-deserved stab of guilt, Gavin climbed into the passenger seat, his feet inadvertently kicking the trash. He'd already told Sage more about his family than he intended. Cassie was off-limits.

"That way," he said, and pointed, acutely aware of the tension his remark had created.

Sage said nothing, leaving Gavin to stew silently. How could he explain to Sage, a virtual stranger, that he'd only seen his daughter a few times while she was growing up? That money for plane trips to Connecticut was hard to spare. In December, he and Cassie's mother would revisit the full custody issue. If Cassie wasn't happy, wasn't adjusting to school, if her and Gavin's relationship didn't improve, she might be returning to Connecticut. Given the current state of his family's finances, he had no idea when he'd be able to swing another visit.

Not a day passed Gavin didn't stare his many failures as a father square in the face and wish circumstances were different.

Picking up the stuffed cat, he set it on top of the coloring book. "Cassie's kind of a neat freak. Always has been."

His explanation appeared to appease Sage for her features softened. "You don't know how lucky you are."

Except he did know. This six-month trial he had with Cassie had been an unexpected gift. The result of her mother's recent remarriage and pregnancy. He hated that he hadn't immediately formed a close bond with Cassie, one like Sage and her daughter obviously shared. And he worried constantly that he'd lose Cassie before he ever really had her.

"Pull into the barn," he told Sage. "That way, you can park in the shade."

"Wow. You really did have some cattle operation." Her gaze roamed the interior of the large barn. "I'm impressed."

"Most of the equipment's gone." They'd sold it off piece by piece over the years.

"Yeah, but it wouldn't take much to start up again." Sage rotated the crank on the hitch, lowering the trailer's front end.

Gavin went around to the rear of the trailer and placed the blocks of wood she'd given him behind the tires. "My plans are to turn it into a mare motel."

"Really?" He could see she'd deduced his plans for the wild mustang. "It would make a good one."

Gavin wondered if he should be less leery of Sage. She seemed genuinely nice and willing to make their agreement work.

"What time tomorrow are we starting?" She shut and locked the trailer's storage compartment.

"We can't head out until Saturday."

"Oh."

"I wasn't expecting you. My day's full."

"Okay." Disappointment showed in her face.

"I do have a free hour in the afternoon. Maybe you can come by. We'll go over the maps and logs and decide on the best area to start looking."

"Sounds good. Any chance I can bring my daughter? She loves horses. I keep promising to buy her a pony of her own and teach her to ride one of these days but just haven't had the time."

"We've got a dead broke horse we use for beginner students. She can ride him if she wants." Gavin had no idea why he made the offer.

"Thank you. That's very nice of you." Her smile returned, brighter than before.

Maybe that was why.

As they were climbing back into the truck, her cell phone rang. She lifted it out of the cup holder and, with only a cursory glance at the screen, answered.

"Hi. I just finished parking my trailer." A long pause followed during which she listened intently, her mouth pursed in concentration. "Yeah, hold on a second." She dug through the pile in the middle of the seat, locating a notebook. "Go ahead." She wrote something down that appeared to be directions, though Gavin couldn't see clearly from where he sat in the passenger seat. "Great. Meet you in fifteen minutes."

Snapping the notebook closed, she started the truck. "I'm sorry to be so abrupt, but I have to leave."

"No problem. Three o'clock tomorrow okay? To meet here," he added when she didn't immediately respond.

"Oh, yeah." She shook her head as if to clear it. "Three o'clock."

After she dropped Gavin off in front of the house, he stood for a moment watching her truck bump down the long sloping driveway leading to the main road.

Apparently she knew someone in Mustang Village.

He didn't like that his curiosity was piqued. He liked the anticipation he felt at seeing her again tomorrow even less.

Sage reached the base of the mountain and merged with the light traffic traveling east. A quarter mile up the road, she spotted a stone sign marking the main entrance to Mustang Village. Next to the sign stood a life-size and very realistic bronze statue of a rearing horse.

Just inside the entrance was a modest shopping plaza with retail stores, a bank, fresh food market, urgent care center and two restaurants, one fast-food, one sit-down. Situated behind the shopping plaza was a commercial building with offices on the first floor and apartments on the second. Stretching beyond that were acres and acres of houses as far as she could see.

What had it been like when all this was once an endless rolling valley at the base of a scenic mountain range? She could almost envision it in her mind's eye.

Gavin's family had probably made a killing when they sold the land, but Sage wasn't sure she could have traded glorious and primitive desert for a sea of commercial and residential development.

A second sign directed her to the visitors' center. She turned into the parking lot, shut off the ignition and, as instructed, waited for her cousin's husband.

As the minutes dragged by, Sage's nervousness increased. She tried distracting herself by observing life at midafternoon in Mustang Village.

It was, she had to agree, a unique and almost genius blending of country life and town life. Cars drove by at a very safe fifteen miles per hour while an empty school bus returned from delivering children home. Exercise enthusiasts walked or jogged or biked along the sidewalks, and people on horseback rode the designated bridle paths networking the community. As the warning signs posted everywhere stated, horses had the right of way in Mustang Village.

Finally, just when Sage was ready to get out of her

truck and start pacing, her cousin's husband arrived, his SUV slipping into the space beside hers.

She greeted him with a relieved hug. He'd been at work when she stopped by their house earlier to drop off Isa, so she'd yet to see him.

"Thank you, Roberto," she told him when they broke apart. "You have no idea how much I appreciate this."

"Happy to help, *primita*."

Calling her "little cousin" always made Sage smile. At five-eight, he was no more than an inch taller than her. When she wore boots, like today, they stood nose to nose.

Not so with Gavin Powell. Even in boots, she'd had to tilt her head back in order to meet those vivid blue eyes of his.

Why had she thought of him all of a sudden?

"We'd better get a move on," Roberto said. "Before he figures out you're in the area and takes off."

"You have the paperwork?" she asked, hopping in the passenger side of his SUV.

"Right here." Roberto tapped the front of his suit jacket.

He'd used his firm's resources to locate Sage's ex—*again*. This time, she assured herself, would be different. Dan wouldn't be able to disappear before they had a chance to personally serve him with the child support demand papers.

She marveled at his ability to jump from place to place, always one step ahead of her. As a horse trainer, a good one, he easily found work all over the Southwest. He was also often paid in cash or by personal check, which had made garnishing his wages nearly impossible.

To her knowledge, this was the first time he'd returned to Arizona in two years.

"He sure picked a nice spot," she observed, taking in the attractive houses with their tidy front yards, each landscaped with natural desert fauna to conserve water. The homes sat on three-quarter acre lots, with small corrals and shaded pens visible in the spacious backyards.

"*Very* nice," Roberto concurred. "And Mustang Village is teeming with horse people, a lot of them with surplus money and a burning desire for their kids to have the best-trained horses. Dan's probably doing pretty well for himself."

"He always has." That was something Sage didn't understand. Her ex could afford the child support. He just refused to pay it.

Another thing Sage didn't understand was his disinterest in seeing Isa. How could a father who'd been devoted to his daughter for the first two years of her life not want to see her? Spend time with her? Be a vital part of her growing up?

"We're here," Roberto said, and maneuvered the SUV into the driveway of a large Santa Fe–style house.

"Do you think he's home?" Sage asked, her worry spiking at the noticeable absence of a vehicle in the driveway.

Roberto grinned confidently. "Only one way to find out."

At Dan's front door, Roberto rung the bell.

Sage read the hand-painted stone plaque hanging beside the door.

The Rivera Family.

His last name, penned with large, bold strokes, reminded her that she and Dan had never married. She'd wanted to, had brought up the subject frequently during their three years together, but Dan had always manufactured some excuse.

Roberto rang the doorbell again. Sage rubbed her sweaty palms on the front of her jeans.

The Rivera Family.

Suddenly it struck her. Family! As in wife and children.

Before her thought had a chance to fully develop, the door swung open, and Dan appeared in the frame, his expectant expression dissolving into a frown the instant he spotted her.

"What do you want, Sage?"

"To make sure you receive a copy of this." Roberto attempted to hand Dan the child support demand letter. "Since you haven't responded to the nine previous ones mailed to you."

He drew back, refusing to accept the papers. "Who the hell are you?"

"Ms. Navarre's attorney."

"Get off my property."

"You owe my client four years of back child support. You can't get out of it just because—"

"Dan, who is it?" A young, strikingly beautiful and very pregnant woman appeared behind Dan, a toddler boy balanced on her hip.

"It's okay, Maria," he said crossly. "I have this handled."

She backed away, a mixture of confusion and concern on her face, then disappeared into the house's dim interior.

The sudden realization that Dan had committed to another woman when he'd refused to commit to her stung bitterly. It shouldn't, Sage told herself. She was over him.

Past that. Moved on. And yet, her heart broke like a dam, releasing fresh pain.

Just then, Dan's cell phone rang. Angling his body away from them, he answered it, speaking in clipped, short sentences. "Hello. Yeah. Not today. Look, Gavin, I'm busy right now. Call you later."

Alarm shot through Sage, leaving her unsteady.

Was that Gavin Powell calling Dan?

She took a deep breath, only vaguely aware of Roberto whispering to her that they weren't leaving until they'd served Dan with the papers.

Slowly, rationality returned. Gavin had no idea Dan was Isa's father. He owned the local riding stables, and Dan was a horse trainer. It stood to reason they knew each other and possibly had dealings together. Clients in common.

Dan disconnected and, pocketing his cell phone, turned back around. "As I was saying—"

"As *I* was saying…" Roberto tried again to give Dan the papers.

He swatted them away. "You're not getting anything from me without proof."

"Proof of what, Dan?" Sage demanded, her voice shaking from residual shock and rising anger.

"Paternity. How do I even know Isa's mine?"

Sage reeled as if physically struck. "Of course she's yours," she sputtered.

"I'm not so sure. You were still seeing that old boyfriend of yours."

"We worked together. That's all."

"Yeah? Well, get the kid tested. Then we'll talk." With that, Dan slammed the door in Sage's and Roberto's faces.

Chapter 3

Gavin opened his front door to a miniature version of Sage, complete with boots, jeans and a floppy cowboy hat.

"Hi. I'm Isa." She displayed a huge smile, not the least bit embarrassed by her two missing front teeth.

"I'm Gavin. Come on in." He stepped aside, and she jumped over the threshold into the living room, landing with both feet planted firmly on a colorful braided area rug.

"Do you have a last name?"

"Don't you?"

"Of course." She giggled. "What's yours?"

"Powell. Why?"

"My mom says I have to call adults by their last name." She assessed him with dark brown eyes in much the same manner her mother had yesterday. "Thank you for having me here today, Mr. Powell."

Her speech sounded rehearsed, probably Sage's doing, but Gage was impressed nonetheless.

He'd once visited Cassie when she was about this age. He and Isa had already exchanged more words in two minutes than he and Cassie had during their first hour together.

In all fairness to his daughter, she hadn't been meeting

an acquaintance of her mother. The man standing before her was her father, a stranger she didn't remember from his last visit three years earlier.

The horse figurine he'd brought as a gift hadn't broken the ice. How was he to know she liked Barbie dolls and dressing up? Their trip to the park had been strained, as were the next three days. How hard it must have been for Cassie to be thrust into the care of a man she barely knew and told, "This is your father."

Love wasn't something that could be manufactured on the spot just because of a biological connection.

The worst moment of that trip was when they were saying goodbye. To his astonishment, Cassie hugged him fiercely and, in a teary voice, asked him not to go. The only genuine moment they'd shared and it had to be when he was getting into the rental car and heading to the airport.

His answer, he couldn't remember it now, had just made her cry.

His next visit three years later was even more strained. And this last time, when he'd picked her up at the airport for her first-ever trip to Arizona, she'd been sullen rather than shy. Nothing much had changed in the four months since.

He must, he told himself, be patient with her. Their dysfunctionality hadn't happened overnight. It wouldn't be resolved quickly, either.

"Where's your mom?" he asked Isa.

"Right here." Sage rushed through the still-open door, pocketing her cell phone and looking completely frazzled. Her high, elegant cheekbones were flushed a vivid crimson, and several tendrils of hair hung haphazardly around her face as if pulled loose by anxious fingers. "I told you to wait for me, *mija*."

"Yes, but—" Isa's eyes widened with delight. "You have a puppy!" She dropped to her knees and opened her arms.

Cassie's puppy went right to her, drawn like iron particles to a magnet, his entire hind end shaking along with his tail. She gathered him into her lap, giggling as he covered her chin with kisses.

"What's his name?"

"Blue."

"But he's brown and black."

"His eyes are blue."

Isa peered into the puppy's face, earning herself more kisses.

"Sorry we're late." Sage shut the door behind her. "I got tied up."

"It happens." Normally, Gavin was intolerant of tardiness. He blamed running a business with strict schedules. But something had obviously thrown Sage for a loop.

She nodded and, pushing one of the flyaway tendrils from her face, offered a pale shadow of the smile that had come so easily and naturally yesterday.

"You okay?" Gavin asked.

"Yeah. Just having a killer day."

He thought she looked more distraught and upset than overwhelmed. "Can I get you and Isa something? A soda or ice water?"

"Water would be great." She sighed as if she'd been waiting all day for just such an offer.

At that moment, Cassie poked her head into the living room. "Have you seen Blue?"

"In here. Cassie, you remember Ms. Navarre. And this is her daughter, Isa."

He'd told Cassie the reason for Sage's visit during dinner last evening and about their plans to capture the mustang. While she'd tried to act as disinterested as she did about everything that concerned him or the ranch— with the sole exception of riding and Blue—he noticed how intently she'd listened to both him and the questions Ethan posed.

Unfortunately, she was still smarting from him asking her to leave him and Sage alone the previous day, and, as a result, talking to him only when necessary.

Okay, he'd handled the situation wrong by embarrassing her in front of company. But how was he to know? He was still at the beginning of a very long and very high learning curve. They both were. Though, as the adult in the relationship, he should be doing better.

Maybe an apology would go over better than an explanation. He'd try later. What could it hurt?

Cassie approached the little girl, and Gavin worried that she might not want someone else playing with her puppy. His concern faded when Cassie knelt down beside Isa and patted the puppy along with her.

"Hi. I'm Cassie. How old are you?"

"Six," Isa muttered under her breath, shrinking slightly.

Strange, Gavin thought. The little girl hadn't been the least bit bashful with him.

Cassie was undeterred. "I'm twelve. Do you like to ride?"

"Uh-huh."

Blue rolled onto his back, his tongue hanging out the side of his mouth, completely lost in puppy ecstasy.

"I have a horse my dad gave me. He's a registered paint."

Isa ah'd appreciatively and blurted, "Your dad said I could ride one of your horses."

"He did?" Cassie raised her gaze to Gavin.

"I thought later I'd let her give old Chico a test-drive."

"I'll take her." A spark lit Cassie's eyes, the first one Gavin had seen in a while.

For a moment, he was struck speechless. "Well…" While confident in her riding abilities, allowing her to be responsible for a six-year-old was an entirely different matter.

But there was that spark in her eyes.

"Come on, Dad. We could have an earthquake, and old Chico would just stand there."

"It's up to Isa's mom."

"Oh, please, Mommy." Isa was on her feet and throwing her arms around Sage's waist.

"I don't know. Isa has only ever ridden ponies."

"Cassie's very responsible." Were his eyes playing tricks on him? Was that actually a smile his daughter directed at him? "If it would make you feel better, we can work on the back patio. You'll be able to see the arena from there. And it's true. Chico would just stand there in an earthquake."

The lines of tension creasing Sage's brow lessened marginally. "All right," she relented after a lengthy pause.

"Can Blue come?" Isa darted back to Cassie.

"Naturally." Cassie scooped up the puppy. "He goes everywhere with me. Even sleeps with me."

The chronic pressure in Gavin's chest eased by a fraction. He was pretty certain something good had just happened between him and Cassie, but he couldn't say what exactly.

Sage stepped forward after the girls left. "We should probably get started…"

"Sorry." He tilted his head toward the kitchen. "Come on, I'll get you that water." It wasn't until they started walking that he noticed she carried a portfolio. "What did you bring?"

"Reports on a few of our recent roundup campaigns. I thought maybe we could talk a little about the techniques we're going to use."

Gavin wasn't sure what techniques the BLM used to round up large numbers of horses on federal land but doubted they'd work on a single horse roaming an urban preserve.

After retrieving his files on the mustang and filling two large plastic tumblers with ice and water, he took Sage outside. Just as he was closing the door behind them, he caught sight of his dad coming into the kitchen. He'd probably been waiting in his room for them to leave so he could start supper.

Another family member Gavin didn't relate to and didn't know what to do about. His father's depression seemed to worsen every year. Short of bringing back his mother, Gavin was out of ideas on how to cure it. Talking got nowhere, and his dad flat out refused to see a counselor, join a support group or consult with his doctor.

Ethan had no better luck than Gavin did. But then, Ethan tried less. Not that Gavin blamed him. His brother had his own problems to deal with since his discharge from the service. Their sister, Sierra, was the only one who could bring their dad out of his shell. But she lived in San Francisco and had come home only once during the past couple years. Something else that depressed their dad.

Outside, in the balmy weather, Gavin tried to put his

concerns aside. It was a beautiful day, he was making plans to capture the wild mustang and Cassie wasn't mad at him anymore. At least for the moment.

It could be, and more often than not was, worse.

"This way."

Gavin escorted Sage to the large patio on the backside of the house. There, they sat at the picnic table where he and his family ate when they took their meals outside. Midafternoon sun filtered through the spindly branches of a sprawling paloverde that was easily as old as his father. Potted cacti and succulents, some of them planted by his mother, nestled along the base of the low stucco wall.

"It's very pretty here," Sage commented, glancing around before opening her portfolio and withdrawing a stack of papers. "The view's spectacular."

She was right. The McDowell Mountains and, in the far distance, Pinnacle Peak, provided a stunning backdrop.

Gavin saw the view a dozen times a day, yet he never tired of it.

He'd once felt that way about the view from the front courtyard, too, which now looked out onto the whole of Mustang Village.

"Do you think the girls are okay?" Sage peered over her shoulder toward the stables.

"If they don't come out in a few minutes, we can check on them."

"All right." She began rifling through her portfolio. A small sound of frustration escaped her lips.

Gavin waited, his doubts growing. Yesterday, she'd impressed him with her confidence, friendliness and intelligence. Today, she was like an entirely different person. Distracted, unfocused and disorganized.

What had happened to her between then and now?

"Here they are." With noticeable relief, she handed Gavin a trio of photographs. "These are from a roundup I participated in this past spring on the Navajo Nation outside of Winslow. We brought in over eighty head of horses and seven burros."

He examined the photos, two of which were aerial shots taken from the inside of what he assumed was a helicopter. The herd of horses, bunched together in a long line, resembled a rushing river as they galloped over a rocky rise and down the other side.

It must have been a majestic and thrilling sight. He could almost hear the pounding of their hooves and feel the ground shaking beneath him as they thundered past. When his great-grandfather had first settled in these parts, mustangs not unlike these had made the valley their home. To have seen these horses on the Navajo Nation would have been like witnessing a living and breathing piece of history.

He flipped to the next picture, and his heart sank low in his chest. In this one, taken from the ground, the horses had been crowded into corrals and were milling restlessly. A few bit or kicked their neighbors. A mare tried valiantly to protect her young foal.

"It's not right, putting the horses through this." Gavin hadn't realized he'd spoken aloud until Sage answered him.

"I know it looks bad. But if we hadn't removed the horses, most of them would have died. Rainfall last winter was half of our annual average. All the area's water sources had dried up."

He studied the photo closer, noting the poor condition of the animals. Underweight, undersized and lackluster, pest-infected coats. It was fortunate the BLM had stepped in when they had. Still, removing animals from their natural environment didn't sit well with him.

"Was there no other way to help them?"

"We tried filling tanks with water. The horses were skittish and refused to drink."

Hearing the girls' animated chatter, Gavin and Sage looked up.

Cassie led Chico from the stables to the small corral beside the arena where Ethan was teaching a class of about a dozen beginner students. They trotted in a tight figure-eight pattern as their parents watched, either relaxing in lawn chairs or standing along the fence.

Isa sat astride Chico, her fists clutching the reins, her feet barely reaching the stirrups of Cassie's youth saddle. Rocking from side to side as he walked, the old horse clopped slowly along, his hips appearing more prominent because of his swayed back. Blue brought up the rear, tripping over his front paws in his attempt to keep up.

Sage watched them, her expression intent.

"Ethan learned to ride on Chico," Gavin told her.

She didn't appear to hear him.

"Isa will be fine."

He was about to repeat himself when Sage suddenly turned around and blinked as if orienting herself. Wherever she'd been the past minute was a million miles from the ranch.

"You want to postpone this?" Gavin's patience had worn thin. According to Sage, they only had a week to capture the mustang, and he resented wasting time.

"No." Picking through the papers again, she removed

a typewritten report and passed it to him. "Not everyone agrees with the bureau's program of capturing feral mustangs and burros. And I won't argue with you, it's an imperfect solution. But I also believe we're doing the right thing. Saving and preserving a part of America's heritage, not destroying it." Her voice rang with unabashed passion.

It was something Gavin understood. He believed in the same thing himself.

After skimming the report, he opened his file and took out the map he used to mark the mustang's territory. Spreading it open on the table, he pointed to the *X*s.

"These are the various places I've spotted the mustang in the last four months. You can see, he keeps to the same territory."

"Which is near the ranch."

"Within three miles, though he's come as close as half a mile. I imagine he's drawn to our horses."

She murmured her agreement. "Where does he get his water?"

Gavin was glad her attention had ceased wandering. "There could be springs, but this is desert country. I've never seen any water in the mountains except after heavy rainfall, which, as you said earlier, has been less than average of late. I'm pretty certain he drinks at the golf course." Gavin showed her the location of the country club on the map.

"You're kidding!"

"They maintain a small reservoir on the back end to feed the ponds on the course and for water in case of a fire. The maintenance people have reported all kinds of wild animals drinking there. Javelina, bobcats, coyotes and even a few deer."

Sage perked up. "Do you own any ATVs?"

"Two. Why?"

"We can use them to round up the horse."

"No, we can't. Motorized vehicles are prohibited on the preserve. And even if they weren't, they make too much noise. He'd hear us coming a mile away and take off."

"How else are we going to capture him? We have to be able to herd him in the direction we want."

"Like my grandfather and great-grandfather did. On horseback."

She shook her head. "That won't work. It'll take too long."

Her complete dismissal annoyed Gavin. "It's that or on mountain bikes."

"I hope you're joking."

"Look, Sage. I'm not the BLM. I don't have helicopters at my disposal."

"Do you know someone with a small plane?"

"Even if I did, I wouldn't enlist their help."

"I'll contact my office. Maybe they can obtain permission from the state for us to use your ATVs."

So much for her little speech about protecting and preserving America's heritage.

"Forget it. The only way we're going after this horse is the same way ranchers have for generations. With ropes and on horseback."

Their gazes connected and held fast. Hers had cooled considerably but revealed little. Gavin was certain there was no mistaking what was going through his mind.

Sage broke the silence. "How exactly are you proposing we go about it?"

"Have you ever heard of a Judas horse?"

"Yes. But I've never seen that technique put to effective use."

"There's a box canyon in the south end of the preserve. Here." Gavin tapped the map with his index finger. "We'll construct a small pen at the base of the canyon and put a couple of our mares in there. Preferably ones in heat."

"How will you construct the pen? Won't you need to haul fencing in?"

"We'll run a rope line. Use any natural materials in the area. We can pack in food and water for the mares, enough to last overnight. If all goes well, the next morning the mustang will be in the canyon with the mares. There's only one way in and out." He circled the narrow opening to the canyon.

"How many of us will there be?"

"Me, you, Ethan, Conner, he's a local cowboy who helps us out part-time, and possibly my partner." Gavin wished he could include his dad but the older man hadn't ridden in years.

Sage returned to the map. "So, we could position two riders at the entrance of the canyon, preventing the mustang's escape, and the other three could trap and rope him."

"That's the plan."

"It might work," she relented with a shrug.

"It *will* work."

"You're still counting heavily on luck."

"He'll come for the mares. I'm sure of it."

Isa's laughter reached them across the open area, once again diverting Sage's attention.

Cassie jogged alongside Chico, urging the old horse into a slow trot that delighted his rider. It pleased Gavin to see his daughter taking her responsibility seriously.

Sage's expression, however, immediately tensed.

She was, he decided, a worrywart where her daughter was concerned. He hoped that didn't cause any problems for them. The risk of danger existed with any trip into the mountains. Greater when a wild and unpredictable animal was involved. The last thing they needed was for one of them to be overly preoccupied. That was how accidents happened.

"What time do we leave tomorrow?" she asked, facing him.

"Right after breakfast. I was thinking seven. It'll be plenty light by then."

"Do you need any help getting ready?"

There was a lot of work involved. Supplies and equipment to assemble and pack. "If you're offering, I accept. But I have a four o'clock lesson and won't be ready to start until after that. Maybe you and your daughter can stay for dinner."

Gavin could use the help, it was true. But after Sage's odd behavior today, he'd grown skeptical and really wanted a chance to observe her in action. He had too much riding on capturing the mustang to take chances with a loose cannon.

"I don't want to impose," she said.

"My dad always fixes enough for an army."

Sage glanced at the girls again, her brow creasing with indecision. "I…guess so. Let me make a phone call."

"My lesson doesn't start for another twenty minutes." He refolded the map and put it back in his file. "How 'bout I meet you in the stables after you make your call."

"Fine." Sage also collected her materials.

As they stood, a pickup truck rolled through the open area in front of the stables at a speed slightly faster than

Gavin would have preferred. Rather than pull behind the stables and park in the area reserved for visitors, the driver came to a dust-billowing stop in front of the hitching rail.

If it were anyone else, Gavin would have a stern word with them. In this case, he simply ground his teeth.

Dan Rivera didn't think rules—*any* rules, not just those at Powell Ranch—applied to him. It came from having a very elevated opinion of himself and his abilities. On the other hand, he *was* a good horse trainer and brought several new customers to the ranch. He was also an astute businessman and had helped Gavin immensely.

So, though it annoyed him, he let the speeding and parking violations slide.

Sage had taken out her cell phone and was punching in numbers. When she caught sight of Dan emerging from his truck, she stopped cold and swore under her breath.

"Do you know him?" Gavin asked.

"Unfortunately, yes." Her hands shaking, she pocketed her cell without completing the call.

Dan headed in the direction of the parents at the fence, several of whom were his clients.

Sage's eyes widened with fright as she tracked his every step. "I need to get my daughter." She started out at a brisk walk.

"What's wrong?" Gavin lengthened his strides to catch up.

"I'm sorry," she stuttered. "We can't stay for dinner after all."

With that, she broke into a fast run.

Sage's heart beat with such force she thought it might shatter. Her ex was on a collision course with Isa, and unless Sage sprouted wings, she wasn't going to get there ahead of him.

Dammit! She didn't want her daughter meeting her father for the first time in four years with no preparation.

Her fault. All her fault. She'd known Gavin had dealings with Dan. She should have at least anticipated the possibility of running into him at the ranch.

"Sage!" Gavin appeared alongside her just as Dan was approaching Isa.

Suddenly, as if a button had been pushed, everything slowed to a crawl and each detail crystalized into sharp focus. Sage watched, horrified and helpless, as Isa trotted along the corral fence within a few feet of Dan. He stared ahead at the parents watching Ethan's class. Then all at once, Sage's worst fears were realized. Dan turned his head and looked directly at Isa.

Oh, God! Please don't let him say something hurtful.

Sage stumbled to a stop. She tried to breathe but her fire-filled lungs wouldn't expand.

The moment—which seemed to last an eternity—abruptly passed.

Dan continued walking without so much as breaking a single step.

He hadn't recognized his own daughter!

"You bastard!" Sage's previously stalled breath came in ragged bursts.

"What the hell's going on?"

She'd forgotten about Gavin. "Nothing."

"That wasn't nothing."

Sit. She needed to sit before her knees gave out. "It's personal."

"If you have issues with Dan Rivera, I want to know."

Sage had to get out of sight. Immediately. Dan may

not have recognized Isa, but if he saw her, he'd put two and two together.

She spun on her heels and hurried to the stables, praying Dan wouldn't decide to go in there.

Gavin was right behind her. The moment they were inside, he reached for her arm.

"Sage."

"Can you go ask Cassie to bring Isa here?"

"Not until you tell me—"

"It's none of your business."

His intense blue eyes drilled into her. Held her in place. "If this involves Dan, it most certainly is my business."

"Why?" she snapped. "Because he's the local horse trainer?"

"Because he's my partner in the stud and breeding business. The one I'm starting with the mustang. And he's also my financial backing."

Shaken to her core, she retreated a step. "No, no, no. We're not working together." She shook her head vehemently. "The deal's off."

"The hell it is." His voice rose. "You agreed."

Her reply was cut short by Cassie leading the old horse into the stables, Isa still sitting astride him. Both the girls' faces registered alarm.

"Dad? What's going on?"

Chapter 4

Sage was still shaking. She only half heard the exchange between Gavin and his daughter, too caught up in her own whirling emotions.

"Everything's fine," he answered Cassie's question with admirable calm.

"It didn't look fine." She faced him, her puppy tucked beneath one arm, the old horse's reins wrapped in the fingers of her free hand. "It looked like you were arguing."

"We were just talking."

"Yeah." Cassie's narrowed gaze pinged between Sage and her father.

Fortunately, Isa was oblivious to everyone and everything around her save the horse.

"Chico, you're such a good boy." She leaned forward over the saddle horn and gave the horse's neck an affectionate squeeze. He lived up to his reputation by bearing the attention with gentlemanly grace. "Did you see me riding, Mama?"

"I did, *mija.*" Sage went over and placed a hand on Isa's knee. "You were awesome."

The minute Dan paid the back child support—and he would, she'd see to it—she was going to buy Isa that pony. She should have purchased one sooner, but the cost of keeping and feeding a second horse was more than she could comfortably afford on her income.

Damn Dan again for denying Isa the money that was rightfully hers. And damn him for putting both her and Sage through the ordeal of a paternity test—though she suspected it was just another postponement ploy.

Last evening, her cousin and Roberto had tried convincing her that a positive paternity test would only strengthen her case against Dan. They were right, of course. The knowledge, however, didn't lessen her angst.

"Are you sure?" Cassie demanded, returning Sage to the present.

"Ms. Navarre and I were just discussing the best method to go after the mustang."

"Loudly."

Sage bit back a groan. Gavin talked to his daughter as if she was Isa's age. Did he not see how astute Cassie was and that very little got past her?

The sound of distant voices reminded Sage of her and Isa's precarious situation. She had to remove them from sight before Dan noticed them. She began looking for another way out of the stables.

"You okay, Mama?"

"Just a little tired." She sent Isa a reassuring smile. In truth, Sage was perspiring profusely, probably from the giant invisible fist squeezing her insides.

She still couldn't believe Dan had failed to recognize his own daughter. Granted, children changed a lot between two and six. But even so…

"If it's none of my business," Cassie grumbled, "say so."

Gavin quirked an eyebrow. "If I do, will you get mad?"

"Honestly, Dad." She expelled an irritated sigh.

Sage didn't blame her. She'd tried reasoning with Gavin, too, and it had gotten her nowhere. How he managed not to chase away every customer on the place with his confounding obstinance was a mystery.

"Fine." Cassie deposited Blue on the ground by her feet. He immediately stumbled over to Gavin and launched an assault on his boot, gnawing the rounded toe. Gavin bent and scratched the puppy behind the ears.

Interesting, thought Sage. He was tolerant of small, defenseless dogs, passionate about the plight of wild horses and hadn't mentioned her meltdown to his daughter.

Which meant he wasn't all bad.

Figures.

If only he weren't in partnership with her ex.

That was one shortcoming Sage couldn't overlook or dismiss regardless of how good-looking she found him.

Fresh thoughts of Dan squashed whatever fleeting and irrational attraction she felt toward Gavin. Her glance strayed yet again to the stable entrance, and her ears strained for the sound of his truck starting up and leaving.

No such luck.

Sage began to fidget, her mind searching for an excuse to leave—if not the ranch, then at least the immediate vicinity.

Gavin beat her to the punch. "Cassie, why don't you take Isa inside for a little while?"

"What about Chico?"

"I'll unsaddle him and put him away."

She frowned. "You told me if I rode a horse, it was my responsibility to walk him out, brush him down and put him away."

"We'll make an exception today."

"This is pure bull—"

"Cassie." His expression grew dark.

"—droppings," she finished with a glare.

He took the reins from her and turned to Isa. "You ready to get off, young lady?"

"Do I have to?" Her bottom lip protruded in a disappointed pout.

"'Fraid so." Sage lifted Isa from the saddle, relief surging through her.

"Tell you what." Gavin patted the little girl's head once she was standing. "You can ride Chico again the next time your mom brings you out."

"Really?"

"As much as you want."

"Tomorrow?"

He laughed. "Okay by me, but you'll have to wait until we get back from our trip into the mountains."

"Can I, Mama? Please?" Isa clasped her small hands in front of her.

"We'll see."

Sage was doubting the wisdom of bringing Isa back to Powell Ranch ever again. Not with Dan coming and going like he did. "Tia Anna and Tio Roberto were going to watch you. Take you to the movies." She put a hand on Isa's shoulder and nudged her along. "Come on, I'll go with you and Cassie. We both need to wash up."

Was there a less conspicuous route to the house? She'd ask Cassie the second they were away from Gavin.

Before she took so much as a step, he said, "Stay. We can finish our...talk."

Not exactly an order, but more than a request.

Sage's stomach sank. She should have expected this— Gavin wasn't a man easily put off. And any objections she made would only further delay the girls leaving.

Choosing the lesser of two evils, she murmured, "All right, I'll stay," and sent Isa off with Cassie, praying Dan was too preoccupied with his clients to glance in their direction.

"Sorry about that," Gavin told Sage once they were alone. "She doesn't generally use bad language. Or if she does," he added wryly, "it's not around me."

Sage fought the need to pace. Gavin's problems with his daughter didn't concern her. She had enough of her own to worry about. "Isa's been around livestock enough to have heard the word *droppings*."

How long would it take the girls to reach the house? Three minutes? Five?

"I should probably have another talk with my brother. He's the bad influence on Cassie. Too many years in the Marines."

Gavin led Chico over to the hitching rail and slung the reins over it. The old horse just stood there. If he did realize he wasn't tied, he didn't care. Gavin unbuckled the girth and let it drop. Chico heaved a tired sigh, and his eyes drooped closed.

"I'm also sorry I raised my voice earlier." Gavin pulled the small youth saddle off Chico's back and held it in one hand by the horn. "When you said you weren't going with us to capture the mustang, I lost my temper." He removed the saddle blanket next. "But you gave as good as you got."

She didn't disagree.

"Cassie and I are still working out the kinks in our relationship," he said after returning from the tack room, minus the saddle and blanket.

"My mother frequently reminds me that's why children were put on this earth."

Sage was tired of discussing Isa and Cassie. They weren't the reason Gavin had detained her. Trying not to be obvious, she peered over her shoulder. No sight of Dan or Isa. Still, she couldn't relax.

When she turned back around, it was to discover Gavin staring at her.

"What exactly went on back there?" he asked. "I take it you know Dan Rivera."

Sage thought fast. If she told Gavin about Dan, he might understand and not insist they work together. One glance at the determined set of his square jaw promptly squashed that idea. He could possibly refuse to help her capture the mustang. After specifically requesting this assignment from her supervisor, she couldn't return to Show Low with an empty trailer.

Though it galled her, she was going to have to level with Gavin. At least a little.

"Dan Rivera is Isa's father."

"Wow." He pushed his cowboy hat back and rubbed his forehead. "Not the answer I was expecting."

"He hasn't seen Isa in four years or had any contact with her whatsoever."

Gavin nodded as if he understood, only he couldn't possibly.

"I didn't want him talking to Isa without me…preparing her first."

"Did you know he was here?"

"I knew he lived in Mustang Village. But not that he was your partner or that he'd be here today."

Gavin removed a halter from a peg on the wall and swapped it out for Chico's bridle.

"I realize Dan being my partner is awkward for you," he said.

"More than awkward."

"But I don't see how it makes a difference."

She stared at him over the horse's neck. "I just told you he's my ex. My *estranged* ex."

Gavin began brushing Chico. "Look. We capture the mustang this weekend like we planned. Afterward, during the rest of your stay, Dan and I work with the mustang while you and he decide whatever it is you need to about Isa. Then, when you leave, he and I go back to business as usual."

Sage was certain it wouldn't be that simple. In fact, she could guarantee it. First thing Monday she was contacting the Child Support Enforcement Agency and having garnishment papers sent here. If the Powells owed Dan any fees or commissions, she'd be able to attach them. A move like that would surely put a strain on Dan and Gavin's partnership.

If all went well and the DES moved at their usual speed, she'd be long gone by the time the papers arrived.

Something Gavin mentioned earlier came rushing back to her. "Did you say that Dan was going with us to capture the mustang?"

"Yeah."

"Well, he can't. Not if you want me along."

Gavin considered that for several seconds. "Are you going to sic the authorities on me for capturing the mustang on my own?"

Sage regretted having made such a big deal about the law. "There has to be another solution."

"How about you and Dan put your personal differences aside for one weekend?" Gavin ran the brush over the old horse's rump and down his back legs.

Could they? It wasn't as though Isa would be going with them on their trek into the mountains. "Even if I agree," she said, "I'm not sure Dan will."

Not after yesterday. He'd probably expect her to serve him with the child support orders again.

"Do you want to talk to him or should I?"

As much as Sage wished she could refuse accompanying Gavin on the mustang roundup, she had a responsibility. She'd also given Gavin her word.

A low groan involuntarily escaped her. How had she wound up in this predicament?

Gavin set the brush on the hitching rail. "Maybe we both should talk to him."

Sage shook her head, mortified at the prospect. "I don't think so."

When she'd phoned Dan this morning to tell him the DNA testing facility she'd contacted required a sample from him along with Isa, he'd hung up on her. Yesterday, he'd slammed the door in her face. No guarantee what he'd do if she approached him with Gavin in tow, requesting he put their personal differences aside.

"You sure?" Gavin asked. "Because he's coming this way."

"What? No!"

Sage whirled around and panicked at the sight of Dan strolling up the aisle with a woman and a teenage boy about Cassie's age.

"I have to leave." Even as Sage recognized how cowardly she sounded, she started off in the opposite direction of Dan. She refused to deal with him. Not until the paternity test was done and not in front of people.

People being Gavin Powell.

This wasn't like her. She didn't run away from problems, she faced them. But Dan's cold treatment of her and unreasonable demands had really shaken her. Sage long ago admitted her part in their breakup. She was hardly a perfect person. But infidelity wasn't and never had been one of her faults. That he should imply as much outraged her. It also hurt.

"Wait." Gavin drew up beside her, Chico trotting to keep pace.

She didn't slow down.

"Sage, he's not following us."

She dared a backward glance. Dan and his companions had stopped in front of a stall, observing the occupant and conversing. She doubted he'd spotted her. Still, she took no chances and continued hurrying.

Gavin reached over and, placing a hand on her shoulder, maneuvered her in front of him. "He won't see you this way."

Assistance was the last thing she'd expected from him. Not when two minutes ago he'd been insisting she speak to Dan.

"Which way to the house?" she asked when they emerged on the other end of the stables.

"We're not going to the house. Not yet."

"You may not be, but I am."

"Come on."

Before she could object, he took her hand and guided her toward a fenced pasture with several noticeably pregnant mares.

Sage might be distraught but she couldn't help noticing the confident ease with which his fingers held hers. Firm, yet gentle and not entirely unpleasant. Neither was the sensation of walking beside him. Men with his height and brawn could be intimidating and overbearing. If anything, the response Gavin's nearness evoked in her was that of being sheltered and protected.

She'd all but forgotten what it felt like.

His stoic expression gave no clue to what was going through his mind or if being close to her was similarly affecting him.

"Where are you taking me?" she asked in an effort to steer her thoughts in a different—and safer—direction.

"First, we're putting old Chico away. He won't mind spending a night with the girls. Then, we're heading inside for dinner. Later, you can help me and Ethan pack for tomorrow. Cassie will watch Isa."

Just as they'd agreed to earlier. Before Dan had driven onto the ranch. Except now she wasn't so inclined to go along.

"And at some point," he continued, "when we find a few minutes alone, you're going to tell me exactly what's going on with you and Dan."

"I don't think so." Sage came to a grinding halt. The abrupt movement separated Gavin's hand from hers.

She told herself she didn't miss his touch.

He opened the gate to the pasture, and the old horse dutifully meandered through it, far more interested in what the feed trough might hold than the mares.

"Look, Sage." Gavin shut and latched the gate. "I'm going to capture the wild horse. I need your cooperation and you need mine to get your job done. Dan's my business associate and partner. I'm pretty sure I can convince him to work with you. But I need to know what's going on. I'm not asking for your life story or all the gritty details. The *Reader's Digest* version will do fine."

His blue eyes assessed her closely. It surprised her to see compassion and sympathy in their arresting depths. Not judgment.

Slowly, she relented.

"Okay. Isa and I will stay for dinner, and I'll help you and Ethan pack." She told herself she owed him that much for helping her evade Dan.

How much of her guts she would spill during their "few minutes alone," however, remained to be seen.

Hand-holding aside, Gavin was still Dan's partner, and she didn't trust him.

Chapter 5

Gavin tried to remember the last time a woman had shared dinner with his family. With the exception of his sister, Sierra, whose previous visit had been almost two years ago, it was...

No one. Not after his mother died and neighbors and friends stopped coming around.

The Powell men, he noticed, were all having different reactions to Sage and her young daughter, including himself. Ethan had assumed the role of host, asking Sage questions about her job and living in Show Low. Gavin's father was polite, though guarded, having not yet decided how big a threat these intruders were to his orderly world.

Sage had definitely threatened Gavin's orderly world, but for entirely different reasons. She was a mystery, exasperating one moment and fascinating the next. It had been a lot of years since he'd felt the sweet tug of attraction. That the woman should be Sage, an unsuitable choice for many reasons, confounded him—and intrigued him.

Once inside the safety of the house, she still hadn't relaxed. Not until Dan's pickup rolled out of the ranch some twenty minutes later. Whatever he'd done to her and Isa must have been very hurtful for Sage to have reacted like she had. Especially after four years.

His common sense warned him to steer clear of her. That she had emotional baggage. More than just carry-on.

But then there was that sweet tug.

"How long have you worked for the BLM?" Ethan asked, and proceeded to shovel an impressive bite of spaghetti into his mouth.

"Eight years." Unlike Ethan, Sage picked at her meal, consuming only half of what she pushed around on her plate.

"What made you decide to work for them?"

"A friend actually convinced me to apply."

"Did she also work for the BLM?"

"Um, he did, yes."

It was less that the friend was a man than the hesitancy in Sage's voice that roused Gavin's curiosity. He'd like to hear the parts of the story she was omitting.

Ethan continued chatting amiably with their guests. He'd always been the more outgoing one, with Gavin preferring to listen rather than talk. Ethan was equally willing to talk about himself and considered himself an open book. Except when it came to his leg. That was a topic he didn't discuss, even with his family.

"Have you always had horses?"

"Actually, no. Not until community college when I took a riding class because I thought it would be an easy A." Sage gave a small laugh. "Turns out, it wasn't so easy. But I loved the class and now horses aren't just my job, they're my life."

"My papa's a horse trainer."

At Isa's announcement, Sage's fork clattered to her plate. Sending an embarrassed glance around the table, she picked it up.

"Really?" Ethan winked at Isa then went for seconds of the tossed salad. "That's neat."

"What kind of horse trainer?" Cassie asked.

She and Isa had become fast buddies, which was more than Gavin could say about any of the kids at school. Principal Rodgers had told him Cassie didn't relate well to her peers. She related well to younger children, as evidenced by her busy babysitting schedule, and had taken Isa under her wing from the moment they met.

"I don't know." Isa looked questioningly at Sage.

"Western equestrian mostly," she replied.

"He lives in Mustang Village," Isa added with a bright, lopsided smile. "That's why we came here. So I can see him."

"The only horse trainer I know of in Mustang Village is—"

Gavin shook his head but his brother didn't notice.

"—Dan Rivera."

"That's him." Isa jiggled gleefully in her seat.

Sage paled.

"No fooling?" Ethan grinned. "He was just here—"

"The other day," Gavin cut in.

"No, he—"

"Yes, the other day," he repeated, and shook his head again.

This time, Ethan saw him and shut up.

"Cassie, why don't you and Isa help me serve the dessert?" Gavin's father suggested, rising from the table. "We have chocolate pudding."

Both girls jumped up to help.

If Gavin didn't know better, he might have thought his father was intentionally diverting a disaster.

The remainder of dinner passed without incident,

though the quizzical stare Ethan aimed at Gavin was hard to ignore. When they were done, their father recruited the girls' assistance again, this time to clear the table and load the dishwasher.

"Do you mind keeping an eye on Isa while her mom, Uncle Ethan and I pack for tomorrow?"

To Gavin's relief, Cassie was agreeable.

"Come on, pip-squeak." She didn't have to ask twice. Isa was hot on her heels in a heartbeat, and the two of them began carting dishes to the sink.

Sage remained subdued as she, Gavin and Ethan walked to the stables. It had grown dark during dinner but their path was illuminated by two exterior lights, one on the back porch and the other mounted above the entrance to the stables. Inside, Gavin flipped a switch and more lights came on, startling some of the horses that weren't used to so much activity after dark.

Gavin extracted a handwritten list from his pocket as they approached the tack room. "I was thinking two packhorses should be enough."

While he and Ethan collected and debated over the various equipment and supplies they would be taking, Sage carried three large canteens to the water spigot outside and filled them. She had only just returned when Ethan's cell phone rang.

He answered it and after a brief, cryptic conversation ended with "See you in half an hour."

"Going somewhere?" Gavin asked.

"Is it a problem? I can stay if you need me to."

"No, it's all right. There isn't much left." If not for wanting to get Sage alone so they could finish their earlier conversation, Gavin might have waylaid his brother and pumped him for more information. This was the third time in the past two weeks he'd left after receiving a phone call and without saying exactly where he was going.

They hurried through the remainder of the packing. "Come on and walk with me," Gavin said the moment Ethan was gone.

"Where?"

"I need help carrying the feed for the mares we're leaving in the canyon overnight." He didn't hurry in the hopes she'd take a cue from him and relax. She didn't. He decided to try a different tactic.

"Cassie's only been living with me since the summer. Before that, she was with her mother full-time. In Connecticut."

"That's quite a ways from Arizona."

They reached the barrels in the hay shed behind the stables where the grain and pellets were stored.

"Her mom moved to Manchester not long after Cassie was born. I only got to see her about every three years. Not by choice. I was young when she was born. Barely twenty-one. My mother had just passed away after a long illness. Money was scarce. We'd sold off most of the ranch two years earlier along with our cattle operation. I didn't have a job, and the only thing I knew how to do was raise cattle."

"Why are you telling me this?"

"You mentioned that Dan hasn't seen Isa in four years. I just thought it might help if you—"

"Dan didn't want to see Isa. And trust me, he's had plenty of chances. He may not want to see her now, which will really disappoint her. You saw at dinner how excited she is."

Gavin had seen. And he had to admit, he didn't understand his partner. He'd have given his right arm to be a bigger part of Cassie's life during her childhood. Maybe then they'd have the kind of close relationship he yearned for.

Setting down the scoop he'd been using to fill the sack with pellets, he removed his cell phone from his belt and dialed a number. When a familiar female voice answered, he said, "Hi, Maria, is Dan there?"

"What are you doing?" Sage hissed.

Gavin angled the phone away from his mouth. "We're leaving in the morning at 7 a.m. sharp. The problem or issue or whatever's going on with you and Dan has got to be resolved by then. There's too much riding on capturing the mustang for it not to be."

"More than you know."

Gavin pressed the disconnect button on his phone. "Tell me."

She remained stubbornly quiet.

"How can I help with Dan if you don't level with me."

"I don't see how you can help."

"He's an intelligent man whose priority is to make money. He'll do what's right for our partnership."

"Dan doesn't give a rat's hind end about anyone but himself."

Gavin didn't agree with Sage. He'd seen Dan go above and beyond for his wife, son, friends and clients. But Sage's anger at him was clearly real and deep and, in her mind at least, justified.

"I admit, he's egotistical. But he's basically a decent guy."

"Yeah. Well how many decent guys do you know who refuse to pay their court-ordered child support and haven't for almost four years?"

Her outburst stunned Gavin into silence. Dan didn't strike him as someone who turned his back on fiscal and moral obligations. If anything, it was the opposite. Which was why Gavin trusted Dan enough to become his partner.

"I'm…sorry, Sage." What else could he say? "I can understand why you didn't want him to see Isa today."

"It's complicated," she replied meekly.

"I'm sure it is."

"I don't understand him."

Neither did Gavin. He may not have visited Cassie as often as he'd wanted to, but he'd never failed to send so much as one child support payment or even been late, regardless of how strapped the family had been for money.

"I'm pretty sure I can convince him not to come with us tomorrow."

"You said before he's your partner and financial backing and entitled to go."

"He is. And the extra man would come in handy."

"Then why take the chance?"

"Because four of us working well together will be better than five, two of whom are at odds."

"I can handle Dan without your interference."

"Is that so?" Gavin scratched his chin thoughtfully. "Because earlier today you had no problem with me interfering."

"Dan caught me off guard," she defended herself. "Tomorrow, I'll be ready."

She put up a brave front. Her eyes gave her away. She wasn't ready to face Dan and less ready to work with him. Gavin couldn't risk their expedition into the mountains going awry.

Taking out his phone again, he punched Dan's number. This time, Dan answered rather than his wife. Gavin skipped any customary preambles. "I don't know if you're aware of this or not, but the BLM agent who arrived yesterday, the one who will be going with us to capture the mustang, is someone you know. Sage Navarre."

Gavin tried not to read anything into the lengthy pause that followed. Beside him, Sage rubbed her palms nervously along the sides of her jeans.

He began to doubt the wisdom of his plan.

Not that he and Cassie's mother got along famously. A part of him still resented her for the pressure she and her parents had skillfully applied on him during the vulnerable time in his life after his mother died. But when they did speak, he was always civil and agreeable for Cassie's sake *and* his own. He didn't want to give her mother any reason to deny him visitation or turn his daughter against him.

"Do you really need me to go with you?" Dan asked, his tone revealing nothing.

"We can manage with four of us." That was their original plan anyway before Sage arrived.

"Then I'll stay home and go with you next time."

"If all goes well, we won't need a next time." He and Sage exchanged glances. Hers was hopeful.

"Good luck," Dan said, and hung up after a quick goodbye. Not at all like him. He usually talked Gavin's ear off.

"He's not coming."

Sage's shoulders sagged. "Thank you."

"No problem."

She smiled, the first honest one she'd given him since they met.

The radiance from it went straight to his heart where it warmed the dark corners left cold for so long.

In that moment Gavin knew he was a man in serious trouble.

Sage stood to the side, pulling her jacket snug against the early morning chill. She'd like to be more help, and had offered repeatedly, but the fact was she'd probably be a hindrance. Gavin, Ethan and Conner, their cowboy friend, were a well-oiled machine. They saddled up the horses, hefted the panniers onto the pack saddles, then loaded the supplies, equipment and feed. Their efficiency let Sage know this was hardly their first expedition into the mountains.

Ethan's next remark confirmed it. "Remember that time Dad took our Boy Scout troop on a pack trip to Pinnacle Peak?"

"I'm still mad about that," Conner joked, loading a five-gallon jug of water. "You guys left me and Gary Cohen at the bottom of that ravine for five hours. Without food or water. We thought we were goners."

"Not our fault you went looking for a shortcut."

"Your dad told us to. Said if we were going to keep bellyaching, we could just figure out a way home on our own. What kind of Boy Scout leader does that?" Conner shook his head, but there was laughter in his voice.

"He didn't think you'd really take off."

"Gary used our only match to set our shirts on fire and signal for help with the smoke."

"And it worked." Ethan clapped Conner affectionately on the back as he walked past. "We found you."

Sage was certain Conner and his friend were never in any real danger and had more fun than he was letting on.

"I didn't talk to your dad for a whole year. Which was pretty hard considering he was also our baseball coach."

Chuckling, Gavin covered the bulging panniers with a large plastic tarp. He and Ethan had decided on three packhorses in total, two of them mares they intended on leaving overnight. The heavy tarps covering the panniers would protect the feed, equipment and supplies from damage or falling out along the trail, which had been described to Sage as challenging.

"It's a miracle any of us survived to grow up," Conner said good-naturedly. "If your dad wasn't trying to kill us on the trail, he was working us to death on the baseball field."

"Those were the days." Ethan's smile was wistful and, Sage noted, a little sad.

So was Gavin's.

"It was a shame about your mom," Conner confessed, securing a galvanized steel tub to the top of the pack saddle frame with a piece of twine. "Don't think your dad's ever gotten over her."

Neither brother commented.

After a moment, Gavin glanced around. "We should get a move on. It's plenty light now. You ready, Sage?"

"Yeah." She nodded, curious about Gavin's mother but not wanting to ask. The man they'd been describing in their stories didn't at all resemble the quiet and subdued one she'd met at dinner the previous night.

"Mount up!"

Sage noticed that Ethan climbed onto his big bay gelding from the right side rather than the left, as was usual. She promptly forgot about it when Avaro began acting up.

"Quiet, girl," she soothed. After not being ridden for

three full days, one of those spent cooped up in a trailer, the young horse was, as the saying went, feeling her oats.

Sage, not so much. Despite Gavin's conviction that they would capture the mustang, she remained dubious. In all her time at the BLM, she'd never seen a single horse willingly submit to capture. Gavin's mustang would be no different.

There was considerable shifting, prancing, nipping and scuffling until order was established and the pack-horses grew accustomed to their loads. Drawing stares from the few regulars out this early on a Saturday morning, they rode through the ranch and out a gate behind the empty cattle barn.

Avaro refused to settle down and tested Sage's patience. The mare's behavior worsened as they rode along the pasture where the Powell broodmares and their young trotted along beside the fence.

At the far end of the pasture, Ethan turned his horse onto a dirt road that bore the imprint of hundreds of horse hooves. Within minutes, they were in the foothills. Soon after that, the road narrowed to a trail that rose upward at a steep angle. They automatically formed a single-file line, the horses walking nose to tail.

Sage chose to bring up the rear, not sure how Avaro would act with another horse so close behind her and in unfamiliar surroundings. Her worries proved unfounded. Avaro attacked the steep trail with the same enthusiasm she did everything else, instinctively following the pack mare behind Gavin.

At a fork in the trail, they took the higher, more rugged branch. Very soon, all the horses were noticeably laboring. Stopping atop a rise, they let their mounts rest. During their ascent, Sage had been intent on the trail and watching where Avaro placed her feet. Looking around, she gave a small surprised gasp.

The view was nothing less than spectacular.

Behind them lay the ranch and Mustang Village, nestled in the heart of the valley. Ahead of them stretched the mountains, a series of peaks and gullies that went on as far as the eye could see. To their right was the city of Scottsdale and beyond that, Phoenix. The metropolitan area stretched for miles and miles, bordered on all sides by deep brown and vibrant green mountains not unlike the one they were on. A dazzling blue sky hung overhead.

"I'd love to see this at night with all the city lights."

"I'll bring you if you want," Gavin said.

Sage's remark had been offhand, but he'd taken it seriously. "I probably won't have time while I'm here."

He shrugged and turned to face forward in his saddle.

Had her easy dismissal of his invitation hurt him? She told herself no, that Gavin wasn't a sensitive man. But guilt ate at her nonetheless. He'd only been trying to be nice.

"How much farther?" she asked when Gavin and Ethan were finished discussing the condition of the trail, which had deteriorated since the summer monsoons.

"About another hour." Gavin pointed. "See that butte over there? The box canyon is on the other side."

It looked far away. Really far. And the going a little treacherous. Okay, a lot. Sage figured she'd better have some water while she could and unwound her canteen from where it hung on her saddle horn.

Avaro began pawing the ground.

"Let's see if you're still raring to go when we reach the top of the next rise," she muttered, and rehung her canteen.

Conversation was at a minimum during the rest of the ride. Partly because they were so spread out and partly because of the noise generated from seven horses' hooves hitting the hard, rocky ground simultaneously.

Sage spotted wildlife everywhere she looked. Hawks, rabbits, coyotes, lizards and even a king snake. Any larger animals, including the mustang, surely heard them coming from a mile away and were long gone. Except for javelina.

"Look over there," Gavin said.

At the bottom of a ravine, a small herd of about eight or nine of the wild pigs scuttled through the brush.

Dropping his reins, Ethan cupped his hands around his mouth and made an odd grunting sound. The two largest javelina stopped, the row of inky bristles on their back standing straight up.

"Boars," Gavin told her.

"Do you hunt them?" she asked.

"Not since I was a kid. My grandfather used to take Ethan and me. We lost interest in high school."

"Sports?"

"That and rodeoing."

"What were your events?"

"Everything. But I was best at roping and steer wrestling."

"Did Ethan rodeo, too?"

"He was one of the top junior bull and bronc riders in the state."

"Did he compete professionally?"

"No." Gavin shook his head. Before Sage could ask why, he told her. "My mother got sick. After she died, Ethan joined the Marines and I took over running the ranch."

His expression shut down, letting Sage know the subject was closed.

"Come on," Ethan called over his shoulder, and urged his horse ahead.

The rest of them followed without any encouragement.

Sage didn't know the Powells well, but after spending three days in their company, she'd reached the conclusion that whatever happened to Gavin's mother had profoundly affected the entire family—in ways they were still grappling with even today.

Chapter 6

One well-placed step at a time, the horses descended what had to be the steepest trail so far. Sage leaned back in the saddle, instinctively balancing her weight.

At the bottom, the riders continued to the entrance of the box canyon, the walls of which rose five stories high. Progress was slow, hampered by a particularly rugged patch of ground.

"Not much farther," Gavin announced.

Sage refrained from crying out with joy. She considered herself a competent horsewoman and spent many hours a week on Avaro. None of those hours were a tenth as grueling as this morning's ride had been. The constant up and down had strained her back and legs and knees especially. Fifteen minutes ago she'd developed an aggravating stitch in her side.

To her annoyance, Gavin, Ethan and Conner didn't appear any worse for the wear. Then again, they'd grown up in these mountains and probably took ranch customers on trail rides like this one all the time. Customers who surely fared worse than her.

That didn't stop her from hiding her aches and pains and utter exhaustion.

"How's this spot?" Ethan asked when they reached the tapered end of the canyon.

The panniers were heavy, even empty. When Sage was done, she went in search of rocks and anything else that might come in handy.

After some debate, Gavin and Ethan selected a natural shelter along the canyon wall for the location of the pen. Though the ground was uneven, the overhang would provide adequate shade.

Sage studied the shelter as she carried rocks to it. Would the mares be safe? She wouldn't want to leave Avaro in the wild overnight.

"What about predators?" she asked Gavin. "Any risk?"

"Not likely."

"But not impossible?"

"Quit worrying, Sage."

He hefted a rock at least twice the size of the ones she'd found and lugged it over to the pile. Ethan laid out the pen, marking the four corners with some of the rocks while Conner untied a bundle of metal fence posts.

Sage paused to watch. There was something about men at work that struck a chord in her—reminding her that they were bigger, stronger, more physically capable than women. It was also…sexy.

Gavin was sexy.

The sound of Ethan driving fence posts into the ground with a rubber mallet drew her attention away from his brother. As soon as he was finished with one post, he started on the next. Sage carried more rocks to the pen, ignoring the nagging twinge in her back.

This will pass, she thought, *with a hot bath and a couple of aspirins.*

All at once, Ethan lost his balance and went down on his knees, the rubber mallet flying from his hands. He let out a deep "Oomph" as he pitched forward onto all fours.

Sage dropped her rock and started toward him. "Ethan! You okay?"

Gavin was instantly beside her, his hand on her arm restraining her. "Leave him alone," he said in a soft voice.

Ethan was already picking himself up and dusting himself off.

"He could be hurt," she protested.

"He won't want your help. Or mine, for that matter."

"Are you crazy?" She noticed Conner hadn't moved, either. What was wrong with them? They all three were taking this macho guy thing way too far.

Gavin bent and retrieved her rock. "It's important for Ethan that he do things on his own."

"Come on, Gavin. Enough already. It's not like he's disabled."

"Not disabled." He placed the rock in Sage's hands. "But he does have a prosthetic leg."

Sage stared at Gavin, speechless. Then at Ethan. She recalled him mounting his horse from the right side and rubbing his knee after they'd dismounted.

"I'm...sorry." She wished she weren't holding the rock so she could bury her face in her hands. "That was insensitive of me."

"Relax. You didn't know."

Ethan had finally stood and was retrieving the rubber mallet he'd dropped. He went on hammering the next fence post as if nothing out of the ordinary had happened.

"I can't believe he still rides," Sage said. "And shoes horses."

"Why not?"

"Because, it...must be hard."

"It is."

"Then why—?"

"This is what we do, Sage. We're cowboys. Always have been and always will be. Losing our ranch, our cattle, our valley to a residential community isn't going to stop us."

He walked away then.

"Gavin, wait!"

He paused. Turned. Only his eyes weren't on her. They narrowed, then widened. "Ethan," he said. "Conner."

His brother and friend looked up from their work. Sage looked, too, and saw what they did.

The mustang. Not a hundred yards from them.

Sage's heart stilled. Before it could start beating again, the jet-black horse tossed his head, whinnied and galloped away, his hooves clattering on the rocks.

So much for her theory that he'd left the area to find a new territory.

"Sage. Hold on a minute." Gavin hurried to catch up with her.

She made it hard for him by not slowing down.

They'd returned to the ranch thirty minutes ago after a long ride back. In that time, they'd unsaddled the horses and put them up, then assembled the equipment for tomorrow. Sage had kept to herself for the most part, both on the ride back to the ranch and afterward.

Gavin let her stew in silence. He had no problem with their differences of opinions, on wild horses, on how to raise their kids and whether or not Ethan should be allowed to live his life in the manner he chose. People didn't always agree.

But when it came to the mustang, he and Sage needed to reach a compromise if they were both going to achieve their goals.

"Okay, I get it. You're mad."

"I'm not mad." She slowed her steps. "It's just that…" They neared the parking area where she'd left her truck that morning. Stopping, she fished her keys from her pocket and depressed the remote door lock. "This whole day has been a disaster."

"Disaster?" He gave her a crooked smile. "Trying, maybe."

She glared at him. "The ride was pure torture."

"I warned you."

"Yes, you did." Her posture sagged. "And then there was Ethan. I totally botched that."

"Come on." He reached for her hand.

"I want to go home." She remained rooted in place, though she didn't withdraw her hand.

He took that as a good sign. "I won't keep you long. I promise."

As they walked, he tried not to dwell on how soft her skin felt or how perfectly her fingers fit inside his. He also ignored the stares from Ethan and Conner and the regular customers milling around the open area. Let them reach their own conclusions. He was too busy enjoying Sage's touch, the first intimate female contact he'd had in over two years.

"Are we going to the house?" she asked.

"The front courtyard. We can talk privately there."

"It's beautiful," she said when they entered the courtyard through a squeaky wrought iron gate.

"My grandfather built it for my grandmother not long after they were married."

A series of three circular steps extended from a large oak door to the spacious courtyard floor. In the center sat an elaborate fountain, though water hadn't run in it for several years. Paloverde and desert willow trees grew side by side outside the low stucco wall, like soldiers standing guard. In the distance, clearly visible between the trees, was Mustang Village.

"It needs some work, I'm afraid." Gavin automatically glanced around.

Many of the red clay tiles were cracked from age, and the trees were in dire need of trimming. The stucco wall hadn't seen a replastering or fresh coat of paint in two decades.

"What's a little disrepair when you have something this charming?"

Sage was being kind. It made him like her all the more. Made him dislike having to let go of her hand.

He escorted her to a pair of chairs tucked in the corner of the courtyard and facing a chipped and weathered Mexican chimenea.

"When my grandparents got older and slowed down," Gavin explained, "my father built these chairs for them. He used leftover boards from the original house my great-grandfather built."

Sage ran her fingertips along an armrest.

Gavin wondered what it might feel like to have those same fingertips caressing him with such delicateness.

He cleared his throat. "It was really more of a shed than a house. There are photographs of it hanging in the hall. My great-grandfather died before the house was finished. Took my granddad five years to complete it."

"That's a great story."

"My father spends a lot of time out here when the weather's nice. And Cassie when she's in a mood." He gestured to the chairs, and Sage sat down.

"When did your family come to the valley?"

"1910." He dropped down beside her. "Ethan, Sierra and I are the fourth generation of Powells to run the ranch."

"Sierra? You have a sister?" Sage looked at him, her brown eyes large and inquisitive.

Gavin was captivated. "Uh…yeah." Sierra. They were talking about Sierra. He had to remember. "She lives in San Francisco."

"How'd she wind up there?"

"That's where the company she works for is based. She visits every chance she gets." He was exaggerating. During the past two years, Sierra had gone to great lengths to put as much physical and emotional distance between her and the rest of them. No one understood why.

"What is it you want to talk about, Gavin?" Sage asked. "I'm guessing it's not your family."

"Actually, it is." He adjusted his hat, buying himself another few seconds. Discussing the past wasn't easy for him. "Twelve years ago, my mother was diagnosed with heart disease. Within months, her health deteriorated. The doctors considered her a good candidate for a transplant. There was only one snag. My parents didn't have adequate health insurance to cover the costs."

He loosened his fingers, which had curled into fists, and continued.

"Dad tried borrowing the money. All the banks turned him down. Ethan and I were too young to be of any financial help. Our neighbor, Bud Duvall, offered to bail us out. At the time, my parents considered him a godsend. He bought all of our land, except for the house, barn, bunkhouse, stables and thirty acres of pasture. He agreed to let us use the land rent free for our cattle operation and then sell it back to us once my mother's heath improved. Interest free."

"Except that didn't happen," Sage guessed.

Gavin swallowed. Even after all these years, Duvall's betrayal still left a bitter taste in his mouth.

"The transplant was successful. But after a few months, my mother's body began rejecting the donor heart. Eventually, an infection developed. She lacked the strength to fight it off. Even if we'd had the money for a second transplant surgery, which we didn't, the transplant board considered her too high a risk. A few weeks later, she died."

"Oh, Gavin." Sage pressed a hand to her lips.

"Cassie was born during the last week of my mother's life. I had no idea that Sandra was even pregnant. We'd only dated a couple months before she broke up with me and didn't see each other after that. I found out about Cassie when she was six weeks old. Sandra's parents hired an attorney, and he showed up at the ranch one day. They wanted to make a deal. I'd give up all custody of Cassie so that Sandra could move with her to Connecticut and live with her parents. In exchange, I wouldn't have to pay any child support."

"And you agreed?"

"Hell, no. But I was young. Twenty-one. My mother had just died. Our cattle business was on the brink of bankruptcy. I wasn't in any position to be a father. As much as I hated to admit it, Sandra's parents were capable of giving Cassie more than I ever could."

"You're her *father*."

"Which is the reason I didn't give up my rights. I paid child support and insisted on visitation."

"Good for you."

"Except I seldom visited. Every three years was all I could afford."

"At least you saw her."

He guessed from her tone she was thinking of Dan.

"I was still a stranger to her."

"Not anymore."

That was debatable. There were times when he and Cassie argued, she looked at him as if she didn't know him from the man behind the deli counter at the local market.

"Mom's death was just the beginning," he continued. "Ethan joined the Marines, his way of coping with the grief. My dad sunk into a deep depression, one he's never come out of. And Sierra, hell, she was just sixteen. Still in high school."

"Which left you to step up and take charge of the family."

"It was my idea to turn the ranch into a public riding stable. We had to do something after Duvall sold our land to an investor."

"I thought you said you had an agreement with him."

"He didn't honor it."

"What about an attorney? Couldn't you have fought the sale?"

"We hired one. Turns out there were a lot of loopholes in the contract. All of them favoring Duvall. My dad had been so anxious to get the money for Mom's transplant surgery, he didn't read the fine print."

Sage reached over and touched Gavin's arm. After a moment, he covered her hand with his.

They sat in silence for several moments before she spoke again.

"You should be commended, Gavin. You've done a great job providing for your family."

"Not that great. We barely get by." His gaze traveled the courtyard, taking in the numerous repairs that needed doing. "I might have been satisfied with that indefinitely. Except something changed this past summer. Something that's made me determined to not only keep the ranch but fix it up into something I'd be proud to pass down to the next generation of Powells."

"Cassie came to live with you."

"Sandra remarried two years ago. They had a baby girl in March. By July, Cassie was here."

"She doesn't like her new sister?"

"Are you serious? You saw her with Isa. She loves kids and, from what Sandra says, doted on the baby. Next to riding horses, the thing she seems to like best is babysitting. She's got quite a nice side business going with some of our customers' children."

"What's wrong then?"

"It's her stepdad. They don't get along. At all. I understand he's strict. Sandra and her parents have always spoiled Cassie. And she's twelve. The school principal is continually reminding me that preadolescence is a challenging age."

"If she is spoiled it doesn't show. She seems like a great kid to me."

"She is a great kid. A little willful at times."

Sage smiled softly. "Like father, like daughter."

There it was again. That radiance warming his insides. He resisted. Sage wasn't the wisest choice for a romantic relationship even if he was in the market for one.

"Believe it or not, Cassie's the one who asked to come out here. I wish I could say she wanted to see me as much as I did her. The real reason was Sandra and her husband had decided to send Cassie to a boarding school in Massachusetts. She was already attending private school, thanks to her grandparents. I guess they figured boarding school wouldn't be much different."

"Excuse me for being rude, but that sounds, well, insensitive."

"It was. Cassie felt like Sandra chose her husband and new child over her."

"What kid wouldn't feel that way?"

"Rough as it's been on her, I'm grateful. It gave me the chance to be a real dad to her. If she adjusts well and chooses to stay permanently, Sandra's told me she won't object. Of course, she could go back on her word." Gavin had only to remember how low she and her parents had stooped in the past. "But I'm not going to let myself worry about that till it happens."

"I hope it doesn't," Sage said.

Gavin echoed her sentiment. "I know I have a lot to learn about parenting. I say the wrong things, lecture when I should be listening. But I love her and have sworn to do right by her. Give her everything a kid her age needs."

"I still don't see how any of this—"

"With the mustang, I'll be able to bring in more revenue. For Cassie. And to make this place into something other than a ramshackle old house and a falling down barn."

"I do understand how important it is for a parent to provide for their child."

"It's more than that. Powell Ranch isn't just a home. It's our legacy."

"Like being cowboys and keeping the tradition alive," Sage said thoughtfully.

"Exactly."

"You're counting an awful lot on that mustang."

"I'm also counting on your help capturing him."

Her expression hardened. "And Dan for his financial backing."

So much for winning her over. "I know what I'm asking of you isn't easy. To work with your ex-husband—"

"We were never married." Dark emotion flashed in her eyes.

"Sorry." He shouldn't have assumed, especially given his own circumstances. "Dan's loss."

She regarded him for several seconds, then the valley below. "It is really pretty here. Even with all the houses and buildings. I can see why you'd fight to keep it."

He read between the lines. "You can't put your differences with Dan aside."

"Actually, I think I could. Him, on the other hand..." She shrugged. "Doubtful."

"He was agreeable when I talked to him yesterday."

"He won't be much longer. And I'm not sure you will, either."

"What's going on, Sage?"

"I didn't come to Mustang Valley solely for the horse. Or to arrange for Isa to meet her father." She smoothed her ponytail, the gesture a nervous one. "Dan owes me, owes Isa, a considerable amount of back child support."

He waited for her to finish, his stomach tightening with each second.

"I'm going to collect it. Do whatever's necessary. Like you are for Cassie. Things might get awkward and unpleasant."

Gavin could see where they would.

"It's possible..." She rose. "No, I'll be honest with you. It's very likely you'll be involved."

"How?" He also rose.

"I wish there was another way. You have no idea how much. But I have to think of Isa. She has a right to the money Dan owes her."

"Tell me."

"You'll be receiving garnishment papers from the state soon."

Gavin sank back into his chair. "How soon?"

"I'm guessing by the end of the week."

He could easily imagine Dan's reaction.

Sage placed a hand on Gavin's shoulder. "I hope your agreement with Dan is in writing and ironclad."

It wasn't, but he didn't tell her that and barely noticed when she walked away.

Chapter 7

The ride to the canyon on Sunday was every bit as demanding for Sage as the previous day. Not so for the men. Ethan and Conner, leastwise. Their spirits soared as the four of them navigated the same steep trails and jagged terrain. When conversation was possible, they talked about what techniques they'd employ to capture the mustang, confident of returning to the ranch in a few hours with their prize in tow.

Sage said little. Neither did Gavin. Not to her, anyway.

Okay, she deserved the silent treatment after the bombshell she'd dropped on him yesterday. If he'd just talk to her, she'd apologize. Tell him how she hated putting him and his family in a bad position. They were innocent bystanders. Like her and Isa. Victims of Dan's selfishness. She had no choice except to report any possible payees to the Child Support Enforcement Agency.

A turn on the trail tickled her memory. Up ahead, she recognized the entrance to the box canyon and silently rejoiced. Ahead of her, the three men simultaneously craned their necks to see into the canyon. Sage did, too.

"You spot him?" Gavin asked Ethan. He was leading the gelding, the lone packhorse they'd brought along.

"Not yet."

The horses increased their pace, no doubt picking up

on their riders' eager anticipation to reach their destination. Sage patted Avaro's neck. The mare had once more started out the morning acting up, then quickly calmed, for which Sage and her sore muscles were grateful.

Five minutes later, they finally had a clear, if distant, view of the mares in their makeshift pen.

From what Sage could tell, there was no sign of the mustang. She tried to stave off disappointment. He could be hiding beneath the rock ledge or behind a rise.

Gavin reined in his horse, causing Sage to stop, as well. He reached behind him, removed a pair of binoculars from his saddlebags and lifted them to his eyes. After several moments of scanning the canyon in every direction, he lowered the binoculars.

No one asked what he'd seen. The answer was clearly written on his face.

The mustang wasn't in the canyon.

Sage rolled her sore shoulders and sighed. All this work for nothing. She should have insisted on contacting the city about using the ATVs. Now, they had no choice.

"How are the mares?" Ethan asked.

"They look okay from here."

As the group started out again, the mares spotted them and began whinnying, their high-pitched calls echoing through the canyon. Avaro and the gelding both answered back.

Near the pen, they dismounted and tethered their horses.

Conner was the first to reach the mares, who pressed eagerly against the sagging lines. "Come here!" Motioning everyone over, he pointed at the ground.

There was no need to clarify. Sage could see what had raised his interest. Hoofprints. Lots of them. Outside the pen and all around.

The mustang might not be here now, but he'd returned at some point during the night.

Gavin pulled on one of the pen's lines, which hung loosely in his hand. "He tried to get to the mares."

"Or they tried to get out," Ethan said.

"Probably both," Conner added.

Gavin raised his gaze to the canyon walls. "You can bet he's not far."

"And that he'll be back."

"I'm counting on it."

Conner meandered over to where the bottom line was anchored to the thick root of a shrub growing between two boulders and began untying it.

Sage assumed to disassemble the pen.

Shouldn't someone locate the halters first so the mares wouldn't get loose?

Gavin checked the level of water they'd left for the mares, absently stroking the head of the nearest one.

Sage waited for him to dump the remaining water so they could load the tub and take it home with everything else.

Ethan returned to the packhorse, his limp every bit as pronounced as before, and started unfastening the ropes securing the pack saddles. "Sage, how about a hand with this?"

She hurried to help him, mentally calculating how long it would take them to pack up and get back on the trail. How long until she could soak away her aches and pains in another hot bath.

Together, she and Ethan lifted the heavy plastic tarp. Beneath it, in the panniers, was a five-gallon jug of water, a large sack of pellets, additional line and some of the same equipment they'd brought yesterday.

Sage stared at the items in disbelief.

"I thought..." Words failed her.

"What?" Ethan looked at her over the horse's back, his expression innocent.

Irritation flared. Were he and his brother taking her for a fool? Then it struck her. "You're leaving the mares here another night."

Gavin came up beside her.

She faced him, accusation in her voice. "You planned this all along."

"We considered the possibility it might take more than one night to lure the mustang into the canyon and came prepared."

"That's not what you told me."

He reached past her and dug into the pannier, removing the sack of pellets. Hefting it into his arms, he carried it to the makeshift pen.

"I can't come back tomorrow." Sage chased after him.

He set the sack on the ground and straightened. "Why not? You said you had a whole week. It's only been four days."

Sage swallowed. She wasn't going to tell him about the paternity test and the appointment she'd made for her and Isa. "I have a previous commitment."

"All day?"

"In the morning."

"Fine. We'll ride out after lunch. Ethan, can you get someone to cover your classes?"

"I'll ask Rebecca."

Gavin returned his attention to Sage. "Will that give you enough time for your commitment?"

His matter-of-fact attitude irked her. They were supposed to have the mustang by now.

She should have known it wouldn't be that easy.

"You can bring Isa with you to the ranch." He bent down and stepped between the lines, entering the pen. The mares immediately crowded around him, sensing that food was coming. "My dad will keep an eye on her. Cassie can take her riding again on Chico."

"No." Sage quashed the panic bubbling in her and hissed, "What if Dan's there?"

"He won't be."

"And you know this for sure?"

Thankfully, Gavin lowered his voice. "I talked to him last night. He's going to Casa Grande for the day to meet with a potential client."

Well, that much was a relief at least.

Gavin poured the pellets into the trough. The mares, unable to wait, reached in for bites.

Sage reconsidered as she watched. The paternity test might be stressful for Isa. If so, an afternoon at the ranch would do her good.

"What if the mustang isn't here again tomorrow?" she asked.

Gavin climbed out of the pen and straightened to his full height. Sage had to tip her head back to look him in the eyes. Those killer blue eyes. She wasn't sure what disconcerted her the most, his height, his proximity or the way in which he studied her.

"Then we'll come back Tuesday."

"On ATVs."

His brows drew together. "We've had this discussion already."

"I think we should reopen it."

To her annoyance, he walked away from her, *again,* and back toward the packhorse.

Ethan and Conner, busy repairing the makeshift pen, stopped to stare openly at Gavin and Sage.

Rather than go after him, *again,* she, called out, "Like you said, I only have a few days left. We need to make the most of them."

"Forget it. The city won't move fast enough. Too much red tape."

"I'll see if my supervisor can expedite the request."

"No."

She did go after him then. "Gavin, this isn't a one-man operation. You don't get to make all the decisions."

He stopped unloading the equipment and glowered at her. Glowered! "I know these mountains. Every inch. And I know this horse. I've spent four months tracking his every move. You couldn't capture him with ATVs if you had a whole fleet of them. Do you have any idea how big this mountain range is?"

"No, but—"

"Over ninety-thousand acres. That's a lot of ground to cover. And I guarantee that horse can go places you can't begin to on an ATV."

Despite his annoying tone, what he said made sense. If only he weren't so stubborn.

"Fine. One more day. But if that mustang isn't here tomorrow afternoon, I'm calling my supervisor." She had no intention of spending her entire vacation in Mustang Valley chasing a horse that obviously didn't want to be chased.

Gavin smiled. The same devastatingly handsome smile he'd given her when they first met. To her embarrassment, a fluttery sensation in her middle left her mildly weak-kneed.

This was bad indeed.

She thought she heard one of the other men chuckle. When she looked over, Ethan was coughing into his hand. Ignoring him *and* Gavin, she threw herself into helping unpack.

Soon, they were done. The mares, tended and secure in their repaired pen, weren't happy to be left behind and whinnied their protests. Sage searched the canyon as they rode out, hoping for a repeat appearance of the mustang. She wasn't alone.

Unfortunately, wherever he was, nearby or not, he remained well hidden.

Sundays were evidently a slow day for the ranch. A few people were grooming or walking out their horses, and a pair of teenagers rode in the arena.

Gavin joined Sage just as she was putting Avaro up in her stall. Though he appeared friendly enough, she doubted their truce would last.

"I'm not trying to make your job harder," he said when she'd shut the stall door.

"If that's an apology, it needs a little work."

"It's not."

Was this irritating man really the same one who'd left her weak-kneed earlier? "What do you want, Gavin?"

"To make a deal with you. If the mustang isn't in the canyon tomorrow, I won't object to you calling your supervisor."

"Then you agree we can use ATVs."

"No. Only that the BLM can contact the city."

Realization dawned. "You think they'll refuse our request."

"There's a good chance of it. The city isn't known for bending the rules."

"I guess we'll see." Sage spun on her heels. She didn't get far.

Gavin quickly fell into step beside her. "Okay, I'm a jerk. I admit it. But you're being selfish."

That brought her to a halt. "Selfish?"

"You want to avoid Dan, and you have every good reason. But that's no excuse to force a method of capturing the mustang on me that not only has an ice cube's chance in hell of working, it's damaging to the environment and dangerous to the wildlife."

"This is getting us nowhere." She refused to acknowledge the grain of truth in what he said.

"There's a trail ride and picnic this afternoon. We have it every third Sunday of the month for our customers and their guests. Everyone brings their own food and drinks. We head out about four, ride for an hour, stop, eat and then come back, usually by seven or seven-thirty."

"That's nice, but what does it have to do with the mustang?"

"Yesterday you mentioned the view of the city at night. This would be your chance to see it."

She blinked in astonishment. "Are you inviting me?"

"And Isa."

"Why?" she blustered.

"Because I thought maybe if we…socialized some, it might improve our working relationship."

She almost laughed. "You're joking."

He shook his head. "Not at all."

"Let me think about it."

"Take your time."

He left her then, and she watched him stride leisurely out of the stables, the impressive width of his broad shoulders filling the jacket he wore. She'd watched those shoulders for two days now on the trail.

It wasn't a hardship, then or now.

Was she crazy to even consider going on the trail ride? Her weary body screamed yes.

Except Isa would love it. Have the time of her life. Sage had yet to tell her about the paternity test tomorrow, waiting for the perfect opportunity. Of course, she was procrastinating.

She could do it this afternoon, on the way back to the ranch. If she used the right words, downplayed the test, played up the trail ride, Isa might respond better. Be less scared.

And maybe "socializing" with Gavin *would* improve their relationship.

She hurried out of the stables. When she found him and accepted his invitation, her repeat reaction to his sexy, satisfied grin had her reconsidering her motives and cursing her vulnerability.

Sage still hadn't told Isa about the paternity test, and they would be at Powell Ranch in less than twenty minutes. She started to speak, only to have her courage desert her. How did one explain to a six-year-old that her father insisted on proof she was his biological daughter?

One didn't, obviously, and neither would Sage. She'd give some other reason for the test. A simplified version of the truth Isa would understand.

As her daughter prattled on about Chico and seeing Cassie, another mile came and went. Sage stared at the road, at the passing landscape, half listening.

A memory from two years ago suddenly sprang into sharp focus. Isa had fallen from the swing set at preschool and broken her arm. The bones hadn't healed correctly and after ten days, the orthopedic surgeon recommended rebreaking the arm.

It would hurt. A lot. Isa would cry. But it had to be done or she would be left with limited range of motion in that arm. Preparing Isa for the procedure had been one of the worst times in Sage's life. But then, thirty minutes later, it was over. Isa, sucking on a lollipop, sported a pink fiberglass cast of which she was quite proud. A week later, she'd forgotten all about the pain.

Maybe it would be the same with the paternity test.

Sage turned off Pima Road and headed east on Dynamite. Less than fifteen minutes until they reached the ranch.

"*Mija,* Mama has to talk to you about something important."

Isa stopped her animated chatter. The stuffed cat, named Purr-o, came to rest in her lap. "What?"

"We, you and I, have an appointment tomorrow morning."

"Where?"

"At a testing facility." *Smile,* she told herself, *and relax.*

"We have to take a test?"

"Yes."

"Like a spelling test?"

"More like a medical test."

"I'm going to the doctor?" Fear widened Isa's eyes.

"No, not a doctor. I swear." Sage reached over and stroked Isa's hair. "And the test won't hurt at all. Someone called a technician will just take a small sample from both of us."

"What kind of sample?"

She went on to explain the procedure in terms Isa could comprehend. "It'll only take a few minutes, and I'll be right with you the whole time."

Isa hugged Purr-o to her chest. "Do I have to?"

Here was the question Sage had dreaded the most.

"You remember Mama telling you about the money Papa pays for you?" She'd briefly mentioned the child support to Isa, omitting the part about Dan not paying for four years. "We need to have the test done in order to get the payments."

Isa's small brow knitted in confusion.

"You see, the test results will go to…" Sage paused, worried she might be overexplaining. "Will go to Papa."

"Why?"

"He asked, and I said yes."

Isa scowled and stuck out her bottom lip.

"Really, sweetie pie, the test won't hurt a bit. Afterward, when your papa pays the money, I'll buy you a pony."

Bribing her child. Could she be a worse parent?

"Will I get to meet Papa?"

Another question Sage had dreaded and one she was even less ready to answer.

"Soon. Maybe while we're here visiting Tia Anna and Tio Roberto."

First bribing and then lying to Isa. Sage truly was a terrible parent.

"Can you call him?" Isa asked out of the blue.

"What?"

"Papa. Can you call him and tell him I want to see him?"

Sage took her eyes off the road to study Isa. "Are you sure?"

Isa nodded vigorously.

"O…kay."

"When?"

"Well, I—"

"Now?"

What would she say to Dan? What would she say to Isa when Dan refused?

"Please, Mama."

With shaking fingers, Sage picked up her phone and dialed Dan's number. Relief flooded her when the call went straight to voice mail. Then shame at her relief.

"Dan," she said after the beep, "this is Sage. Call me as soon as you get this message. It's about Isa. Sorry, *mija,*" she said, gratefully disconnecting.

The delay was temporary, she reminded herself. Soon enough, she'd have to deal with Dan. If only to keep her promise to Isa.

"Are you excited about the trail ride?"

"Yeah, I guess."

Isa's response couldn't be more glum. The poor kid was having way more thrown at her than she deserved.

Sage pressed a hand to her chest and the knot of misery lodged there. She didn't cry a lot. Being a single mother, the sole support of her child, financially and emotionally, had toughened her up. But the past few days had severely weakened her defenses.

"What kind of pony will I get?" Isa asked, her tone marginally brighter. "Will it be a mustang?"

"Probably not." Sage fought the tears pricking her eyes. "Mustangs are big. And too wild for a little girl."

"Chico's big."

"But he's old. And very tame."

"Like Black Beauty." The movie was one of Isa's favorites.

"A little."

She concentrated on the end of the month, when she and Isa would head home in Show Low, with the first of the delinquent child support payments in the mail. She didn't consider Dan and his unlikely visit with Isa, having heard his fabricated excuses once too often.

By the time they reached the entrance to Powell Ranch, Sage was dry-eyed.

"There's Cassie and Blue." Isa bounced excitedly in her seat, her former happy self once more.

Thank goodness.

Cassie waved them over. Sage pulled to a stop and pushed the button to lower Isa's window. "Can Isa go with you while I park?"

"Sure. Come on, pip-squeak."

Isa bailed out of the truck, charging Cassie and throwing her arms around the older girl. Blue, connected to Cassie by a leash, jumped up on Isa's legs and begged for attention. Isa bent and scooped him up in her arms.

Her delighted laughter floated through the open window, acting like a balm on Sage's bruised emotions.

She drove slowly to the parking area behind the barn, carefully avoiding all the people and horses. The trail ride and picnic was obviously very popular with the ranch clientele. She spotted Ethan and Conner. Gavin, however, was nowhere in sight.

Just as well. Sage didn't want another confrontation with him.

Slipping the truck into an empty space, she shut off the engine and opened the door. Rather than get immediately out, she waited, needing one last minute to compose herself before facing people.

Flipping down the sun visor, she checked her reflection in the small mirror.

Wonderful. Her mascara had run and left black smudges beneath her eyes. She searched among the pile of toys and folders and CD cases for a tissue. There was none. Using the cuff of her shirtsleeve, she dabbed at her ruined makeup.

Later, she would find humor in the situation. At least no one was nearby to see her.

"You okay?"

She started at the sound of Gavin's voice. Where had he come from?

"Great," she mumbled, issuing what she hoped was another forgivable lie.

"You don't look great." He stepped closer, in between her and the open truck door.

"Allergies. Something must be in bloom."

"Here." He removed a red kerchief from his back pocket. It was clean and folded in a tidy square.

She turned it over in her hand, hating the idea of messing it and impressed by his sensitivity. "Thank you, but—"

"Go on," he urged. Kindly. Sweetly.

It was a little more than Sage could handle. Even as she wiped at her eyes, fresh tears spilled. Then a sob escaped, which she quickly swallowed. She could not, *would* not, break down. Not in front of Gavin.

Before she quite knew what was happening, she was being lifted from the truck and onto the ground...then into Gavin's arms.

Every shred of common sense she possessed urged

her to step away. She hardly knew him. Not really. One personal conversation didn't make them intimate friends.

Except his arms had settled comfortably around her and held her close with just the right amount of tenderness.

"Everything's going to be all right," he murmured in her ear.

"You don't know," she protested, a catch in her voice.

"I don't have to know. You're a strong woman. You'll get through it, whatever it is."

How long since a man, since anyone, had held her and offered her comfort? Been a shelter during a storm?

Maybe Dan, in the early days of their relationship. She honestly couldn't remember. Gavin, with his broad chest providing a very nice, very welcoming place for her to lay her head, was wiping away every memory of every man that came before him.

His hand drifted to the middle of her back and pressed lightly. Sage's own hands rested awkwardly at the sides of his denim jacket. For one brief second, she allowed herself to imagine what it would be like to circle his middle with her arms and nestle fully against him.

Crazy. And highly inappropriate. Certainly not the kind of thoughts a crying woman had about a man.

Except she wasn't crying anymore.

"Sorry about that," she murmured, and slowly began to disengage herself.

"Don't be." He halted her by tucking a finger beneath her chin, tilting her head up and bringing his mouth down on hers.

Her arms, no longer awkward and indecisive, clung to him as she gave herself over to what quickly became the most incredible kiss of her life.

Chapter 8

Kissing Sage hadn't been Gavin's intention when he first spotted her sitting in her truck, struggling not to cry. He was only going to ask if he could help.

But then he caught sight of her face and her lost expression, completely unlike the capable and fearless woman he'd come to know. Taking her into his arms, on the other hand, had been a conscious act. If there was ever someone who'd needed holding, it was Sage in that moment.

Now, leaning in, drawing her close…that was something he couldn't explain and didn't want to.

Not while they were fused together, hungry for each other.

Her lips, soft and pliant and incredibly delicious, molded perfectly to his. Then, they parted. That was all it took for Gavin's thinly held control to snap.

Wrapping his arms more tightly around her, he angled his head and tasted her fully. She responded by pressing herself flush against him, her fingers curling into the hair at the base of his neck. He seared the feel and taste of her into his memory because he would not soon forget this day.

Or her.

Stopping occurred to him. After all, there were people—lots of them—within a few dozen yards of her truck. But the next second she rose up on her tiptoes and traced the outline of his jaw with her fingertips. Gavin quit trying to be responsible for his actions and worrying about proprieties. Instead, he let his instincts take over. They served him well.

When he thought he couldn't possibly get more lost in the moment, want a woman more than he did her, the inevitable occurred.

They were interrupted.

"Mama, Mama!"

Gavin reluctantly released Sage just as Isa came racing across the parking area, Cassie and Blue not far behind.

"Over here, *mija*."

"What are you doing?" Isa's large brown eyes traveled from her mother to Gavin.

"Getting our food." Sage reached into the truck's cab and removed a small soft-sided cooler and two plastic bottles of vitamin water.

"Can I carry it?"

"Sure."

Isa took the cooler and bottles. She didn't appear to notice the vivid flush staining her mother's cheek or the unsteadiness in her voice.

Gavin did and grinned. He couldn't help it. He rather enjoyed knowing he was the cause of her discomfort.

Sage scowled at him.

He didn't let it faze him. She'd participated in their kiss every bit as much as he had. And enjoyed it every bit as much, too.

His grin died when he caught Cassie staring at them with a much-too-knowing look on her face.

Shoot. He might have some explaining to do later. For now, he chose to pretend nothing was out of the ordinary. Not easy to do when the past five minutes had been extraordinary.

"What did you bring to eat?" he asked Isa.

"Leftover chicken, fruit salad, tortillas and chocolate cookies," she answered proudly.

"Enough for me, too?"

The little girl looked dismayed. "I don't know."

"Don't worry." He tugged on her earlobe. "I was joking with you."

"You can have one of my cookies."

"Now, that's an offer I won't refuse."

Sage slammed the truck door shut and pocketed her keys. "We should probably get going."

Isa trudged out ahead of them, the cooler slung over one shoulder and the water bottles clutched to her chest. Cassie walked along beside her, Blue obediently trotting at her heels.

Gavin tried not to read too much into Cassie's silence. It hadn't occurred to him to speculate how his daughter might react to a new woman in his life since the prospect had been nonexistent until now.

Considering that Sage was leaving soon *and* was his business partner's ex, those chances were still pretty nonexistent.

Two more last-minute arrivals pulled into the parking area. The occupants of the vehicles waved as they hurried into the stables to saddle their horses. Already riders were assembled in the open area in front of the arena, some mounted, some gathered in small groups. All of them excited.

Gavin liked the monthly trail rides and picnics, and not just because they were his brainchild. Something about them reminded him a little of when he was young, back before his mother got sick and Mustang Village was built. Families from various ranches in the area would gather together a few times a year for similar trail rides and picnics.

Gavin spotted his brother helping one of their regular students, and his thoughts turned contemplative.

Also in those long-ago days, Ethan had both legs and his best friend was Clay Duvall. Gavin remembered the two boys, no more than eight or nine, fishing in the river while everyone else ate and relaxed under the shade of nearby trees.

Now Ethan wore a prosthetic leg, their mother was gone and neither of them had spoken to Duvall since his father sold the Powells' land to the investor.

Times change, and all the wishing in the world couldn't restore what had been taken from them. The best Gavin could do, for himself and his family, was take whatever life dealt them and adapt.

Until he was on solid financial ground, until his and his family's future more secure, until he knew if Cassie was living with him permanently or returning to Connecticut, he had no right getting involved with *any* woman, much less Sage.

But then, there was the kiss.

"We should talk about what happened back there," she said.

"Why spoil it with talk?"

"It was a mistake."

"There you go."

"Gavin."

He chuckled at her exasperated tone, which earned him another scowl.

"I don't want you to get the wrong idea."

He had a lot of ideas at the moment, none of which felt wrong despite his earlier attempt to convince himself otherwise.

"Kissing men I barely know isn't something I do."

"So, I'm special?"

She groaned.

"Relax, Sage, it was no big deal."

"It wasn't?"

Her dismay made him grin.

"Are you kidding?" He came to a halt. When she did, too, and he had her full attention, he said in a sober voice, "I can't remember when anything was a bigger deal."

For a moment, her eyes softened, and he saw what could be between them if things were different. But then she closed her eyes and drew in a breath. When she next looked at him, the resolve was back—as was an emotional shield he didn't have to see to know was there.

Gavin and Sage found the girls in the stables.

"Hey, Dad!" Cassie had already saddled old Chico and Barbie Doll, her favorite horse, well before Isa arrived so they'd be ready to go. "Can Isa and I ride around while you get ready?"

"It's up to her mom."

"Sure." Sage lifted Isa onto Chico. "Don't go far."

Cassie tucked Blue into the front of her jacket, adjusted the zipper over his head, then mounted. No sooner was she seated than the puppy's head popped out.

"You be careful you don't drop him," Gavin warned.

Cassie tried to push Blue back inside her jacket. He resisted. What would she do when he got bigger?

Gavin refused to think about Cassie returning to her mother's after the holidays and not seeing Blue grow up.

"Maybe Isa and I can go with you tomorrow to capture the wild mustang."

"You have school."

"Uh-uh. Fall break."

Oh, yeah.

He was inclined to let Cassie come along. His grandfather and father had taken him on rides in the mountains when he was much younger than twelve. Isa, he was less sure about.

"Can we, Mama?" she asked.

"I'm afraid not, sweetie pie."

"Please," she begged.

"No. You're too young."

Gavin recognized the tone. It was the same one his mother had used on him when further arguing was useless.

He hesitated telling Cassie she could come along if Isa couldn't.

Fortunately, Cassie spoke up.

"It's okay, Isa," she said good-naturedly. "You can stay with me. We'll go riding. And afterward, you can help me clean stalls."

Isa was appeased, judging by her happy smile.

Sage wasn't. "Okay. But not without adult supervision."

"My dad will watch them," he offered.

"Grandpa?" Cassie's mouth fell open.

"I'll ask him." It wasn't easy getting his father out of the house, but he had a soft spot for Cassie who, Gavin suspected, reminded him of Sierra.

"Fifteen minutes!" Ethan hollered from where he stood at the entrance to the stable. "Fifteen minutes!"

"We'd better hurry and saddle up."

They joined the group just in the nick of time. Gavin hoped Ethan remembered to bring their picnic dinner. If not, Isa's cookie might be all he got to eat until they returned.

Duty dictated he check on all the riders, not just Sage, and there were quite a few of them. Thirty-four, he determined after a quick head count. This was their largest monthly ride yet.

For the first time since he and his family had decided to turn what was left of their ranch into a riding stables, Gavin dared to believe he might actually carve out a decent life for himself and Cassie.

Once he had ownership of the mustang, that was.

The riders went mostly single file through the gate leading from the back pasture to the trailhead. Ethan rode in front, Conner in the middle and Gavin brought up the rear. Just as he was dismounting to shut the gate after the last rider, he noticed Sage.

Avaro was acting up again. Worse than earlier in the day. Ears pinned back, she bared her teeth at the horse beside her and threatened to kick the one behind her. Sage did a prompt and thorough job of removing Avaro a safe distance away. Holding the mare in position, she waited for Gavin.

"It might be best if I rode with you."

He was happy to oblige.

Spotting a fresh wound on Avaro's neck near her shoulder, he asked, "What happened there?"

"I think she got in a fight with her neighbor in the next stall. One I'm sure she started and that won't be her last." Sage sighed wearily.

Some mares were unbothered when they came into heat. Others, like Avaro, became cranky and aggressive.

"We have a small pen near the pasture. We could put her in there if you want."

Sage considered his suggestion, then shook her head. "She doesn't like to be alone. And she's something of an escape artist. Twice, when I've put her by herself, she's jumped the fence in order to be with other horses."

No small feat considering her compact stature.

"Why don't we put her in with the mares? They're less likely to agitate her than the geldings in the stables."

They'd reached the branch of the trail that would take them into the mountains.

"Do you mind? I don't think she'll bother the mares or foals."

Gavin agreed. Avaro was hardly paying any attention to Shasta.

"If it doesn't work, we can always put her back in a stall."

"Thank you." Sage's expression had gone soft again.

It was fast becoming Gavin's favorite one.

"About...the kiss."

He smiled. "You really are going to talk about it."

"Don't you think we should?"

"Tomorrow. When we return from capturing the mustang."

"Or tonight when we get back from the ride."

She drove a hard bargain.

Gavin was about to tell her as much when his cell phone rang. Reception was iffy out here so he reined Shasta to a stop. Sage also stopped, her glance traveling ahead to the riders stretched out in front of them. Isa and old Chico were plodding along. Cassie rode directly behind them, chatting with another girl. All was well.

Removing his phone from his pocket, he checked the display. All was evidently not well. His glance cut to Sage, then he flipped the phone open.

"Hello, Dan."

She sat straighter in the saddle, her lips compressed to a thin line.

"Is it true?" Dan demanded. "Are Sage and Isa on the trail ride with you?"

"Yes." Gavin didn't tell Dan exactly how close Sage was to him.

Dan swore in Spanish. "I agreed not to go on the roundup when you asked me. Nothing was ever said about them participating in ranch activities."

One of his clients must have mentioned the woman from the BLM. There'd been quite a stir about Sage and the mustang the past few days.

"It's no big deal," Gavin explained patiently. "When we got back from the mountains today, I invited them on the trail ride. Simply being hospitable."

"I don't want that bitch and her kid anywhere near that ranch unless it's to go after the mustang, you hear me?"

There was much in what Dan said that infuriated Gavin, starting with calling Sage a derogatory name and ending with the barely concealed threat.

"We'll talk tomorrow." Unable to continue the conversation, he disconnected and pocketed his phone.

"Like I said—" Sage gathered her reins "—kissing was a mistake." Nudging her mare into a walk, she set out after the others.

It wasn't, Gavin thought, following at a much slower pace.

But his choice of business partners was sure starting to look like one.

Gavin perched on a rock at the outskirts of the circle, eating the cookie Isa had given him. Everywhere he looked, horses were tethered to bushes and low hanging branches. This spot was one the group often chose for their picnics because of the ample level ground and breathtaking view.

The sun was at that moment slipping behind Pinnacle Peak. From where he sat, the top of the peak glowed a brilliant russet as if a fire burned within its core. Gavin had witnessed this eye-popping spectacle many times, but it never failed to amaze and inspire him.

Ethan limped over and claimed the rock next to Gavin's. The past few days had been hard on him. Fortunately, he was physically fit, thanks to the Marines and years playing sports and rodeoing before that.

Though his brother would be the last to complain, Gavin wasn't fooled. Ethan hurt and should probably see his doctor. Gavin kept his mouth shut, however. Experience had taught him his brother would go when he was damn good and ready.

"What time are we heading out tomorrow?" he asked, passing Gavin a bottled water.

"Between noon and one," he answered. "Sage has some business to take care of in the morning."

Ethan rubbed his knee where the prosthetic leg was attached. "Okay. But we have to get back at a halfway decent hour."

"You have plans?"

"I do."

His brother's mysterious comings and goings were increasing in frequency. "How soon until you're ready to tell me what it is you're up to?"

"Soon."

Gavin respected his brother's privacy, but he was also worried. "Be careful."

"I am." Ethan's gaze darted to Sage, who was chatting with a middle-aged couple. Nearby, Cassie supervised as children took turns playing with Blue. "I take it you and Sage are getting along better."

"What makes you say that?"

"I noticed you earlier at her truck. Looked to me like you were well on the way to resolving your differences."

"How much did you see?"

"Enough."

"She was upset. Dan's been giving her grief."

Ethan took a long swig of his water. "You sure you want to get involved with her? Dan's our financial backing. They may not be together anymore, but that doesn't mean he'll be okay with you dating her."

"We're not going to date."

"Then explain the kiss."

"It was an accident."

"I don't think he'll be any less angry with you just because your mouth *accidentally* collided with hers."

Ethan was right. "Dan called me when we were riding out. He's furious that Sage and Isa came along on the ride."

"What are you going to do?"

"Not let things get out of hand."

"Is that possible?"

"It's what Sage wants."

"I'm not hearing a lot of conviction in your voice."

His brother could always read him better than anyone else.

"Even if we weren't counting on Dan's money, I'd still steer clear of Sage."

"Why?"

"She lives in Show Low for starters," Gavin said quietly. His family, he knew, was frequently the topic of conversation with their customers despite his efforts to keep their private life just that.

"She can move."

"Her job is there."

"She can find a new one. Or transfer."

"I'm not in a position to date."

"Because of Cassie?"

"Partly."

Ethan snorted dismissively. "I'm pretty sure Sage likes kids."

"I have nothing to offer a woman. Financially," he clarified when Ethan started to object.

"How do you know money's important to her?"

"It's important to me." Gavin was a holdover from the dark ages, according to some people, but he'd been raised to believe a man should provide for his wife and children.

"There's another solution," Ethan said contemplatively, "if you really care for her."

Gavin's curiosity got the better of him. "What?"

"Sell the ranch."

He could tell by Ethan's grave expression, this was no joke. "Forget it."

"Before you get bent out of shape, listen to me." Ethan leaned forward, his elbows propped on his thighs, the empty bottle of water dangling between his legs. "Dad has no interest in the ranch anymore. Neither does Sierra. I'm only here because you need help."

Was that true? Gavin had always assumed Ethan's love for their family's home ran as deep as his.

"I don't have the authority to sell the ranch. It's in all of our names." Their father had deeded the remaining property equally to Gavin, Ethan and Sierra a year after their mother had died.

"I'd sign off if you want to sell," Ethan answered. "And I'm pretty sure Sierra would, too."

"No."

"I'm just saying, if you ever wanted to move. Like to Show Low."

"No," Gavin answered more emphatically. He'd buy out his brother and sister before selling the ranch. Maybe that was what they secretly wanted. "Are you tired of working with me?"

Ethan shrugged. "It's not like I'm doing anything else. Or *can* do anything else." He chuckled mirthlessly. "Not much call for one-legged bull riders or police officers." Those were the two professions Ethan had considered before joining the Marines. "It occurred to me, if we sold the ranch, maybe we could all start fresh."

What Gavin heard was "quit fighting a losing battle."

"I don't want to sell the ranch," he said. "Not yet. If the stud and breeding business tanks, then maybe I'll…" The words stuck in his throat. Gnashing his teeth together, he forced them out. "Think about it."

"First things first." Ethan clapped Gavin on the back and rose. "Gotta capture the mustang."

Gavin also rose. Evening was falling fast, and it was well past time to head back. "All the more reason to keep things professional with Sage."

Except it wouldn't be easy. As he walked the picnic area, supervising the cleanup and helping the younger riders onto their horses, he couldn't keep his eyes off her or his mind from reliving their kiss.

Chapter 9

Ten minutes into the return ride, Avaro started acting up again. After she bit yet another horse, Sage removed them from the line and waited until all the riders had gone ahead. Then, like before, fell into place beside Gavin.

Being with Shasta made little difference. Avaro pranced and fought the bit until sweat broke out on her neck and foam gathered at her mouth.

"I don't understand," Sage complained to Gavin. "She wants to be with the other horses, then kicks and bites them."

"It doesn't help that we have two stallions at the ranch."

"Probably not." Sage tugged on the reins. "I can't wait to get home."

"I'm sorry your trip isn't turning out the way you hoped it would."

"It's not your fault."

"You sure? You've been mad at me more than once."

She hadn't been mad earlier when they were kissing. Maybe at Isa for interrupting them.

"Dan's insisting on a paternity test. He's suddenly decided Isa may not be his."

"Is that what upset you?"

"I told her about the test on the way here."

"That must have been hard."

"It was awful. There's no chance the test won't come back positive. I'm just furious at Dan for putting us through it."

Avaro chose that moment to rear on her hind legs and thrash out with her front ones.

Fortunately, no other riders were nearby, except for Gavin who acted quickly and turned Shasta away.

Sage was mortified. And annoyed. Mostly at herself. She should have known better than to bring Avaro on a ride when the horse was in heat.

"There's another trail going back to the ranch," Gavin suggested when Sage once again had control of the horse— temporarily, she was sure. "We can take it if you want."

"Good idea."

"The trail's a little rough," he warned. "And it'll be dark soon."

"I can handle it."

He nodded. "Wait here for me. I'll tell Ethan."

"Can Cassie watch Isa? I hate to impose—"

"She won't mind." Gavin nudged Shasta into a trot.

"Tell her I'll pay," Sage hollered after him.

Avaro immediately started to prance in place and whinny. At one point, Sage noticed something moving from the corner of her eye. She scanned the eastern rise. A dark shape moved along the rocky ledge. In the next instant, Avaro distracted Sage by tugging hard on the reins. When Sage next looked at the rise, whatever was there, if there'd been anything at all, was gone.

Shadows, she told herself. The last smoky rays of daylight dancing across the mountains.

Gavin returned, and Avaro promptly quieted.

Soon, they came upon a narrow trail Sage hadn't noticed before. It was, as Gavin had informed her, steep and rough.

At the bottom, the ground gave way, probably washed out from a recent flash flood. Gavin's mare cleared the ditch effortlessly, landing solidly on the other side. He turned around and waited for Sage.

Avaro balked. Dropping her head, she snorted at the ditch, which was easily four feet wide and two feet deep, then pawed the earth with her right front foot, dislodging chunks of dirt and small rocks.

"Come on, girl," Sage soothed, increasing the pressure of her calves. "You can do it."

Avaro disagreed and tried backing. Not an easy feat with her head considerably lower than her hind quarters.

"No, no." Sage prodded her forward to the edge and clucked her tongue.

All at once, Avaro launched herself in the air and popped over the ditch. As she hit the other side, she stumbled and nearly went down. Sage hung on. Barely. For several seconds, her surroundings were a blur. Then, thankfully, everything righted itself.

"You okay?" Gavin was on the ground, hurrying toward her, his horse's reins hanging loose.

"Yeah. I'm fine." She didn't mention her heart, which was beating a hundred miles an hour. "How's Avaro?"

The mare's legs trembled violently. It could be aftershock. Or worse. For all their great size, horses were delicate creatures and easily injured.

"See if she'll walk," Gavin instructed.

Sage gave Avaro her head. The mare obediently took one step. When it came to putting her other foot down, she resisted. Worried, Sage climbed off. Gavin was already beside the horse, squatting down to examine the suspect leg.

Sage stood behind him, watching over his shoulder as he ran his hand over Avaro's knee and down to her fetlock. When he finished, he stood and lifted her hoof, examining the underside.

"What do you think?" Sage asked.

"Hard to tell. I don't see a rock stuck in her shoe, and she doesn't appear to have any tenderness. Could just be residual pain. She landed pretty hard."

"Tell me about it." Sage was feeling her own residual pain.

"See if she'll walk now." Gavin straightened.

And just like that, they were as close as they'd been when they kissed earlier.

Gavin was thinking the same thing, Sage could see it in his eyes.

Funny, after all her talk about maintaining a strictly professional relationship, what she wanted most to do was press her lips to that very stubborn, very delectable mouth of his.

She bolstered her resolve…for all the good it did her. Avaro rubbed her head against Sage's arm, momentarily unbalancing her. Gavin came to her rescue by placing a hand on her shoulder and steadying her.

He had great hands. Strong, yet gentle. Sensitive and confident. Whether he was checking a horse for injuries or leading her away from a potentially awkward situation with Dan.

"Steady now," he murmured.

"I'm, uh, good. F-fine, really." Stammering? She didn't stammer.

"You sure?"

All right, already, her mind screamed. *Either kiss me or let me go.*

Making the choice for him, she lifted her face and raised her arms.

Gavin abruptly stepped back, his hand falling to his side.

Sage's cheeks burned. She covered her blunder by mounting Avaro. "Come on, girl."

Gavin also mounted, though he didn't immediately move or speak.

She was about to make a snappy comment, one she hoped would cover her embarrassment at being rejected after practically throwing herself at him, when she followed Gavin's gaze to a trio of riders approaching from the opposite direction.

Avaro stared at them, ready to spring into action, every muscle in her body tense.

Gavin also stared. And there was no mistaking the ice-cold fury blazing in his eyes.

"Evening," the man in the lead said, a congenial smile on his face. "You folks having a problem?"

Gavin didn't respond.

The man halted in the middle of the trail, as did his two companions riding behind him. "Can we help?"

"You've already helped enough," Gavin ground out.

Sage didn't understand what was going on but recognized an insult when she heard one. Whoever this man was, Gavin disliked him intensely, though the feeling didn't appear to be mutual. That, or the man was considerably more adept at masking his baser emotions.

"How you doing, Gavin?" one of the young cowboys asked.

The other one tugged on the brim of his hat. "Gavin." His gaze fell on Sage. "Ma'am."

So, they all knew each other. Interesting.

Sage studied the one in front. He was probably around her age, his companions a few years younger. He was also handsome, wore clothes a cut above the rest and rode an exceptionally fine-looking gelding.

"My horse stumbled," she informed him, curious to see how this chance meeting would play out.

"Is she all right?"

"Appears to be."

"Isn't this the night of your monthly trail ride?" the man asked Gavin. "Where's the rest of your group?"

Rather than answer, Gavin said, "I'm surprised to find you here. As I recall, you don't much like being out in these mountains after dark."

The man smiled.

There was little room on the narrow trail. As a result, they stood facing each other, the three newcomers on one side, Gavin and Sage on the other. In order for them to pass, someone was going to have to move. From the rock hard set of Gavin's jaw, she doubted it would be him.

"We've been tracking that wild horse."

"Stay away from him." Gavin's voice took on a lethal edge. "He's mine."

The man rubbed the back of his neck, the casual movement tipping his hat forward. "Unless you can prove ownership, I don't believe there's any law saying I can't go after him."

"There is," Sage spoke up. "Only agents of the BLM can capture feral equine. If you *do* go after that horse on your own, you're breaking the law."

"No fooling?" The man's smile stretched wider as he

apprised her from his higher vantage point. "How do you know that?"

"I'm Sage Navarre, a field agent with the Bureau of Land Management."

"Nicely played, Gavin." He chuckled with obvious good humor. "Did I say we were tracking a horse? I meant stray calves."

"Kind of late for that, isn't it?" Gavin asked with unmistakable challenge. "Calves are hard to spot in the dark."

"You're right." He regarded his companions. "How 'bout it, boys? Ready to head back?"

"Whatever you say, boss."

He inclined his head at Sage. "Good night, Ms. Navarre. It was a pleasure." The amused light in his eyes dimmed when he looked at Gavin, and his expression became almost sad. "Give my regards to your father. And your sister the next time you talk to her. I hope they're both doing well."

"They are, no thanks to you."

The man simply nodded.

"'Night, Gavin," the second cowboy said. "Ma'am."

With a wave, all three men turned their horses around and headed back up the trail the way they'd come.

For several moments, Gavin didn't move.

"I think I can ride now." Sage waited a full minute, then attempted to break the silence again. "Or, we can stand here all night if you prefer."

Gavin busied himself checking his saddlebags.

"I know it's none of my business," she went on conversationally, "but he seemed nice. And genuinely concerned about your dad and sister."

Another minute of silence passed.

Sage grew impatient and expelled a long breath. "It's pretty clear you have some history with him—"

"That was Clay Duvall."

Something about the name rang a bell. Try as she might, she couldn't place it.

Gavin urged Shasta into a walk. Without looking back at her, he said, "His father's the one responsible for my family losing their land."

Ah, yes. That would explain the animosity.

"The SOB used the proceeds from the sale to build a rodeo arena, and now he's making money hand over fist."

Sage said nothing, for there was nothing *to* say.

Neither did Gavin, which made the ride back to the ranch incredibly long and tense.

Gavin stood at the kitchen sink, staring out the window and sipping his coffee. The first gray streaks of dawn were just appearing in the eastern edge of what promised to be a clear, cloudless sky. A breeze rolled off the mountains, the mild gusts catching tree tops and teasing the branches. It was going to be another beautiful fall day.

Maybe it was also going to be a lucky day, and they'd find the mustang in the box canyon.

He still hadn't gotten over the shock of running into Clay Duvall last night on the trail and discovering he was also tracking the horse. Good thing Sage had been there and warned him off. If not, Gavin might have lost his composure and done something stupid. Again. He and Duvall had tangled before. Verbally and physically.

Gavin inherited his temper from his grandfather, as well as his penchant for staring out the kitchen window and a fondness for strong coffee. Not that his grandfather could brew a decent pot to save his life. Gavin wasn't much better. Nor was Ethan. Their father, on the other hand, could outcook most people. If not for him, they'd probably starve.

Draining the last swallow, Gavin surveyed the empty kitchen. He was usually the first one up, with Ethan a close second. Cassie woke next, on the days she didn't have school, and his father last, crawling out of bed just in time to fix everyone breakfast before they headed off in their different directions.

Hearing footsteps, he looked up, expecting to see his brother.

"Morning, son."

"Hey, Dad." Gavin rinsed his empty mug and set it in the dish rack to dry. "Trouble sleeping?" His father frequently suffered from insomnia, a side effect of his chronic depression according to the doctor.

"No. In fact, now that I think about it, I slept straight through the night."

That was a change. As was the smile on his father's face. Granted, it wasn't much of a smile, but the first real one Gavin had noticed in a while.

"Coffee?" he asked, and reached in the cupboard for a clean mug.

"Half a cup. I need to cut back on my caffeine."

"Since when?"

"I'm not young anymore. Need to take care of my health if I expect to outlive you."

Had his father just made a joke?

Gavin passed him the mug, half-full as requested. "I thought Ethan would be up by now."

"He got home pretty late. I suspect he's sleeping in."

"You have any idea where he's going lately?" Gavin slid a chair out from under the table and sat beside his dad.

"The obvious answer would be a woman."

"Except you don't think so."

"My guess is he's breaking horses."

"Why won't he say anything?"

"He's afraid of failing."

Gavin mulled that over a bit. "Who do you suppose he's breaking horses for?" Powell Ranch wasn't the only one to succumb to progress or economic hardships in recent years.

"Clive Curtis maybe?"

That would explain the late hours. The Curtises lived twenty miles southeast of Mustang Valley.

Gavin would have liked to continue the conversation with his father but Cassie chose that moment to stumble into the kitchen, Blue tucked under her arm. He'd given up telling her she couldn't let the puppy sleep with her.

"Morning, honey," he said. "You're up early, too."

Seemed everyone except him was on a different schedule today.

"Hi, Dad. Hi, Grandpa." She gave each of them a quick, one-armed hug en route to the refrigerator where she poured herself some orange juice.

Another surprise. Cassie didn't voluntarily dispense hugs.

An unexpected pressure pushed against the inside of Gavin's chest. It was, he realized after a moment, contentment. For the first time in a very long time he experienced a sense of family and with it, a rightness with the world.

Capturing the mustang and launching his stud and breeding business suddenly took on a whole new importance because this feeling wasn't something he wanted to lose. Ever.

"You don't mind watching Isa this afternoon, do you?" he asked Cassie.

"Can we go riding?"

Remembering the girls' request to go on the mustang roundup with him and Sage, he answered, "No farther than the pasture."

"Of course, Dad." She gave him a pained expression.

"I appreciate it. And so does Isa, I'm sure."

"She's a cool kid."

"She's not the only one." He smiled at his daughter.

She returned it, tentatively. But, like her grandfather earlier, it was genuine and directed straight at Gavin. The pressure against his chest grew heavier, squeezing his heart.

Or, was it the other way around? Had his heart suddenly grown bigger?

"I'll keep an eye on them, too," his dad offered. "You think you and Isa would like to go to that new ice cream parlor in town?"

"Seriously?"

"Seriously," her grandfather replied, his glance cutting to Gavin, his eyebrows raised in question.

"I'm told the Pralines and Cream is really good. Why don't you bring a gallon back with you?"

Cassie lifted Blue out in front of her, his hind legs dangling, and gave the puppy's nose a kiss. "You hear that, Blue? We're going to the ice cream parlor."

"He has to stay in the truck," Gavin's dad warned.

She responded with another pained expression.

A loud, impatient knock on the back door interrupted them.

Gavin got to his feet. "Probably Conner," he said, assuming their buddy had arrived early.

Way early, he thought, glancing at his watch.

Except it wasn't Conner at the door. Instead, Javier waited, his expression a mixture of excitement and worry.

"Señor Powell." Javier spoke only broken English and was sometimes difficult to understand. For a while, when he first came to work for the Powells, he'd lived in the old bunkhouse next to the barn. "Hurry. It is the horse."

Gavin reached for his jacket on the coatrack beside the door. "Which one?"

Perhaps one of the broodmares had delivered early, or a customer's horse injured itself. Mishaps and accidents weren't uncommon where animals were concerned.

"El caballo salvaje." Javier made a motion with his hand for Gavin to hurry. "You must come now."

"The mustang?"

"Sí. He is here."

Gavin fumbled with his jacket zipper.

"Where?" His father had risen from the table to stand beside Gavin. Cassie was with him.

"The pasture. With the mama horses."

The mustang was on the ranch!

"Get Ethan," Gavin told his father, then raced after Javier.

Maybe they didn't have to go to the box canyon today. Maybe, by some miracle, they could capture the mustang right here on the ranch.

He and Javier reached the outskirts of the pasture in mere minutes. Gavin slowed from a dead run to a jog, then to a complete stop. His breath, which had been coming fast and furious, was completely swept away. There, not thirty yards away in front of them, was the mustang. Standing motionless, black head held high in the air, his stance fearless, he confronted the intruders. Then, as if deciding they were of no great importance, he pranced in a circle, only to stop and arch his neck, his ears pricked forward.

"He's incredible."

"Sí," Javier agreed, his tone reverent.

Gavin remembered reading long ago in high school that the ancient Greeks believed Poseidon gave man the horse. There had been a photograph in the text book of a marble statue by a famous sculptor. Gavin remembered little about the myth. But he did remember the stature of the horse, with its regal head, small yet powerful build and flowing mane and tail that resembled tongues of exploding fire.

He thought if Poseidon had indeed given man the horse, that first one must have looked something like his mustang.

Trotting back and forth in front of his audience, both the equine and human ones, the horse shook his head as if to draw attention to himself.

"I'll be damned," Ethan said, appearing beside Gavin, jacketless and his shirt only half-buttoned.

"Sí," Javier repeated.

The broodmares, along with Avaro and old Chico, had congregated at the end of the pasture. The mares huddled a safe distance away, old Chico nearby. Avaro, on the other hand, alternately pressed against the fence, the rails cutting into her chest, or reversed her position and presented her backside to the mustang.

He reared, twisted the upper half of his body, and whinnied.

"I can't believe he ventured this close." Ethan tucked his loose shirttails into his jeans.

"Avaro's in heat." Gavin observed the courtship ritual with keen interest.

Ethan did, too. "I'd say he's in love and that it's mutual."

The mustang kicked up his hind legs, warning everyone else to stay away from his prize.

At the sound of approaching footsteps, Gavin looked over his shoulder. His father and Cassie hurried toward them, their eyes wide with astonishment.

"Oh, my gosh!" Cassie drew up beside Gavin and clutched his hand in both of hers. She hadn't done that since she was three.

He only this moment realized how much he'd missed it.

"You think the two of us can manage to surround and rope him?" he asked Ethan.

"I don't know. Lots of space out there."

"We should try."

"Hell, yes. Can't let an opportunity like this pass."

"I'm not thinking he'll cooperate."

Ethan chuckled. "You'd be disappointed if he did."

"We'd better hurry. I don't care how much in love he is, he's not going to stick around for long."

They no sooner started for the stables when Javier shouted, "The horse. Look!"

Gavin turned, afraid the mustang had run off. What he saw was the last thing he'd expected—Avaro sailing over the fence to join the mustang, her front legs tucked tight beneath her body.

All five of them stared, slack jawed.

"Who'd've thought it?" Ethan finally muttered.

Gavin remembered how high the mare had jumped when she popped over the ditch yesterday and Sage's warning that she was an escape artist. "Dammit. I should have seen this coming."

"Don't blame yourself," Ethan said philosophically. "You had no way of knowing."

The two horses, united at last, galloped off toward the mountains, quickly shrinking to matching specks on the distant rise.

"We'd better saddle up and go after them. I'll call Conner. Tell him to get here fast."

"What about Sage?" Ethan asked. "You going to call her, too?"

Gavin could. He still had the business card she'd left with him that first day. "I will. Later. She has an appointment this morning."

"This is pretty important."

So was the paternity test, and she didn't need any distractions. Especially when there was nothing she could do.

"Let's ride out first. Follow their tracks. Avaro may have once been wild but not for the past three years. Chances are good she won't go far. She may even come back on her own after she and the mustang…" He glanced at Cassie. His daughter probably figured out what was going on. Nonetheless, Gavin wasn't ready to talk "sex" in front of her. "After a while," he finished.

"Should we cancel classes today?" Ethan asked.

"I'll cover you," their father volunteered. "Javier can handle the trail rides, if there are any."

Wayne Powell was a decent horseman, or had been at one time, and was certainly capable of instructing the beginner and intermediate students. It was just that he hadn't shown any interest in riding for years.

"You sure?" Gavin asked, uncertain how many more shocks he could take in one day.

"Cassie can help."

"And Isa, too," she piped up, excited at being included.

"You don't really think Avaro will come back on her own, do you?" Ethan remarked while he and Gavin were saddling up.

"It's possible."

Gavin was grasping at straws. But the alternative was telling Sage her horse had disappeared, and he was hoping like hell to avoid that.

Chapter 10

While not exactly shabby, the testing facility was far
from state-of-the-art. Sage had been expecting something
along the lines of an urgent care clinic. Instead, the facility was four storefronts down from a chain grocery store,
had darkly tinted windows and a sign out front advertising Walk-ins Welcome.

She'd phoned Roberto the moment she'd seen the
place, sitting in her parked truck and staring at the tinted
windows. He'd assured her that, besides being the closest testing facility to Mustang Valley, it came highly recommended.

Once inside, Sage had to admit the staff treated her
and Isa professionally and tried to make both the chain
of custody documentation process and the testing procedure itself as painless as possible. Her only complaint
was having to wait…and wait…for the clerk to finish
with the three people ahead of them, for a room to become available, for the technician who conducted the test.

Sage had pulled Isa close to her in each room they
were asked to "Have a seat." She did it in part because
the thermostat was set at a temperature suitable for pen-
guins and in part because Isa was nervous. Sage even
more so, though she had no reason to be.

The test was simply a nuisance. A hoop to jump

through. In her overactive imagination, however, she envisioned ridiculous, impossible scenarios, ones where the test came back negative and she was insisting to Dan that some terrible mistake had been made.

Finally, they were done. Sage watched the technician package her and Isa's swabs and affix the labels.

"You should have the results in two to three business days," the technician told them. "After the other party comes in."

"Do you know when that will be?"

The man smiled patiently. "Couldn't tell you."

Of course not. She wasn't sure why she'd even asked.

After thanking him, Sage and Isa left the room and traveled the long hall. Pushing open the door to the reception area, she held it for Isa—who walked straight into Dan.

"Oh!" Sage automatically reached for her daughter, and the two of them took a step back. "You're here," she sputtered.

He glowered at them. "Have you finished with the test?"

"Yes." Why hadn't she asked him when he was coming? Then they could have avoided this…inconvenience.

"I saw you at the ranch," Isa said, her head tilted back to peer at him.

Dan ignored her in favor of Sage. "We need to talk."

She fumed. Not "*Can* I talk to you?" or "Do you have a minute?" No, he'd issued the order as if her sole option was to obey.

Worse, he'd snubbed Isa. His own daughter. For the second time.

"Come on." He began walking to the other side of the reception area where no one sat. When Sage didn't immediately follow, he glared at her and repeated irritably. "Come on."

Anger built inside her. She wanted nothing more than to tell Isa, "This rude and selfish man is your father, and you should be glad he wants nothing to do with you." Next, she'd lead Isa out the front door, never to see the bastard again.

Except this wasn't the time or place. Reluctantly, she sat Isa in one of the chairs with a magazine, told her to wait and joined Dan.

"What is it?" she asked, purposefully infusing weary irritation in her voice.

A young woman sat across the waiting area, cradling a baby in her lap. She made no effort to hide the fact she was straining to hear Sage and Dan's conversation.

Sage fought for composure.

"I don't want you hanging around Powell Ranch," he said.

"I've been assigned to round up the mustang. I *have* to hang around Powell Ranch."

"But you don't have to go on trail rides."

Understanding dawned. He didn't want her mixing with his clients, word spreading that he had a daughter, one he didn't acknowledge or support. Bad for business and his image.

In that moment, she despised him. More than she'd thought possible.

"You have no say over what I do or where I go."

"This is a tricky situation, Sage."

"Cough up the money and Isa and I will be gone in a flash."

"I don't have it." His face reddened, from anger or embarrassment or frustration, she couldn't tell.

"I find that hard to believe, Dan. You live in a nice house, drive a new truck and seem to have plenty of clients."

She caught a glimpse of Isa, sitting with the unopened magazine in her lap and watching them with unblinking eyes. Sage's heart constricted. Her little girl didn't deserve this.

Reining in her temper, she vowed to stick to her original plan. No scenes.

"I won't give up, Dan. Not until you pay the child support."

"My disposable income is currently tied up in other ventures," he said.

"Other ventures?"

"The Powells, for one. Horses, for another."

"I don't care where your money is. Isa and I have been more than patient and aren't waiting any longer."

"You have no choice."

She stared at him, hardly recognizing the man before her. "What happened, Dan? You used to adore Isa."

An undefinable emotion flickered in his eyes.

All at once, she knew. Something she should have figured out long ago. "It's your wife."

"What are you talking about?"

"You met her while we were still together."

"Big deal. We weren't involved."

"Liar. That's why you're insisting on the paternity test. You think I could have been unfaithful because you were."

"Don't go there, Sage," he growled.

Too late. She'd already gone. And the guilt written all over his face proved she'd uncovered his dirty secret.

"On second thought, I'm glad Isa won't ever know you."

Turning her back on him, she went to her daughter—*hers,* not theirs—and held out a hand. Isa took it, her sweet face marred by confusion and nervousness.

"Is he my daddy?" she whispered, casting a furtive glance at Dan.

"We'll talk outside, *mija.*"

As they approached the door, it swung opened.

Dan's pregnant wife stood on the other side, their little boy in tow.

Both she and Sage came to an abrupt halt, their gazes assessing each other and the children at their sides. Judging by the other woman's look of disdain, Sage and Isa came up short.

Sage refused to step aside. Petty, but she didn't care. As a result, Dan's wife had no choice but to skirt around them. She did so, giving them a wide, wide berth.

The feeling's mutual, Sage thought.

Telling herself it would be worth it in the end, she trudged out the door and to the parking lot.

If only she didn't have to go back to the ranch today, she'd take Isa somewhere fun. They could forget all about this morning. But she did have to go back. For the mustang. The same mustang Gavin would use in his stud and breeding business. The business where Dan's money was supposedly tied up.

The irony of the situation didn't escape her. By doing her job, helping Gavin, she was actually hurting Isa's chances of recovering the money Dan owed.

Opening the passenger side door, she helped Isa into the truck and buckled her seat belt.

"Who was that lady and little boy?" she asked. "Is he my brother?"

Sometimes, like right now, Sage wished Isa wasn't so smart for her age. She'd have to explain. Isa was entitled to the truth. At least, a simplified version.

"I saw a park up the road with some swings and picnic tables. Why don't we go there and Mama will tell you everything. Okay?"

Gavin, Ethan and Conner had just returned from searching for Avaro when Sage pulled into the ranch. He wished he had something better to tell her. Unfortunately, they not only hadn't found her horse, they lost the tracks a mile into the mountains.

With school on fall break, there were more than the usual number of people for a Monday, many of them kids. Maybe because of that, and the fact he was distracted by the morning's events, he hadn't noticed Cassie right away as he walked from the stables. Why would he? She didn't hang around with the kids who came to the ranch. She didn't hang around with anyone her age.

Until today, apparently.

A group of middle school students, mostly girls, were playing some sort of game in the open area in front of the arena. Cassie was smack-dab in the center, participating. And laughing. Blue nipped at her heels as she ran, then spun and shrieked gleefully when another girl grabbed the back of her shirt.

It was a sight Gavin had only dreamed of seeing.

He committed it to memory for the next time Cassie's mother asked how their daughter was doing.

Isa fled Sage's truck the moment it was parked and ran straight for Cassie. Reaching her, the little girl flung her arms around Cassie's waist and clung to her as if they'd been separated for years instead of hours. Cassie gave Isa's back a comforting pat, much like the ones Gavin had given her when she was young. He couldn't hear what the two were saying, but he suspected whatever Cassie uttered was the right thing, for Isa slowly extracted herself and smiled…through her tears.

She'd been crying.

Hearing footsteps behind him, Gavin turned around to see Sage approaching. By the expression she wore, she'd also been through an emotional wringer, though her eyes were dry. He assumed the paternity test hadn't gone well or had been a lot tougher than she'd anticipated.

"Hey," he said when she approached.

"Hi."

He went to her and cupped her cheek in his palm, stroking her smooth skin with the pad of his thumb. Ethan had already figured out there was something between Gavin and Sage. Who cared if anyone else figured it out, too?

She didn't pull away. Covering his hand with hers, she leaned into him, tucking her head into the crook of his neck. Gavin's other arm came up and circled her protectively. She felt good nestled against him. More than good. She felt as though she'd been designed to fit precisely there, and he'd only been waiting for her to show up.

They stood like that for several moments. Gavin was glad he could give her what she needed. He also dreaded having to add to her troubles.

"You're a good man, Gavin Powell," she murmured, her warm breath caressing his exposed neck.

"No, I'm not. I've made a lot of mistakes in my life."

"Who hasn't? But you do the best you can."

"So do you."

"I wish I didn't have to involve you in my problems. I'd hate for there to be any...repercussions."

Gavin thought of Dan's warning phone call the previous night. "Did Dan say something to you?"

"He showed up at the testing facility just as we were leaving. Along with his wife and son."

"Was Isa there?"

"Yes. He was terrible to her."

That explained the tears. "I'm sorry, honey." When she didn't immediately respond, he asked. "What else?"

She sighed and withdrew.

He'd have preferred to continue holding her but it was impossible. "Sage?"

"He threatened me and, indirectly, your family if I didn't stay away from you and the ranch, other than going after the mustang."

Maybe holding each other out in the open wasn't such a good idea after all. Dan's clients were obviously feeding him information. Gavin and Sage would have to be more discreet in the future. But not stop. He had every intention of holding her again *and* kissing her.

"Don't worry about Dan," he said.

"I wish it was that easy. He won't back off."

"No, he won't. But right now, we have a slightly bigger problem."

"What's that?"

"Sage, I'm sorry." He swallowed before continuing. "Avaro escaped early this morning."

She didn't immediately speak. When she did, she struggled. "H-how? Was the f-fence...broken?"

"No. She jumped it. We've been out looking for her. Came back because we knew you were arriving soon."

"I don't understand." Her hand rested at the base of her throat. "We put her in with other horses so this wouldn't happen."

"The mustang was here."

"At the ranch!"

"Outside the pasture. That's when she jumped the fence. Javier, Ethan and I saw the whole thing. We were going to go after the mustang, try to rope him, but then Avaro escaped, and the two of them ran off. I didn't call you, I knew you had the paternity test. And I figured it was better that we went after her right away."

"We have to go back out," Sage said in a rush.

"As soon as we saddle up a horse for you and fresh ones for Ethan, Conner and I. Dad will keep an eye on the girls. He's also packing us a lunch and some drinks."

"Mama, look at Blue's new collar." Isa came running over, the puppy patiently coping with his bumpy ride. Cassie came, too. "He outgrew his other one already." Isa took one look at her mother and stopped suddenly. "What's wrong?"

"Avaro's missing," Sage told the girls. "We're leaving now to look for her."

"Can we come?" Cassie asked.

"That's not a good idea," Gavin said.

"Why not? The more people looking, the better the chance of finding her. Right?"

"We'll handle it, Cassie. You and Isa are going to stay here with Grandpa."

"Not fair." Her bottom lip protruded stubbornly.

Isa set the puppy on the ground, went over to Sage and hugged her. "Poor Mama."

Sage stroked the girl's hair. "You be good for Mr. Powell, promise?"

Isa nodded.

"How 'bout you head into the house," Gavin suggested. "Fix yourselves some lunch."

Sage kissed the top of Isa's head, then she and Gavin started toward the stables.

Cassie accompanied Isa, though storming off was probably a better description. Gavin put the incident from his mind. He'd make amends later.

At the moment, finding Avaro took precedence.

Gavin peered through the binoculars, hoping to see a movement among the overgrown brush in the rocky ravine below. They'd been riding the Tom Thumb Trail for the past two hours, with no more luck than before.

"See anything?" Sage asked. She sat astride one of the ranch's more dependable horses, a gelding Ethan had broken to ride right before he joined the Marines.

"No," Gavin answered, and lowered the binoculars. "Nothing."

"Damn. Where could she be?"

About a million and one places, but Gavin didn't voice the thought aloud. Sage was already plenty worried.

"Let's keep going." He loosened his reins, the only cue his horse needed. The mare, an older sister of Shasta from the same original mustang lines, started up the trail, her head lowered, her powerful front legs digging into the steep and uneven ground.

They'd split into two groups for the afternoon search. Gavin and Sage in one, Ethan and Conner in the other. As well as looking for Avaro, Ethan and Conner were going to the box canyon to retrieve the mares. There was no point in leaving them another night. The mustang would not likely return now that he had Avaro.

Gavin's cell phone suddenly rang, startling him. Though far from any tower, he sometimes got reception in odd little pockets throughout the preserve. How good the reception was depended on the weather.

He reined in his horse and removed his phone from his pocket. His brother's name appeared on the display. Skipping any preamble, he answered brusquely, "Find her?"

"Not yet. What about you?"

"Nothing."

"How's Sage holding up?"

Though his back was to her, Gavin sensed her gaze on him. "Well enough."

"Conner and I are just getting ready to head over to the canyon."

"I think we'll check out the reservoir at the golf resort." It was a long shot, but worth investigating.

"I doubt my phone will work after this. I'll send up a flare if we spot the horses."

"I'll do the same."

Disconnecting, Gavin continued along the trail. Sage didn't ask about the call, the gist of which was probably obvious from listening to his end of the conversation. Not three minutes later, his phone rang again. Hoping it was Ethan with good news, Gavin was surprised to see his father's number appear on the display.

"Hey, Dad. Everything okay?"

"No, it's bad. The girls are missing."

Chapter 11

"Missing!" Panic ripped through Gavin.

"I've been searching for the last twenty minutes." Worry strained his father's voice. "The girls aren't anywhere on the ranch."

"Are they on horseback or foot?"

"Horseback. Javier said he saw them riding Chico and Barbie Doll along the back pasture about an hour ago."

"Why didn't he stop them?"

"He didn't know. It wasn't his job to watch the girls. It was mine." His father sounded desperate. "I screwed up. I lay down for a nap."

"A nap?" Gavin snapped, unable to help himself. His father had a habit of sleeping in the afternoon. But why today of all days? "Dammit, Dad."

Avaro escaping with the mustang paled in comparison to this crisis.

"What is it?" Sage had nudged her horse close to Gavin's. "Tell me," she insisted.

Gavin held the phone away from his mouth. "Cassie and Isa are apparently riding in the preserve. Alone."

"Apparently!"

"Javier saw them head out about an hour ago."

"And your dad was napping?" Her voice rose with growing agitation.

"We'll find them. Don't worry." He had to stay calm. Think clearly. "They couldn't have gotten far, and I know every inch of these mountains."

He did, it was true. But there were a lot of mountains in this range.

"Javier and I will saddle up right away," his father interrupted. "I'll alert Rebecca in case the girls come back."

"And I'll call Ethan. He and Conner are on their way to the box canyon." He tried to think of where Cassie might take Isa. "You and Javier ride the west ridge. The picnic site is one of Cassie's favorites places."

"Please tell Sage how sorry I am."

He glanced at her. She was leaning forward in the saddle, hanging on his every word.

"We'll worry about that later," he said. "Contact the sheriff's office before you and Javier leave. Report the girls missing."

Gavin and his father discussed several last details, then disconnected. Contacting Ethan next, Gavin filled in his brother with clipped, urgent sentences. They agreed he and Conner should continue onto the box canyon as that route ran south of the ranch. Between all three search parties, they'd have much of the preserve's northern section covered.

"If you find them, send up a flare," Gavin said. "I'll do the same."

He hesitated after disconnecting. There had to be more he could do, someone he could call to help beside the sheriff. They had friends in the area. People who would come to their aid. Unfortunately, time wasn't on their side. At most, ninety minutes of daylight remained.

He didn't want to think about how cold it got in these mountains at night.

"What possessed Cassie to take Isa on a ride?" Sage blinked back tears, fighting for composure.

Gavin didn't defend his daughter. She knew better, and there was no excuse for taking Isa with her. He recalled Cassie storming off to the house, angry she couldn't go with them to search for Avaro. He should have taken a moment to talk to her and explain.

"This isn't just Cassie's fault or my dad's. It's mine, too. But we can divvy up the blame later, after she and Isa are home."

"Does Cassie carry a cell phone?"

"She lost it last week, and I haven't replaced it yet. No reason. She hasn't been off the ranch, what with school on break."

Gavin cursed the lousy stroke of luck. Taking out his binoculars, he scanned the distant rises. It was unlikely he'd spot the girls from their position at the base of a large hill. Still, he tried.

"If I told Isa once, I told her a thousand times not to go anywhere without checking with me first." Sage rubbed her temple with trembling fingers. "This morning at the testing facility…she was so upset afterward. She might be acting out."

He reached over and grasped her hand. It was cold and clammy. Like his. "We're going to find them, honey. And they'll be just fine. I promise." He squeezed her fingers, hoping that the more pressure he applied, the more she'd believe him.

"Can we go now? Please."

He started to put his phone away, only to have it ring again. Thank God he had decent reception.

"It's Ethan." Heart hammering, he answered the call. "Yeah."

"I have an idea." Static on the line made it hard for Gavin to hear everything. "Extra manpower for the search."

"Tell me." He angled the phone in an attempt to improve the connection.

"Clay Duvall."

"Who?" Gavin heard his brother. He just thought he had to be mistaken.

"Duvall. He'll help us. And he has a half-dozen men working for him he can recruit."

Every nerve in Gavin's body screamed no. He didn't want to involve Duvall or have anything to do with the man. Not after his and his father's betrayal.

Except that Ethan was right. There was an unspoken code among the cowboys, times when differences were put aside. This was one of them. And Duvall would come through.

Swallowing his pride and resentment, which was far from easy, Gavin instructed his brother, "Call him."

"I already did. He and his men are on their way."

Leave it to Ethan to know the right thing to do.

"Have them check out the northwest rim first."

Gavin and Sage continued on the Tom Thumb Trail for another half hour. They encountered only two sets of hikers, neither of which had seen any other riders, much less two children on horseback. In between, Gavin and Sage didn't talk much. That left each of them to cope with their guilt and anxiety in silence.

On every rise that afforded them a decent view, they stopped. While Gavin glassed the area with his binoculars, Sage hollered for the girls. Her shaky voice carried, echoing off the sheer rock faces. There was no answer, not that Gavin expected one. He felt certain his father and Javier would locate the girls at the picnic site.

He hadn't yet decided on Cassie's punishment, his mind too filled with thoughts of finding her and Isa. His daughter would no doubt be unhappy with him. Resent him. And she would probably want to return to her mother at Christmastime, if not before.

At least she would be safe.

All at once, Gavin saw it. There, to their left, a tiny missile climbing skyward, a column of orange smoke trailing behind it. His relief was so strong, his chest hurt.

"Look!" he shouted.

"Thank God," Sage said from behind him, and burst into tears.

Noting the southern location of the flare, he pulled out his cell phone to call Ethan. The display registered no signal. He resisted the urge to fling the phone into the ravine below.

Instead, he said, "Let's hurry." They had less than an hour of daylight left.

"Where are they?" Sage asked as they pushed their horses for more speed up the steep hill.

"Near the box canyon." Five miles at least from the picnic site.

"Do you think they're all right?"

He refused to think Cassie and Isa might be in trouble or injured. "I'm sure they are."

Only, he wasn't.

"How long will it take us to get there?"

"Forty-five minutes if we haul ass."

It was the longest forty-five minutes of Gavin's life.

Too soon, the smoke from the flare dissipated, leaving him uncertain as to Ethan's exact location. Every ten minutes he tried to reach his brother. Always, the infuriating "no service" message flashed on his phone's display. When they got within a quarter mile of the entrance to the box canyon, he cupped his hands to his mouth and shouted his brother's name. No one answered.

Shit.

"Where are they?" Sage asked. She'd held herself together well during their rough-and-tumble ride. But stress and exhaustion showed on her face and in the weary slump of her shoulders.

"They can't be far."

"Are you sure the flare was launched around here?"

"Positive."

A shrill whistle came from a ridge some two hundred yards to the east. Gavin swung around in the saddle and immediately identified the three riders.

"Who are they?" Sage asked.

"Clay Duvall and two of his men. They must have followed the flare, too."

Duvall waved from his position in front, and Gavin raised his hand in reply.

At that moment, another flare appeared in the sky, not more than a mile away by Gavin's estimation. He smiled for the first time all day. When he next saw his brother, he was going to give him a big kiss and not care who saw.

"Isn't that coming from inside the box canyon?" Sage stood in her stirrups, straining to see.

"The far end, I'd say." He could have kicked himself for not thinking of it earlier. "I bet the girls went after the mares and Ethan found them."

"Or after the *mustang.* They did ask to go with us."

He grumbled. "When I get hold of Cassie, I'm going to wring—"

"Hug her. You're going to hug her."

"Yes," Gavin conceded. "But rest assured, there will be a loss of privileges."

They hurried the remaining distance to the canyon with nightfall chasing them the entire way.

Ethan sat astride his horse about a quarter mile past the entrance.

"Where are they?" Gavin asked when he and Sage drew near.

"At the pen. They're okay."

Sage sighed.

"Is Conner with them?"

"He's over there." Ethan pointed to a spot fifty yards away.

Conner tipped his hat.

"Why isn't one of you with the girls?" Sage demanded.

"Because we found more than your two daughters." Ethan's grin stretched from ear to ear. "Your mare's tied up at the pen."

"Really!" Sage's anger vanished, replaced by surprise.

"And something else," Ethan said, grinning even wider.

Excitement exploded inside Gavin as the reason for his brother's exuberance hit him.

"The mustang's here."

Ethan chuckled. "Looks like we're having us a wild-horse roundup tonight."

Sage had never been on a horse roundup quite like this one. It wasn't just the lack of helicopters and manpower. The techniques the men used reminded her of another era altogether, when cowboys had only their ropes and their wits at their disposal.

Clay Duvall, the neighbor whom Gavin held a grudge

against, had arrived with his two wranglers. So had Gavin's father and Javier.

Sage stayed with the girls and watched from their vantage point atop a rocky peak near the mares' pen. She would have rather been a part of the roundup but conceded she possessed neither the roping skills required, nor the experience. These eight men, even with their differences and dislike of each other, knew what to do without being told. They might have been on a hundred roundups together considering how well they worked as a team.

"Mama, I'm sorry," Isa apologized for the third time in a meek voice. She sat huddled beside Sage, hugging her drawn up knees.

"We'll talk later, *mija*." And they would. But for now, Sage wanted to watch the roundup. What she could see of it. Dusk had already fallen. Complete darkness wasn't far behind.

Gavin, Ethan, Conner and Clay Duvall circled the mustang on their horses, having driven him away from the mares and to the farthest corner of the canyon. The remaining men formed a second outer circle. Their job was to stop the mustang if he tried to escape—which he did, every few minutes.

Avaro whinnied from where she was tied to a branch, agitated by all the horses and activity.

"Watch out!" Cassie hollered.

The mustang had tried to cut between Gavin and Ethan in a frantic dash for freedom. They quickly stopped him by blocking his escape route. Frustrated, he galloped in a circle, head lowered and hind legs kicking.

"Why don't they catch him?" Isa asked.

"They're tiring him out so he won't fight so much and it'll be easier."

"How long will that take? I'm hungry."

Sage wanted to tell her daughter she should have thought of food before riding off with Cassie, but didn't.

The mustang was stubborn and determined. He was also outnumbered and fast becoming exhausted. Each attempt he made to break loose was immediately thwarted and further depleted his energy.

Minute by minute, foot by foot, the circle surrounding him closed. Suddenly, Ethan threw his rope at the mustang…and missed. Angry, the mustang let out a high-pitched squeal and ran in the opposite direction, only to be stopped by the men waiting there. Sage lost track of him after that. It was too dark to see more than thirty feet beyond where they sat.

"Heads-up," Gavin shouted. "He's coming your way."

In the next instant, the mustang materialized in front of Sage and the girls as if formed from thin air. He seemed as surprised to see them as they were him and pawed the ground menacingly.

Sage stared, her attention riveted. He was truly a magnificent sight, and her heart swelled with wonder.

"He's beautiful," Cassie whispered.

Sage started to rise, compelled by an emotion she couldn't define. It was as if the horse demanded she honor him with a show of respect.

The rope came from nowhere, sailing through the air to land squarely around the mustang's neck.

She barely had time to realize what was happening when another rope flew by, also hitting its mark.

The mustang summoned the last of his strength and fought his constraints. Thrusting his head from side to side, he reared, came down and reared again, his breathing labored.

Gavin leaped to the ground. His horse, trained in calf roping, slowly backed up, pulling the rope connected to his saddle horn taut.

Ethan also dismounted. As the remaining men on horseback closed the circle, he and Gavin approached the mustang.

"Easy, boy." Gavin spoke softly, his hand raised in front of him. "It's going to be all right."

The mustang didn't agree and bared his teeth.

"I'm not going to hurt you."

"Watch he doesn't bite you," Ethan warned.

Gavin stopped five feet in front of the horse. Sage sensed in him the same wonder she'd felt earlier. She thought for a moment he might dare approach the horse and lay a hand on him. He didn't, which turned out to be a smart move. The horse reared again, this time slicing the air with his front hooves.

"He likes you, bro," Ethan said with a chuckle.

"It's mutual." There was no humor in Gavin's voice, only admiration.

They stared at each other, he and the horse. And then something magical happened. The horse stopped fighting. Maybe he was tired. Or maybe he decided he'd met his match. Sage preferred to think the horse and man had come to some kind of understanding.

Gavin let out a long, satisfied breath. "What do you say we take him home?"

The trip back to the ranch was arduous. Isa became whiney and cranky halfway there. Probably due to hunger and fatigue and, possibly, fear of what punishment lay ahead of her. The mustang, with both ropes still tied around his neck, and Gavin and Ethan at the end of each one, refused to cooperate. Every step he took was only because he had no choice.

Sage had always assumed the horse was an escapee from either the Indian reservation or a nearby ranch. Seeing him now, his reaction to his captors, it was clear he'd had little or no human contact for a very long time, if ever.

Could he be, as Gavin believed, the last descendant of the wild mustangs that once roamed this area?

No, that was impossible. Right?

Conner, Javier and Gavin's dad brought up the rear, each of them leading a mare. Gavin's two horses carried the remaining equipment and supplies in their hastily loaded pack saddles. Clay Duvall and his wranglers had taken a different trail, one that would lead them back to his place. Before parting, Ethan had thanked his neighbor warmly and shook his hand. Gavin's father hadn't been quite so friendly, though his brief conversation with Clay Duvall was civil enough.

Not Gavin. His entire exchange with the other man consisted of a nod, and a terse one at that.

Eventually, the lights of Powell Ranch came into sight. Not long after, they reached the pasture fence.

"Where should we put him?" Ethan asked.

Gavin pondered their captive. "I'm thinking the round pen. It has the highest fence on the property."

A high fence would probably come in handy, considering what Avaro had done. And the mustang was far more determined to regain his freedom.

When they reached the stables, everyone dismounted. It was decided that Conner and Javier would unsaddle all the mounts and put them up for the night. The girls went with Gavin's dad into the house, assigned to helping him throw together a quick supper for everyone.

Getting the mustang into the round pen proved to be a process. With Gavin pulling him, and Ethan behind guarding his back, they managed to get him through the narrow gate after ten long and exhausting minutes. When they finally shut the gate, both men were sweating and Ethan was limping badly.

He rubbed his knee and grunted in pain. "I'm surprised he's got that much energy left after all we put him through."

"I'm not." Gavin stood at the fence.

The mustang put on a show, trotting back and forth and snorting with frustration. Every few seconds, he would stop and glare angrily at Gavin.

Sage went to stand beside him. "He won't be easy to tame. You have your work cut out for you."

Gavin smiled with pleasure.

Conner carried over the galvanized steel tub they'd brought back from the canyon. He pushed it under the bottom railing of the round pen. Uncoiling a nearby hose, he filled the tub with water. From a safe place on the opposite side of the pen, the mustang eyed the hose as if it were a poisonous snake.

Sage knew from BLM roundups that feral horses seldom drank right away. "By morning," she said, "he'll be thirsty."

Javier came, too, bringing a thick flake of hay which he pushed under the bottom railing next to the tub.

The mustang stretched his head forward, his nostrils flaring, but he didn't move from his spot. No worries. He would also eat by morning, if not sooner.

"How old do you think he is?" Sage asked.

"Hard to say without a closer inspection. But my guess is he's young. Three. Five, maybe."

Sage thought so, too.

When Gavin's dad rang the dinner bell fifteen minutes later, everyone was still standing at the railing, transfixed. The mustang had yet to move from his spot.

"I don't know about you guys, but I'm hungry." Ethan clapped Conner on the back. "You, too, Javier." He dragged the smaller man along. "Eat with us."

The three of them strolled to the house, continuing their loud and lively conversation.

Gavin was slow to move.

"Come on." Sage rested a hand on his shoulder. Like everyone else, she was feeling happy. For a day that had started out awful, it had certainly ended on a high note. "We've got some celebrating to do."

"We do." He turned toward her. "And I want to start now."

His ice-blue eyes, so dark in the moonlight, swept over her face. She had only seconds to prepare before his arm circled her waist, and he drew her flush against him.

A small gasp escaped her, not of protest but delight— at his actions and her reaction to them. Her instincts told her this kiss would be nothing like their previous one... and infinitely more exciting.

Her instincts weren't wrong.

Even before his mouth came rushing down to claim hers, she tensed in eager anticipation. For an instant, when his lips first met hers, she thought her feet had truly left the ground.

The impracticality of any romance developing between them became a distant, insignificant concern as his arms secured her more snugly to him and his tongue sought entry. She opened herself to him, sighing softly as he explored her mouth, melting inside and out as the kiss went on and on.

He was incredibly skilled, demanding but also giving. Oh, yes, giving. The effects of his generosity cascaded through her, lighting tiny sparks at each nerve ending. She could, and did, lose herself. In his masculine scent. In the feel of his muscles bunching beneath her fingers. In the caress of his breath on her cheek as he broke off the kiss, groaned, then returned for more.

Good, because she wasn't ready to stop, either.

He angled her sideway and the next thing she knew, he'd pinned her between him and the round pen. His hands, large and strong, cradled her face, their callused palms stroking her cheeks with a gentleness that touched her as much as it excited her.

The mustang, undoubtedly confused at what his human captors were doing, snorted angrily and pawed the ground.

Gavin slowed the tempo of their kiss but didn't stop.

"Dad! Sage!" Cassie's voice carried from the house. It was followed by more ringing of the dinner bell. "Hurry. We're hungry."

Gavin slid his mouth from Sage's, only to tickle her earlobe with his lips and teeth.

"We'd better go," she murmured, as reluctant as him for the moment to end.

He closed his eyes, collected himself and stepped back.

She moved from the railing on legs a little unsteady, gave the mustang one last look and started toward the house.

An acute awkwardness settled over them—only until Gavin took hold of her hand and linked their fingers.

Sage supposed they had a lot to talk about. It was very unlikely their relationship would go anywhere. Even if she resolved her differences with Dan, she and Isa were leaving in a matter of days.

Suddenly the prospect of going home to Show Low didn't hold nearly the same appeal as it had this morning.

Chapter 12

"Can we stand next to the pen?" the reporter asked.

"I don't think that would be a good idea." Gavin pushed his cowboy hat back and scratched his forehead thoughtfully.

"Why not?"

"He got mad at the last reporter and bit him on the… right cheek."

"Cheek as in…" The reporter grimaced.

"Yeah, that one," Gavin confirmed.

The woman camera operator giggled, then sobered when the reporter glowered at her.

"How about we stand over here?" The reporter relocated a respectable distance away from the pen. "Sal, can you get a shot of the horse in the background?"

"No problem."

Gavin was happy to oblige them. Given his choice, he'd rather the mustang not be filmed up close. Part of him worried that someone would recognize the horse and come forward, claiming ownership.

He still had no idea who'd leaked the story to the news media or why, though his suspicions were leaning toward Conner. He certainly understood the interest. It wasn't every day a horse was found roaming an urban preserve. There was also his family's long-standing ties to the valley, and that the horse was captured as a result of searching for two lost girls.

"Are your daughters here?" the reporter asked as the camera operator positioned them according to the best light. "I'd like to interview them, too."

"Only one of the girls is mine. And she's not here now."

Gavin's father had taken Cassie with him to Scottsdale for a dentist appointment. After that, they were running errands, which included the bank, the post office and, lastly, the warehouse food store. They'd be gone for the rest of the afternoon. Cassie despised their monthly stock-up shopping trips. She despised the unpacking of everything they brought home even more. Accompanying her grandfather was part of her punishment for taking off without permission or telling anyone about it and, Gavin thought, a fitting one.

Cassie had tried her best to sweet-talk him out of it, saying if she and Isa hadn't gone in search of the mustang, they'd have never found him. The argument got her nowhere. Funny thing was, she hadn't been all that mad at Gavin. Once she realized there was no swaying him, she backed off.

He wasn't sure he'd ever understand the twelve-year-old female mind.

"The other girl," Gavin continued, "is the daughter of…" He hesitated, not sure what to call Sage. After their fiery kiss last night, he didn't think of her as just the BLM agent who'd come to Mustang Valley to assist with rounding up the horse.

That was, however, what he told the reporter. The man, the whole world, didn't need to know about Gavin and Sage's relationship. Not yet. Certainly not until they'd figured it out themselves. Besides, if Dan got wind of their involvement, no telling how he'd react.

"Who else went with you on the roundup?" the reporter asked.

"My brother, a buddy of ours and..." Again Gavin hesitated. "Some neighbors."

He appreciated Clay Duvall's help. However, he was nowhere ready to bury the hatchet. Bud Duvall had ruined the Powells' lives, and Clay had profited every bit as much as his father from the sale of their land.

The reporter continued to fire questions at Gavin about the mustang. He answered, squinting into the early afternoon sun. He didn't much like being interviewed and would have refused under different circumstances. Except his phone hadn't stopped ringing all day. And the callers weren't just reporters or folks curious about the mustang. Many were potential new customers interested in taking lessons or boarding their horse. After the first TV news segment ran on the midday edition, people started inquiring about breeding their horses to the mustang.

Gavin couldn't believe it. If only a percentage of the callers became actual customers, the increase in revenues would be enough to make a difference in his family's lives, if not change them completely.

It would take time. Nothing happened overnight. He might even be able to buy Dan out eventually.

The idea appealed to him on many levels.

So, for those reasons and others, he tolerated the various reporters and patiently answered the same questions again and again.

Ethan sauntered over during the interview, a wide grin

splitting his face. He was enjoying the attention they were receiving considerably more than Gavin.

Distracted, Gavin tripped over his next sentence.

The reporter told the camera operator to cut and glanced backward. "Is that your brother?"

"Yes."

"Mr. Powell!" The reporter gestured at Ethan. "Mind if we interview you, too?"

"Naw, that's all right."

"I'm sure our viewers would enjoy hearing about how a man with only one leg manages to work as a cowboy."

How did the reporter know that? Gavin hadn't mentioned it. Damn Conner, if indeed it was him.

Ethan's grin dissolved. "My brother's the one in charge of the ranch and the mustang. It's him you need to talk to."

He walked away, leaving the reporter confused and irritated.

The interview progressed poorly after that. Gavin's cell phone ringing twice didn't help. While the reporter and camera operator were getting into their van, Ethan's red Dodge truck rumbled past.

Gavin's irritation spiked. Fine, the reporter had been a jerk, but this wasn't a good day for Ethan to be playing hooky. They were far too busy.

Gavin's cell phone rang yet again. As he spoke to the potential new customer, reciting boarding rates and lesson fees, Sage arrived. He forgot all about his caller as memories of their kiss filled his mind.

She drove behind the barn to park. He walked over, meeting her halfway. He noticed she carried a briefcase.

"You here on business?" he asked, half joking.

"As a matter of fact—" she smiled brightly "—I am."

He was tempted to take her in his arms. Common sense prevailed.

"My supervisor wants me to email him pictures of the horse. And I brought some paperwork for you to complete in order to start the adoption process."

"Great." They headed toward the round pen and the mustang. "Where's Isa?"

"Not coming today. I felt she needed a couple days away from the ranch and Chico to help drive the lesson home."

"I bet she's taking that hard."

"Very."

"You will bring her back." Gavin stopped himself from adding, *before you leave*. He didn't want to think about Sage returning to Show Low.

"Yes, of course." She glanced at the arena and stables. "Where is everyone?"

By *everyone*, Gavin knew she meant his family. The ranch was crowded today and not just because of the reporters. All the regulars also wanted a peek at the mustang. He'd had to station Javier near the round pen in order to run interference.

"Dad took Cassie into Scottsdale. Ethan left right before you arrived. I have no idea when any of them will be back."

At the round pen, the mustang greeted him and Sage the same way he did everyone else—by lowering his head, snorting and backing himself into the farthest corner.

Sage set her briefcase on the ground, opened it and removed a digital camera. "Have you thought of a name for him yet?"

"No. Been too busy."

"It needs to be something really special." She stood on the bottom rung and powered up the camera. At the small noise, the mustang raised his head, his ears pricked forward, and stared intently at them. "Would you look at that. Am I wrong, or is he posing?"

Gavin laughed. "Who'd have guessed he's a ham?"

Three pictures later, the mustang had enough. He trotted back and forth in the pen, a shower of soft dirt exploding from beneath his feet. Sage continued taking pictures until she had at least two dozen. Stepping down from the railing, she reviewed the pictures, sharing them with Gavin.

Heads bent close together, they commented on each shot. It was hard for Gavin not to lean in and steal a kiss from her. She must have sensed his thoughts, or was having similar ones herself, for she tilted her head to gaze at him, invitation in her eyes.

Oh, hell, Gavin thought, *why not?* Who cared about propriety?

He reached for her—only to be distracted by a vehicle roaring to a dirt-spitting stop not far from them. He glanced up to see who it was with the lousy timing and cursed under his breath.

Dan Rivera pushed open his truck door and emerged, his booted feet hitting the ground with purpose.

Beside him, Sage stiffened.

"It's all right," Gavin murmured. "He didn't see anything except us looking at the pictures you took."

Not entirely true but a plausible excuse if Dan should question them.

He didn't and marched toward them, scowling at Sage.

Gavin had been expecting Dan. He'd called his partner last night to give him the good news. Dan had said he'd be over later in the day. Too bad later in the day coincided with the exact moment Gavin had decided to kiss Sage.

"What are you doing here?" Dan directed the question at Sage.

Gavin didn't like the man's tone. He was about to reply when Sage cut in.

"I brought papers for Gavin to sign." She held up the camera. "And to take pictures for our files."

Dan made a noncommittal grunt, then went over to the railing and peered through the bars.

Sage's mouth tightened with suppressed tension.

"Why don't you wait for me in the house," Gavin said in a low voice, his back to Dan. "The door's unlocked. There's leftover sandwiches in the fridge if you're hungry or help yourself to a cold drink."

"I will not run and hide," she said between clenched teeth.

He admired her tenacity. "That's my girl."

"Nice-looking horse," Dan commented when Gavin went to stand with him at the railing.

They discussed the horse's merits, along with the problems they would face breaking him to ride.

"I'll start tomorrow," Dan said.

Gavin's hackles rose. "We agreed that Ethan would be the one to train him."

"Your brother's got a bum leg."

Sage inhaled sharply.

"Which doesn't slow him down one bit," Gavin replied.

"This horse is too valuable to risk screwing him up."

Okay, now Gavin was mad. Dan typically talked tough, it was part of his two-faced salesman personality. Insults, however, were another matter.

"Ethan's the best there is with a horse in these parts."

"That's debatable." Challenge sparked in Dan's eyes.

He had Gavin over something of a barrel, and they both knew it. Without Dan's money, Gavin couldn't afford to construct the mare motel, which would cost in the tens of thousands of dollars.

For the second time in recent days, he felt trapped by his and Dan's partnership agreement.

"No reason you and Ethan can't work together."

Dan made another disgruntled sound. After a few more minutes of observing the mustang, he announced, "I have an appointment with a client," and left without so much as a "See you later."

The air surrounding Gavin and Sage felt suddenly lighter and clearer.

"Let's get out of here." He took her arm.

"Are you sure? It might not be a good idea to be seen with me. Someone's bound to tell Dan."

"At the moment, I don't care about him."

"Strong words for someone you're in partnership with."

"Yeah, well, that remains to be seen."

Sage set her briefcase on the kitchen table and removed her jacket. After Dan's rude behavior at the round pen, she'd expected to be distraught, if not downright furious. She was neither. Something inside her had changed the past few days. Dan was losing his ability to yank her emotional chains.

It was a step. A huge one.

She glanced over at Gavin, a tenderness stirring inside her. He was responsible for this change in her. At least, in part.

"Water?" he asked, opening the fridge.

"Thanks."

He plucked two bottles from the shelf and handed one to her. It was then she noticed the scowl.

"Are you upset about Dan?" she asked.

"I don't like the way he treated you. Or his attitude." Shrugging off his jacket, he hung it on the coatrack. His hat landed on the countertop.

"Me, either. But it could have been much worse."

"I don't see how."

She unscrewed the lid on her water. "Attitude aside, he wasn't argumentative and he didn't make a scene. Which is more than I can say for the last two times he and I were together."

"I can't believe he insisted on breaking the mustang." Gavin braced his hands on the countertop. "That wasn't in our original agreement."

"It's because you're getting all the attention. And new customers. He doesn't like that." When Gavin didn't respond, Sage went over and placed a hand atop his. "I'd say forget about him, but he's your partner and you can't. So do the next best thing. Forget about him *for now.*"

"He shouldn't have talked to you the way he did," Gavin repeated.

"With any luck, it'll be the last time he talks to me for a while."

"What about Isa?"

Sage removed her hand. They really should be going over the adoption paperwork. She'd promised her cousin she'd be home by four.

"She hasn't mentioned Dan since our talk yesterday after the paternity test. I think once we get home, I'm going to have her see a counselor. A professional can probably help her deal with Dan's rejection better than I can."

"We, my family, saw a counselor before and after my mother's heart transplant surgery and again when she died. He did a lot for us. For me and Ethan and Sierra. Dad's still struggling."

Wanting to dispel the somber mood they'd fallen into, Sage opened her briefcase and removed a manila folder. Before she could lay the papers out on the table, Gavin removed the folder from her grasp and tossed it aside.

"We need to go over those," she protested.

He took her by the shoulders and held her in front of him, his intense gaze boring into her. "It's not just Dan. I wouldn't let anyone or anything hurt you, Sage. Not if I could help it."

"I know that." And she did. She trusted him. It should have come as a surprise considering they'd met only a short time ago. Somehow, it didn't.

"I can give you a dozen reasons why a relationship between us won't work." He paused, drew a breath.

"Are you asking me out?" she blurted.

"To start with." He raised his hand to her face and brushed away a stray tendril of hair. "We can go from there."

"Gavin, I…"

"Don't say no. Not without giving me a chance."

"I wasn't going to say no."

His mouth lifted in a half smile. "You weren't?"

"These last days at the ranch, capturing the mustang, being with you, your family, they've been the best I've had in over four years."

"Even with the arguing?"

"Even with that." She looked away, suddenly shy. "I'm not sure I can walk away."

"Don't."

Whatever else was on her mind to say would have to wait because he kissed her then and conversing was the last thing on her mind.

This wasn't their first kiss, yet, in light of their recent confessions, it felt like it. Discovering how much he cared, that he, too, wanted to continue seeing her, ignited a new intimacy between them. A connection that wasn't there before.

Within seconds, the kiss went from warm and tender to off-the-charts hot. When his lips abandoned hers to seek the sensitive skin beneath her ear and along the column of her neck, she let out a tiny, needy moan. Her body, responding without any direction from her, curled into him.

He kissed her again, groaned, then pulled away. She saw the lines of tension etched in his face, recognized the effort it took for him to exercise control.

"Gavin?"

"We should probably quit while we still can. While I still can."

He desired her *and* cared about her. The combination was a heady one and gave her the courage to voice what was in her heart.

"Why?" She slipped into his arms, aligned her hips with his. "You did say your family would be gone for hours."

That was all the persuading he needed. Scooping her up, he held her against his chest. She stifled a laugh. No man had picked her up like this since…maybe not ever.

He carried her out the kitchen, through a rustic great

room and down the hall. She caught only glimpses of the house as they stole into its recesses. Photographs and pictures adorning the walls. A bathroom with—was that a claw-foot bathtub? Doors leading to bedrooms, one with clothes strewn over the floor and plastic horse figurines on a bookcase that had to be Cassie's.

At the last doorway he stopped and gazed down at her questioningly.

He was giving her the chance to say no. She could and there would be no repercussions. Gavin was above all an honorable and decent man.

"Put me down," she said. "Please."

He did as she requested, disappointment and acceptance in his eyes.

"Not here, silly!" Really, he was so sweet. Something of a dolt at times, but sweet. "On the bed."

He picked her up again. "You're going to drive me crazy."

How did he know that was her plan exactly?

The bedroom was large, more like a suite. A set of French doors, bracketed by a pair of sheer drapes, looked out onto the courtyard where she and Gavin had sat and talked the other day. In the center of the room was a queen-size four-poster bed, probably constructed by Gavin's father or grandfather. Shutting the door with his foot, he crossed the room and lowered her onto the patchwork quilt spread. The room was neither messy nor tidy but rather a comfortable in-between.

He stood over her, his hands at his sides, his gaze casting about.

"Wait here."

Wait? Sage pushed to a sitting position, instantly alarmed. Maybe *he* was having second thoughts.

Going to the armoire, he opened the door, pulled out a drawer and rummaged through the contents.

Ah! He wasn't having second thoughts at all.

Finding what he was searching for, he came back to the bed. "Sorry about that." He dropped a condom packet on the nightstand.

Sage looked over at it and burst into laughter as she read the name aloud. "Rainbow Delight?"

"It's a long story. Has to do with a high school buddy's bachelor party last spring."

"I can't wait to hear it."

He tugged at his shirt, yanking it from his pants. "It's the only condom I've got. If you don't—"

"Are you kidding?" She jumped to her feet and reached for the top button on his shirt, quickly unfastening it. "I happen to love rainbow colors."

No sooner did Gavin have his shirt off than he went to work on hers. Once she was out of it, he lowered her onto the quilt. In one easy motion, he removed her boots. Then her jeans.

"Nice," he murmured, his expression darkening as he took in the sight of her wearing just her bra and panties.

It wasn't fair that he should have all the fun.

"Come here, cowboy." Looping her arms around his neck, she tugged him down on top of her. His weight felt good as they sank together onto the mattress.

The remainder of their clothes disappeared in a blur.

"Cold?" he asked, covering her body with his. "We can get under the covers."

"No. This is perfect."

She snuggled deeper into his embrace, not wanting to miss the sight of Gavin fully naked for anything, even a little chill. He was splendid. Long, lean limbs. Hard muscled planes. Strength coupled with gentleness. Male perfection at its finest.

He seemed to appreciate her every bit as much as she did him. Skimming his hand along the length of her, he explored the hollow at the small of her back, the curve of her hip, the subtle expanse of her thigh.

"You're so beautiful."

She started to object, then decided not to. He was telling the truth. She could see it in his face. Hear it in his voice. To him, she was beautiful.

"Make love to me, Gavin," she murmured, lifting her hips in invitation as she brought his mouth to hers.

He groaned in response, his hands moving more frantically now. Kneading her breasts, cupping her buttocks, sliding between her legs. Then, his mouth was everywhere his hands had been, tasting, teasing, coaxing soft sounds from her.

She murmured his name, urged him to stop, then pleaded with him not to. His hands, his mouth, his warm breath caressing her soft feminine folds, became too much. She quickly climbed toward climax. A moment later, she tumbled over the edge—only to fall softly.

"That was…mmm."

He slowly kissed his way up the length of her body until they lay face-to-face, their legs entwined. "I agree."

Closing her fingers around his erection, she began stroking him. "You're beautiful, too."

He smiled.

It promptly vanished when she told him to, "Lie back," and took him into her mouth. He stopped her after only a few minutes.

"Party pooper," she complained.

"Darling, the party's just starting."

He pressed her into the mattress, simultaneously reaching for the condom on the nightstand. Sheathing himself, he parted her legs and entered her. The sensation of him filling her, stretching her, was exquisite. And addictive.

She wrapped her legs around his middle, arched her back. There was no slowing down. Neither of them tried. Moments later, she sensed his muscles tightening.

"Sage." He lifted his head, sought her gaze and held it fast.

Emotions exploded inside her. This was what it should be like between a man and a woman. What it had never been like for her before.

Gavin. He made the difference.

He clung to her and buried his face in her neck. She held him tight as he found his release. Soon, his breathing slowed, and he started to roll off her.

"No."

"I'm too heavy."

"I don't care."

"Sage."

She liked all the different ways he said her name. In anger. Frustration. Affection. Tenderly. She liked the way he said it in the throes of passion the best.

"What?" She sifted her fingers through his hair, sunlight from the window glinted off the black strands.

"We're going to figure things out. With us."

"I'm not worried."

"We have the mustang. Dan's going to pay you the back child support. Everything will work out."

Her response was to give him a peck on the lips.

Within seconds they were back where they started, hands frantically roaming and hungry for each other.

"Sure there aren't any more of those rainbow color condoms left?" she purred.

"I'll look."

He got up, only to go still.

"Is something the matter?"

"Listen."

A door slammed in another part of the house, followed by voices.

"Oh, shit." Sage started scrambling, digging through the quilt for her underwear. "Someone's home."

"It's just Cassie and my dad."

"*Just* Cassie and your dad?" Where the hell was her bra? "I will not be caught in bed with you."

Gavin laughed.

"This isn't funny."

"Relax." He bent and helped her gather their clothes. "I have an idea."

"It had better be a good one." She squirmed into her panties.

He nodded at the French doors.

It just might work, she thought.

Dressing as quietly as possible, they tiptoed out the French doors and into the courtyard. Sage winced when the latch made a loud noise as it clicked shut. Outside, she went weak. They were going to pull this off.

"Dammit!" She slapped her forehead.

"What?"

"My jacket and briefcase are in the kitchen. Your family's going to know."

"Relax."

"I can't."

Gavin grinned and hooked her by the arm. "Come on."

"How's my hair?"

"A lost cause."

Great. Just great.

They hurried around the house to the kitchen door, Sage attempting to finger comb her hair with one hand. The moment of truth came too soon. She prepared herself to be the object of curious stares and the subject of much speculation.

Except Cassie and Gavin's dad, who were busy unloading groceries, didn't seem the least bit surprised to see her or notice that anything was amiss.

She was almost let down. Almost.

Chapter 13

Sage couldn't stop shaking. It was over. Finally. Not just the meeting, which had lasted an hour, but the whole wretched ordeal.

"Congratulations, *primita*." Roberto slung an arm over her shoulders as they walked from the upscale office building in north Scottsdale to the parking lot.

"Thank you so much." She smiled up at her cousin-in-law. "I really appreciate everything you've done for me and Isa."

The paternity test results had arrived bright and early that morning. Dan wasted no time. His attorney—Sage hadn't realized he retained one—contacted Roberto, and a meeting was set up for after lunch.

"I'm just glad it's over and done with," Roberto said. "Now you can enjoy the rest of your vacation. Speaking of which, what are you going to do?"

"I haven't thought about it." What a lie! Until the call from Dan's attorney, she'd been thinking of Gavin and their incredible afternoon together yesterday almost to exclusion.

He'd called her last night and again this morning. They'd talked like a couple of teenagers, soft and low. He'd chuckled, she'd giggled. Isa had looked at Sage in confusion while her cousin Anna rolled her eyes knowingly.

Sage couldn't remember the last time she'd felt so young. Or, so good. What should have been an embarrassing situation when they were nearly caught by Gavin's dad and daughter had turned into an enjoyable dinner with the family, followed by several goodbye kisses that left Sage walking on air—or should she say, driving on air—the entire ride home to her cousin's.

She decided to enjoy it while it lasted. Once she returned to Show Low and two hundred miles separated her and Gavin, it would be difficult to recapture the feelings she was having now.

"I've got another appointment." Roberto kissed her on the cheek, said, "See you tonight" and then headed to his car.

Sage waved at him before getting into her truck. She'd barely started the engine when her cell phone rang.

"Hi." She cradled the phone to her ear, anticipating hearing the rich timbre of Gavin's voice.

"Did I interrupt you?"

"We just finished the meeting."

"How'd it go?"

"Unbelievably well. Dan and I agreed on a new monthly amount, and he's going to pay an additional sum toward the back child support he owes. It'll take him almost three years to catch up, but at least Isa will have the money."

"That's great. I'm really happy for you both."

Unfortunately, there was always a downside. "I just wish Dan wanted to see her."

"He still doesn't?"

"No. I agreed to visitation, naturally, and we came up with a schedule. He made it clear Isa wasn't to come here.

If anything, he'd go to Show Low. I got the impression that wasn't going to happen very often."

"Poor kid."

"Has he said anything to you?" Sage inserted her key in the ignition.

"About Isa?"

"No. The mustang or your partnership." She hadn't mentioned Dan's remark about his money being tied up elsewhere.

"We talked this morning. Decided on which mares we'd breed first and set a price for stud fees. He has a few clients interested."

"Okay, good." She relaxed. It was impossible for her not to dwell on what effect her relationship with Gavin would have on his and Dan's. Not that Dan knew anything—or ever would if she could help it.

"I finished filling out the adoption paperwork. Was thinking maybe I could drop it off tonight."

"You don't have to drive all the way into Scottsdale for that."

"I wasn't. I was going to drive all the way into Scottsdale to pick you up for dinner."

"Really?" She brightened.

"Ever been to P.F. Chang's?"

"Once. I love Chinese food." Sage mentally rummaged through her suitcase contents and the clothes she'd brought with her. No dresses or shoes besides boots and sneakers. Maybe Anna had a dress and a pair of heels she could borrow that were suitable for fine dining.

"Six o'clock okay?"

She held the phone closer, imagining Gavin in dress clothes. He would leave her breathless. "Perfect. See you then."

Grinning foolishly, she started the truck and headed toward the exit. She hadn't quite reached it when her phone rang again. Ready to ask Gavin what he'd forgotten, she slowed when she recognized her boss's number.

"Hi, Steve. Did you get the pictures I emailed?"

"Yeah, thanks. They're great."

"I just got off the phone with Gavin Powell." Since Steve's conversations usually lasted several minutes, she pulled into the nearest empty parking space. "He's completed the adoption papers. I'll get them later today and overnight them tomorrow."

"Forget it. You don't need to bother with that. There's been a change in plans."

Sage didn't like the tone in Steve's voice. She'd heard it before, and it usually preceded the delivery of bad news. "What change?"

"We're going to follow regular procedure with the mustang. Auction him to the public."

"W-why?"

"The media attention. Did you watch TV last night?"

"A little."

She'd seen the evening broadcast at Gavin's. Both broadcasts, in fact. Everyone had crowded together in the great room, laughing and ribbing Gavin mercilessly. They'd also congratulated him on doing such a great job.

"This horse has made big news, and not just statewide," Steve continued. "National, too. One clip's gone viral on the internet. The office can't keep up with all the phone calls."

"What does that have to do with Gavin Powell adopting him?"

"Money, of course. With all the media attention, this horse will bring a considerably higher price than usual at auction. And positive publicity for the bureau. We can use both."

"But you already agreed," she protested, anticipating Gavin's reaction.

He would be devastated. And angry. At the BLM and also at her. Hadn't she assured him there would be no problem adopting the mustang?

"Nothing's in writing," Steve said, easily dismissing her objection.

"You gave your word."

"Even if I wanted to let Powell adopt the horse, which I don't, it's out of my hands. The head of the department won't let an opportunity like this one slip by without making the most of it."

Sage rubbed her aching forehead. All she could think of was Gavin. His plans, his dreams, his hopes for the future about to disintegrate before his eyes.

"You can't do this, Steve. Please. Gavin Powell and his family are the ones who captured the mustang, and it wasn't easy. More than that, he's the one who originally contacted the BLM. We owe him."

"He still can own the horse. He just has to win him at the auction."

Except Sage knew the Powells didn't have the money. Not if the mustang went for the large sum Steve and the department head were obviously hoping he'd bring.

"It's not fair."

"Few things in life are," Steve answered caustically. "Why do you care anyway?"

"The Powells are nice people." She hoped he didn't notice the hitch in her voice. "And we—I—promised them."

She considered going above Steve's head, making a case on the Powells' behalf to the head of the department.

Except what good would that do? As Steve had said, it was the head of the department who'd decided to publically auction the mustang.

Damn, damn, damn! This couldn't be happening.

She closed her eyes, holding her tears at bay, guilt tearing her up inside.

"Do you have Powell's number?" Steve asked. "I'm going to call him now."

"No! Let me tell him."

The news would be bad enough. Worse coming from a stranger. Besides, this was her fault and her responsibility to handle. Afterward, she'd advise Gavin on the ins and outs of the auction, help him prepare.

At least he'd have the coming week. In that time, Gavin could breed the mustang to a few of his mares.

Then, she remembered. Avaro was in heat. She'd probably mated with the mustang during their little adventure. They could breed Avaro to the mustang again, just to make sure. And Sage would give Gavin the foal. There was also the new business he was getting because of finding the mustang. It wasn't all bad, she reasoned.

Only she doubted Gavin would see it that way. Nothing could make up for losing the mustang.

"Are you sure?" Steve asked. "I'd be happy to call him."

Sage glanced at her watch, made a mental note to call her cousin and check on Isa. "I'm on my way there now."

"Okay. I'll see you tomorrow."

"Tomorrow?" Her heart jumped. "Are you coming to Mustang Valley?"

"No, you're bringing the horse here."

"I… I'm on vacation."

"Not till Friday. Which means you're on the BLM's clock through tomorrow. We need you to transport the horse here as soon as possible so we can begin processing him. PR wants to really pump up the advertising. The auction's a week from Saturday. We don't have much time."

"Steve." Sage was aware of the pleading in her voice. "Give the Powells a few days with the horse. I'll bring him up Monday morning."

"Impossible."

She had no choice. Not if she wanted to keep her job. The idea of rebelling, of telling her boss to shove it, was appealing. Also unrealistic. She had a daughter to support and eight years with the BLM. Decent jobs like hers, ones with benefits, weren't easy to come by.

"Fine," she said, sick to the bottom of her soul. "I'll call you tomorrow when I'm on the road."

Wiping her watery eyes, she put the truck in gear and drove to Powell Ranch. After calling Anna and telling her she'd be late, Sage concentrated on coming up with the best and kindest way to tell Gavin about the mustang. In the end, she decided to be honest and straightforward. Sugarcoating or dancing around the topic wouldn't lessen the terrible blow, merely postpone it.

Gavin was nowhere to be seen when she arrived at the ranch and parked. Spying Javier leaving the arena on horseback, she went after him. A glance at the empty round pen made her think the mustang had been moved to a more permanent location.

Except it wouldn't be permanent.

Javier told her Gavin had gotten a phone call a little bit ago and went into the house. She resisted the urge to run, choosing a brisk walk instead. At the back door, she knocked. And knocked again. In between she chewed a thumbnail. Where was he?

At last, Gavin answered the door. His cell phone dangling from his fingers.

"Hey, what are you doing here?"

"I dropped by to—" The stunned look he wore stopped her. She stepped over the threshold, afraid Steve had changed his mind and called Gavin about the mustang. "Is everything all right?"

"No." He motioned her inside. "I just got off the phone with—"

"I'm sorry," she blurted, and threw herself in his arms.

"You know?"

"Yes, my boss called me. I told him I wanted to tell you myself."

Gavin set her gently aside and held her at arm's length. "Tell me what?"

"About the mustang."

"I don't know what you're talking about."

"That wasn't my boss on the phone with you?"

He frowned in confusion. "Why would your boss call me?"

Oh, no! She'd jumped to the wrong conclusion. This wasn't going anything like she'd planned.

"Then who was it you were talking to?"

"Dan," Gavin said solemnly. "He's terminating our partnership agreement. Said he doesn't have the money now that he has to pay you the back child support."

The strength went out of Sage's legs. She stumbled to the table, pulled out a chair and dropped into it.

"That bastard," she said, covering her face with her hands. "That dirty bastard."

"I don't care. Not that much. He's been a pain in the ass from the beginning. And now I'm not so sure I need him anymore. Not with the mustang."

Sage groaned.

Gavin sat in the chair next to hers. "What's wrong, honey?"

He was being so nice. She didn't deserve it. "This is terrible. Awful. I'm still in shock."

"Forget it. Dan's not worth the trouble."

"Not Dan." She reached for Gavin's hand and folded it between hers. "My boss called me right after I talked to you. He's ordered me to transport the mustang to our Show Low facility. Tomorrow."

He sat back. "Why?"

"Because he's...the mustang...is going to be publically auctioned a week from Saturday. The department head changed his mind. They aren't going to let you adopt the mustang outright."

He stared at her, disbelief written on his face.

"You'll have to bid on him like everyone else. I'm sorry." She squeezed his fingers. "I would give anything for this not to have happened."

Gavin stood, went over to the sink and looked out the window.

Sage sat, waiting quietly, respecting his need for a few minutes to himself.

When he turned to her, his expression was that of a defeated man.

She rushed to him and hugged him fiercely.

While he held her in return, the strength and passion and conviction that was Gavin had seeped out of him.

The mustang didn't want to go in Sage's trailer. That made two of them. Gavin didn't want the mustang to go in Sage's trailer, either.

As she'd informed him yesterday, Gavin had no choice. According to the law, the mustang belonged to the federal government. If he tried to harbor the horse illegally, there would be serious repercussions. So, he complied, as much as it galled him.

"Watch out!" Ethan called a split second before the mustang's right rear hoof sliced the air in what was two inches shy of a deadly kick.

It had taken five of them, Gavin, Ethan, their dad, Sage and Javier, forty minutes to put a halter on the horse and drag him to the trailer. Gavin's shoulders would be sore for a week, and his dad sported a bright red welt across his wrist. If not for the gloves they all wore, their palms would be ripped to shreds from rope burns.

"Let's try this again."

Gavin positioned himself to the right of the mustang and tossed his rope to Javier on the other side. Ethan gripped the rope attached to the mustang's halter and wound it around an opening in the side of Sage's trailer. The two of them proceeded to engage each other in a game of tug-of-war, with the mustang having the advantage.

Slowly, Gavin and Javier drew their rope taut across the mustang's hindquarters. They were ready for him when he bucked. They were also ready for him when he stopped.

"Now!"

Knowing he'd want to escape the rope irritating his back legs, they forced him forward one reluctant step at a time. Ethan aided the process by pulling on the lead rope. The mustang resisted, grunting and squealing and putting all his weight in his back legs until he was almost sitting on the ground. Exhaustion eventually wore him down.

No graceful entrance into the trailer for him. He charged ahead, landing with a resounding thud and banging into the sidewall.

Sage, who had been waiting for just this moment, slammed the trailer door shut behind him.

They breathed a collective sigh of relief. So did the crowd that had gathered to watch.

"Good job, Dad." Cassie ran over to peer at the mustang through the open slats in the trailer.

"Not so close," Gavin warned her, taking off his gloves and wiping his damp forehead with his sleeve. To Sage, he said, "I'll be glad when school starts up again next week."

"No, you won't. You like having her around."

She was right. "Maybe I should go with you. He could give you trouble on the drive."

"I'd like that except..." She smiled sadly.

"More BLM policy?"

"'Fraid so. I can't even take Isa with me."

"Call me when you get there."

"I will." She made her farewells to Gavin's family, promising to see them tomorrow.

He slung an arm over her shoulders and walked her to the cab of her truck. No one paid them much attention, evidently accepting that he and Sage were a couple and deserved a private goodbye.

"I'm sorry."

"For what?" he asked.

"This." She waved a hand at the trailer and mustang. "It's all my fault."

"I don't see how."

"I promised you ownership."

"None of us saw this coming."

"You have every right to be mad at me."

"I'm not."

No, he wasn't mad at her. But Dan? Hell, yes. For his

treatment of her and Isa, and the slimy way he'd terminated their partnership agreement.

Gavin was also mad at himself. Like his father, he'd put his trust in someone untrustworthy, blinded by the prospect of easy money.

"It's ironic," Sage said. "If the girls didn't wander off, we might not have captured the mustang for weeks. It was them being found in the canyon with him that's generated all the media attention. Otherwise, he'd be just another feral horse."

"Yeah." Ironic and unlucky.

"What are you going to do?"

"I'm not sure." A lot had happened in the past day, and he'd yet to process it all.

She circled his waist with her arms and rested her head on his chest.

He stroked her hair, which she wore loose rather than in her customary ponytail. He enjoyed running his fingers through its thickness, pictured it fanned out on his pillow.

"I'll miss you."

"Me, too," she murmured, her face pressed into his jacket.

One thing they had agreed on last night was that Sage would return to Mustang Valley after dropping off the horse. Not only to finish her vacation but to be with him. Where they'd go with their relationship from there remained to be seen.

"Not to pressure you, but I really hope you'll go to the auction. If only so we can spend the weekend together."

"Now, there's an offer I can't refuse."

The truth was, he had a lot to consider before deciding. On the one hand, it would kill him to watch someone else buy the mustang. On the other hand, it would kill him worse if the going price turned out to be something he could have afforded and he wasn't there.

If only he was more certain the potential new customers who'd called or come by would still be interested in doing business even if the mustang wasn't on the ranch. If only he had a spare couple thousand dollars tucked away somewhere.

"I hate to go." Sage expelled a long, mournful breath. "But I need to leave now if I don't want to be driving that highway at midnight."

Hooking a finger under her chin, he lifted her face to his. Their relationship was still brand-new and each kiss an exciting discovery.

Would it still be like this when they'd kissed a hundred times? A thousand?

If he wanted a future with Sage, and he did, he needed something worthwhile to offer her. Financial stability. A decent home in good repair. A profitable livelihood. Owning and operating a successful stud and breeding business could provide all that and more.

As long as he had a worthy stallion.

Preferably the mustang.

After yet another kiss, a "Drive careful" and last smile, he stood and watched as Sage drove away, the horse trailer bumping along behind her truck.

Seeing his brother strolling toward the stables, Gavin hollered to him. "Ethan!"

"What's up?" he asked when Gavin drew near, buckling the front of his farrier chaps.

"I'm calling a family meeting."

"Now?"

"Yeah, now." They hadn't had one since after their mother died.

"About what?"

"The mustang. I want to buy him at the auction."

Ethan grinned. "Let's do it!"

Their dad made a pot of fresh coffee for the meeting, which took place an hour later at the kitchen table. It was just like the ones they had years before, except instead of Sierra sitting to Gavin's left, his daughter did.

She'd been surprised when he asked her to take part in the meeting. "You're family," he'd said in response, and she smiled even bigger than when he'd given her Blue.

Maybe he'd get the hang of this parenting thing, after all.

Gavin laid out the files containing the ranch's bank statements and past year's income and expense reports in the middle of the table.

"Does Sage have any idea how much the mustang will go for?" his father asked after Gavin had summarized the condition of their current finances.

"Not really. She says the BLM has never had a situation like this before."

"I don't think the horse will go for that much," Ethan said confidently. "Sure, he's a novelty and generated a lot of attention. But once people see what a handful he is, they'll rethink owning him."

Gavin hoped his brother was right. "What we have to figure out is how much cash we can raise without putting the ranch or the family in jeopardy."

They debated the issue hotly for some time, rereviewing the income and expense reports, making projections for the next year and brainstorming ideas on how to increase revenues and cut corners.

Finally, they decided on an amount. Gavin wasn't sure it would be enough.

"I have some money set aside," his father said quietly. "I want you to have it."

"You sure, Dad?"

"It's not much. Twelve hundred dollars. Leftover from your mother's life insurance policy. I know she'd want you to have it."

Gavin was deeply touched. "Thank you."

"I have some money, too," Cassie piped up. "Fifty-three dollars and twenty-five cents. From babysitting."

"Sweetheart, I don't want to take your money."

"You said I was family."

"Yes, but—"

"I want to help, too. I can get more babysitting jobs." She gazed at him with heartfelt earnestness.

Gavin tried to figure out what he'd done to deserve such a fantastic kid.

"Okay. Thank you." Because it meant so much to her, he'd accept her babysitting money and make it up to her another way.

"I guess that's it." Ethan lifted his coffee mug in a toast.

Everyone clinked mugs, except Cassie. She raised her glass of juice.

Gavin glanced around the table, astounded at the differences one short week had made in their lives.

The mustang had managed to unite them as a family, give them a shared dream, help Gavin and Cassie grow closer and, maybe most important, bring Sage to him.

This was only the beginning. There were more changes, good ones, on the way. He could feel it.

All he had to do was outbid the competition at the auction.

Chapter 14

Gavin fingered the piece of card stock in his hand. On it was printed his number—one hundred and twenty-nine. So many bidders. He'd seen one individual with a number well into the two hundreds. And at least three times as many spectators were in attendance. According to talk, this was the most well-attended auction in the history of the BLM.

It was also the first one with TV news reporters and camera operators.

"Where's Sage?" Cassie asked, holding on to Gavin's hand as they strolled the auction grounds.

Ethan and their dad stayed behind to run the ranch. While Gavin was pleased his dad was taking a more active role in the family business, he missed the home-cooked meals. Frozen pizza and microwave lasagna just didn't taste as good.

"I don't know." Gavin scanned the crowd for Sage. He considered calling her cell phone then decided against it. She was working today. "She said she'd find us before the auction started."

Which was half an hour away.

The knot in Gavin's stomach tightened. All the assurances Sage had given him this past week weren't enough to relieve his agitation.

"Cassie!"

At the sound of her name being called, both Cassie and Gavin came to a halt. Isa appeared, running toward them and dragging her aunt Anna and uncle Roberto with her. Gavin had met Sage's cousin and cousin-in-law twice during the past week and liked them very much. He thought they might like him, too.

"Hi," Anna said a little breathlessly when they met up.

"Good to see you again." Gavin shook Roberto's hand. "I didn't know you were coming."

"Spur-of-the-moment decision."

"Dad and I drove up last night," Cassie announced over the top of Isa's head. The younger girl had attached herself to Cassie, and they'd need a crowbar to pry them apart.

"Have you seen the mustang yet?" Anna asked.

"Several times."

Gavin had planted himself at the mustang's pen shortly after the main gate was opened and stayed put for nearly an hour. As much as he'd wanted to, he couldn't prevent other people from inspecting the horse—from outside the pen. No one dared step inside, not if they valued their safety. Gavin secretly cheered the mustang's aggressive temperament. Anything to make him less appealing to prospective bidders.

"We thought we'd walk over to see him." Roberto craned his neck in the direction of the horse pens.

"Cassie and I will go with you," Gavin offered.

He commented on several of the other horses up for auction as they walked down the long aisle between the pens. Anna and Roberto murmured polite replies, typical of nonhorse enthusiasts.

"Isa, check out these horses." Cassie and Isa darted

to a pen containing two mares, one gray, one paint. "My dad's buying them."

"Are you?" Roberto asked.

"Maybe." Gavin came up behind Cassie. "If they sell for the right price. I'm trying to preserve mustang bloodlines, and I'm thinking they might make good breeding stock."

All the broodmares in the world wouldn't do him any good if he didn't win the mustang.

He'd transferred four thousand dollars into the ranch's checking account yesterday. Surely that would be enough. Sage seemed to think it was four or five times the amount he'd need.

The mustang had been placed in a separate pen, far away from the other horses. Spectators were standing two and three deep when they got there, an increase from earlier.

Anna, Roberto and the girls wormed their way closer. Gavin stayed behind, glimpsing the mustang now and again when someone moved. Lights flashed as cameras went off. Annoyed at the unwanted attention, the mustang lowered his head and pawed the ground.

A young man with more brawn than brains reached through the bars and barely escaped having his hand bitten.

Soon, Gavin thought, this will all be over and I'll take my horse home.

"I'm hungry," Isa complained some minutes later when the thrill had worn off for her.

"Me, too." Roberto pressed a finger to the tip of her nose.

"If we're going to eat," Gavin said, "maybe we should

do it before the auction starts." He wasn't really hungry but he could use a cold drink.

After finishing their meal of hot dogs and potato chips, they made their way to the bleachers, which were already two-thirds filled, and found seats that afforded them a decent view.

Gavin's phone rang soon after they were seated. "It's Sage," he said, and answered, "Hey."

"Where are you?"

"In the stands." He told her which section. "Can you get away?"

"No. Not till later, unfortunately."

He could hear the disappointment in her voice. It matched his own.

What would it be like when he returned to the valley tomorrow and she remained in Show Low?

They'd talk tonight. Make some definite plans. No, tomorrow would be soon enough. He'd rather celebrate tonight, which they would. In style.

"Call me when you're done. We'll meet you by the chuck wagon."

"Good luck," she said, her voice soft and warm. "But I know you won't need it. That horse is yours, Gavin. He's been yours from the moment you saw him."

He felt the same way.

Pocketing his phone, Gavin reread the auction flyer for the third time, only to be distracted by a lone man climbing the bleacher stairs. He didn't look like the usual horse auction patron, not with his tailored slacks, dress shoes and expensive jacket.

As he took a seat three rows in front of them, he turned to speak to an old-timer beside him.

"James," Roberto suddenly called out. "James Bridwell."

Glancing behind him, the man gave a brief wave of acknowledgment when he spied Roberto.

"You know him?" Anna asked.

Gavin was wondering the same thing.

"We run into each other on occasion. He's an attorney with a firm in Scottsdale."

An uneasiness Gavin couldn't explain came over him. Why should it matter that an attorney from Scottsdale was at a BLM horse auction?

Except he couldn't shake the feeling that it *did* matter. A lot.

The feeling intensified when he noticed the man also held a card stock bidder's number.

"Sold to bidder…"

Gavin held up his number for the auctioneer to see. "129."

"You won!" Cassie tugged on his jacket sleeve.

He smiled down at her, admittedly caught up in the excitement. "We probably don't need another mare."

Except he would need them, when he brought the mustang home.

As Sage had predicted, the horses at the auction were all going for one to two hundred dollars despite the enormous crowd. Gavin dared to hope. Surely the mustang wouldn't bring much more than that. He patted his pocket, the one containing his checkbook, and thought again of the balance.

It would be enough.

The attorney sitting in front of them hadn't bid on one single horse. He wasn't alone. According to the snippets of conversation Gavin picked up from his neighbors, many people had come solely to see the mustang auctioned.

He tried to shake off his uneasiness, telling himself the attorney wasn't important.

The auction continued. Thirty minute went by. Forty-five. At one point, the auctioneer's singsong voice started to crack. Burros, managing to be both scruffy and adorable at the same time, were also sold. Cassie was naturally enamored, as was most of the crowd, and wanted one.

Finally, they announced the mustang was up next for bid. Excitement rippled through the stands, and the noise level instantly increased. Gavin's right leg beat a frenzied tattoo.

A minute passed. Then three. Clanging noises came from the holding pens behind the auctioneer's booth, followed by shouting. More noise, more shouting, and the gate was at last thrown open.

The mustang emerged, and he was none too happy.

Nostrils flaring, feet prancing, head shaking, he fought the three men who dared try to restrain him with their ropes. Oohs, aahs and whistles emanated from the crowd, which incited the mustang even more. The wranglers, three of them, did their best to control a living, breathing tornado.

Sage entered the arena behind the men and horse, acting as an extra hand and spotter in case of trouble.

Gavin paid little attention while the auctioneer extolled the mustang's merits. Everything and everyone took on a strange, surreal quality. That changed the instant the bidding began.

The auctioneer called for five hundred dollars to start.

When no one responded, he called for four hundred. Then three.

Someone offered two hundred. Like a gun shot at the start of a race, they were off. From that moment on, the bidding came fast and furious.

Gavin didn't jump right in. Instinct told him to wait and see what everyone else did first. Within seconds, the price jumped to six hundred. Then seven. He raised his number in the air. One of the auctioneer's helpers standing outside the arena saw him, pointed at him and called out his bid.

Immediately, he was beaten. He bid once more, only to be outbid again. Each time he went higher, vaguely aware that the price for the mustang had reached a thousand. Then two thousand. That was okay. He still had plenty of money.

One by one, the less serious bidders dropped out. When the going price reached three thousand dollars, only three people remained. Gavin, a middle-aged woman and the attorney.

The attorney?

Gavin had been too involved to realize the attorney had been bidding against him.

At thirty-five hundred dollars, the woman dropped out.

The mustang began to paw the ground impatiently as if urging Gavin to hurry up.

"Thirty-eight hundred," he called out.

"Do I have thirty-nine?" the auctioneer asked.

No one responded. The attorney was on his cell phone, speaking to someone.

Elation surged inside Gavin. His hands shook. The mustang was his!

In the arena, Sage grinned and gave him a thumbs-up sign.

"Going once, going twice—"

"Four thousand dollars," the attorney shouted.

"Do I hear forty-one hundred?"

Four thousand was all Gavin had in his checking account. Fighting panic, he called out, "Forty-five hundred." He couldn't lose the mustang. Not when he was this close. Somehow he'd come up with the other five hundred dollars.

Then, he remembered he'd also bought the two mares. Son of a bitch. He was screwed.

The attorney continued talking on his cell phone, then waved his hand wildly in the air.

"Five thousand dollars!"

"Going once," the auctioneer sang into the microphone.

There was no way Gavin could match that amount, much less beat it.

"Going twice."

Pain sliced through him. This couldn't be happening. The horse was supposed to go for hundreds of dollars, not thousands.

"Going three times."

He crumpled his card-stock number into a ball and threw it on the bleacher floor beneath his feet.

"Sold! To number 238."

The words rang like a death toll in Gavin's ears.

"Gavin!"

He slowed at the sound of Sage's voice. Not that he'd been walking fast. He couldn't, his feet weighed a thousand pounds each.

She ran to where he, Anna, Roberto and the girls milled on the fringes of the thinning crowd.

"I couldn't get away any sooner," she explained in a rush. "I had to help the wranglers with…" She took his hand, pressed her free one to his cheek. "It's crazy. I still can't believe he went for that much money."

Gavin wanted to comfort her. She seemed to need it. Except there was only cold emptiness inside him.

"Do you know who bought him?" he asked in a flat voice.

"Not the owner's name. The man who bid on him was acting as an agent. I might be able to find out in a few days, once the paperwork is processed. Steve will tell me."

Her boss. The name penetrated the thick haze surrounding Gavin's brain.

"Cassie?" Where had she gone? He searched the immediate area, spotting the two girls with their heads together by the chuck wagon. "Come on, honey," he hollered. "We need to get on the road."

"You're leaving?" Sage asked. "So soon? I thought we'd…have some time together."

He'd thought that, too, when they were going to be celebrating.

"I need to get the mares home."

"That's right. You bought two new horses."

Breeding stock he wouldn't need now.

Dammit. The mustang was his. He'd tracked him, captured him, pinned his entire future on owning him.

"Can I help you load them?" Sage offered.

"I can manage, thanks."

On some level he recognized he was putting distance between him and Sage. She realized it, too.

"Please, Gavin. Talk to me before you go." Her fingers entwined in his were warm and coaxing.

Anna must have read the situation. "There's a little petting zoo right up the road. Why don't Roberto and I take the girls there?"

Sage smiled her thanks.

Gavin muttered a distracted "Okay." He was still reeling and really didn't want to talk to Sage. Or anyone for that matter.

She accompanied him to his truck and trailer. Climbing in, he drove very slowly through the grounds to the horse pens.

Loading the mares didn't take much time. Gavin had chosen well. For wild horses, these two possessed relatively calm dispositions as well as striking looks. It was a shame they wouldn't be able to combine their desirable qualities with those of the mustang.

All at once, the barrier holding his emotions in check broke. They crashed over him with a force that left him shaking. Anger. Frustration. Resentment. Disappointment.

Devastation.

He slammed the trailer door shut harder than necessary. The startled mares flinched and bunched toward the front.

"There are other feral stallions for sale," Sage said gently. "They come in all the time."

Gavin shook his head.

"I know they won't be the same—"

He cut her off. "I'm not interested in another horse."

"You may feel differently later."

"I'm not interested," he repeated harshly.

They got back in his truck and drove to the main parking lot. Anna and Roberto hadn't yet returned with the girls. Gavin selected a spot in the half-empty lot, parked and turned off the engine. He and Sage said nothing for several moments. He hoped it would last, that she would give him a break before pressuring him.

She didn't.

"I was thinking, I can relocate to Mustang Valley. Live with you, if you're willing," she added shyly. "My house is on a month-to-month lease so I can leave anytime. And I have family in the Phoenix area."

If the mustang were in the trailer with the mares, Gavin would be having an entirely different reaction. He'd grab Sage, kiss her, tell her how happy she made him. As it was, the cold emptiness inside him grew only colder.

"What about your job?"

"If the BLM doesn't have an opening in their Phoenix office, I'll find a new one."

She was going to make him say it, strip him of his pride and leave him bare to the bone.

"I can't afford to support you while you're looking."

"I wouldn't expect you to," she answered breezily. "I'll have extra money coming in now that Dan's paying me."

Gavin ground his teeth. He wished she hadn't brought up her ex's name. If he and Dan were still partners, Gavin would have been able to outbid the attorney.

"I'd rather you didn't live off his money."

"It's not like that. He owes me. I've supported Isa for years when he should have been paying."

Splitting hairs, in his opinion.

"Don't you want to keep seeing me?" She was finally getting past all his excuses and to the heart of the matter.

"*Keep* seeing you," he said. "Not be the reason you're uprooting your entire life."

"I was thinking of it as more like creating a new one."

It was then he noticed the tears forming in her eyes.

Much as he wanted to, he wasn't ready to make the kind of commitment she was asking of him. He might have been, if the day had ended differently.

Instead, he said, "Let's talk about this in a week or two. After I've had a chance to meet with the family. Examine our options."

"You can still go ahead with the stud and breeding business." She looked at him appealingly. "With a new partner."

"Who?"

"Me."

He recoiled as if she'd slapped him across the face. "I won't take money from you."

"But you would from Dan."

"That was different."

"Why? Because he's a man?"

"Because he's not someone—" Gavin started to say, *I love,* but stopped himself. This wasn't the time to admit his feelings for Sage, give her cause to have expectations he couldn't meet. "Someone I have an intimate relationship with," he said instead.

He'd let her down. She'd been hoping for a declaration of love. Everything in her expression told him so.

Gavin shifted and stared out the driver's side window.

"You blame me for losing the mustang."

"No."

"I misled you. Assured you he'd sell for a fraction of what he did."

"Sage, I don't blame you."

Only he did. A little. He'd counted on her being right. On her experience and connections with the BLM. It wasn't anything he couldn't get over eventually. Her intentions had been honest and sincere, after all.

He probably wasn't being fair to her, but he'd lost so much today and wasn't thinking his clearest.

"I get that you don't want to take my money. I also get that you're a traditional kind of guy. That you feel a responsibility to take care of any woman in your life, even if she doesn't need taking care of."

He closed his eyes, wishing she would stop talking. Let him go home and sort through this mess before wringing a decision from him.

"We'd make really good partners," she went on, "if you think about it. I know we don't always agree, but look at it this way. Your strengths balance my weakness and vice versa."

"Sage—"

"I'll come down next Friday. We can hash out the details."

The more she pushed him, the more she made him feel like a complete failure.

"I don't want to think about this now," he snapped, hating himself for his lousy temper.

She pursed her lips, her way of asking when *did* he want to think about it?

"I would feel a whole lot better if we just didn't make any decisions for a while." He was surprised how reasonable his voice sounded considering the turmoil raging inside him.

At that moment, an SUV pulled up beside them. Not her cousin's vehicle. This one had a BLM insignia on the door.

"Oh, great," Sage muttered when a man stepped out and came over. "It's my boss." She opened the door and got out.

Gavin did, too, and she introduced them.

"Sage, I'm glad I found you before you left." He motioned for her to join him a few feet away. "You got a minute?"

Gavin shoved his hands in his jacket pockets and kicked at a small rock at his feet. He didn't intend to eavesdrop, but Steve's deep voice carried.

"I need you to transport the mustang to the new owner tomorrow."

"Where?"

"Outside of Scottsdale. Not far from that place where you went on your vacation. I'll have the exact address for you in the morning."

Mustang Valley?

Learning that the new owner of the mustang lived near him and that Sage would be the one to deliver the horse was the final blow.

Gavin returned to his truck, vaguely aware that he was staggering.

What a fool he'd been, to think he could turn things around and create something significant for him and his family. His mother's illness had sent them into a downward spiral from which they would never recover. He should have known better than to try.

Without realizing how he'd got there, he found himself sitting behind the steering wheel, his hand on the key, poised to start the ignition. Wait. He couldn't leave. Cassie wasn't back yet.

He jerked when the passenger side door opened and Sage stood framed in it. "Steve's gone."

Sound came from his mouth, an unintelligible reply to her statement.

"Gavin, I... I'll refuse the assignment if you want me to. I just figured, well, I'll take good care of the horse."

He didn't answer. The fragmented thoughts whirling inside his head refused to come together into something coherent.

"I'll come by the ranch with I'm done."

Another SUV pulled into the parking lot then, this one her cousin's. He saw Cassie in the backseat. She was reading a book to Isa.

Cassie.

She was his priority now.

Maybe he *should* consider buying a different wild stallion. Salvage as much of his original plan as he could.

"Gavin?" Sage leaned into the truck. "Did you hear me? I'll come by the ranch tomorrow."

He shook his head. At her confused expression, he got out and circled the truck.

She smiled when he reached for her. It disappeared when he held her at arm's length.

"You don't have to," he told her, striving to keep his voice gentle. He remembered that from when his mother was sick. The doctors had always delivered bad news in low, quiet tones. "In fact, it might be best if you didn't."

"What are you saying?"

"I care about you. More than you realize." He squeezed her shoulders. That was another thing the doctors had done. They'd placed reassuring hands on him and his family. "But we were foolish to ever think we could make a go of this."

Dismay filled her eyes. "We *can*."

"There are too many obstacles. The distance—"

"I told you, I'll move."

He shook his head. "I need time, Sage. I'm not the kind of person who can pluck a plan B out of the air. It's important that I build the business, the ranch and my home into something meaningful before I can share them with you."

"That's what people who care about each other do. They build meaningful homes and businesses. Together."

"I wasn't ready to be a father when Cassie was born. I loved her but I was incapable of giving her what she needed. I regret that and am doing my damnedest to make up for it."

"I know how important she is to you. I have a daughter, too."

"When I commit to you, Sage, it will be when we're both ready. Not before and not just you."

She stiffened. "How long will that take? Because some people are never ready and use it as a convenient excuse."

"I don't know." He wouldn't lie to her. "And asking you to wait is unfair."

"I would, you know." Her features crumbled.

He was probably committing a huge mistake by letting her go.

Hadn't he accused Dan of the same thing?

Pride was Gavin's downfall. A downfall of all the Powell men. He couldn't change the way he felt, however. Not even if it resulted in an end to his relationship with Sage.

The SUV door opened, and Cassie emerged.

"Dad?"

"Yeah, honey."

She walked toward him, casting uncertain glances at him and Sage. "Are we leaving?"

"In a minute."

"Bye, Ms. Navarre." She gave Sage a tentative wave, then continued to Gavin's truck. It was obvious from Cassie's woeful expression that she'd deduced at least some of what was happening. So, probably, had Anna and Roberto, for they didn't emerge from the SUV.

Sage tried to smile at Cassie. She couldn't, not with her lower lip trembling. "This isn't at all how I thought today would end," she said to Gavin, and wiped her nose.

"Me, either."

"I love you, Gavin, and I think you're making a terrible mistake."

His chest ached. He wished she hadn't said that. Wished he could say it back to her because it was true.

"Sage—"

"I just wanted you to know in case we don't... Just in case." She touched her cool fingertips to his cheek. "It still can be different. You have only to stop me from walking away."

He opened his mouth to say the words. They got stuck in his throat and wouldn't come out.

With a last sad look, she went to her cousin's SUV and climbed in, sitting in the seat next to Isa. He stood and watched as Roberto drove away. Sage's tear-stained face appeared briefly in the window.

The next instant, she was gone, along with a sizable chunk of Gavin's heart.

Chapter 15

It hadn't taken long for the road to Powell Ranch to become familiar. As Sage drove it today, quite probably for the last time, memories came flooding back with each familiar landmark she passed.

She'd traveled this same stretch of pavement on the day she met Gavin. It was right along here that she'd told Isa about the paternity test. Leaving the valley with the mustang had been the worst memory, until today. She was bringing him back, only not to Gavin's.

So much had happened in only a few short weeks.

Damn Gavin for allowing her to leave last night. Why did she have to go and fall for such a stubborn man? Stubborn, irritating, always convinced he was right and prideful. She'd like to wring his neck with that last one.

He was also strong, dependable, honest to a fault and trustworthy. Mostly, he put his family above all others. Fine qualities in a man and the reason she'd fallen in love with him.

It was possible, in her effort to make amends for her part in him losing the mustang, she'd gone overboard and pushed too hard. Her enthusiastic suggestions had come off as criticisms. Gavin asked for time and space to work through his problems on his own terms. Instead of respecting his wishes, she'd invited her and Isa to move in with him, thrown money around, *Dan's* money at that, and suggested she and Gavin become business partners.

In hindsight, she'd been insensitive to his needs.

He hadn't exactly been sensitive to her needs, either. His rejection of her was brutal. Cruel. She hadn't deserved that even if she did unintentionally insult him.

What a mess. A stinking, miserable mess.

As if voicing his opinion on the matter, the mustang kicked the side of the trailer. The bang reverberated through the truck all the way to the cab.

"Yeah, yeah, we're almost there."

Signs for Mustang Village and the drive leading to Powell Ranch passed in a blur—from tears, not the speed at which she drove. Blinking, she removed a tissue from the travel-size box on the console and wiped rather ineffectually at her eyes.

The new owner of the mustang didn't live far. She dug around in the pile of papers beside her, searching for the one with the address and the attorney's phone number in case she got lost.

A sudden gust of wind caught the horse trailer and pushed it hard to the left. Sage compensated by twisting the steering wheel to the right. It had been like that the past sixty miles, her battling the strong winds sweeping across the highway.

More familiar landmarks prompted more memories and more regrets. Lost in thought and not paying attention, she yelped in surprise when another gust of wind grabbed her truck and shoved her over the center line. Reacting quickly, she swung the steering wheel too far to the right, causing the truck to swerve off the road. The right front tire ran over a pile of nasty-looking debris. Almost immediately, the truck began to weave.

Sage applied the brakes, careful to come to a slow rather than sudden stop so the trailer wouldn't fishtail. The truck rocked unevenly, making a loud thump, thump, thump, as she scouted for a safe place to pull off the road.

"Oh, hell," she grumbled, "I do not need this."

The trailer, which had ridden so easily behind her truck the entire time, now dragged like a two-ton anchor. When she finally came to a complete stop, the right front of the truck dipped at a sharp angle.

Under normal circumstances, she could change a flat tire with no problem. The horse trailer complicated the task considerably. She'd have to unhitch it, change out the tire, then rehitch the trailer. Not easy, but not impossible.

She peered back down the road. Powell Ranch was only a mile away. If Gavin was there, he'd come and help her. She had no doubt of it despite their awful breakup.

Taking out her cell phone, she dialed a number. Not his, the attorney's. Seeing her again, seeing the mustang, would be too difficult for Gavin, and she didn't want to put him through any more grief.

The attorney answered on the third ring, and she told him about the flat tire. He put her on hold and returned a couple minutes later, informing her his client would be there shortly and driving a white Ford crew cab pickup. She was to sit tight and wait for him. Under no circumstances was she to attempt to change the flat tire herself.

Fine. She could do that.

More than one person driving by stopped and asked if she was all right. Sage thanked them and told them help was arriving any minute.

After a while, she decided to get out and check on the mustang. Snorting at her and pawing the floor, he let her know how displeased he was about the delay and how much he disliked riding in trailers.

"Sorry, buddy, I don't like this, either."

More vehicles passed. Sage pushed her hair out of her face. The wind instantly blew it back. When she looked up, she saw a familiar truck approaching from the direction of the ranch. As it drew closer, there was no mistaking the driver.

Gavin.

What was he doing here?

He drove slowly past her, pulled off the road in front of her and parked. She wavered between throwing herself in his arms and storming off in a huff. He opened his door, got out and strolled toward her, stopping briefly to look inside the trailer.

The mustang kicked the sidewall, his way of saying hello.

"Hi." He smiled at Sage, though it was a pretty weak one.

"Hey."

"I was on my way to the feed store."

He seemed as uncomfortable as she.

He was also hurting, it showed in his eyes.

Join the club.

"What happened?" he asked, going around to the front of the truck and examining the flat.

She came up behind him and stood a little too close. His powerful build, his height, the attraction that had flared between them right from the start, overwhelmed her, and she had to step away.

"The wind caught the trailer. I overcompensated and ran over a pile of debris." She didn't mention she'd been thinking of him when it happened. "The owner of the mustang is on his way here now," she said, hinting it might be best for him to leave.

"No reason we can't get started. Where's your jack?"

"I'm supposed to sit tight."

He ignored her. "Is it in the toolbox?" Without waiting for her to answer, he climbed into the bed of the truck and held out his hand to her. "Key?"

Since arguing was useless, she handed him her key ring. "Think we should get the mustang out?"

He unlocked the toolbox and removed the jack. "If we do, I'm not sure we can control him with just the two of us."

Actually, there would be three of them. But who knew if the new owner was any kind of cowboy? He might have no experience with horses and purchased the mustang for other reasons.

Gavin unhitched the horse trailer and set up the jack. He'd just started pumping the handle when a white Ford pickup driving down the opposite lane slowed and then stopped.

"I think he's here," Sage said, worried at how Gavin would react to the man.

He didn't look up from his task. Not even when the truck door opened and the man stepped out. Sage recognized him instantly.

Shock coursed through her. *Impossible! It can't be him.*

He strode toward them, his gait purposeful, his cowboy hat angled low over his eyes.

She braced herself for what would surely be an ugly confrontation.

Behind her, the noise from the cranking jack stopped. The next sound she heard was Gavin swearing.

"Ms. Navarre." Clay Duvall inclined his head at Sage. "Gavin. You folks need a hand?"

"Hell, no," Gavin said curtly. "We don't need a hand." He didn't care if Clay Duvall now owned the mustang. The man wasn't lifting so much as a pinky to assist him and Sage.

"Where's your spare?"

"Get back in your truck, Duvall."

Duvall acted as if he hadn't heard Gavin. He went to the rear of Sage's truck, stopping momentarily to examine the mustang. For once, the horse didn't kick or attempt to bite.

Gavin pumped the jack handle harder.

Kneeling on the ground between the truck and trailer, Duvall bent to peer at the spare tire attached to the truck's underside. "Do you have a wrench, Ms. Navarre?"

Sage started for the toolbox.

"Stay there," Gavin growled. To Duvall, he said, "I'll remove the spare."

"I'm already down here," Duvall answered pleasantly enough, though there was unmistakable tension in his voice. When no one immediately responded, he climbed back to his feet. "No problem. I have a wrench in my truck."

"You knew I wanted that horse."

Duvall stopped midstep and turned around. "You weren't the only one."

Gavin straightened. "I tracked him for months."

"And again, you weren't the only one."

Gavin was taken aback. He'd assumed only a few residents in the valley knew about the mustang and that he alone was interested in capturing him. "You have no use for that horse."

"Actually, I do." Duvall appeared remarkably calm.

Gavin, in comparison, was holding on to his control by the thinnest of threads.

"I figure with his temperament, that fellow will produce some nice offspring for my bucking stock."

"What bucking stock?"

"For my arena. And to lease out to local rodeos. I started the business six months ago. I thought you knew."

"Why would I know or care what kind of business you started?"

"Because of Ethan."

"What about him?"

"He's been helping me."

The words struck Gavin like a rain of fire. Ethan? Helping Duvall? How could his brother talk to, much less help, the son of the bastard who ruined them?

"You're lying," Gavin ground out.

"Ask him yourself."

Gavin would do more than ask Ethan when he saw him next. He'd knock him flat to the ground.

"Are you all right?" Sage's voice, soft in his ear, reached the part of his brain still functioning normally.

He should answer her. She was worried about him. Because she cared. Even after the rotten things he'd said to her last night.

"Yeah, I'm fine." Except, he wasn't.

Learning Duvall owned the mustang was bad. That he'd recruited Ethan...

Gavin couldn't take any more. The fury building inside him boiled over.

"It's not enough that you took our land and our livelihood. You have to take my brother's loyalty, too?"

"I didn't take anything from you."

Technically, Duvall was right. At least about the land and their livelihood. His father was the one to do that. But Ethan? So what if he and Duvall were once best friends? That didn't excuse Duvall going behind Gavin's back or Ethan's betrayal.

"And as far as your brother helping me," Duvall continued, "you'll have to talk to him about that."

"Oh, I will," Gavin assured him. "Count on it."

The flat tire wasn't changing itself. All of a sudden, he wanted the hell out of there. But he wouldn't abandon Sage, leave her with that slimeball.

Digging through her toolbox, he found the lug wrench and went over to the flat tire, now elevated well off the ground thanks to his furious pumping of the jack handle.

Duvall followed him, peered over Gavin's shoulder as he struggled to loosen the frozen lug nuts. "For the record, I didn't agree with what my dad did to yours."

Gavin didn't answer, taking his frustration out instead on his task. The air might have a nip to it but sweat beaded along his brow and ran down his neck.

"It's one of the reasons I haven't spoken to him in years."

Gavin paused, digested that information, then resumed loosening lug nuts. He'd heard rumors about Duvall and his father, though he didn't realize they'd become completely estranged. Not that he cared.

"You used the money you got from the sale of my family's land to bankroll your rodeo arena."

"I didn't. I used income from selling my share of the cattle business. I refused to have anything to do with my dad after he sold your family's land to the investor, including taking money from him."

Now, that was something Gavin hadn't heard.

But again, he didn't care. The hard shell surrounding his heart wouldn't let him forgive any of the Duvalls or feel sorry for their troubles.

He felt it then, Sage's hand on his shoulder. Warm. Soft. Gentle. Offering him her unspoken support. Letting him know she was there for him.

It was what he'd wanted from her last night, what he needed now, today, more than ever.

When this was over and Duvall had left, he was telling Sage he loved her. What she'd said was true. They could build a future together. Everything didn't need to be in place first.

"You and your family weren't the only ones who suffered at the hands of my father," Duvall said.

Gavin stood, Sage still by his side. His feelings for her might have changed his thinking, but they hadn't affected his anger at Duvall one tiny bit.

"Maybe not. But you still have your money and your rodeo arena. And now you have my brother's loyalty and my horse. What else of mine do you want, Duvall?"

"Your friendship."

"That will never happen."

"Why the hell not?" The question erupted from Sage's mouth, the corners of which turned down in an impatient frown.

Both men stared at her, Gavin in confusion and Duvall in mild amusement.

"Sage, you don't understand—"

"I do," she interrupted. "I understand perfectly. This man's father did a terrible thing to your family." She pointed to Duvall. "Not him, his father. When he was what? Nineteen? Twenty? All right, fine. You've held him accountable. Blamed him for his father's actions. Angry people do that. But the man's trying to apologize, for pity's sake. The least you can do is listen to him. Ethan obviously did."

"Don't compare me to Ethan."

If she heard Gavin, she paid no attention. "Your brother's been able to put his anger aside in order to help Mr. Duvall at whatever it is they're doing. If you weren't so pig-headed—" she jabbed a finger in Gavin's chest "—you'd realize you could work with him, too."

"Are you crazy?"

"A little, I suppose. But sometimes, crazy ideas are the best ones. He has the mustang. You have the mares. Seems to me you could strike up a partnership. Can't be any worse than the one you had with Dan."

The idea was preposterous. Insane.

Gavin glanced at Duvall, who shrugged.

Was he actually considering it?

Should Gavin?

"I really only want to breed him," Duvall said. "Don't need him on my property. He could just as easily stay at your place. And I could bring my mares there. If you ever finish building that mare motel."

Ethan must have told Duvall about their plans.

They could get started on the construction right away, using the money they'd pooled to buy the mustang. It would be a risk but when didn't gain require risk?

There was only one drawback. He'd be betting everything that Duvall wasn't cut from the same cloth as his father.

Gavin gazed at Sage, taking in the features of her

lovely face. Something inside his chest shifted. It was, he realized, the hard shell surrounding his heart melting.

She smiled, her eyes telling him, *Take the leap. I'll be with you the whole way.*

"Okay," Gavin said, and did something he wouldn't have believed possible in a million years. He extended his hand to Duvall. "We have a deal."

Duvall shook Gavin's hand firmly. "Good."

"We'll write up the agreement later."

"I'm not worried about it." Duvall grinned. "Let's find that wrench and get this gal of yours on the road."

"Think you can turn this truck and trailer around?" Duvall asked Sage when they were done changing the flat tire. "Take that horse to Powell Ranch?"

So, Gavin thought, Duvall meant what he'd said. He was letting Gavin take the mustang home.

"Piece of cake." Sage jumped into her truck after saying goodbye to Duvall.

The two men watched her head down the road.

"She's something else," Duvall said. "If I were you, I'd grab her up before another man does."

Gavin thought that was pretty good advice.

"You want to come by tomorrow for supper?" The spontaneous invitation appeared to surprise Duvall as much as it did Gavin.

"What time?"

"Six o'clock. Bring your whole family."

They shook hands again, then started toward their trucks. "Clay," Gavin called after him.

"Yeah?"

"Thanks."

Clay touched the brim of his hat, checked oncoming traffic and jogged across the street.

Cresting the top of the long drive, Gavin studied the ranch with fresh eyes. The house, the grounds, the barn and stables might be in need of repair, but they were strong and solid and built to weather the worst storms. Like his family. Like him.

He would fix the place up. A little at a time in the Powell tradition. For Cassie and Sage, too. If she'd have him.

He found her behind the old cattle barn, soon to be the new mare motel.

"I wasn't sure where you wanted to put him up tonight," she said, meeting up with Gavin at the rear of the trailer.

"I'm not sure, either." He unlatched the trailer door. "Let's see what kind of mood he's in."

The mustang backed out, not charged out, as was his customary exit. And rather than fight the lead rope, he stood, surveying his newly permanent surroundings. With a satisfied snort, he lowered his head and bumped Gavin's arm in what could be considered affection. At least, that was what Gavin chose to believe.

Sage laughed. "I think he's happy."

"He's not the only one."

Over in the pasture, Avaro whinnied. The mustang turned to look at her, his regal head raised high in the air. The other mares bunched together at the fence. He was special. They knew it, and he knew it.

"Principe," Sage said.

Gavin spoke enough Spanish to recognize the word. "Prince. That's a good name for him. Prince of the McDowell Mountains."

"I'm happy for you, Gavin."

With his free arm he hooked her by the waist and hauled her against him. Both she and the mustang were startled by the abrupt move. Both also quickly settled, Sage into Gavin's embrace.

"I've been an idiot the last couple of days."

"Glad you came to your senses."

"If not for you, I wouldn't have Prince."

"You'd have caught him on your own eventually."

"No, I mean now. Your idea that Clay and I become partners, it was…"

"Genius."

"Half-genius." He bent and brushed her lips with his.

"What?" She withdrew, feigning insult.

He pulled her back into his arms. "Clay will make a great business partner. I have someone else in mind for my *life* partner."

"Are you sure?" she asked hesitantly.

"Move to Mustang Valley. You and Isa. Marry me. Make this rambling old place into a home again. I know it won't always be easy. I can be stubborn sometimes."

"Sometimes?" she chided.

"I love you, Sage."

She repeated the sentiment, in a whisper against his lips, right before she accepted his proposal with a kiss.

Epilogue

Three months later

Gavin and Sage sat in the courtyard on chairs his father had built for his grandparents, enjoying the view and each other's company. They held hands, as was typical when the two of them were within touching distance. Sunlight poured through the branches of the trimmed trees and glistened off the water trickling down the center column of the fountain.

Those weren't the only changes around the Powell house.

At Gavin's urging, Sage and Isa had moved in. They'd done so shortly after she started her new job with the Game and Fish Department. At the same time, Ethan moved out, though he went only as far as the old bunkhouse behind the barn. The weekend warriors who were helping them construct the mare motel, all friends and neighbors, including Clay Duvall, also lent their talented manpower to converting the bunkhouse into a cozy apartment.

Isa had her own bedroom, as did Cassie. She'd returned to Connecticut for the two weeks over Christmas, then flew home early January right before school started. Gavin hadn't known when he put her on the plane if she'd be back. Cassie had called him Christmas day to deliver the good news. Next to Sage setting a wedding date for May seventh, it was the best present he'd received.

That left one empty bedroom in the house. Gavin thought it might make a nice nursery when they were ready to add to the family. Next year, maybe. When Sage was more settled in her new job, the stud and breeding business operating solidly in the black and the wild mustang sanctuary they were starting this spring fully operational.

Prince, as everyone called him, was still a handful but he knew his job on the ranch and did it well. Nine mares were already carrying his offspring, one of them Avaro. Ethan continued the task of training Prince—when he wasn't teaching riding classes or breaking horses. Dan and his family left Mustang Valley and moved to Casa Grande. Ethan, the only other experienced horse trainer in the area, had picked up many of Dan's former clients.

As far as Gavin knew, no one missed Dan. Certainly not he and Sage. As long as the child support payments came like clockwork, he hoped to never see the man again. Sage, of course, had left the door open for him to visit Isa. Maybe someday he'd realize what a treasure he had in the little girl. Well, his loss was Gavin's gain.

Bringing Sage's hand to his lips, he kissed the sensitive skin at her wrist.

"I was thinking," she said wistfully, her gaze taking in the view of the valley below. "The courtyard might make a great place for the wedding ceremony. Late afternoon. When the sun is just setting."

"Sounds good to me."

"Anna offered to lend me her dress."

He imagined Sage in a white wedding gown and coming down the steps into the courtyard. The picture made him smile, as did the small, precious item he carried in his pocket.

"I guess that's everything," he said.

"All the important stuff."

"Except for one." He reached in his pocket and pulled out a diamond-and-emerald ring. "My father gave me this today."

Sage gasped.

"It belonged to my mother. Dad said he'd be honored if you wore it." Gavin got out of the chair and went down on one knee in front of Sage. "So would I. Deeply honored."

"Oh, Gavin. Yes!" She extended her left hand for him to place the ring on her finger. "It's beautiful. I love it. I love you."

He stood and pulled her to her feet, sealing their now official engagement with a kiss that conveyed everything in his heart more than words ever could.

As they walked into the house to show off the ring to the rest of the family, Gavin swore he could feel the presence of his grandfather and great-grandfather. In the pictures that hung in the hallway. In the tiles beneath their feet. In the walls that had sheltered and protected five generations of Powells—and would continue to for many more generations to come.

* * * * *

With over seventy books published and millions in print, **Lenora Worth** writes award-winning romance and romantic suspense. Three of her books finaled in the ACFW Carol Awards, and her Love Inspired Suspense novel *Body of Evidence* became a *New York Times* bestseller. Her novella in *Mistletoe Kisses* made her a *USA TODAY* bestselling author. Lenora goes on adventures with her retired husband, Don, and enjoys reading, baking and shopping...especially shoe shopping.

Books by Lenora Worth

Love Inspired Suspense

Men of Millbrook Lake

Her Holiday Protector
Lakeside Peril

Fatal Image
Secret Agent Minister
Deadly Texas Rose
A Face in the Shadows
Heart of the Night
Code of Honor
Risky Reunion
Assignment: Bodyguard
The Soldier's Mission
Body of Evidence
The Diamond Secret

Visit the Author Profile page at Harlequin.com for more titles.

THAT WILD COWBOY

LENORA WORTH

To my nephew Jeremy Smith, who has become a true cowboy.

Happy trails, Jeremy ☺

Chapter 1

This was a bad idea on so many levels.

Victoria Calhoun stared up at the swanky stone-faced McMansion and wondered why she somehow managed to get all the fun jobs. Did she really want to march up to those giant glass doors and ring the bell? Or should she run away while she still had the chance? She really hated dealing with cowboys.

Especially the rhinestone kind.

Especially the kind that got drunk in a bar and kissed a very sober, very wallflower-type of girl and didn't even remember it later.

Yeah, that kind.

But it had been a few years since that night in downtown Fort Worth. He hadn't remembered her then and he wouldn't remember her now. They'd danced, had some laughs and shared some hot kisses in a corner booth and then, poof, he'd moved on. Like two minutes later.

I've moved on, too. Enough that I don't have to stoop to this just because some sexy, sloshed cowboy kissed me and left me in a bar.

Victoria decided she was pathetic and she needed to leave. She'd have to make some excuse to Samuel but her boss would understand. Wouldn't he?

In the next minute, the decision was made for her. The

doors burst open and a leggy blonde woman spilled out onto the porch while she also spilled out of the tight jeans and low-cut blouse she was wearing. The blonde giggled then started down the steps to the curving driveway, but turned and giggled her way back to the man who stood at the door watching her.

The man wore a black Stetson—of course—a bathrobe and...black cowboy boots with the Griffin brand, the winged protector, inlaid in deep rich tan across the shafts. It looked like that might be all he was wearing.

Guess if you lived on a five-thousand-acre spread west of Dallas, you could pretty much wear what you wanted.

Victoria wanted to turn and leave but the sound of her producer's voice in her head held her back. "V.C., we need this one," he'd said. "The network's not doing so great. The ratings are down and that means the revenues are, too. Sponsors are pulling away left and right on other shows and soon the bigwigs will be cutting shows. The ratings will go off the charts if we nab Clint Griffin. He's the hottest thing since Red Bull. Go out there and get me some footage to show our sponsors, while I keep pushing things with his manager and all the bothersome lawyers."

So Samuel wanted some good footage? After trying to make an appointment by leaving several voice messages, Victoria had decided to do her job the old-fashioned way—by using the element of surprise. Since this was just a little recon trip and not the real deal, she could have some fun with it. She lifted the tiny handheld camcorder and hit the on button. And got a sweet, sloppy goodbye kiss between Blondie and Cowboy Casanova that should make Samuel and the sponsors, not to mention red-blooded women all over the world, sit up and take notice.

She remembered those lips and the way he pulled a woman toward him with a daring look in his enticing eyes. Remembered and now, filmed it. Revenge could be so sweet.

Blondie giggled her way to her convertible, completely ignoring Victoria as she breezed by. Clint Griffin stood with a grin on his handsome face. He waved to Blondie and didn't notice Victoria standing underneath a towering, twisted live oak.

"You come back anytime now, darlin', okay!"

Victoria rolled her eyes and kept filming. Until she got closer and saw that the cowboy in the bathrobe was staring down at her.

"Hello, there, sweetheart," he said, his steel-gray eyes centered on his close-up. "Who are you? *TMZ, Extra, Entertainment Tonight?* Oh, wait, *CMT,* right?"

Victoria stopped recording and held out her hand, both relief and disappointment filtering through her sigh. "I'm Victoria Calhoun. I'm from the television show *Cowboys, Cadillacs and Cattle Drives.* We're part of the Reality Network."

Clint Griffin lifted his hat to reveal a head full of light brown curls streaked with gold and then took her hand and held it too long. "TRN? Get outta here. Did my manager send you as some kind of joke? 'Cause I'm pretty sure I told that fellow on the phone the other day that I'm not interested."

Obviously, he didn't have an inkling of ever being around her or kissing her in a bar long ago. Or maybe his whiskey-soaked brain had lost those particular memory cells. Good. That would make this a lot more fun and a whole lot easier.

Yanking back her hand, Victoria wanted to shout that

he was the joke, but she needed this job to pay for her single-and-so-glad lifestyle. "No joke, Mr. Griffin. My producers want to do a few episodes about you. But then, you obviously already know that, since our people have been trying to negotiate with your people for weeks now."

"So I hear," he replied, his quicksilver eyes sliding over her with the slowness of mercury. Probably just as lethal, too.

Forever grateful that he'd tightened the belt on his robe, Victoria waited while he put his hat back on his head and walked down another step and stared right into her eyes. "Honey, you're too pretty to be on that side of the camera." He reached for her recorder. "Why don't you let me film you?"

His teeth glistened a perfect white against the spring-time sunshine while his gray eyes looked like weathered wood. His thick brown-gold hair curled along his neck and twisted out around the big cowboy hat. The man had the looks. She'd give him that. Even in an old bathrobe and just out of bed, he oozed testosterone from every pore. And his biceps bulged nicely against that frayed terry cloth.

Angry that he looked even better with that bit of wear surrounding him like hot red-pepper seasoning, Victoria tried to compare this man to the young cowboy who'd messed with her head all those years ago. Young or old, Clint Griffin still had it.

But she didn't come here to gawk.

"No, no." She pulled her hand and the camcorder away before he could grab it. "That's not how this works, Mr. Griffin."

"Call me Clint and come on in."

Victoria wondered at the sanity of entering this house

without her crew, the sanity of making any kind of deal with this man, verbal or otherwise. Would she come out later, all giggly and dazed like the woman who'd just left?

A forbidden image shot through her sensibilities.

Job, Victoria. *You need this job, remember?* Her boss had hinted at a nice salary change if she nabbed Clint Griffin.

"I'll wait for you to…uh…get dressed so we can talk."

He looked down and let out a laugh. "Mercy me, I am half-nekked. Sorry about that."

He didn't look sorry, not the least little bit.

His cowboy charm grated on her big-city nerves like barbed wire hitting against a skyscraper window. "It's okay. I did kind of sneak up on you. But I did try to call first. Several times."

"Did you? I'll have to find my phone and check my messages. Been kind of out of commission for a few weeks." He grinned at that. "That's me, I mean, out of commission. The phone works just fine. If I can keep up with it."

She knew all about him being out of commission but she figured he had his phone nearby at all times. His life was in all the tabloids. Rodeo hero parties too hard and gets arrested after a brawl in a Fort Worth nightclub. A brawl that involved a woman, of course. Apparently, his phone wasn't the only thing he didn't bother to check. Rumor had it if he didn't check his temper and his bad attitude, he'd lose out on a lot of things. One of them being this ranch.

What a cliché of a cowboy.

He motioned her inside. The foyer was as expected—as tall as a mountain peak, as vast as a field of wheat. But the paintings that graced the walls were surprising.

A mixture of quirky modern art along with what looked to be serious masterpieces. And here she'd thought the man didn't know art from a postcard.

Maybe someone else had picked these out.

Victoria pictured a smartly dressed, brunette interior-design person. A female. She imagined that most of the people in Clint Griffin's entourage were females. Or at least she'd gathered that from all the tabloid stories she'd read about the man. He'd probably seduced the designer into bringing in the best art that money could buy to show he had some class.

Victoria wasn't buying that. She'd researched her subject thoroughly. Part of the job but one of the most fascinating things about her work. She loved getting background information on her subjects but this had been an especially interesting one. When Clint's name had come up in a production meeting, she'd immediately raised her hand to get first dibs on researching him. That, after trying to forget him for over two years.

Rodeo star. Hotshot bull rider, and all-around purebred cowboy who'd been born into the famous Griffin dynasty. Born with a silver brand in his mouth, so to speak. Money wasn't a problem until recently but that rumor had not been substantiated. Credibility however, had become a big deal. *Former* rodeo star, since he'd retired three years ago after a broken leg and one too many run-ins with a real bull. Country crooner. Shaky there, even if he could play a guitar with the same flare as James Burton and sing with all the soul of Elvis himself, he only had one or two hit songs to his credit. Rancher. She'd seen the vastness of this place driving in. Longhorns marking the pastures, Thoroughbred horses racing behind a fence right along beside her car, and a whole slew of hired hands taking care of business.

While he lolled around in boots and a bathrobe.

But his résumé did impress.

Endorsement contracts. For everything from tractors to cars to ice cream and the next president. His face shined on several billboards around the Metroplex. Nothing like having one of your favorite fantasies grinning down at you on your morning drive.

Women. Every kind, from cheerleaders to teachers to divorced socialites to…giggly, leggy blondes. He'd tried marriage once and apparently that had not worked.

And again, Victoria wondered why she was here.

"Come in. Sit a spell." He pointed toward the big, open living room that overlooked the big, open porch and pool. "Give me five minutes to get dressed. Would you like something to drink while you wait? Coffee or water?"

"I'm fine," Victoria replied. "I'll be right here waiting."

"Make yourself at home," he called, his boots hitting the winding wooden stairs. He stopped at the curve and leaned down to wink at her. "I'll be back soon."

Victoria wondered about that. He'd probably just gotten out of bed.

Clint got in the shower and did a quick wash then hopped out and grabbed a clean T-shirt and fresh jeans. He combed his hair and eyed himself in the mirror while he yanked his boots back on.

"No hangover." That was good. He at least didn't look like death warmed over. The tabloids loved to catch him at his worst.

But he'd had a good night's sleep for once.

The determined blonde named Sasha had obviously given up on him taking things any further than a movie and some stolen kisses in the media room and had fallen asleep sitting straight up.

She'd probably never be back, but she'd be happy to tell everyone she'd been here. Since he'd had the house to himself all weekend, he'd expected her to stay. But... they almost never stayed.

And now another woman at his door—this one all business and different except for the fact that she wanted him for something. They almost always did.

He thought of that Eagles song about having seven women on his mind and wondered what they all expected of him.

What did Victoria Calhoun expect of him?

This was intriguing and since he was bored... The woman waiting downstairs struck him as a no-nonsense, let's-get-down-to-business type. She didn't seem all that impressed with the juggernaut that was Clint Griffin, Inc. He didn't blame her. He wasn't all that impressed with him, either, these days.

But the executives and the suits had sent her for a reason. Did they think sending a pretty woman would sway him?

Well, that had happened in the past. And would probably happen again in the future.

It wouldn't kill him to pretend to be interested.

So after he'd dressed, he called down to his housekeeper and ordered strong coffee, scrambled eggs and bacon and wheat toast. Women always went for the wheat toast. He added biscuits for himself.

When he got downstairs Victoria wasn't sitting. She was standing in front of one of his favorite pieces of art, a lone black stallion standing on a rocky, burnished mountainside, his nostrils flaring, his hoofs beating into the dust, his dark eyes reflecting everything while the big horse held everything back.

"I know this artist," she said, turning at the sound of his boots hitting marble. "I covered one of his shows long ago. Impressive."

Clint settled a foot away from her and took in the massive portrait. "I had to outbid some highbrows down in Austin to get it, but I knew I wanted to see this every day of my life."

She gave him a skeptical stare. "Seriously?"

It rankled that she already had him pegged as a joke. "I can be serious, yes, ma'am."

She turned her moss-green eyes back to the painting. "You surprise me, Mr. Griffin."

"Clint," he said, taking her by the arm and leading her out onto the big covered patio. "I ordered breakfast."

"I'm not hungry," she said, glancing around. "Nice view."

Clint ushered her to the hefty rectangular oak table by the massive stone outdoor fireplace, then stopped to take in the rolling, grass-covered hills and scattered oaks, pines and mesquite trees spreading out around the big pond behind the house. This view always brought him a sense of peace. "It'll do in a pinch."

She sank down in an oak-bottomed, cushioned chair with wrought-iron trim. "Or anytime, I'd think."

Clint knew all about the view. "I inherited the Sunset Star from my daddy. He died about six years ago."

She gave him a quick sympathetic look then cleared her pretty little throat. "I know… I read up on you. Sorry for your loss."

Her clichéd response dripped with sincerity, at least.

"Thank you." He sat down across from her and eyed

the pastureland out beyond the pool and backyard. "This ranch has been in my family for four generations. I'm the last Griffin standing."

"Maybe you'll live up to the symbol I saw on the main gate."

"Oh, you mean a real griffin?" He leaned forward in his chair and laughed. "Strange creature. Kind of conflicted, don't you think?"

Before she could answer, Tessa brought a rolling cart out the open doors from the kitchen. Clint stood to help her. "Tessa, this is Victoria Calhoun. She's with that show you love to watch every Tuesday night on TRN. You know the one about cowboys and cars and cattle, or something like that."

Tessa, sixty-five and still a spry little thing in a bun and a colorful tunic over jeans, giggled as she poured coffee and replied to him in rapid Spanish. "She's not your usual breakfast companion, *chico*."

Clint eyed Victoria for a reaction and saw her trying to hide a smile. *"Comprender?"*

"Understand and speak it."

Okay, this one was different. "Coffee?" Clint shot a glance at Tessa and saw her grin.

"I'd love some," Victoria said, thanking Tessa in fluent Spanish and complimenting the lovely meal.

Clint watched her laughing up at the woman who'd practically raised him and wondered what Victoria Calhoun's story was. Single? Looked that way. Prickly? As a cholla cactus. Pretty? In a fresh-faced, outdoorsy way. But when she smiled, her green eyes sparkled and her obvious disapproval of him vanished.

He'd have to make sure she kept smiling. But he'd also have to make sure he kept this one at arm's length.

"We have toast or biscuits," he said, serving the meal so Tessa could go back inside and watch her morning shows. "Tessa's biscuits make you want to weep with joy."

To his surprise, she dismissed the skinny toast and grabbed one of the fat, fluffy biscuits. After slapping some fresh black-cherry jam and a tap of butter on it, she settled into the oversize chair and closed her eyes in joy.

"You're right about that. This is one amazing biscuit."

"Try her scrambled eggs. She uses this chipotle sauce that is dynamite."

"I love spicy food," Victoria replied, grabbing the spoon so she could dollop sauce across her cluster of eggs.

Clint hid his smile behind what he hoped was a firm stance of boredom. But he wasn't bored at all. For someone who'd insisted she wasn't hungry, she sure had a hearty appetite. He sat back and enjoyed watching her eat. "Where did you learn to speak Spanish?"

She lifted her coffee mug, her hand wrapped around the chunky center, bypassing the handle altogether. "This is Texas, right?"

He nodded, took in her tight jeans and pretty lightweight floral blouse. "Last time I checked. I mean, where did you go to school?"

She gave him a raised eyebrow stare. "In Texas."

"Hmm. A mysterious…what are you? Producer, docu-journalist, director?"

"All of the above sometimes. Mostly, I'm a story producer, but I've worked in just about every area since joining the show a few years ago, first as a transcriber and then as an assistant camera person."

"Are you always this tight-lipped?"

She finished her eggs and wiped her mouth. "Yes, especially when my mouth is full."

And it sure was a lovely mouth. All pink, pouty and purposeful. He liked her mouth.

He waited until she'd scraped the last of her eggs off the plate and let her chew away. "When was the last time you had a good meal?"

She squinted. "I think yesterday around lunch. Does a chocolate muffin count?"

"No, it does not." He loaded her plate again. "So you television people like to starve?"

"I'm not starving. I mean, I eat. All the time. I just got busy yesterday and…well…the time got away from me."

"You need to eat on a regular basis."

She gave him a look that implied he needed to back off. "I'm supposed to be the one asking the questions."

Clint drank his coffee and inhaled a buttered biscuit. Then he sat back and ran a hand down the beard shadow on his face. "Okay, fair enough. So, now that you've had some nourishment, why don't we get down to business? Why do you want me on your show? And I do mean you—not the suits." He leaned over the table, his gaze on her. "And what's in it for me?"

Tilting her head until her thick honey-streaked brunette ponytail fell forward toward her face, she said, "That's three more questions from you. I think it's my turn now."

Clint liked flirting, but business was business. "You don't get off that easily. You came looking for me and I'm not signing on any dotted lines until I know what the deal is with this television show. And I'm certainly not making any decision this early in the morning. At least not until you answer *my* three questions, sweetheart."

She glared at him and grabbed another biscuit.

Chapter 2

Victoria rubbed her full stomach and wished she'd resisted temptation with those incredible biscuits. She was not a leggy blonde, after all. More like a petite and too-curvy brunette. And she had a job to do.

She also had another temptation to resist.

Him.

He smelled like freshly mowed hay. With his hair still damp and his five-o'clock shadow long past that hour, he looked as dangerous and bad as his reputation had implied. But he also looked a little tired and worn down.

Long night with the blonde?

Squaring her shoulders, she took in a breath and got back to business. After all, she was burning daylight just sitting here chewing the fat with this overblown cowboy.

"Okay, my producer, Samuel Murray, is a whiz at doing reality television. He has several Emmys to prove it."

Clint nodded, leaned forward. "I got trophies for days, darlin'. And my time is valuable, so why should I sign up to have you and that fancy camera poking around in my life?"

How to explain this to a man who obviously thought he was so above being a reality?

"Well, you'll get instant exposure. You'll become famous all over again. You can revive your—"

Clint got up, stomped around the flagstone patio floor. "My what? Rodeo career? That's been over for a long time. My songwriting? That's more of a hobby, according to what I read in the papers and heard on the evening news." He lifted his hand toward the vast acreage behind the yard. "This is it for me right now. Just a boring cattle rancher."

"Don't believe everything you hear and read," Victoria replied, surprising herself and him. Why should she care how he felt or what he thought? "And the viewers love anyone who is living large." She indicated the house with a glance back at it. "And it certainly seems as if you're doing just that."

Once again turning the tables on her, he asked, "And what do you believe? What have you read or heard about me? How am I living large?"

Should she be honest and let him know upfront that she despised everything he stood for? That beginning with high school and ending with a called-off wedding and later, one long kiss from him, she'd dated one too many cowboys and she'd rather be in a relationship with a CPA or a grocery store manager than someone like him? That she thought he was one walking hot mess and a complete fake?

"No need to answer that," Clint replied, his hands tucked into the pockets of his nicely worn jeans. "I can see it in your eyes. You don't like me and you don't want to be here, but hey, you have a job to do, like everyone else, right?"

Victoria didn't try to deny his spot-on observation. "Right. If we can work together, we both win. I get a nice promotion and you get the exposure you need to put your name back out there, so to speak."

Clint lowered his head and gave her a lopsided grin. "Meaning, I can either make the best of this offer or I can show myself in a bad light and make things worse all the way around."

She'd thought the same thing, driving out here. If he acted the way the world thought he acted, he wouldn't win over any new fans. Or they'd love him and watch him out of a morbid fascination with celebrities doing stupid things. Watch him to make themselves feel better, if nothing else. Why the world got such a perverse pleasure out of watching others have public meltdowns was beyond her. Victoria valued her own privacy, which made her job tough sometimes. Filming someone in a bad light had not been her dream after college. But a girl had to earn a paycheck. She'd get through this. Right now she needed Clint Griffin to help her.

"I won't lie to you," she said, hoping to convince him. "This could work in your favor or it could go very bad. But I think people will be fascinated by your lifestyle, no matter how we slant it."

"Oh, yeah." He turned to grab his coffee then stared out over the sunshine playing across the pasture. "Everybody wants a piece of Clint Griffin. Why is it that people like to watch other people suffer?"

Wondering how much he was truly suffering, Victoria watched him, saw the pulse throbbing against the muscles of his jawline. Hadn't she just thought the same thing—why people liked to watch others suffering and behaving badly?

She ignored the little twinge of guilt nudging at her brain and launched back into trying to persuade him to cooperate.

"I think people like reality television because they get

to be voyeurs on what should be very private lives and they see that celebrities are humans, too."

He turned to look at her, his eyes smoky and shuttered. "They like to watch people hurting and trying to hide that hurt. They like to see someone who's been given everything fail at it anyway. That's why they watch."

"I suppose so," she conceded. "It's a sad fact, but today's reality television makes for great entertainment. And I do believe you'd make a great subject for our show."

"In spite of your better judgment?"

"Yes." Victoria believed in being honest. But she couldn't help but notice the shard of hurt moving through his eyes. "You'd be compensated for your time, of course."

"At what price?"

The look he gave her told her he wasn't talking about money. Did this shiny, bright good ol' boy have a conscience?

"You've heard the offer already but you could probably name your price."

He stared at her then named a figure. She tried not to flinch. No surprise that he was holding out for more. "I'll talk to Samuel. But I think we can come to an agreement. I can't speak for the network and the army of lawyers we have, but I can report back and have someone call you or meet with you and your handlers."

He laughed, shook his head then offered her a hand. "No dice, darlin'. I don't have a lot of handlers these days except for my manager, who also acts as my agent. But I've already informed him and your army of lawyers, as you called them, that I'm really not interested in your show."

"What?" Victoria didn't know how to respond. She

would have bet a week's pay that this ham of a man would have jumped at the chance to preen around on a hit television show.

But he didn't seem the least bit interested or impressed. He actually looked aggravated.

Victoria's head started spinning with ways to sway him. Should she stroke his big ego and make him see what he'd be missing—a captive audience, loyal female followers and his name back in the bright lights?

She couldn't go back to Samuel without at least a promise that Clint Griffin was interested. "Look, you'd be in the spotlight again. You could write your own ticket, sing some of your songs. All we want to do is follow you around on a daily basis and see how the great Clint Griffin lives his life. And you'd make a hefty salary doing it. What's not to like about this?"

"You said it yourself," he replied, obviously done with this conversation. "People like to get inside other people's private affairs and… I might be dumb but I'm not stupid. I've been on the wrong side of a camera before—both the tabloid kind and the jailhouse kind. That's a can of worms I don't intend to open." His chuckle cut through the air. "Heck, if I want attention I'll just get into another brawl. That always gets me airtime."

Victoria could tell she was losing him. "But I thought you'd jump at this chance. The pay is more than fair."

He whirled and she watched, fascinated as his expression changed from soft and full of a grin, to hard and full of anger. Her heart actually skipped a couple of thumps and beats. Even if she didn't like him, she could see the star potential all over his good-looking face.

"I'm not worried about the pay, darlin'. I know everyone and his brother thinks this ranch is about to bite the dust, but this isn't some I'm-desperate-and-I-have-to-save-the-ranch type story. The Sunset Star will always be solid. My daddy made sure of that. It's just that—" He stopped, stared at her, shook his head, stomped her toward the open doors into the house. "It's just that I need to take care of a few things before I settle down and get back to keeping this place the way my daddy expected it to be kept. And I don't need some reality show to help me do that."

"But—"

He held her by the arm and marched her and her equipment toward the front of the house. "But even though you're as cute as a newborn lamb and you seem like a good person, I'm not ready to take on the world in such an intimate way."

Victoria's panic tipped the scale when he opened the front door. "What if you just give me a week? One week to follow you around. Just me. No crew? I'll edit the footage and let you have the final say."

"No."

"What if I double the offer?"

He stopped, one hand on the open door and one hand on her elbow. "Can you do that or are you just messing with me?"

"I can do that," she said, praying Samuel *would* do that. "We really want you for this show."

Clint glared down at her, his nostrils flaring in the same way as the black stallion in his favorite piece of artwork. "I don't know. Maybe Clint Griffin is worth even more than that. You must want me pretty bad if you're willing to give me millions of dollars just so you can follow me around."

She blushed at the heated way he'd said that. But she

was willing to play along. "I do. I mean, we do. I can't go back without a yes from you. I might get fired."

"And that'd be so horrible?"

"Yes. I'm a single, working girl. I have bills to pay. I have a life, too."

"Then film your own self."

"I can't do that. I was sent out here to film you, to get you to become a part of our highly successful television series. You'd be a ratings bonanza."

"Yeah, I've heard all that." He leaned close, so close she could smell the scents of pine and cedar. "And yes, I would." He let her go, leaving a warm imprint on her arm to tease at her and tickle her awareness. This was so not going her way.

Victoria gave up and took in a breath. She'd failed and now she had to tell Samuel. He would not be pleased. She started down the steps with the feeling that she was walking to her own execution.

"Hey," Clint called. "C'mere a minute."

Victoria whirled so fast, she almost dropped her camera. "Yes?"

"Would this contract include anything I wanted in there? Would I have a say over what goes in and what stays out?"

She swallowed and tried not to get too eager. "Uh, sure. We can put whatever you want into your contract—within reason, of course."

He leaned against a massive column and crossed his arms over his chest, giving Victoria a nice view of his healthy biceps. "Come to think of it, I do have a non-profit organization I could promote on air to get some exposure. That might be good. And I could certainly put the money into a trust for my niece. I'll have to consider that possibility, too."

Victoria was all for good deeds, but good deeds didn't always make for good ratings. He couldn't go all noble on her now. She needed bad—the bad-boy side of him. Or did she really? "Charities? You? On air?"

"Yes, charities, me. On air. I might be a player, sweetheart, but believe it or not, I'm also a human being."

"Really now?"

"Really. Yes. I tell you what, you come back with a contract I can live with and I just might sign on the dotted line." His grin stretched with all the confidence of a big lion getting ready to roar. "And I just might give you a little bit of what you want, too."

Before she could stop herself, she blurted, "Oh, yeah, and what's that?"

He moved like that roaring lion down the steps and got to within an inch of her nose. "My bad side," he said, his eyes glistening with what looked like a dare.

"You're on." She backed up, glad she could find her next breath. She would not let this womanizer do a number on her head. She had to work with him, but she didn't have to fawn all over him. Or put up with him fawning all over her.

Clint laughed and shook her hand. "We'll see, sweetheart."

Victoria knew that might be as good as she could get today. She'd be back all right. And she'd have a strong contract in hand and a couple of lawyers with her to seal the deal.

She might be dumb herself, but she wasn't stupid either. She had to get Clint Griffin to star in *Cowboys, Cadillacs and Cattle Drives* or she might be out of a job.

She didn't want her last memory of working on the show to be Clint Griffin turning her down. And honestly, she didn't want things to end here. The man had somehow managed to intrigue her in spite of his wild reputation and in spite of how he'd treated her during their one brief encounter. But she was interested in him on a strictly professional level.

Victoria wanted to see what was behind that wild facade.

And she wanted to get to know Clint a little better in the process, too.

Temptation, she told herself. Too much temptation.

But this was a challenge she couldn't resist.

Clint seemed to see the conflict in her soul.

"Whaddaya say, darlin'? Ready to rodeo?"

"I'll get back to you within twenty-four hours," she replied.

He tipped his hand to his forehead and gave her a two-finger salute. "I'll be right here doing Lord knows what," he called. "Think about that while you're negotiating on my behalf."

Victoria hurried to her Jeep and tried to drown out the roar in her head with some very loud rock music, but she heard his satisfied chuckle all the way back to the studio.

Chapter 3

Victoria approached Samuel Murray's office with trepidation mixed with a little self-serving hope. She didn't want to disappoint her boss, but part of her wished Clint Griffin would turn down any and all offers. That way she wouldn't have to ever be near the man again. Why on earth had she thought this would be a good idea?

He gave her the jitters. Victoria was usually cool and laid-back about things but after spending an hour or so with him, she needed a bubble bath and a pint of Blue Bell Moo-llennium Crunch ice cream.

How was she going to explain to the show's producer/director and all-around boss that she'd failed in her scouting mission? Samuel had hired her right out of film school as a junior shooter and transcriber, but after watching her follow the head camera operator around, he'd promoted her because he liked her confidence and her bold way of bringing out the "real" in reality stars. Victoria worked with her subjects until they felt uninhibited enough to be honest, even with a roving camera following them around. What if she couldn't do that with Clint? What if he messed with her head and made a fool of her? Or worse, what if he became too real, too in-her-face? What if Clint became much more than she'd ever bargained for?

And why was she suddenly so worried about this? She always did heavy research on her subjects, always had an action plan to get the drama going. But this time, with this man, she was too close, her old scars still too raw to heal.

"*You're* behind the camera," she reminded herself as she pulled into the parking garage of the downtown Dallas building where the TRN network offices were housed. That meant she had to be the one in control of the situation. "And you need your job."

Unlike Clint Griffin, Victoria didn't have land and oil and cattle and a reputation to keep her going. She had to live on cold hard cash.

Her parents had worked hard but had very little to show for it. Money had always been a bone of contention between her mother and father and in the end, not having any had done them in. They'd divorced when she was in high school. That had left Victoria torn between the two of them and confused about how to control her life. She'd been making her own decisions since then, but she'd never told Samuel that she'd honed her negotiation skills and her ability to soothe everyone from dealing with her parents.

She didn't envy Clint Griffin his status in life, but she'd had some very bad experiences with men like him. Pampered, rich, good-looking and as deadly as a rattlesnake in a henhouse. She still had post-traumatic dating stress from her high school days and a typical Texas-type cowboy football player who had turned out to be the *player* of the year, girlfriend-wise. She'd been number three or four, maybe.

But high school is over, she reminded herself. *And you're not sixteen anymore.* More like pushing thirty and mature beyond her years. Realistic. After high school, she'd dated for a while and finally found another cowboy to love. But that hadn't worked out, either. He'd called off the wedding minutes before the ceremony because he couldn't handle the concept that she might have a career. And she couldn't handle his demand that she give it all up for him.

So when a very drunk Clint Griffin had planted that big, long kiss on her a few weeks after she'd been jilted, she'd needed it like she needed a snakebite. But that hadn't stopped her from enjoying his kiss. Too much.

She didn't have the California-dreaming, making-movies career she'd hoped for, but she was free and clear and she was still good at making her own decisions. Victoria prided herself on being realistic. Maybe that was why she was so good at her job. She couldn't let the prospective subject get to her.

After hitting the elevator button to the tenth floor, Victoria hopped in and savored the quietness inside the cocoon of the cool, mirrored box. The dinging machine's familiar cadence calmed her heated nerves. Still steaming from the warm summer day and the never-ending metro-area traffic between Dallas and Fort Worth, she rushed out of the elevator and buzzed past Samuel's open office door then hurried to her own overflowing cubbyhole corner office. At least she had a halfway good view of the Reunion Tower. Halfway, but not all the way. Not yet. She'd go in and talk to Samuel later. Right now she just needed a minute—

"I know you're in there, V.C.," a booming voice called down the hall. "I want a report, a good report, on your scouting trip out to the Sunset Star Ranch."

And now that he'd shouted that out like a hawker at a

Rangers baseball game, everyone within a six-block radius also knew she'd been out in the country with a rascal of a cowboy.

Grimacing around the doorway at Samuel's grandmotherly assistant, Angela, who was better known as Doberman since she was like a guard dog, Victoria shouted, "On my way." Looking around for her own assistant, Nancy, she almost called out for help but held her tongue.

Everyone screamed and hollered around here for one reason or another, but one thing she'd learned after working for Samuel for three years—she couldn't show any fear or he'd devour her with scorn and disdain. Samuel didn't accept failure. But he might accept an almost contract from Clint Griffin.

Samuel pointed to the chair across from his desk. "Take a load off, V.C."

Victoria stared down at the stack of old newspapers in the once-yellow chair then lifted them to the edge of the big, cluttered desk, careful not to disturb the multitude of books, magazines, DVDs and contract files that lay scattered like longhorn bones across the surface.

"So?" her pseudo-jolly boss asked, his bifocals perched across his bald head with a forgotten crookedness. What was left of his hair always stayed caught back in a grayish-white ponytail. He looked like a cross between George Carlin and Steven Tyler. "What's the word from the Sunset Star?"

Victoria settled in the chair and gave him her best I've-got-this look. "We're close, Samuel. Very close."

He squinted, pursed his lips. "Very close doesn't sound like definite."

"He's thinking about it but he haggled with me about the contract. He wants more money."

"How much?"

Samuel always got right to the point.

"Double what we offered."

"Double?" Samuel's frown lifted his glasses and settled them back against his slick-as-glass head. "Double? Does he think we're the Mavericks or something? We're not in Hollywood and we don't have basketball-player money. We work on a budget around here."

"Well, that budget had better have room for Clint Griffin's asking price or we won't be featuring him on our show. He's interested but only if we pay his price and only if we highlight his favorite charitable organization."

Samuel sat back on his squeaky, scratched, walnut-bottomed chair and stared over at her with a perplexed glare, then let out a grunt that brought his bifocals straight down on his nose. "Charities? We've never done nonprofit work. We need drama and conflict and action. People behaving badly. Ain't any ratings in do-gooder stuff."

Victoria nodded, considered her options. "I told him I'd talk to you and then we can both talk to him. At first, he wasn't interested but I tried to explain the advantages of signing on with us."

Samuel's frown lifted then shifted into a thoughtful sideways glance. "Such as exposure on one of the highest rating shows on cable? Such as endorsements that will make him blush with pride? Such as——"

"I mentioned some of the perks," she said, wishing again Samuel hadn't sent her to do this work. Where were all the big shots and lawyers when a girl needed them? "I also pointed out that he'd appreciate the money, of course."

"You mean he badly needs the money."

"I was trying to be delicate since that is only a rumor

and hasn't been confirmed. He denied that the ranch is in trouble. I think most of his trouble might be personal."

Samuel snorted at that. "You don't have a delicate cell in that pretty head, V.C. But you're perfect to persuade Cowboy Clint that he needs to be a part of our team."

"So you sent me because I'm female, Samuel? Isn't that against company policy...being sexist and all?"

"I didn't mention anything about that," Samuel said, looking as innocent as a kitten. "I sent you to just get a feel, to see the lay of the land. This man makes the supermarket tabloids on a weekly basis. Now he's playing all high and mighty?"

Victoria pushed at her ponytail. "I got a feeling that Clint Griffin doesn't give a flip about any reality show and I saw the lay of the land, and frankly, the Sunset Star seems to be thriving. I think the man just likes to make a commotion. I'm beginning to wonder if all those rumors aren't the truth after all. He's certainly full of himself."

"There is always truth in rumors," Samuel said, repeating his favorite saying. "You need to go back out there. Something isn't connecting here. He's hot right now because he's a headline maker. He'd be stupid to turn down this offer."

"He's not stupid," Victoria said, remembering Clint's words to her. "He's smarter than he lets on, I think."

Samuel grabbed a pen and rolled it through his fingers. "I'd say. He played you, V.C. Which is why you need to get right back on that horse and convince him to take the deal before he asks for even more money."

"I can't, not until you tell me yes or no on the asking price. And I mean his asking price, not what our team has offered. I know we can afford that, at least."

Samuel squinted, looked down through his bifocals.

"Now we bring in the lawyers and his manager," he replied, a dark gleam in his brown eyes. "You gave him a nibble. I'd bet my mother's Texas Ware splatter bowl, he's talking to his people right now."

Victoria wondered about that. Did he really want this kind of exposure? Or did he need it in spite of how he felt about doing a reality show? She figured Clint Griffin had already forgotten about the whole thing, including meeting her and having her camera in his face.

He kept remembering her face. It had been two days since Clint had met Victoria Calhoun but he hadn't heard a word back from her about the so-called deal she wanted to offer him with *Cowboys, Cadillacs and Cattle Drives*. He'd talked to his accountant, his manager and even the family minister, but he still hadn't decided about taking on this new venture. His accountant's eyes had lit up at the dollars signs mentioned. His manager's eyes had lit up at the possibility of asking for even more dollars. Greedy, both of them. The minister—probably sent by Clint's mother to check on him concerning other areas of his life—had lit up with the possibility of more funding for some of the church mission work.

Everyone wanted something from Clint. Either to take over his soul or save his soul.

And all he wanted was one day of peace and quiet. Just one. He'd had the house to himself all week but he'd had more people dropping by than ever. He needed to get out of the state of Texas, just to rest.

Or to be restless and reckless.

But it'd be worth taking this deal to have a little fun on the side with that perky but slightly buttoned-up camera operator and production-assistant-story-time-girl-Friday named Victoria.

He'd have to make up his mind soon. Clint knew offers such as this one came and went by the dozen. But an interesting working woman? Well, he hadn't been around many of those lately. It'd be worth his trouble to have some good times with her. That and the nice salary he'd get for agreeing to this.

He could secure a good future for his only niece, fifteen-year-old Trish, or Tater, as he always called her. His little sweet Tater.

Still, taking on Victoria Calhoun would mean having to deal with one more female in his already full-of-females life. And he hadn't exactly asked how anyone else around here would feel about constant cameras in their lives.

Clint listened to the sound of girly laughter out by the pool, his eyes closed, his mind in turmoil while he sat in the shade of the big, open patio, watching the steaks sizzle on the grill. With a cowboy hat covering his face to shade him from the bright glare of the afternoon sun, he listened to the women gathered for a quick swim before dinner.

"Well, he said he'd take me to the party."

That would be Tater. The young, confused, teenage one.

"But did he *ask* you to the party? Because you wanting him to take you and him asking, that's a whole different thing."

That would be Susan. Or Susie. The bossy older one.

"Take, ask, what does it matter? I want to go with him but he treats it all like a joke."

"It is a joke. Men like to treat us that way."

"You two need to quit worrying about boyfriends and get outta that water and help me finish dinner."

And that would be Denise. Denny—the nickname she hated. The divorced, even older one.

Man, he loved his sisters and his niece but sometimes they got on his last nerve. Favorite, Forceful and Formidable. That's how he labeled them in the pecking order, youngest to oldest.

"Can't a man get some shut-eye around here without all this squawking?"

"And you, Mister Moody. You need to turn those steaks 'cause your mama is on her way over right now."

Clint opened one eye and squinted up at the one he liked to call Denny just to irritate her. Tater technically belonged to Denny, but everyone around here was trying to advise his niece on how to get a date for the summer party coming up in a few weeks. "Mama? You invited Mama for a cookout?"

"She does live right over there—sometimes," Denise said, one hand on her hip while she pointed toward the white farmhouse near the big pond at the south end of the yard. When he'd built this house, their stubborn mother had insisted on staying on out there. "And she does come for dinner at least once or twice a week."

"And she doesn't like to see her grown son lying around like a lazy donkey," Clint added, groaning his way out of the big lounge chair. "I sure enjoyed having the house to myself this week. Y'all need to take Mama to visit Aunt Margaret in Galveston more often."

Denise gave him an impish smile. "I might consider that since I'm mighty tired of finding feminine clothes scattered all over this house each time I come back home. Not a good role-model-type thing for your niece."

"I don't mind the parties," Tater said on an exclamation-point holler. "I'm old enough to handle things like that if y'all would just quit trying to ruin my life."

"You have a good life," Susie said with her infamousness sarcastic tone of voice. "Enjoy being young and carefree. Adulthood isn't all that fun."

Denny shook her head at her younger sister. "You know, you need a better attitude."

"You don't know what I need," Susie retorted before she went back to scrolling on her phone.

Clint held up both hands, palms out. "I have no idea what any of you are talking about."

"Right." Denise turned and flipped the steaks herself, as was her nature with all things.

Control. Everyone around here wanted control but they were all out to control. Especially him.

Clint put his hat back on his head and sat back down in his chair, wondering when exactly he'd lost control of his own life. Maybe taking on this crazy reality show would serve them all right. At least then he could call the shots himself.

Two whole days and Samuel was on Victoria to go back out to the Sunset Star Ranch. Okay, so she was accustomed to using a handheld camera to get a few shots when she went out on a scouting assignment, and she was used to going on these missions by herself since she'd been more than a production assistant from day one. Samuel depended on her spot-on opinions of people and he also appreciated that she stayed in shape for the physical part of her job, which sometimes entailed lugging cameras of all sizes that often weighed up to twenty-five pounds, or running around with hair and makeup, or soothing an angry castmate, or maybe, just maybe, getting a good scene without anyone having a real meltdown.

But mostly Samuel depended on her to ease a subject into becoming a reality star. One small camera, no pressure and nothing on the air without a consent release. That was part of what her job required and most days, this was the best part of that job. Discovering someone who'd make a great star always got her excited. Looking into someone else's life and seeing the reflection of her own pain in their eyes always made her thankful for what she had and how far she'd come. Her job allowed her to create stories out of reality and in the process, she'd seen some amazing changes in people who started out all broken and messed up and ended up whole and confident again.

But for some reason, coming to talk to Clint Griffin again made her break out in hives. She didn't think she could fix him without destroying part of herself.

"Get over yourself," she whispered as she parked her tiny car and started the long hike up to those big double doors. She'd just reached the top step when the front door burst open and a young girl ran out, tears streaming down her face.

The girl glared at Victoria then stomped into a twirl and glared up at the house. "I hate this place."

Victoria wasn't sure what to say, but when she heard someone calling out, she stood perfectly still and went into unobtrusive camera-person mode. This was getting interesting.

"Tater, come back here."

She sure knew that voice. Surely he wasn't messing with high-schoolers now.

The girl let out a groan. "And don't call me Tater!"

Then another voice shrilled right behind Clint, obviously addressing that heated retort. "Tell her to get back in here and finish helping me set the table."

The woman whirled past Victoria in a huff of elegance. She had streaked brown hair and long legs and a dressed-to-impress attitude in a white blouse dripping with gold and pearl necklaces and a tight beige skirt that shouted Neiman Marcus. So he also dated lookers who knew which hot brands to wear.

By the time Clint himself had made it to the open door, Victoria was boiling over with questions and doubts, followed by a good dose of anger. She couldn't work with this man.

Clint stared down at the driveway, where the two other women were arguing, and then turned to stare at her. His mouth went slack when he realized one of these things was not like the others. "Victoria?"

She nodded but remained still and calm, her leather tote and one camera slung over her shoulder. Let him explain his way out of this one.

Before he could make the attempt, two other women—one pretty but stern and definitely more controlled in jeans and a blue cashmere sweater over a sleeveless cotton top, and the other smiling and shaking her beautiful chin-length silver bob—virtually shoved Clint out of the way and completely ignored Victoria.

Clint put his hands on his hips and listened to the chattering, shouting, finger-pointing group of women standing in his driveway. Then he turned to Victoria with a shrug. "I can explain."

"Yeah, right," she retorted. "Do you have a harem in there, cowboy?"

"I only wish," he replied. "You want reality. Well,

c'mon then." He took her by the arm and dragged her down the steps and pushed her right in the middle of the squawking women. But his next words caused Victoria to almost drop her tiny not-even-turned-on video recorder.

"Victoria Calhoun, I'd like you to meet my mother, my two aggravating sisters and my hopping-mad niece. This is my reality."

Chapter 4

Victoria did a double take. "Excuse me?"

"Turn on that little machine," Clint replied, pointing to her handheld. "Get this on tape, darlin'." Then his voice grew louder. "Because this is my life now."

All of the women stopped talking and stared at Victoria.

"What did you say?" the oldest one asked, giving Clint a sharply focused, brilliant gray-eyed appraisal.

"Mama, this is Victoria Calhoun. From TRN. She works on that show y'all like to watch. *Cowboys, Cadillacs and—*"

"*Cowboys,*" the fashion plate said, her angry frown turning to a fascinated smile. She went into instant star mode. "Really?"

"Really," Victoria replied, wondering how his entire family had turned out to be females. And thinking this explained a lot about the man. He was obviously spoiled and used to being pampered with so many women around.

"I love that show," the starlet woman replied, her attention now centered on Victoria. "But why on earth are you here?"

"She's probably filming us," the young rebel replied, her eyes a lot like Clint's mother's. "Did you get all of that? Are you gonna put that on television?" She turned in a panic. "I will die of embarrassment. I so don't want anyone to see that on TV. Uncle Clint?"

"I haven't filmed anything yet," Victoria replied in a calm voice. "I came out a few days ago, scouting, and took a few candid shots. But... Mr. Griffin was the only one here."

He gave her a look that said, "Right," but he didn't call her out on getting the leggy blonde on tape because if he said anything he'd have to confess to having a leggy blonde here. "That's true," he said. "And if you'll all come in the house, I'll explain everything."

Victoria took that as her invitation to go inside with them. Had he made a decision? Probably not, since he hadn't bothered to tell his family...or her...about it.

The older-looking sister in the casual outfit gave Victoria a look that suggested she hated this idea and she wasn't going to budge. "Somebody go and check on the steaks," she said, waiting for Victoria to get ahead of her in the procession. "I think we need to set an extra plate for dinner."

"No, I couldn't—"

"I insist," Clint's mother said.

Victoria knew that motherly tone. No arguments.

"I'm Bitsy," the silver-haired lady continued. She guided Victoria toward the back of the house. "We're having supper out on the porch by the pool. Do you eat meat?"

Stunned, Victoria nodded. "This is Texas, right?"

Bitsy chuckled, gave her son a quick glance. "Last time I checked. But my granddaughter—the one we call Tater—has decided she's a vegan. So I always ask."

Polite and elegant. Manners. This woman was a true

Texas lady. A society dame, Victoria thought. What a nice contrast to Clint and his bad-boy ways. But why were they both here together?

Clint sat at the head of the long pine table and took in the women surrounding him. How did a man escape such a sweet trap? He turned to Victoria, conscious of her quiet reserve. She observed people and watched the exchange of comments, criticisms and contradictions that was dinner at the Sunset Star. What was she thinking? That she needed to run as fast as her legs would carry her? Or that this was certainly fodder for her show?

He decided to ask her. "So, you think we could entertain people with our little family dynamic?"

Her green eyes locked horns with him. "Oh, yes. You have an interesting family dynamic."

He chuckled, drained his iced tea. "We ain't the Kardashians, darlin', but we love each other."

He saw the hint of admiration in her eyes. "I can see that, I think. But all of this chaos makes for good television."

"Uh-huh." Chaos, hormones, mood swings and his man-view. Couple that with all the mistakes he'd made and how his family clung to those mistakes like a rodeo pro clinging to a bucking bronco and well, who wouldn't want to see that on television? That would make for great entertainment. But did he really want to reduce his family to ridicule and embarrassment just to make a buck or two? Hey, that was what this popular show was all about and his family was kind of used to it anyway.

Victoria perked up. "Have you decided to accept our offer?"

"I've been waiting to hear back from you on that account."

She gave him a surprised frown. "We were waiting to hear back from your lawyers—"

"Forget the lawyers. This is my decision."

"Well, I'm here now and we can decide, once and for all."

"Did you come all the way out here to pin me down?"

"Yes, I did. My boss wasn't happy with me the other day."

"He can't blame you. We have a whole passel of lawyers and one greedy manager looking into the matter but I told them to hold off. So this is my decision and my fault if I decide not to participate. Which I haven't decided. Yet."

"So you are interested?"

"Maybe." He nodded toward his mother at the other end of the table. "But ultimately it will be up to her and the rest of them."

"And here I thought you were the master of your domain."

"An illusion. I'm just the dog-and-pony show."

"Having family here will add to the drama of the show."

"Maybe. We do have lots of drama around here. But I'm not so sure I want to put my family through anything that will make them uncomfortable. Or rather, anything more."

Her disappointed look didn't surprise him. Maybe she was just like everyone else. Greedy and needy and clueless about leaving a trail of stepped-on people behind her. Maybe he was the same way himself.

She leaned forward. "When we first thought of you,

we didn't know you had family here. I was under the impression you lived alone in this big house."

He fingered the condensation on his glass. "I did for a while. The old family home is on the other side of the property. My folks lived there for many years. Then my daddy passed and my sister got a divorce and my other sister lost her job and…"

"You took them all in?"

"They kinda came one at a time. Mama didn't really want to move into this house, so she stays out in the old place by the pond, but we see her just about every day. Denise didn't want to move in but after her divorce, well, she couldn't afford her own overblown home. So I finally convinced her by asking her to help me out around here. She's the ranch manager but she does her own thing on the side. She has an online business selling clothes. The latest is Susie. She lost her high-fashion job in California, even though she'd tell you she was a struggling actress, so she came home for a visit about a month ago and…she stayed." He grinned and lowered his voice. "But, bless her heart, she still thinks like a Californian."

Victoria's smile indicated she enjoyed bantering with the best of them. "And dresses like one, too."

"Yep. She wants to be a star but she was forced to find a real job between auditions and bit parts. Rodeo Drive— not quite my kind of rodeo, but it paid the bills until the owner up and shut everything down."

From down the table, his mother tapped a spoon on her glass. "Clint, are you going to explain about this television show or do I have to read about it in the local paper?"

He let go of Victoria's gaze and looked at his mother. Bitsy Griffin hated scandal of any kind. She valued her privacy so much, she'd rather stay in that old farmhouse than stay in the nice room he'd fixed up for her upstairs. So what made him think she'd ever agree to a television crew filming her every move? And his every scandal?

Denny glared at him, always in perpetual distrust of any man, especially her playboy brother, who'd introduced her to her playboy husband, who'd become her ex-husband but was still very much a playboy. Too many issues with that one.

"Let me lay it out on the table," he said, holding his breath and bracing for a storm of catty protests. "Ms. Calhoun came out here the other day as a representative of the show and offered me a contract to appear in several episodes of the show. We talked about the offer and discussed the pay. I told her I'd have to think about it."

"And it never occurred to you to tell us this?" Denny asked, fire burning through her eyes.

"I'm telling you now," he replied, a heavy fatigue drawing him down. "I never agreed to have any of you on the show anyway. If I decide to do this that doesn't mean any of you have to participate."

"Did you invite her to come and explain to us?" Susie asked, her long nails tapping on the table, her brown eyes full of interest.

"No, he didn't," Victoria said, sitting up in her chair. "I came back to see what he'd decided and to answer any questions he might still have. I didn't know…about all of you."

"Of course you didn't," Denny said, her tone bordering on hostile. "My brother likes to keep us all a secret. Gives him more of a spotlight."

"Look," Clint said, holding out a hand in defense. "I'm sorry for not telling y'all. That's because I had to think long and hard about this before I said anything. I know how rumors get started, some of them right here at this table."

That quieted everyone.

"Would we have cameras around twenty-four hours a day?" his mother asked, her tone caught between interest and exasperation.

"No," Victoria answered. "We'd frame each episode. That means we'd plan it out to tape show segments at a certain time, say for an event such as this. But we won't be here every day, all day." She glanced around the table. "We'd do a few episodes and see how it goes."

Clint nodded at her, impressed with her calm, professional tone.

"What do you expect from us?" Denny asked, still glaring.

Instead of turning snarky, Victoria smiled. "Our viewers love Texas. They want to see how a real cowboy lives. You know, the horses, the homes, the cattle. Oil and everything that entails. The saying that everything is bigger in Texas pretty much sums up this show. We like to show off our stars."

Denny didn't look happy. "So you'd be exploiting us?"

Clint gave her a warning look. Denny sent back a daring look.

"We don't want to exploit anyone," Victoria replied. "But we do want good ratings. Good ratings mean better sponsors and more dollars and not getting canceled. So I get to keep my job."

Susie shot Clint a greedy glance. His ambitious little sister would be all over this like a duck on a June bug. "Well, I *am* unemployed right now and I do have some acting experience. I'm available."

"We haven't reached that part," Clint retorted. "And

you know I'll take care of you while you're looking for work."

"I don't want to be taken care of," his sister said on a hiss of breath. "I can take care of myself. But I would benefit from being featured in this show." She shifted her gaze to Victoria. "Of course, I don't come cheap."

"Susan," her mother said, a hand on her daughter's arm, "let's not get ahead of ourselves. This is your brother's house, but we all have a say in this since we live on the property."

"It's your property, Mama," Denny said. "He could have asked before he allowed these people out here."

"He didn't allow anything," Victoria said. "I came looking for him because he didn't return my calls."

"And why exactly did the powers-that-be send *you?*" Denny asked, a killer glare in her brown eyes.

Victoria didn't skip a beat. "My boss is Samuel Murray and he is both the producer and director of *Cowboys, Cadillacs and Cattle Drives.* He sent me—his production assistant and story producer—because I've done every job on the show from camera work to hair and makeup to just being a gofer for food and drinks. He trusts me to scout out people who will be able to handle being on a reality show."

For the first time since her hissy fit earlier, Tater spoke up. "And do you think we're those kind of people?"

Victoria shot Clint a glance that reassured him and terrified him. "Yes. Yes, I certainly do."

"I'll walk you to your car," Clint told Victoria after they'd cleared away the dinner dishes.

They were alone now and at least she'd survived the scrutiny of his overly protective family. They'd all lis-

tened, intrigued and repulsed in turn, and she believed
they were curious enough to want to try this. Susie obviously wanted to be a part of things and was ready to sign
tonight. Denny refused to even discuss it. But Victoria
wasn't sure she'd convinced his mother, or Tater for that
matter, to open up their lives to the world. And honestly,
Victoria couldn't blame them. There was a reason she
stayed on the other side of the camera.

"Thanks," she told him now, putting her guilt and
her own reservations out of her mind. "That was a great
dinner."

His self-deprecating smile sizzled with charm. "I almost burned the steak."

"The steak was just right but I was talking about the
undercurrents around the table."

"Oh, I see. You'd like to get that on the screen?"

"That's the kind of family interaction we dream about
getting on TV."

"Keep dreaming then, darlin'." He strolled her to her
car then leaned back against it to stare down at her. "I
don't think my girls are quite ready for prime time."

Victoria didn't want to lose this chance, especially
after meeting his family. At first, she'd only been intent
on showing Clint Griffin in his worst light because she
wanted to reveal him for the player he'd always been.
She'd wanted nothing more than to expose his shenanigans to the world because viewers loved to see others in
misery. But she had a gut feeling that showing him interacting with all of his female relatives would send a new
message and make the ratings skyrocket. Women loved a
man who knew how to handle women. It was a bit sexist
but true. Clint's handling of his many girlfriends would
contrast nicely with how he interacted with his family.

Plus, everyone loved watching notorious people having meltdowns. It was a sad paradox, but it was there. She had every reason to want to cash in on that.

"What can I do to convince you?"

"I'm almost in," he said, nodding. "But even before you showed up tonight, I was gonna explain it to all of them and ask them to let me work around them—not include them, unless they agreed to it."

"Susie seems interested," she pointed out. "And she does have an impressive acting résumé from what she told me."

"Yes, that and an ego the size of our great state," he said on a guarded chuckle. "I'll have to think about bringing her in but she just might work out and she does need some means of an income."

"We could start with you," Victoria replied. "We'd just coordinate scenes with you, doing your thing. Nothing too hard. Then we'd ease into the family stuff."

"Me?" He puffed up. "Well, that's what you came for, right?"

Right. But she was getting more than she bargained for. Just being in the same space with him upped her ante and made her have interesting, dangerous daydreams. "You don't seem too worried, either way. Your picture is in the papers a lot and you make the local news on a weekly basis. This would just be another day at work for you."

"With one infraction or another, yep."

She tried another tactic. "Maybe you don't want people to know that you're really a decent man who's trying to hold his family together, a man who takes in his sister and niece because they're going through a rough patch. A man who takes in his other unemployed sister to save her pride. Or a man who makes sure his widowed mother has a home when she needs a place to get away and be by herself."

"You got all of that from dinner?"

Victoria couldn't deny what she'd seen with her own eyes. "I got all of that from watching you and your family and asking you questions. I think the viewers would be surprised, too."

His gray eyes turned to silver and swept over her with a liquid heat. "Well, I like to surprise people."

She wondered about that while she tried to shield herself from that predatory gaze. "So, what if we just go with taping you first and then see how everyone else feels?"

"How 'bout I think it over and call you tomorrow?"

Victoria needed more than that. She'd like to march triumphantly into Samuel's office first thing in the morning and tell him she'd nabbed the infamous Clint Griffin for their show. But that would have to wait. "Okay. Call me early. I have a busy day tomorrow."

"I have your card," he replied. "I'll get back to you."

How many times had she heard that from a man?

Victoria left knowing she'd never see him again unless she subscribed to all the papers and magazines in town. He'd go on being him and she'd miss out on getting it all down on tape.

A shame, too. She really liked his mother.

Chapter 5

"Okay, I'm in."

Victoria held her cell to her ear and rolled over to stare at the clock. Five in the morning? "Clint?"

"Yeah. I'm in. I've thought about it and I like this deal. But at the price I named and with the stipulations I requested."

Victoria sat up and pushed at her hair. Greed didn't seem to stop this man, but who was she to judge. She wanted him for the show. "Have you been up all night thinking about how you'll spend this money?"

"No. About an hour or so. Couldn't sleep. Old habits die hard. But yes, I've got big plans. You know, always think big. This is Texas and I plan to give the masses what they want, but the money will mostly go for a cause dear to my heart and maybe a few other things."

Not sure what her boss would think, she let out a sigh. "Well, okay. I'll tell Samuel and he'll have our lawyers get with you to draw up the contract."

"With stipulations," he replied again, his tone as clear and precise as the silence that followed. "Highlight my nonprofit, Griffin Horse Therapy Ranch—better known as the Galloping Griffin—and don't tape anyone in my family who is off-limits."

"Got it." She needed coffee to continue this conversation. "Is that all?"

"Like I said, I want to showcase a couple of organizations I've been involved with and… I want to secure my niece's future. Nothing so underhanded and horrible, see?" He went silent and then said, "It's not like I'm going to use the money to start that harem you mentioned. Or open a bar or hold a toga party at my house. Although, I wouldn't mind seeing you in a toga, understand."

His bad-boy attitude obviously came out during the wee hours of the night. That image got her fully awake and back to business.

"It depends on how the stipulations can be highlighted as part of the show. But I'll leave that up to you and the lawyers. Samuel will want to sit in on the meeting, too."

"And you. I want you there."

"I don't usually—"

"I want you there."

His husky request in her ear singed the skin on her neck and left it all tingly and warm. "Okay. I'll let you know the time and place."

"Good enough. See you then."

Victoria tapped her phone and ended the call. Knowing she wouldn't be able to go back to sleep, she got up and padded to the kitchen for coffee. Samuel would be happy but she didn't have that sense of joy she usually felt when they were about to work with a new subject. In fact, she felt something new and disturbing and difficult to accept.

She was still attracted to Clint Griffin.

That would never do, she decided. Never. Slamming down a hammer of self-control on her carried-away imagination, she stomped to the coffee pot and hit the on button. On that distant night, she'd enjoyed kissing the man, but she'd chalked that up to being young and naive. She had not come looking for him to become the next reality star because, honestly, one kiss long ago had not shaped her whole adult life. She'd been attracted to him that night, attracted to the tension and intensity of the man and to the notion that he'd even noticed her. But what he'd really noticed was the nearest female and the chance to flirt with her and maybe take her home.

When Victoria, still bruised from being left at the altar, had turned him down flat, he'd walked away without so much as a backward glance.

Victoria had been hurt, yes, but she'd gotten over that and made a life for herself. Even after her groom had left her at the altar, she'd managed to brush herself off and get on with life. After a while, she'd been glad she hadn't married so young and she'd sure been glad she hadn't had a one-night stand with Clint Griffin. Now she was happy to be independent and free.

Or she had been until Samuel had come to her with the notion of trying to get Clint for the show. Of all the cowboys in all of Texas, why had Samuel stumbled on this one and decided he'd be perfect? Seeing Clint again after such a long time had brought out all of her anxieties and self-doubts. So she was using the old revenge tactic to get back at him. But would it be revenge if he became a ratings winner?

"This is such a bad idea," she mumbled to her wilted red geranium plant. It sat on the wide kitchen window with a lonely sideways tilt. Why her mother always brought her plants to kill was beyond Victoria. But she watered it anyway and begged it to stay alive. "Plant, what do you think about Clint Griffin?"

The plant's one wrinkled flower took that moment to shed a few limp petals.

"That's what I thought, too."

Victoria turned back to her coffee and grabbed a Pop-Tart and stuck it in the toaster. She'd get a shower and get into the office so she could warn Samuel about the few noble requests their bad boy wanted in the contract.

And she'd certainly have to brace herself to get through the next few weeks. Life with a self-centered cowboy wouldn't be easy. Even if this one looked as if he hadn't been back on the horse in a while.

"He wants everyone in on this except his immediate family?"

Samuel stared at Victoria, his eyes bulging with disbelief. "We need those women to spice things up, V.C. Now what do we do?"

Victoria had been in the same meeting but she and Samuel had stepped outside to let Clint talk things over with his people. Clint had announced in no uncertain terms that he didn't want his sisters or his niece to be a part of the show. At all. And she wasn't sure if this was coming from him, or his mother and sisters. She wondered how Susie with the stars in her eyes felt about this.

"You heard the man," she replied to Samuel. "He's trying to protect his family."

Surprising, but he'd been adamant. She glanced back through the windows to the conference room. He had his head down and was talking low to one of the suits.

When she remembered how good he'd looked in his jeans, boots and button-up shirt while he was playing hardball with them earlier, she had to swallow back the lump of awareness that caught at her throat each time she was around the man. Clint Griffin was bad news. She couldn't wait to get *that* on tape so women everywhere would agree with her.

Or fall in love with him.

Samuel's snort of disdain brought her out of her gossamer-revenge-tinged daydream. Her boss wasn't ready to concede anything just yet, but he still wanted Clint. Even with charity events and a hands-off family.

"Yeah, right. So far, he's managed to keep his relatives out of the limelight but we've found 'em now. I get his need to protect his womenfolk, but the world wants to see the interaction you described to me. We like people pushing at tables and breaking bottles. We need people shouting at each other and making scenes in public places. It's the kind of stuff that makes or breaks a reality television show. We know that, but we don't have to tell them that. Meantime, you can work on loosening his stubborn stance."

Victoria wasn't so hot on that idea, so she decided to stall Samuel's own stubborn stance. "Then in the meantime, we need more cowboys and less family. Just until I can figure something out. We can create more outings, more bar scenes, a party atmosphere."

Sam thought that over. "He does like to party, right?"

"Right. That's why we went after him."

"Then we'll start there. Take him out to a bar and have at it."

Victoria always managed to let Samuel think things were his idea. Maybe that was why he thought she was so good at her job. But hey, it worked. And she had to make this work.

Clint Griffin in a bar. Worse than any bull in a china shop. What could go wrong with that? Only about a million things.

Victoria waded through her warring thoughts and remembered *she* needed and liked a paycheck. "I'll get right on it."

"Good. Promos for the first episode go out in two weeks. We'll use that bit you did when you found him the other day—the bathrobe scene. Get a release on that one right away."

Nothing like a little pressure to get her going.

"You haven't even signed the contracts."

"We will." Samuel glanced back toward the men gathered in the other room and gave her that special smile that meant his wheels were turning. "We get him in, get him going, and I'm thinking the fans will be so excited, the family will want in on this eventually. And soon our Cowboy Clint will want to stay with us for a long time to come."

"He won't like us trying to entice his family."

"He'll like the money and the notoriety, though. You just watch. I bet he'd sell out his mother for this."

"He hasn't so far."

"Money brings out the mean and greedy in people, V.C.," Samuel reminded her. "And in this case, Clint Griffin might be the man to save us. I can predict a lot of mean and greedy in his future once the numbers come in and that will allow a lot of mean and greedy for leverage to save our show."

Victoria went back to her office to wait for Clint's final adjustments and thought about her conversation with Samuel. A sliver of regret nudged at her, making her want to run into the conference room and tear up that contract. Was it worth disrupting a man's life just to save a reality show? Just to get a little bit of satisfaction that amounted to mean and greedy revenge?

Yes, if you also want to save your job.

Since she didn't have a choice in the matter, she gathered her notes and equipment and decided she'd order in and spend the rest of the day and evening preparing for the weeks ahead. She planned to find all the ammo she could to push at Clint Griffin so she could get to the real man underneath all that testosterone and bravado. The man she'd witnessed kissing that blonde and inviting Victoria in to be next in line. Was he trying to put on a good front because of his family? Or was he up to something else entirely?

What did she care anyway? Her job was to get in, get the shots and do the edits that would play up the drama. After all, reality television was all about the drama. She could cut and paste and get the worst that this man had to offer and people would still love watching. She just hoped his family didn't form a revolt.

Clint wandered down the wide hallway of the Reality Network production rooms, fascinated with the whole studio thing. He'd had a little experience in studios, mostly cutting demos or sitting with some artist who wanted to record one of his songs, but nothing all that big or exciting. He'd been trying to get back into songwriting again lately, so this might give him the push he needed. If he could write a song and sing it on the show he might get a few nibbles from Nashville. Not for the money, but because he enjoyed writing songs. His daddy hadn't agreed with Clint having a creative side so he'd gone back and forth between writing songs and riding broncs.

"You need to get those notions out of your head, son," his father had advised. "You're a Griffin. We work the land, tend our herds. Rodeoing will give you an outlet for all that pent-up frustration. That and a good woman." But not a good song. No, sir.

Yeah, his daddy knew a thing or two about horses and…women. Too many women.

"Guess I inherited that from you at least," Clint mumbled to himself now.

He noticed the framed posters on the walls, most of them showcasing some poor celebrity who'd just signed an agreement like the one he'd inked minutes ago. Had he sold his soul again?

When he came to an open door down the way, he glanced in and saw Victoria sitting at her desk jotting notes to beat the band. Her hair was down around her shoulders today, tangled and tempting. She wasn't all painted up like a lot of the women he knew. She looked natural and girl-next-door. Innocent in some strange sweet way. Flowered shirts and soft-washed jeans, nice sturdy boots. One silver thread of a necklace dangling against the *V* of her shirt. A necklace with some sort of intricate token weighing it down.

"Wanna go to lunch?" he asked before he had time to think. To ease his eagerness, he added, "You can start picking me apart today. Film at eleven or something like that."

She looked shocked and kind of cute. She'd obviously been deep into plotting out his future. Now she lifted her hand through all that twirling hair and asked, "You want me to go to lunch with you? Right now?"

He glanced at his watch. "It's twelve-thirty in the afternoon. Lunch, dinner, whatever you want to call it. I'm hungry."

Her green eyes darkened at the quiet that followed

that comment. And suddenly Clint was hungry for one thing. Her mouth.

That tempting mouth spoke. "I…uh…sure, I could eat."

And he could kiss. Her. Right. Now.

Clint blinked and laughed to cover the shock of attraction moving like heat lightning throughout his system. "Okay, then, let's go." He turned to glance down the hall, sure someone had seen that rush of awareness sparking up the back of his neck.

"I know a great place on the corner," she said. He turned back and watched as she grabbed a tiny laptop and several piles of papers and magazines, and shoved them into that big brown bag she carried. "But no taping. This is just you and me, getting to know each other. I'll take notes, though. I have a lot of background questions."

"Ask away," he said through a smile. That way, he could stare across the table at her without looking too obvious.

When she breezed by, a hint of something exotic and spicy filled his nostrils. Then he watched her retreat, enjoying the way her jeans curved around her feminine body.

Nice.

And since when did he *not* notice a woman's posterior?

But this woman had something he couldn't quite figure out.

She wants you.

Yep, but she wants you for a different reason than all the rest. She wants you as a means to an end. She's using you so her show will stay on the air a little longer. Nothing personal.

And that was the thing that just might drive him crazy.

* * *

The sandwich shop did a chaotic dance of lunch-hour service, the spicy scents coming from the kitchen making Victoria's stomach growl. But she wasn't sure she'd be able to eat a bite with Clint sitting across from her.

Already, the downtown women were giving him the eye.

And already, she was remembering why she didn't want to be here with him.

What have I signed on for? she thought. *Why did I jump at this chance when Samuel presented it? I should have declined and found someone else, someone better suited for the show.*

But who could be better suited for a down-and-dirty reality show than the man sitting across from her?

"So, what's good here?" he asked, completely oblivious to her inner turmoil. "The steak sandwich sounds great but so does the tamale pie."

Victoria shut down her jittery nerves and pretended to read over the menu. "I love the tamale pie."

"Then pie it is," he said, grinning over at her. "I'm not hard to please."

She stared at him for a minute before responding. A minute that only reminded her of all the reasons she shouldn't be here with him. "Why did you ask me to lunch?"

Surprised at her blunt question, he drew back. "Do I have to have a reason?"

"I'd think you have a reason for every step you take."

He put down his menu and braced one arm on the back of his chair. "You really don't like me very much, do you?"

Wishing she'd been a little nicer, she shrugged. "It's

not really my job to like you. It's my job to make sure you and I can work together to put on a good show."

He nodded, drank some of his water. "And that's what this is about—putting on a good show."

"Yes," she said, the snark still lurking in her words. "And I believe you're very good at that."

"Whoa." He sat up and leaned his elbows on the table. "You're sure prickly today. Having second thoughts, Victoria? If you don't like me, why do you want to work with me?"

"I just told you," she said, sweat beading on her backbone. She did not want to have this conversation. "Anything I do from here on out is strictly for the show, Clint. I have to make it work."

"And that's always your first priority? Making the show work?"

"Yes. It has to be. It's my job."

"Right." He leaned back and motioned for the waitress. "Get that camera out and watch and learn, sweetheart."

Victoria watched, fascinated, as his frown turned into a brilliant, inviting smile. A smile aimed at the pretty waitress and not her. "Hey there, darlin'. I think we're about ready to order up. I heard from a slightly reliable source that your tamale pie is delicious."

His eyes moved down the girl's trim figure then roved back up to her face. "Nice service around here."

Victoria wanted to bolt out of the sandwich shop. She knew these people, talked to them every day. Now this show-off was milking it for all it was worth.

"The tamale pie is one of our favorite dishes," the college student replied. Her giggly smile merged with her blushing cheekbones.

"Well, I can't wait to sample me some of that."

"And you?" The girl didn't even bother to look at Victoria.

"I'll have the...chicken salad sandwich." And a slice of humble pie.

Clint winked at the waitress then waited for the enamored woman to leave before turning back to Victoria. "What? You didn't tape me putting on a show?"

She gritted her teeth. "I'd have to get that *college student* to sign a release. We can't put everyone you meet in the show."

He reached a hand up to play with the fresh daisy in the tiny vase between them. "Well, then, you'd better bring a whole stack of those forms 'cause once ol' Clint gets started, there sure ain't no stopping him. I intend to make the most of being overexposed to the entire universe."

"Not quite the entire universe," Victoria countered, her pulse tripping over puddles of dread. "But most of the six million or so people in the Metroplex and surrounding areas."

"Do they all watch your show?"

"Not yet, but together we can change that."

He winked at her, too. "That'll get us started then."

Chapter 6

The first day of production was always busy, stressful and chaotic. Usually Victoria loved starting a new project but today her stress level weighed on her like the state of Texas, big and vast and ever-changing.

"Nancy, where's my—"

"Hot-sheet?" Nancy, punk-rock, red spiked hair and black fingernails aside, was an ace assistant. "Right here, boss."

Nancy handed Victoria her notes on the day's production schedule, along with her clipboard and her cup of strong coffee. "Why are you so jittery today?"

Victoria shot a glance at Clint. "I should have never agreed to this."

Nancy giggled. "You mean because of your history with him?"

"I wouldn't exactly call it a history," Victoria said on a whisper. Wishing she'd never mentioned having kissed Clint long ago she put a finger to her lips. "We can't talk about that. He doesn't even remember and I'd like to keep it that way."

Nancy pushed a bejeweled hand through all that red hair and grinned. "My lips are sealed. But I think it's sweet."

"Right, sweet like those chewy little candy things that eventually break your teeth."

Nancy frowned and went about her work, while Victoria sweated in the early morning Texas sun. Taking a deep breath, she shook off her trepidation and decided to get on with her job.

Clint sat in a corner reading over the list she'd given him earlier. She'd decided to frame this segment out by the pool and she'd asked Clint to invite some friends over. His sisters and his niece were supposed to be out of the house and Bitsy had elected to keep to the old farmhouse for the next couple of days. So Clint should be relaxed enough to get into the groove and forget the cameras were even there. She hoped.

Gearing up, Victoria walked around the lighting and camera crew and stepped over cords. She hopped around the main camera operator, who'd be in charge of the B-roll—the head shots and any extra footage they would try to work in today.

Clint looked up as she approached, his eyes moving from her face to her toes in a way that left her feeling stripped and vulnerable, but also warm and…tempted.

"So you want me to just forget about all these people milling around and be me?" he asked, his expression showing signs of fear.

Victoria had to smile at that. The man was big, strong and brawny, and yet he was camera-shy. It was her job to calm him down and get his mind off the cameras. "Yes. Be you, Clint. Entertain your guests and have the kind of party you'd have if we weren't here."

"Really?" He gave her a wink. "Some of that might not be suitable for prime-time television, darlin'."

Victoria's whole being buzzed like a bee to a flower. But she reminded herself this big bee could sting. "Keep it clean. Keep it real. Keep it going. That's what my boss always says."

She did one more visual of the entire pool area. "We want fun, and calamities and honest personal conflicts, but we've always been proud that we don't have to bleep out words or edit too heavily. We do warn parents to keep their young children out of the room, especially when we're doing party segments."

"Cowboys and shindigs just go hand in hand, don't they?"

She nodded. "It seems that way, yes. That's what our show is all about—highlighting the rich and the spoiled and the bigger-than-Texas attitude."

"You know most working cowboys don't have the luxury of a swimming pool or a party every night, though, right?"

"Yes, that's why I put the emphasis on the rich part."

Clint gave her a hard glance then pulled out that charming smile. "I'm not all that rich so I hope I don't disappoint."

Victoria knew better. The man wasn't hurting, not one bit. She'd verified that with several reliable sources, but the rumors that he was losing everything only fueled the hard-to-put-out fire. And made Victoria want to figure him out even more.

"Are you ready for this?" she asked.

He got up, shook his jeans down over his boots. "Yes. Let's get this show on the road. I've got real work to do later today."

"What kind of real work do you do?"

He gave her an exaggerated frown. "Do you really believe all that hype about me going from bar to bar, making trouble and breaking hearts?"

Victoria thought of one heart long ago, but then she reminded herself she was so over that night. "Yes," she said, more to herself than to him.

"Well, then, you'll come with me and you'll watch and learn. This is a working ranch—not just for show."

Victoria's radar went off. "We'll tape that side of you, too, if you don't mind. To show the contrast between the good-time Clint and the Clint who truly does do a day's work."

A disappointed look colored his eyes a dark gray like a quick-passing cloud. "Yeah, that's me. Two different personalities in one broken, tired body." Then he lifted an arm to show off his biceps. "Think I'm still in pretty good shape considering."

"Not bad," she said through a haze of awareness. "Not bad at all." She turned away before he saw the flare of that awareness in her eyes. If Clint even saw a hint of interest, he'd swoop in and do what he did best—enjoy the hunt. When that was over, she'd be left for dead. "Okay, everyone, let's get going," she called out.

When she looked back at Clint, his eyes were back to that knowing, glowing silvery gray. Dangerous. This was going to be a very long day.

Clint decided to give the cameras a good show. And since everyone in this so-called household was fuming at him right about now for agreeing to do this, he planned on making the most out of the situation. He had his reasons for signing up for this crazy show, but no one around here needed to hear those reasons. A man had to keep some things to himself.

His mother had been so conflicted she'd announced she was going back to the other side of the ranch to the old farmhouse and she did not want to see a camera anywhere near that house.

Denny was so mad that she'd taken Tater on an extended trip to the New Braunfels Schlitterbahn to meet up with some of their Louisiana friends. And Susie was piping mad because he refused to let her be a part of things—for now.

He didn't mind Susie chiming in since she was single and looking for work, but he wanted to get the lay of the land and he didn't need his baby sister hanging around and messing with his head when he did it. So now she was off on the other side of the house, lurking and pouting.

Add to that, he couldn't stop thinking about the woman who'd convinced him to do this in the first place. Victoria Calhoun's curvy little body and wild mane of sun-streaked hair were driving him nuts. But her lips were killing him softly.

He still wanted to kiss those lips. Why, he couldn't understand. He'd kissed a lot of women in his life but for some reason he needed to verify what his mind was already telling him—that a kiss from Victoria would either cure him or kill him. And he didn't care which right now.

She came hurrying toward him, her clipboard on her arm, her dark green cargo pants looking more feminine than outdoorsy. And her form-fitting white T-shirt made her look like she was on the prowl instead of on a busy set.

"Ready?" she asked, a long curl of bangs falling across her face. "This is it."

Clint nodded, took a breath. He didn't have a nervous bone in his body but she made him jumpy. "Yep. So I just look into the camera and welcome people into my home, right?"

"Right. We'll give them a quick tour and explain you're about to throw a party out by the pool. Fun in the sun with friends."

"Got it." He knew how to play things up, but he wasn't so sure he could pretend to be having a great time with cameras all around. "I'll give it the ol' college try."

"Give it your honest self," she replied, her smile indulgent. "Just do what you did the morning I met you."

Her expression told him she remembered every bit of that little scene.

"Right. I'll need at least two cheerleaders and a model for that, darlin'."

She shot him a look filled with both anticipation and distrust. "Well, bring 'em on then."

"They should be arriving any minute now."

Victoria glanced around, obviously not all that impressed that he could conjure up pretty women with the snap of his fingers. "Let's get you going on the tour," she said, her mind already racing ahead.

Clint braced himself and put on his game face. He knew the drill. Tease 'em, give 'em a good time, then move on.

A few hours and several takes later, he'd made it through what would be the intro to his time on the show and was now opening the doors to the patio. The party was already going on and the crew wanted to get in some segments before the hot Texas sun settled in the western sky.

"So, there you have it. You've seen my home and now it's time to see how I live in this home. I'm Clint Griffin and I'd like to welcome you to *Cowboys, Cadillacs and Cattle Drives*."

He swung the doors open and did a sweep of the pool

and yard, his hands lifting into the air as he turned to smile into the camera. "Let's go have some fun."

Then he winked at the women waiting for him then stripped off his shirt and headed straight for the deep end of the pool.

But when he came up out of the cool depths of the sparkling water, a fourth woman was sauntering out in front of the cameras, a provocative smile centered on her pretty face.

His little sister Susie was on the set. And the cameras were taking it all in.

"Get her out of here," Clint hissed as he rose out of the water and headed toward his sister.

Victoria followed him, motioning for the cameras to get all of this on tape. They wouldn't be able to use it without a release from Susie, but she couldn't miss recording this little bit of drama.

Clint took Susie—who was clad in a black bikini, her long brown hair falling around her shoulders in soft curls—and pulled her to the side. Quickly wrapping a towel around her, he said, "You weren't supposed to come down right now and you know it."

Susie shrugged, dropped the towel and smiled into the camera. "My big brother neglected to mention that I live here, too, and I like to take a dip in the pool myself." She gave Clint a daring glance. "I don't mind the whole world watching. Just little me, taking a late-afternoon swim." With a swish of her slender hips, she waved to the other women frolicking in the pool and headed for a lounge chair.

"Susie!"

The cameras swung to follow Susie while Clint stalked

toward Victoria. Victoria nodded to the cameras to keep rolling. This was the kind of stuff she needed. If Susie wanted to become a reality star, then who was she to judge the woman.

"Victoria!"

"Yes?"

"Do something! I don't want to have all of America ogling my baby sister."

"She's a grown woman," Victoria replied, wondering why he didn't get the double standard here. "As long as she signs a release, I'm cool with it. And she's beautiful."

"Yes, she is beautiful," he said on a growl. "But no, I'm not so cool with every man alive seeing too much of her."

Victoria automatically went into damage-control mode. "Look, Clint, we can delete the footage with Susie. If you don't like it, it won't go in."

"I won't like it," he said. "I won't."

"Go and play," she cautioned, her calm only a front. "We'll keep the cameras on you and the girls but we'll let Susie think she's being filmed."

He settled down at that. "Why did I think this would be a good idea?"

"It is a good idea," Victoria replied, lying through her teeth. "And it's only the first day. You'll get used to the cameras."

"I doubt that," he replied. "But I do need a drink and some sweet talk. I'll just have to pretend my baby sister isn't watching."

He headed back to the pool and started earning his pay in such a big way that Susie got up, put her hands on her little hips and announced, "Next time, I'm inviting my friends, not yours." Then she stomped past Victoria with a glare and a parting shot. "This isn't reality. It's ridiculous."

* * *

Victoria let out a yawn. It had been a long day. Nestled safely in the spacious pool house, she wondered at the wisdom of staying so near that big stone house across from the pool. But Samuel liked the crew to stay on sight as much as possible to capture any and all incidents. And boy, had they had incidents today.

Susie showing up at the pool.

Denny calling Clint in the middle of the B-roll. His mother coming over and holding a hand over her face as she marched through the house to give him an important package that had been mistakenly delivered to her side of the ranch.

They had most of it on tape and they'd have to delete most of that. It would be tricky, taping around his unyielding family. But Victoria hoped she could keep the segments with Susie. Clint's sister couldn't be much younger than Victoria, but she had the spoiled Dallas socialite routine down pat. And that would make for great television. Well, great reality television anyway. She'd have to do a good job of editing, so Clint could see that the tension between Susie and him was undeniable. As long as she kept it light, however, she thought she could make it work without getting too deeply into family dynamite best left on the cutting-room floor.

And just how far are you willing to go?

This was always the dilemma for her. How long could she keep up this pace? How long could she push to get into people's heads and lives just to keep the ratings up and the sponsors happy?

As Samuel would say, "As long as it takes, sweetheart."

So she gritted her teeth and went back over the raw

footage for today's taping. If she liked what she saw, she'd send it electronically to Samuel with editing suggestions. Then back at the studio, they'd work through the rough cuts to create what would become the footage for the first show highlighting Clint Griffin. He'd lived up to his promise to put on a show. He'd flirted, whispered sweet nothings, had a few drinks and played a few tunes on his acoustic guitar.

Victoria had tried very hard to ignore how smoothly he moved from woman to woman. Now if she could only ignore the beating drums of her heart and how that tune had changed today each time he kissed one of those bikini-clad women.

Because Victoria knew how good that man's kisses could be.

Chapter 7

Clint couldn't sleep. Nothing new there. Normally when he had insomnia he'd get dressed and head into town for some nightlife. Sometimes, he'd stay out all night and sometimes he'd bring the party home.

But lately, even that temptation had gone sour. Maybe he was getting old. The things that used to get him all excited and happy now only made him tired and cranky. And bored.

Then why are you putting on this show for the entire world?

Why, indeed?

He got up and pulled on some sweatpants and threw on an old T-shirt. Maybe a nightcap.

Padding through the quiet coolness of the house, he noticed Tessa's light was out. She deserved her sleep because she was a kind, spiritual soul. She probably slept like a baby.

Susie had long ago left the house to do her own late-night kind of thing, whatever that was. She wanted in on this new gig, but Clint couldn't allow that. Not that he could stop her, technically, but he could stop her with a big brother clarity that would protect her and the rest of the family. His baby sister wasn't known for being discreet.

He had a feeling that after today, however, he'd lose that battle. And how could he blame her for wanting to be noticed? She'd had a good thing going for a while there out in California. Sure she missed the spotlight.

Clint grabbed some milk and a hunk of Tessa's sour cream pound cake and headed out to the patio, where he'd left his guitar. He liked to sit here back in the shadows late at night and stare at the heavens while he tried to come up with another perfect song. Tonight, the moon was as close to full as it could be. It hung bright and punch-faced across the lush blue-black sky. A few bold stars shined around it just to showcase the whole thing.

Beautiful.

Then he was startled by a splash and watched as two slender arms lifted out of the water and two cute feminine feet kicked into a slow, steady lap across the pool. Curious as to who could be swimming at this late hour, he waited to see.

And watched, fascinated, as Victoria walked out of the water and pushed at her long, wet hair.

Beautiful.

Clint took in her white one-piece bathing suit and her glistening skin. The suit shimmered like pearls against the darker pale of her skin. She walked toward a table and picked up a big bright towel, then started drying off. How long had she been here? Did she know he was hidden up under the covered patio?

Clint set down the napkin full of cake and lifted out of the wrought-iron chair. The slight scraping of metal against stone brought her head up.

Her eyes widened. "Clint?" She grabbed the towel again and held it to her.

"Yeah." He walked out toward her. "Didn't mean to scare you. I… I couldn't sleep."

She pushed at her damp hair. "I… I couldn't, either. I

hope you don't mind if I took a quick swim. We have a pool at my apartment building and this helps me settle down."

He moved closer, liking how the moon highlighted her pretty skin and wide pink mouth. "Don't mind at all. Don't let me stop you."

"I'm done," she said, already gathering her things. "I did a few laps and sat awhile—that moon." Her head down, she added, "I just took one last lap and I really should try to get some sleep."

"Sit with me awhile."

She looked as surprised as he felt but nodded. "We could talk about today."

"We could. Or we could talk about something else."

Wrapping herself with the big striped towel, she asked, "What else is there?"

Clint could think of a lot else but he didn't explain that to her. "I don't know. You. Me. I don't know much about you but you know a whole lot about me."

"Just my job. I have to ask the intimate questions so I can understand things and get a storyboard going for the show."

He motioned to two chairs by the shallow end of the pool. "I want to hear how you got this job."

He was shocked that he really did want to know about her life, but he was even more caught off guard because he just wanted to sit here in the moonlight with her and enjoy looking at her.

Full-moon madness?

Or just a man tired of chasing and ready to settle down. But he wasn't that man quite yet, was he?

Victoria thought she should probably go back into the pretty little pool house and call it a night. She'd wondered at the wisdom of staying on-site but in the end, the crew had decided it would be easier to stay on the ranch rather than drive back and forth through heavy traffic each day. Clint had agreed and had graciously offered Victoria and some of the other crew members the use of the pool house. The pool house where she should be right now, working, instead of visiting with her new star.

But something melancholy drew her to Clint. Or maybe his open shirt drew her. Either way, it would be rude to leave now that he had asked her to sit down.

"What's that?" she asked, her gaze hitting on what looked like food. She'd skipped supper and now her stomach growled with a vicious plea.

"Tessa's pound cake," he said, sliding the napkin over to her. "Did you forget to eat again?"

How did he already know that about her?

"Yes," she admitted, comfortable with him knowing. Liking that he'd noticed. "I love pound cake."

He chuckled. "Want something to drink?"

She nodded between bites. "Milk?"

He pushed his glass toward her. "You eat and drink and I'll go get us more food."

"But…"

"Hey, the cameras are off. We follow my rules now, okay?"

"Okay." She sat and glanced around. No one in sight. Then she noticed his guitar on the other table. She'd have to play up that angle because he obviously loved to play the guitar and he had mentioned his songwriting dreams. She liked that about him.

She might even like the way he always took charge and made her feel safe and cared for, too. But she couldn't handle that for too long, she was sure. She was used to being in charge and being in control. And she really liked being single and independent.

Comparing the way Clint Griffin made her feel to her need to take care of herself was like comparing apples to oranges.

She liked both but they were two different things.

By the time he'd returned, she'd polished off the cake and downed most of the big glass of milk. And she'd talked herself out of any notions of a big strong man in her life. How old-fashioned and clichéd did that sound?

He had brought more food. A whole tray full of sliced cake, cold chicken and steak strips, tortillas and chips and salsa. And a bottle of sangria.

"What are you doing?" she asked as he spread out the food with all the flourish of a maître d'.

"I'm feeding you," he replied with a grin. "Now eat up, and between bites tell me about you."

She grabbed a soft tortilla and threw some meat and salsa on it then rolled it tight and started nibbling. Clint poured them both some sangria and pushed a goblet toward her.

After she took a sip, she sat back to stare over at him, thinking he really was a paradox. "Thank you."

"You're welcome. Where were you born?"

"You don't waste any time, do you?"

"I have a lot of catching up to do, remember?"

She nodded, smiled, glowed with a full tummy and a nice calm. "I was born in Dallas, of course."

"But you're not the cowgirl type."

"No, I grew up in a trailer park. It was nice and clean but crowded and…certainly not upper class."

"Class isn't in the upper or lower," he said. "It's all in how you handle life."

She lifted her goblet to him. "A cowboy, a playboy and a philosopher, too. You never fail to surprise me."

"Sometimes, I surprise myself." He gave her a look that seemed to include her in that realization. "But back to you. So what happened with your life?"

"You mean did I have a happy childhood?"

"Yeah, I guess."

"My parents got a divorce when I was a teen so my childhood pretty much ended." She shrugged. "But it wasn't all that great to begin with. I learned to fend for myself since they didn't seem capable of taking care of business."

"That's tough." He pushed more cake toward her then broke off a piece for himself. "But you survived."

Victoria thought about that, memories filtering through her mind like falling leaves. "Barely. My mother worked hard and my dad—he sent a little money but it was never enough."

"Did he leave y'all?"

"He did. He traveled here and there, always looking for some sort of dream. He died never finding that dream, but he sure had some tall tales to tell."

"Don't we all?"

She wiped her mouth and put down her napkin. "I suppose so. I think I like this job because even though our show is based in reality, we always manage to get into people's heads and find out what really matters. Most people have dreams they keep to themselves." She motioned to the guitar. "Like you. You should pursue that again."

"Maybe."

Clint went silent, his head down, so she pushed on. "You have this big vast family. Noise and laughter, shouting and drama. But it's kind of nice to see you all living together. Not what I expected at all."

He shrugged, gave her a soft smile. "I know—it makes for good television."

"No, I mean, I didn't have that growing up. It was quiet and sad most of the time around my house. Like we were mourning."

"Maybe you were."

She glanced out at the lights shimmering in the pool. The water glistened in shades of aqua and azure. A group of palm trees swayed in the wind near a constantly streaming foundation that emptied into the deep end. It felt foreign, being the one on the hot seat.

Finally, she turned back to Clint. "Are you mourning for anything?"

He looked shocked then he gave her an evasive gaze. "I do miss my dad. We didn't see eye to eye, but I thought I'd always have him."

Victoria zoomed in on that admission. Here was something to bring out, something the audience could understand and identify with. So could she.

"I miss my dad, too," she said, hoping to draw him out. But her words were the truth. "He just never got it together and I always wondered what my life might have been like if he'd had a different mindset."

"You might be a different person now," Clint said. "Or I might not have ever met you. And that would have been a shame."

Okay, she needed to steer this back around. "Tell me more about your daddy."

He didn't speak for a minute, then said, "He didn't like me dabbling in songwriting, so I gave it up and became a rodeo star." That evasiveness again. "Among other things."

Back on track, she continued probing. "Did you like being on the rodeo circuit?"

He nodded. "I did. It was dangerous, a challenge, and I had friends all over the place. But a lot of times after a big event, I'd sit in my hotel room, alone, strumming on my guitar." He grinned over at her. "I think I'll write you a song."

Victoria lifted her head, grabbed her towel. This was getting way too intimate for her. A song? Soon he'd have her bawling like a baby. Or worse, pining away like a forlorn lover in a twangy country song. "It's late. I'd better get inside. Early day tomorrow."

"Victoria?"

She didn't dare turn around. How had he dragged that out of her about her father? She didn't miss people. She put people in little compartments and shut the door on her feelings about them. She needed to do that with Clint, too. She also needed to remember she was the one good at digging up secrets. He had no reason to delve into her hidden places.

She heard him lifting off the chair and then she felt his warm touch on her chilled skin. "Hey, your mom must have done something right. You're the real deal, you know."

Putting on a good front, she countered, "What is the real deal to you?"

His eyes washed over her face. "I have a pretty good radar when it comes to judging people. You don't put on any airs and you don't dance around any subject. With you, what you see is what you get. I—"

"What you mean," she said, wishing he'd let go of her arm, "is that I'm not blond and tall and leggy and will-

ing and able. But I'm interesting to you in the same way
a new puppy is interesting?"

He let her go, his face turning somber. "Yeah, I reckon
that's exactly what I meant." Giving her one of those
soft, unreadable smiles, he said, "Good night, Victoria."

Then he turned and went into the house...leaving her
centered underneath the gossamer spotlight of that laughing moon.

Clint stood in the quiet kitchen, his teeth clenched
and his knuckles white against the granite counter. If
he'd finished that apparently awful compliment he'd been
trying to give her, he would have told Victoria that he
liked her. A lot.

But since she had him figured out, or so she thought,
he'd have to quit handing out the compliments and get
on with the show. A few weeks, that's all. A few weeks
to reassure the audience that he was alive and kicking
and—what was it she had said—willing and able.

He sure was and he'd make certain Victoria Calhoun
and company got it all down for the record and for the
world to witness. Keep the attention on his bad ways and
off his good family.

And he'd do his best to make sure she didn't unearth
any more touchy-feely confessions out of him.

Wide awake, he headed back toward the stairs and
his bedroom, but the front door squeaking open caught
his attention.

Susie. At two in the morning.

Hidden in the shadows of the entry hall, he waited
until she'd quietly shut the door and taken off her stilettoes. When she was halfway done with tiptoeing her way
to the stairs, Clint stepped out of the shadows.

"Hello there, Susie-Q."

Her scream lifted to the rafters. "Clint, you scared the daylights out of me."

"I guess I did. Where you been?"

His sister tossed her long dark hair and rolled her eyes. "None of your business."

"It's late. Oh, wait, it's early."

"And I'm over eighteen so lighten up."

"Have you been drinking?"

She giggled. "Maybe."

"Did you drive?"

"No. A friend gave me a ride."

"Where's your car?"

"Where's your brain. Clint, I'm way over your big-brother tactics in case you've forgotten. Now let me go. I'm exhausted."

"I just bet you are."

She whirled with one bare foot on the first stair. "If you've got something to say, just spit it out."

"I'm not your parent," he replied. "And you are an adult. But I just worry about you. You've been clubbing almost since the day you got here."

"Well, there's not much else to do. I'm bored and I'm out of work. What do you expect?"

"I expect you to remember you're a Griffin, for starters."

Susie huffed a laugh. "Isn't that like the pot calling the kettle black?"

Did everyone have to remind him of his own overblown reputation? "Yeah, I guess it is. You're right. None of my business. I just run a hotel here anyway."

"Yes, and now you've invited in a few more people.

With cameras. But then we all know it's so important for your ego—gotta showcase the mighty Clint Griffin."

Anger made him step forward but he stopped and let out a sigh. "Yep, gotta keep up the reputation. Everyone loves a bad boy, right?"

"Right. And you certainly fit that mode." She leaned against the stair railing. "Can I please go to bed now?"

"Sure, honey. Need that beauty sleep."

"I'm just…tired," she said, her tone turning pensive. "I need a life, Clint."

He hated his next words but he spoke them anyway. "If you want to be a part of the show, I guess I can handle that."

Before he knew what had hit him, his sister sailed off the stairs and into his arms. "You are the best brother in the world. I'm gonna tweet this to all my friends."

"No tweeting," he said. "Not yet. We have to make it official. I'm asking for a separate contract for your appearances, so if you do…move out…we won't have anything sticky to worry about."

"I'll stay as long as you need me," she offered with a newfound sense of commitment.

"Right." He knew that wasn't the truth but if having her here taping instead of out there doing who knew what would keep him sane, then he'd make it work. "But make sure your bathing suit covers you up, okay?"

"Right," she agreed, giggling. Then she kissed his cheek and ran the rest of the way upstairs.

Apparently, his little sister had found some wee-hour energy. While he now only had one more headache to add to all his other aches and pains.

Chapter 8

Victoria shouted directions and called out instructions on framing the next shot. As long as she stayed busy, she wouldn't be able to think about Clint holding her so close last night. She'd told herself all night long that he had not held her.

The man had simply touched her arm.

And sent a chain reaction lined with serious heat straight to her heart. That, along with bringing out her own raw emotions and unpleasant memories.

Not good. So not good.

After giving herself a pep talk this morning at breakfast, sometimes out loud, which caused Tessa to stare at her and cluck over her like a mother hen, Victoria now only wanted to finish the few weeks of working with Clint Griffin and get out of Dodge.

When the man himself sauntered out to the breakfast table, looking too late-night for such an early morning, Victoria had to swallow and take in a breath.

She needed to get out and date more.

What else could explain her sudden, agonizing attraction to the one man in the world she couldn't be attracted to? Why him? Why now? Why had the stars lined up to bring her to this point in her life? She still wondered how Samuel had decided on bringing in Clint for the show.

But that didn't matter now. She had a job to do. So she braced herself against feeling anything and glanced back toward Clint and chanted her mantra.

Get in. Get the drama. Then get out. You wanted revenge, so go for it.

Clint nodded to no one in particular then settled that steely gaze on her. Grabbing the cup of coffee Tessa shoved toward him with more clucking noises, he headed toward Victoria.

"I need to talk to you."

Relieved and a little disappointed, she nodded. "Me, too—I mean, I need to talk to you. I'm sorry about last night—"

"Oh, you mean that comment you made? Something about me and models and blondes? Kind of hurt my feelings."

Had she hurt his feelings? Hardly. She saw the smirk behind that confession. He was messing with her. "Seriously, I didn't want you to think—" She stopped, realizing she couldn't admit that they'd had a moment since he had clearly missed the whole heart-to-heart thing. "Oh, never mind. Let's just get on with this segment. Remember, we'll be taping you at work today." She checked her field notes. "We'll do one interview segment and then a couple of on-the-fly type interviews. You seem to enjoy those."

"'Cause those are not scripted out. I mean, I get all antsy when you start throwing all those questions at me."

And didn't she know it. "You've done pretty well so far. You'll get more comfortable as we go, trust me."

He grunted and gave her a *distrustful* stare. "Can't wait, but first I need to tell *you* something."

Was he going to talk about…things…between them? Or the lack of things between them?

"Okay, go ahead."

"I had a talk with Susie late last night or early this morning, whichever way you wanna look at it."

Wondering if this man ever truly slept, she lifted her chin. "And?"

"And I agreed to let her be part of the show, on a limited basis. But I want her contract separate from mine. She wants to be an actor and this might help give her some confidence and some credentials in case she heads back out to La-La Land."

Yet again surprised, Victoria put a hand on her hip and tried not to jump up and down with glee. "Are you sure? I mean, her life will become an open book."

"She wants her life to be an open book. That girl wants somebody to discover her, so what better way than being on a reality television show. It sure worked for what's-her-name? Snooki?"

Victoria was glad to hear he'd agreed, but she wondered if Susie was truly ready for this. "And she's willing to work hard and follow directions? She'll have to be interviewed extensively, too, of course. She might not like how we frame her life, but once she signs on the dotted line, we take over."

He laughed, sipped his coffee. "Hmm. We'll see about that. But I'll make sure she understands."

Victoria could almost guarantee Susie would cooperate. She obviously wanted to take advantage of this situation.

"Susie is a natural and she's very pretty. The camera will love her and if she can show us her portfolio to give us an idea of her credentials, she'll have leverage to negotiate her own contract. We just can't tell my boss I told you that. I'll call the office and tell Samuel to get a contract going right away. We can messenger all the paperwork out today."

"Okay," he replied, his tone still doubtful. "I hope I won't regret this."

"It's not up to you," Victoria said, thinking he kept saying that as if he meant it. "Susie is an adult and she's part of a good family. She'll know what to do."

"I think she's very capable of being a part of things, but I'm more worried about how she'll handle millions of people being in on the intimate details of her life."

"That's what reality is all about, Clint."

He gave Victoria one of those granite-laced stares. "And don't I know it."

"Do you want her in or not?" Victoria asked, time ticking away.

He had a worried, big-brother frown on his face. "She wants herself in, so I reckon I'll have to make it work."

"Okay. We'll talk to her and see how she can organically become part of the show."

"I'm sure she'll have some ideas on that," he replied. "Susie's a steamroller. Just remember that."

"I've handled worse," Victoria said. "Go get some breakfast. When you're ready, we'll head out so you can give our viewers a tour of the ranch."

He grinned. "Once you get past those annoying interviews, this isn't as hard as I thought it would be. I had a good time last night with the girls and they got a kick outta being on the show. Lots of exposure for them, too. They'd all like to come back."

"We'll see." Victoria had the image of Clint buddying up to those models and the one very limber cheerleader emblazoned in her mind. Talk about exposure. Hard to miss all that flirting and cuddling when she'd had to go through the dailies and update Samuel on how the first day had gone. Hard to miss Clint with his hands all over a slender waist here and a tiny arm or two there.

But that was mostly for show, she reminded herself. The man didn't have a committed bone in his big, loose, buff body.

Did he?

Clint forgot the camera was rolling. Forgot he was being cued from a scripted interview sheet. He focused on talking to Victoria, telling her about his favorite spot on earth.

"Yeah, we've got longhorns and some Brangus and if you don't know what either of those are, you can get outta Texas!"

He grinned into the camera and laughed, one hand on the steering wheel of the open-air Jeep and the other hand hanging out the window. "Horses, too. We have good, strong quarter horses for work and a couple of Thorough-breds for going to the races."

The cameraman smiled and made a motion that Clint understood meant to keep on talking. "We have a nice watering hole, full of catfish, bream and bass and heck, we're only a mile or two from the Trinity River. What can I say, I love this place."

Victoria watched his face, glad the camera had gotten that look of anguish mixed with a deep, abiding respect. That was the kind of look and this was the kind of open honesty that could win over even the most hardened re-ality fan. It showed another side of the man who'd played with starlets and socialites in the pool the day before.

When he listed some of the workload and how he and the hired hands all pitched in, she saw him in a different light. The audience would eat this up.

She sure was. But only because she wanted the show to be a big success.

She could envision the scene with him laughing and playfully kissing one of the blondes, followed by the quietness of this Clint. The pride he exhibited today revealed a somber, quiet man who contrasted sharply with the man who'd grinned and made jokes yesterday.

If the edits worked, the whole country would see a glimpse behind the good ol' boy and the partier, to a man who loved his life and wanted to keep it. Maybe he needed to write a song about that.

Great. He'd sure gotten to her. But encouraging him to get back into songwriting would make the show stronger. She jotted down a note on that.

When he stopped the truck and pulled over near a pasture full of bluebonnets, she motioned to the cameraman to follow then she hopped out. "Talk to me, Clint. I'll be off camera, but if you're still talking to a real person, this will go even better."

He turned from the fence and grinned. "I don't mind talking to you one bit." He started to take off his hat, but she stopped him. He shoved it down onto his head then did a fingertip thing with the brim. "So you like the hat, huh?"

"It's not about what I like. We want the best shot and… you look good in that hat." Too good.

He tugged at the hat and winked at her. "Answer the question. So you *do* like the hat?"

She smiled. "Yes, I like the hat. Now tell me about this spot."

He turned back to the pasture, one booted foot caught up in the fence wire. "This is my favorite spot. The big field and the pond right over there—" He pointed back the way they'd come and showed her a different view of the big pond. "The tree line makes a pretty backdrop. I like to go riding back in there." Then he pivoted toward her. "Do you ride?"

Victoria forgot to stay on script. "What? Four-wheelers?"

"Horses, goose."

"Oh." Victoria had forgotten the cameras, too.

This was getting out of hand.

"Yes. I mean, it's been a long time but yes, we used to go to an old riding club down from our trailer park. One of the caretakers taught me how to ride and never charged me a penny." She shrugged. "I'm thinking your horses are probably better cared for and much more expensive than those, however."

"We'll go for a ride. Take a picnic. Have us some fun."

Victoria motioned for the cameras to stop. "Clint, that sounds nice, but we'll have to stage this with someone else in mind."

He did take off the hat then. Holding it against the fence, he finger-brushed his curling hair. "Say that again."

"I can't be in any of the scenes with you and I won't actually be in this scene with you when the edits are done. You'll be talking into the camera and thousands of women will pretend you're talking to them. Only them."

"I get that and I can go with that, no problem. But don't you take time off without a camera around?"

She thought about being out here alone with him and took a minute to swallow back the awareness bubbling up inside her. Putting that tempting image out of her mind, she tried again. "Yes, only I can't go riding in this pasture with you. But that is a great idea for you and someone else. One of your blondes, maybe?" Her mind kept spinning and she let it, hoping it would spin him away. "That'll cause conflict. Which blonde will Clint Griffin pick to go horseback riding?" She grinned and slapped him playfully on the arm. "It'll be better than *The Bachelor.*"

"The...what?" His disgusted expression would have been priceless if the camera had been rolling. "I ask you to go horseback riding and you manage to turn it into part of the show?"

Victoria put on her professional face. "It is part of the show—a good part, and if you have to pick someone to go with you, it will create conflict and drama and then we're off and rolling."

"Off and rolling." He did a grunt and shoved his hat back on. "From the way you're talking, I don't think you've been *off and rolling* in a while, darlin'."

Victoria glared at the snickering cameraman and pointed a warning finger at him. Ethan loved to tease her about her lack of a love life. "Clint, be reasonable. This is how we do things."

"Well, yeah, but I don't have to like it. Arranging my dates now—that wasn't part of the bargain."

"I'm not arranging anything. I'm staging a scene, a segment we can use to show the player Clint Griffin with the rancher Clint Griffin. Frolicking by the pool, but going all soft and romantic on a picnic in the pasture. Does that make sense?"

He turned and stalked back toward the Jeep, his long legs looking mighty good in those worn jeans. "About as much sense as a turtle in a tuxedo."

"Oh, I hope we got that," Victoria said, rushing to catch up with him. "People love good Texas sarcasm."

"I got plenty more where that came from."

Victoria hoped he truly did have more sarcasm to dish out.

And she hoped he'd gotten the message about taking her on a date. Like that would ever happen.

Clint stood in the kitchen, staring at the refrigerator. It was late at night again and he was dog-tired and hungry. And mad. And aggravated. And irritated.

So Miss Victoria Calhoun couldn't take time off to frolic in the pasture, but she could force him to take another woman out there and pretend he was having fun?

Right. Reality TV sure did bite.

He grabbed a chocolate chip cookie and a glass of milk then turned back to get an extra cookie. Maybe he'd run into Victoria out by the pool.

At first, he'd been surprised to hear that part of the production team would need to be here 24/7 most of the time. But then, when he'd realized that included Victoria, he'd immediately offered her the privacy of the pool house. She'd brought along her assistant, Nancy, and a few other female crew members. He'd put the boys in the bunkhouse, thinking he'd have some off-camera time with Victoria.

Yes, it had been an ulterior motive. He wanted to see more of her. The bonus was that she liked to swim late at night and lucky him, he couldn't sleep late at night.

So now he carefully opened the French doors and let himself out onto the long covered patio then found his favorite lounge chair and settled in, cookies and milk in hand.

A few minutes later, he'd almost fallen asleep waiting, but when he heard a light splash he sat up and smiled. His little mermaid was back in the water.

Clint remained still and wondered when he'd decided to pursue this woman. It wasn't like she was his type. But she was cute and cuddly and, darn her, maybe she *was* like having a new puppy. He thought about what type he actually wanted in his life, but only drew a blank. He kept coming back to Victoria and those luscious lips. Lately, he wasn't sure what kind of woman he wanted. Victoria had shattered the prototype.

But she was different and different was good. Different made him feel alive again. Alive and relaxed and... almost human.

Remembering her warning about keeping things between them professional, he chuckled at the notion that she'd find one of the blondes to go on a picnic with him. Most of the women he knew considered Neiman Marcus a picnic. Not the great outdoors. But Victoria, she looked like she belonged out in a field of wildflowers wearing a billowy dress and perfectly aged cowgirl boots. He liked that idea.

Right now he aimed to enjoy watching her swim and then he'd offer her a cookie because he knew she loved junk food. They'd talk and get closer and *bam, boom.* She wouldn't know what hit her. And she wouldn't even know they'd been on a date.

Chapter 9

Victoria did a couple more laps then lifted out of the pool to sit on the warm tiles near the steps. The night was humid and windy, the big Texas moon shining like a lone streetlamp over the distant tree line. She listened to the sounds of frogs calling and night birds cawing, and somewhere out in the pasture, a cow mooing a forlorn call. The wind played across the palm trees with a swishing that fanned the fronds into a frenzied dance and stirred up the fragrant honeysuckle vines running up a nearby trellis. Off in the woods, an owl hooted a lonely call while the tall pines did their own dance.

And then she heard the gentle strumming of a guitar.

"How's the water?"

She jumped and almost slipped back into the water. "Clint, you scared the daylights out of me." And how long had he been there?

"Sorry," he said, getting up to come and stand over her. "Want your towel?"

The way his lazy gaze slid over her, yes, she wanted her towel. "No, I'm okay. But you can't just sneak up on me like that. I thought I was alone."

"I came out onto *my* porch," he said by way of an apology. "Something I do almost every night. I like it when the house gets quiet and you've sent all those squealing, cackling assistants and camera people scurrying back to that trailer y'all call a production room."

"I should be there with them."

"Do they get jealous that you're in the pool house with the other girls?"

"Not really. They're used to strange living conditions and they understand someone needs to be around all the time. Besides, I promised them a pool and pizza party Friday night."

"Did you now? That's mighty nice of you."

She saw his grin and figured he'd join right in anyway. Maybe she could sneak a few shots of him with the crew.

"Have at it," he continued. "But right now it's just you and me. I like talking to you—off camera."

She liked that, too, but she shouldn't. She couldn't. Trying to be polite since it was his pool, she motioned to the tile next to her. "Have a seat then."

He took a step into the water and slid down beside her then splashed water out in front of them. She noticed he was barefoot and wearing cutoff shorts. She also noticed the shadow of the jagged scar running along one knee.

"Did it hurt when you broke your leg?"

"Like a hundred horses stomping on me. Yeah, it hurt."

"You had a long recovery from what I read and heard."

"I'm still recovering."

She let that comment soak in, but she didn't mention that she'd seen him limping after their earlier trek around the property. "Do you miss the rodeo?"

"Sometimes. But it was more of a circus than a rodeo." He paused, squinted up at the stars. "Putting on a show, kinda like this reality show thing. When I was winning, the world was perfect. I had women hanging off me day and night and endorsement deals left and right." He grinned. "I just made you a poem."

"And such a lovely poem, at that."

"I could write you a sonnet or two along with the song I'm working on."

Pretending that she didn't care about the song, she teased, "So you're also like Shakespeare?"

"I have my moments. I have sold a few country songs here and there that could have possibly had deep roots in *Macbeth* or *King Lear.*"

"I'll have to find them and try to decipher what that means, exactly." She could use those tunes for background music on the show.

He chuckled, splashed more water. "Life is full of comedy and tragedy, sweetheart. Sometimes all mixed together."

"Oh, we call that reality," she quipped, loving the banter that always emerged between them.

"I think we're both talking about the same things, yeah. Country music is about reality—hard work and hard luck, broken dreams and lost loves."

Victoria's mind started buzzing. "I did read about your songwriting career in my research. You need to bring that back. We'll have you sing something and play guitar. That would be good for a family night maybe. If we can get your family to agree to be on scene just for that one segment, it'll show the viewers yet another side of you."

He leaned in and gave her a slanted, suggestive stare. "I got a lot of sides to show."

Okay, that comment went over her like smooth whiskey over ice. "I just bet you do."

His smile was thousand-watt. "I like you, Victoria. You make me laugh."

She ignored the pitter-patter of her confused heart.
"Glad to hear that." Should she be honest with him? "I
have to admit, I like you, too. I wasn't sure at first."

He hit a hand to his chest. "You wound me."

She should tell him that *he* had wounded *her,* but that
was water under the bridge. She probably should thank
him for opening her naive eyes and making her see that
she couldn't fall for any cowboy ever again. Especially
this one.

But he wasn't through yet. "And why *didn't* you like
me?"

She had to laugh. "Uh, isn't that obvious? From that
first morning when the blonde giggled her way down
the steps up until when we finally inked the contracts,
I thought you were exactly what the tabloids said you
were."

His expression softened into what looked like humility and embarrassment. "And now?"

"And now I think you're a good man who's used to
having his own way. I think you played until you played
out."

The humility changed to regret. "You've got me
pegged." He got up, reached out a hand. "I guess you
always have a good read on people, being in this line
of work."

Victoria took his hand, aware of the shift in his mood
and aware of the heat of his fingers touching hers. "You
don't like being judged, do you?"

He stood staring down at her, his eyes as gray and
distant as the moonlit sky. "Who does? But this type
of work that you do—isn't that what this is all about?
Being judged? I'll get judged on my partying ways and
I'll get talked about for my other side, too. Everyone will

believe their own reality, not what my life is really like. No one really wants to believe Clint Griffin can have a normal, content life."

"Can *you* believe that?" she asked, wishing she could get this on tape. "Can you have a normal, content life?"

He shifted back, away from her, and she felt a chill covering her. "I reckon that's for me to find out, huh? None of your business."

Victoria heard the hint of anger in his words. "You're right. It is none of my business. I'm just here to make good television."

He swung back around. "Is that really all you care about?"

Turning the tables on him, she replied, "That's none of *your* business." She started gathering her things. She'd been wrong to goad him, but that was her job. Had she become too good at asking the tough questions?

"Oh, I get it," he said, marching behind her as she headed toward the pool house. "You can probe me and pick me apart to get the goods but I'm not allowed to question you. Is that how this works?"

"Yes," she said, turning at the door. "Yes, that's it exactly."

He pushed close, giving her that heated warmth again. "And what if I stopped asking questions and just kissed you?"

Victoria turned, hoping to escape. "That can't happen."

But he turned her around and pressed her against the door. "Oh, yes, that can happen. Kissing tells a man a lot more than talking ever could."

He moved closer, so close she could see the dangerous

determination in his eyes. Gathering strength, she held her hand on his chest. "Clint, stop this."

"Do you want me to stop?"

She was trapped, by him, by the heat coming off him, by her own need to taste what she'd remembered for so many years. "I want you to understand I can't do this. We can't do this. I'm here for a reason—"

"Yeah, to pick me apart."

"No, to do my job."

"You are so good at that job, too." He leaned over her then put both hands on the door, trapping her yet again. "I'm good at a few things myself and I've heard kissing is one of them."

"Clint?"

She'd meant that as a warning but somehow his name on her lips sounded like a plea.

He touched his mouth to her cheek. "Yes?"

He was taunting her, teasing her, making her crazy. "Clint?"

"I've got Tessa's chocolate chip cookies waiting on the table. With milk."

"Clint, stop."

He moved his lips over hers, little feathers of warmth and touch as soft and enticing as that night wind lifting all around them. Even more enticing than cookies and milk.

"Uh-huh."

"Clint, you can't kiss me. We have to stop this."

"No. You don't want me to stop. I can hear your heartbeat hitting against my shirt. I can see the don't-stop in your eyes."

She tried to squirm away but he retreated then moved in for the final capture. "Go then if you want to, if you can't stand this."

That sounded like a dare and a challenge. Deciding to prove to herself—and him—once and for all that he didn't matter in her world, Victoria turned back and tugged his head down to hers. And then she kissed him, and enjoyed the triumph of hearing him make a throaty groaning sound. It was a short-lived triumph, however.

The next thing she knew, he'd pulled her into his arms and was kissing her in a full-on Clint Griffin attack. Over and over.

And instead of getting him out of her head, Victoria fell against him and returned his kisses, measure for measure.

This was even better than she remembered. She forgot all about the cookies and milk. And her resolve.

The next morning, Victoria still hadn't managed to get Clint or his kisses out of her head. In fact, she'd thought about him most of the night. Which meant things would be awkward this morning and the next morning and the next morning.

"What have I done?" she mumbled to the bacon on the breakfast buffet.

Tessa sailed by and gave Victoria a wayward, scared look then said something in rapid Spanish. Something that Victoria interpreted as concern.

No wonder. Victoria needed to quit talking out loud to herself. She had to report in to Samuel today, so maybe she'd drive into the city. They'd been working hard for three days now. No use trying to pretend the days weren't long or strenuous. Taking a break might help clear her head.

And keep her hands off Clint Griffin.

He strolled over to the Danish tray. "Cheese or cinnamon. What's your favorite?"

Being so close to him again did strange things to her whole system. She came alive with a wired-and-ready buzz.

"If it's Tessa's homemade bread, I prefer the cinnamon," she said in her best professional voice. "That was a big hit the other day when we first got started."

"Cinnamon." He grinned, winked. "Sweet and spicy. Reminds me of someone's lips."

Victoria's gasp echoed out over the yard and caused Tessa to cluck her tongue and give Clint a warning look, followed by a colorful litany.

"Tessa thinks I'm flirting with the lady producer," Clint explained. "She is saying prayers for both of us." Then he bit into his Danish.

"Aren't you?" Victoria's breath hissed like a live wire. "We can't... I can't... It isn't professional."

He shot her an innocent, intriguing glance. "What, eating a Danish?"

"You know what. I'm not going swimming in your pool again. Ever."

"Ah, now, that's the highlight of my day. Don't be so mean, Victoria. One of these nights, we'll get in the deep end together."

Shivering against that suggestion, she retorted, "I'm not being mean. I'm trying to remain professional. I didn't come here to be a part of the show."

"You'd be cute on screen with someone picking your brain with those loaded questions."

"This isn't about me. It's your moment to shine."

"I'll shine, all right. I'll jump through hoops during regularly scheduled filming hours. But what I do after hours is my business and I'd like to spend some time with you."

Since the crew had begun to arrive, she shook her head and glared at him. "We'll discuss this later."

"Out by the pool, around midnight. We can test the water. Together."

"No, we will not get into the pool. Somewhere safe without moonlight."

"You're blushing. I've never seen you blush, probably because it's usually dark when we meet up."

"All the more reason to stay away from each other."

"I'll see you later," he whispered. "Much later."

She didn't plan on that. She'd have to resist the pool at night. Grabbing a cinnamon bun, she hurried to her spot as story producer and went over her field notes. After everyone had eaten and gathered, she made an announcement.

"Okay, today we'll introduce Clint's sister Susan Griffin. We'll call her Susie for the show. And she's agreed to let us use some of the footage we shot the other day when she interrupted our pool party."

Clint's easygoing smile turned to a frown. "What? You can't show her in that bikini."

"Yes, they can," his sassy sister said as she sauntered by, wearing short-shorts and a barely there T-shirt. "I signed all the proper papers, agreed to a good salary, and I'm in the show now, big brother."

"I don't like this, Susie. So watch yourself."

"It's not for you to like," Susie said as she waved to one of the production people. A male production person who needed to put his eyeballs back inside his empty head.

"But—"

"Clint, a word?"

He turned to find Victoria giving him the eye. The eye that meant he'd messed up on something. Her arched eyebrows pointed a two-thumbs down frown. "What?"

She motioned him away from what was supposed to be a breakfast scene where he and Susie went over his rules for her being on the show.

"What?" he said on a hiss of frustration.

"You agreed. She's signed the contracts and release forms and she's going to be in this scene with you. Save the conflict for the cameras."

"Oh, I got plenty more conflict where that came from."

"I know and that's good, but don't waste all that energy trying to convince her to *not* be in the scene. You get to lecture her and give her a set of rules so that our viewers will know exactly how you feel." She gave him an indulgent smile. "And one of our producers came up with a great suggestion. We're going to poll our viewers to see how they feel about your rules."

"What?" How many times did he have to say that today?

Victoria patted him on the arm, like he was some sort of disobedient puppy. "We'll take a poll and then we'll announce the votes and see if your viewers agree with you or if they want Susie to stay on the show. Then we'll have a drawing for two lucky winners to come to the ranch for a weekend and be part of the fun."

He almost said "What" again, but changed his mind. "Well, all right then. That sounds like a swell plan. And I'll cooperate fully, I promise."

"You will?"

"Yeah, sure." He leaned close and gave her one of his surefire smiles. "But I want to discuss this further with you, tonight, out by the pool."

Her green eyes widened. "No, no. That's not gonna happen."

"Then we'll just have to see."

"Are you blackmailing me?"

"I'm negotiating with you. I like you better after hours than right now. I can talk to you in private tonight. Just to understand and do my part, of course."

She glared at him, her hands on her hips, her eyes boiling with disbelief. "I will not meet you tonight at the pool, Clint. Susie has agreed to this and...we need to get some promo work going. This poll and a contest are two good ways to bring in viewers."

"And having a happy star who feels like discussing this in detail will make for a better mood on set, don't you think?" He leaned close again. "Be there."

She lifted her chin. "Or?"

"Or, I don't know. I might have to sleep late tomorrow. Or I'll come looking for you at the pool house. I can be loud when I'm trying to find something. Or someone."

He laughed then turned and stomped over to the breakfast table. "I'm ready whenever y'all are."

Chapter 10

"We're already trending on all the social media sites," Samuel gleefully sputtered when Victoria walked into his office later that day. "The poll was a great idea. Drew in people to the website and now they'll want to watch to see who won. I hope you left the crew taping away."

"They're doing background shots and B-roll and scene work. We're making sure all the location releases are signed, too. We've been to one of Clint's favorite hangouts and they've agreed to allow us to tape inside and outside. That'll be on next week's agenda."

"Good, good," Samuel said, his frizzed ponytail fluttering around like a spiderweb. "We'll add that to the second episode to get a just-right story going." He leaned back in his chair and gave Victoria his famous furrowed-brow stare. "So what's your take on the first installment?"

Victoria had to tread very carefully here. Samuel could sniff out an undercurrent like a K-9 could sniff out hidden drugs.

"Well, we start off with Clint opening the front doors and we do a sweep of the house with his comments on the décor and the artwork. Then he takes us out to the pool and he turns from being the narrator and host to frolicking with a few friends there. A lot of flirting, trash talk and a little bit of catty drama between the women who are all after him. That should be a fun start."

As fun as watching cows chewing on their cud.

Samuel tipped his chair back. "Uh-huh, then the scene with Clint describing the ranch and doing his daily work. Let's call that the tender scene. I liked what you did with that so far."

Victoria let out a grateful sigh. "I thought switching to Clint the rancher after seeing him being a playboy might show the audience a new side of our cowboy. His softer, more mature side."

A side that had sure opened her eyes.

"Good, good. But let's keep focusing on his wild side, too. That'll attract the women viewers in droves."

"And don't I know it."

Samuel's brows lifted like sagebrush in the wind. "Something nagging at you, V.C.?"

Had she really said that out loud? "Uh, no. Just that our subject is perfect for reality TV. He seems to love the camera and he sure loves showing off to his many friends. Between Clint and his little sister, Susie, I think we have a hit on our hands."

"Is this getting to you?" Samuel asked. "I mean, I know how you feel about cowboys, especially the ones who aren't really cowboys at all."

And how did he know that about her? Maybe she'd mentioned her distaste several times in the past. "Yes, you do know how I feel. But I'm okay with it. I understand we're exploiting Clint Griffin for the show and as long as he can live with that, so can I."

Samuel scratched his gray beard stubble. "That's great," he replied. "I've already told the brass how well you're doing with this. Pretty impressive. Keep working on him. I get the feeling he trusts you."

Clint wouldn't trust her if he knew her boss was rubbing his hands in glee at the prospect of exploiting him even more. Since when did she care about that, anyway.

Maybe since he fed you and kissed you and seemed to want to do it all again?

"I aim to please," Victoria retorted, her need to do her job warring with her need to kiss Clint again. "Now, to finish up with the final segment of this episode, we'll add a teaser about the bar scene, with Clint dancing and partying. Oh, and we do have the couple of scenes where we introduce Susie. She did great with the preliminary interviews yesterday."

She didn't add that Susie had been flirting like a butterfly with one of the better-looking camera operators. She'd have to watch that one. Ethan was handsome but he was always looking for his next conquest, too.

Samuel bobbed his head. "She's posting a lot of comments all over the internet. Getting a buzz going about her older brother's house rules and the online poll. I like that. Like it a lot."

"I think Susie will bring a lot of younger viewers to the show," Victoria said. "And I've extended an invitation to the rest of the family for some dinner shots."

"You *are* the best," Samuel replied. "Now, get back to work."

She laughed and stood. "I'm going to work on the edits tonight. Get in some forecast bites so the viewers will see that our happy-go-lucky cowboy might be losing some of his rhinestone dust. And with Susie in the mix, things are bound to get dramatic."

"Conflict from the get-go. Can't beat that." Samuel

gave her another one of those burly glares. "You sure everything's all right?"

Victoria had to word her answer very carefully. Everything was great, production-wise. They'd done some rough cuts on the first episode and things were coming together in a good way.

If she could just get Clint off her mind, personal-wise, she'd be on a roll here.

So she fibbed a reply to Samuel. "Great. I'll also work up some hot-sheets for the second episode and I'll get the outline for all five shows mapped out." She shrugged. "I've got a pretty good idea where this is going, but I have to wait and see. And I'll definitely keep the on-the-fly interviews going to foreshadow the drama."

"Okay. How's the crew?"

"Good. We're all settled in. I'm in the pool house, along with Nancy and a couple of the other women. The guys are in the bunkhouse and our trailer. Not too shabby."

"So with you being closer to the house I guess you get to see some of the interaction."

"Yes, more than I care to see."

She turned to leave before Samuel wheedled the truth out of her. She couldn't let him think she was fraternizing with the talent. That was a big no-no in reality television. But it did happen on occasion. If Samuel thought she was getting too close, he'd pull her off this job and plop her into postproduction on some other show.

"Keep me posted," he said.

Victoria felt his eyes burning into the back of her head.

Angela the Hun must have sensed something, too. She pushed at her huge bifocals and pressed her thin lips together, her hawkish brown eyes landing on Victoria with a vulturelike glee. "So what's it like working with that sweet-talking, good-looking Clint Griffin? I could eat him with a spoon."

So not a good image.

"Things are great," Victoria replied. "Does your husband know how you feel?"

Angela laughed. "He sure does. I've been so excited about these episodes I've already got them on my DVR schedule. Bernie'll watch 'em with me and he'll be glad to do it."

Victoria had no doubt about that. Bernie was a sweet man but he seemed perpetually terrified of his overbearing wife.

And she had no doubt that Samuel had asked Angela to question her. He'd be watching her for signs of distress. Which was why she'd better hurry and get her hot-sheets and edits done so she could get back out to the ranch. No telling what might be happening with her gone. Clint could have the whole crew in the pool by now.

Or he could be biding his time until she got back and he could corner her in the dark again.

He was out at the pool.

With one of the blondes.

Clint had decided he'd show Miss Victoria Calhoun that she was so right about him. Right as rain. He was a fun-loving man. He did put himself above others. He did have a bad reputation and he sure did want to use that to his advantage on this show. And even though Victoria had come out and said those things to him, he could see her disdain each time they taped a scene. The only time she'd lightened up was when they'd done the ranch tour scenes. That Victoria had laughed and smiled and asked questions, both for the camera and away from the camera.

And she changed after hours, of course. She'd sure seemed more relaxed once the cameras had shut down. She didn't mind him at all when she'd kissed him with way more bad-girl attitude than blondie here could ever muster up.

Or so he kept telling himself while the lovely Shanna swam around him like a mermaid. Or more like a siren.

Neither Shanna nor Victoria had been here earlier when he'd done some real work. When he'd helped the local vet with a pregnant heifer delivering a calf. The cameras had been on, capturing the whole thing, so at least Victoria would see his more noble side. And probably erase it.

But Shanna here, she just liked his man-with-the-big-house partying side. Maybe he should tell her to get dressed so they could do the town.

Better yet, he'd invite her to the bar tour the show wanted him to make for the next installment. His instructions were to have fun, no holding back. He'd been doing that for years because as long as the attention was on him and just him, the rest of his family wouldn't be scrutinized. He hoped.

"Just do your thing," Victoria had told him earlier today.

Not sure what his thing was anymore, Clint laughed and whispered sweet nothings into the blonde's cute ear. "Shanna, I want you to be my special guest at the Bar None tomorrow night. How do you like that?"

Shanna giggled then dipped under the water and came back up right in front of Clint. "I think we're gonna have us a blast, that's what I think."

And to show him how happy she was to be included, she tugged him down and planted a wet kiss on his mouth.

Clint kissed her back then lifted his head and grinned from ear to ear. Until he looked up and saw Victoria standing there, staring at him.

Her heart shouldn't beat like an angry bird flapping its wings on a glass wall, but Victoria couldn't stop the quickening of her pulse while she stood there watching Clint with another woman.

A woman who was definitely more his type.

She did a visual of the entire pool area. Nancy had done a good job of keeping things going in her absence. The cameras were on and rolling and production seemed to be steady. Susie was nearby in her own little world, chatting right into the camera. Of course, Ethan was holding that camera and he seemed to be asking Susie all kinds of questions.

Well, good. Ethan was trained like the rest of the crew to ask open-ended questions to get a subject talking. Victoria only hoped Ethan would remember that fine line they all lived with. He couldn't become too friendly with the talent. Susie would eat him for breakfast.

Maybe she should listen to her own advice, Victoria thought, her gaze meeting Clint's. His expression held defiance and resignation, as if he'd just given up trying to be all things to all people and had finally settled into being himself.

That was what she needed, Clint Griffin being Clint Griffin. His bad side was his best side, for the tabloids and television.

But she did like those little glimpses of his quiet side, too. She'd enjoyed the tour of the ranch and the crew had gathered some great shots of the vast property. The little drive had given her new insight into Clint's personality. Telling herself to just go with it and get her work done, Victoria headed straight toward the pool house.

Ethan saw her and held his big camera to the side. "V.C., where you been? We're getting some smoking-hot footage here."

Victoria cringed at the nickname the crew called her, thanks to Samuel. "I went into town to the studio. Got a lot of editing done. Looking good so far."

"I'll say." Ethan turned back to Susie. "So you were talking about Texas and California. As different as day and night, but why?"

Victoria turned away and headed toward the pool house, but not before she saw Clint push past the blonde and swim away. Now why was he doing that?

Because the cameras were on Susie right now.

So was this all for show, after all? Or was he just already tired of juggling time with his many girlfriends? And why should she care?

The cool confines of the long rectangular pool house gave Victoria a sense of contentment. At least she had a relative amount of privacy in here. The combination kitchen and living area was decorated in light, airy colors. More nautical and sunshine than Western and shotgun. She was amazed that this place was even needed, since the house had seven bedrooms, according to Clint. And he'd probably been in every one of them.

Stop thinking that way.

It didn't matter who Clint dated or didn't date. Victoria had to put that out of her mind unless thinking about that allowed for better scenes with more conflict.

Boy, she sure loved her job.

Ignoring the shouts of glee and loud splashes coming from the pool area, she immersed herself in work. An hour later when she heard a knock on the door, she figured her assistant had locked herself out.

But Nancy wasn't on the other side of the door.

Clint gave her a sheepish grin, one arm up against the door frame. His eyes shimmered a rich, steel gray. "I guess you saw us in the pool?"

Victoria wanted to blurt out "Yes, I sure did." Instead, she nodded, trying to overlook that he'd had a shower and smelled really good. "I saw. Looked like Ethan was getting some great footage. Susie seems to be going with the flow, too."

He frowned at that. "Better than going with the flow. I think she intends to take over the whole show." Shrugging, he said, "That one always was ambitious."

"And you're not?"

His frown deepened. "My daddy always told me I didn't have any ambition. Said I had lazy bones."

Victoria heard the hurt and disappointment behind that comment. Why was it when she heard such confessions, her first reaction was to get them on tape? To make up for her own self-serving thoughts, she said, "Well, I think you've proved him wrong."

He lifted away from the door. "Can I come in?"

"Why don't I come out there," Victoria replied. "So no one will think we're manipulating the script or anything."

Clint glanced around at the now-empty backyard. "I think they've all headed to town for pizza."

"Without me?" Victoria didn't really care, but she was hungry.

"You like pizza?"

"Of course. Doesn't everyone?"

He laughed at that. "We could catch up with them."

She shook her head. "Not a good idea. You can't get too chummy with the crew. That can lead to trouble."

He waited for her to shut the door then motioned to their usual talking spot. "You mean the kind of trouble you and I just about got into the other night."

Victoria's cheeks blushed hot. "Yep. That's exactly the kind of trouble I'm talking about. It's just not something we want to deal with. So you can't demand I meet you at the pool every night."

He leaned back against the patio table and stared over at her. "Or maybe it's just not something *you* want to deal with?"

"You're right. I don't have time for it."

He didn't look as if he believed her. "So you say. But remember what I told you."

"That you'd walk off the show if I don't meet you here so we can have our after-hours chat time? Yeah, I remember."

"And here you are."

His triumphant glance reminded Victoria of why she needed to avoid this man when work hours were over. "I only came out here to remind you, Clint. It can't happen."

He stood up, his hands on his hips. "That's just plain silly. I need to talk to you each day, about the show, about me, about us."

"No us." She turned back to the pool house. "I have to respect the unspoken rules or my crew won't *respect* me."

He was right behind her. "And what about how I feel?"

She whirled, surprised to see the look of misery on his face. But if she didn't drive her point home right now, she'd be too tempted to follow his lead. "What about you? You're doing a good job of living up to your reputation.

That's why we wanted you for this show. You can handle that without me to reassure you or stroke your giant ego, right?"

He backed away toward the house, walking backward a couple of steps. "Absolutely. Not a problem. Forgive me for thinking you and I might be able to become friends."

"Clint, that kiss was a little too friendly." She could see she'd made him mad. But he looked confused and hurt, too. But she couldn't give in. "That's the way it has to be."

"So you won't do any more late-night swimming?"

"No." She'd miss that and their late-night talks, too. "I have to do what I came here to do—make you a reality TV star."

He let out one of his famous disapproving grunts. "Got it. Don't worry, sweetheart. You haven't even touched the surface. I'll make sure your viewers have a show to remember."

"Good. And you'll let Susie be Susie? She's going to be a big part of the show."

"Far be it from me to stand in my little sister's way to stardom. I'm doing a favor for the whole family. They'll all thank me one day." Then he stopped and put his hands on his hips. "But things between you and me? That ain't over."

Victoria hurried back inside and let out a long breath. She'd just been challenged. And as much as it would bother her to see him with someone else, that's the way it had to be.

At least until they were finished with production on the show.

Chapter 11

The next few days became a little more of a routine. Now that the first episode had wrapped, postproduction work took priority. Thankful for the reprieve and the mindless hours of editing and going over interview materials, Victoria tried to ignore how her heart bumped and banged a little more each time Clint was around. Watching him on the screen was hard enough, but seeing him in the flesh was even worse. Time and again, she wondered why she'd agreed to this. But she had to admit, the show was looking good. She wanted to tell him this but she'd do that later when it was absolutely necessary.

Right now they were avoiding each other and everyone had noticed.

"He sure stares at you a lot," Nancy kept pointing out. "He might not remember you from that night long ago, but I think he's got a thing for you, boss."

"He's got a thing for anyone female," Victoria replied. "Just ignore him."

"Easier said than done," Nancy quipped. "He's a cool drink of Texas water, in case you haven't noticed."

She'd noticed all right. But Victoria kept that thought to herself. "Get used to it," she told Nancy, but more to benefit herself. "We've got at least four more weeks of this."

Nancy turned glum but went about her work. "At least we get to look at him for a while longer."

Now Victoria was in her usual spot at the kitchen table, her laptop humming as she went over dailies and texted or emailed suggestions back to Samuel and the boys in the control room. Some scenes worked out wonderfully while others had to be tweaked for a rough cut. It was always a delicate balance, deciding how to slice and cut to get a final installment, but they were managing. She finished a string-out to send to Samuel and the studio team.

Now she watched the video of Clint on the ranch tour. He laughed and teased the crew. He smiled into the camera, but that day, he'd been mostly smiling at her. She'd interviewed him with an in-depth clarity, enjoying the pride in his words as he talked about the history of the Sunset Star Ranch. Now she'd become genuinely interested in that history. It was a true Texas tale of bravery, hardship and survival. A story Victoria longed to tell.

She always tried to sneak in a bit of dignity with each new subject they found. Samuel let her get away with it as long as the show focused on the conflict and drama of human nature.

That never went out of style.

But that day on the ranch tour, she'd seen a side of Clint that made her get all warm and sentimental. A side she kept refusing to believe. It probably had more to do with the stories he'd told and the beautiful country they'd explored than her feelings for Clint. Just seeing the horses, the herds of cattle and the oil wells pumping away showed Victoria something that the world had never seen. Clint loved this ranch.

And there were two very different sides to the man.

She'd come here knowing the power this man held. She'd thought about that power for years now. But she'd braced herself against all that enticing charm. Until they'd ridden across the ranch together. Until he'd tried to kiss her and she'd deliberately kissed him back. Until she'd realized he could be a really nice man when the mood hit him.

Playing with fire.

She went back to her work. She didn't want to get burned. Ever again. But she couldn't stop watching the way Clint had laughed and flirted with the camera during that waltz across Texas. The ranch tour segment would be a nice contrast to the swimming pool scenes. She'd end the first episode with Clint silhouetted against the backdrop of a burnt-orange sunset, his hat tilted back as he surveyed his land. A lone stallion would run by and gallop off into that sunset. Then Clint would turn and smile at the camera and start walking toward home.

Victoria dove back into the technical aspects of her job and tried very hard to put the main attraction out of her mind.

An hour later, she heard people talking out on the patio. Curious, she glanced out the big window that gave a great view of the pool. Clint was talking to his sister Denise. So Denny and Trish were back. That would add a new wrinkle even if they stayed off camera.

Victoria was about to go back to work when she heard Denise's angry voice.

"Did you give any thought at all to Trish? How do you think this will make her feel?"

Clint lifted his chin. Defiant as always. "You know I did since we discussed this before you left. I won't allow her on screen. The crew knows that. It's in the contract."

Denny put a hand on her hip. "I'm not talking about Trish being part of the show. I'm worried about how her friends will react when they see her…her uncle making a fool of himself. What if they tease her? What if they say bad things about you and our family?"

Clint scowled at his older sister. "We discussed all of this, Denny. Trish is fifteen, not five. She can handle things a lot better than you and I ever did. Besides, you know why I decided to do this."

"I know what you think, but I don't buy it. You're not doing this for Trish. Her future is secure without you selling out for some stupid television show."

"I want to make sure she's always taken care of. You know that." He stalked and paced then turned back to his sister. "This extra money will go straight into an account for her trust fund. You have to know why I think this is so important."

"Better than you'll ever understand," Denise retorted. "It doesn't matter now. You'll do what you want no matter what anyone says. And as always, I have to take care of business." She whirled at the French doors into the house. "I've always taken care of her, Clint. Me. And I'll keep on doing that, no matter what."

"Denny?"

His sister kept on walking.

Victoria ducked out of sight before Clint turned around.

That's sure good conflict, she thought. Too bad they couldn't get that little exchange on tape. Denny seemed like an overly protective mother, which was understandable. But why was she harassing Clint for wanting to set up a trust fund for his niece?

Victoria almost opened the door to ask him.

Then she caught herself, appalled that she hadn't considered Clint's stance. "He's protecting his niece. She's off-limits." She jotted that down even while she whispered it to herself. Off-limits, overly protective. Normal for any family. But why did Denise begrudge him doing this to help with Trish?

An intuition born of watching people and understanding human nature made Victoria wonder if there wasn't something more between Clint and Denny. What was it they weren't saying to each other? And how could she find out?

Clint sat in the big, worn leather chair in his daddy's office. His office now.

Remembering his gruff, tough father always made Clint moody and unsettled. He'd loved the old man, but the old man had never liked Clint. His father, Clinton Henry Griffin, was a fourth generation Texan with roots as deep and wide as the old oak tree out in the back pasture. Clint had followed in that tradition but he wasn't his father. Clint Henry, as friends had called his father, had lived and breathed ranching. His daddy had been noble and giving and strong and hard-working.

And hard to emulate.

Clint loved the ranch but he'd always wanted more. So he'd rebelled in a big, public way. And that rebellious nature had stayed with him and, as it turned out now, served him well. Let everyone think he was a player. His family knew the truth.

He wanted something more now, too, but it had nothing to do with roping cattle and tilling hay. And it surely had nothing to do with being the star of a reality TV show.

Denny was right about protecting Tater. But he was

right in doing this to earn money for Tater's future. She was the youngest of them and he wanted to take care of her. All of this would be hers one day, if he stopped right now and preserved it for her.

He should be thanking Victoria for making him think about how this extra money could help with a lot of things. But especially with Tater's future. This would be a gift from him and only him. That was what made this so important.

Victoria Calhoun had managed to invade his life with her in-your-face exposure, but she'd also brought a fresh presence to this big lonely house. Now he wanted to get to know her better and it was driving him crazy.

But that wasn't such a good idea. He knew it. She knew it. And his big sister Denny would soon know it if she saw them within ten feet of each other. Their attraction was probably the best kept secret on this set.

He turned back to the computer and went back to work on the monthly farm reports. Denny handled most of the household and rental accounts, but he enjoyed keeping track of the ranch.

A knock at the office door brought his head up. His niece stood at the door, hesitant and hopeful. Her long light brown hair curled around her shoulders and her eyes held a hint of a made-up look. When had she started wearing makeup? When had she slendered up and turned into a young lady?

"Tater? I was wondering when you'd come give your uncle a big hug."

His niece stood back near the door. "I need to talk to you."

Okay, so no hug. Tater wasn't much of a hugger anyway. She was blunt and to-the-point, just like the rest of the Griffin clan.

"Have a seat," he said, noting her frilly blouse and hot-pink jeans. "You must have done some shopping down in New Braunfels. You look nice."

"You know, I'm almost ready to start driving," Trish said in response.

Clint leaned back in his chair, the love he felt for his niece overwhelming him. "Driving? I can't believe you're all grown up."

She tossed her golden brown hair and made a face. "Everybody around here thinks I'm still a kid. I want to go to the summer party with Eric Holland but mom thinks he's too old and too wild."

Clint had to hide his smile. He'd heard the same thing about himself most of his life. "How old is that Holland boy anyway?"

"He's almost eighteen but he's not that much older than me. Mom says I should just go with a group but I'll be sixteen this fall and a junior now. I want to go on a date. A real date where he picks me up and we go out to dinner and parties."

Clint knew where this conversation was going. "You want me to run interference with your mama, right?"

Tater's pretty hazel eyes lit up like a sunny sky. "Could you, Uncle Clint? I think she'll listen to you."

Not so sure about that, Clint nodded. "Yeah, maybe. But be prepared if she refuses, okay?"

"I have to go to the party with Eric," Tater replied, her big eyes imploring him. "I'll die of embarrassment if I can't. He'll find someone else and I'll lose him forever."

And how could he say no to that pretty face and that angst-filled plea?

"Nobody's gonna die of embarrassment around here. I'll see what I can do," he replied. "Just don't rattle your mama's chains until I get back to you."

She stood, triumphant in her victory, her hands in front of the ruffles cascading down her shirt. "I have one other favor to ask."

"No, no limo," he said with a grin.

"It's not about the party. Eric's already got a limo for us and some other friends."

That scared the daylights out of Clint but he held his poker face. "What's up?"

"I want to be on the show. I mean, Aunt Susie is having so much fun and she's like a celebrity all over Twitter and Facebook. So are you. I'd like that myself. I mean, at first I hated the idea but now…well… I'd like to be on the show."

Oh, boy. Clint felt a whole passel of trouble brewing. In a house with women, drama was an everyday occurrence. And now he'd added to the mix by doing this reality show, maybe because he was bored with life. No, correction there. He'd agreed because he thought this would be an easy way to secure Tater's future and some of his pet projects. Maybe he should have thought long and hard before signing that contract, though. Maybe his big sister was right after all.

"I can't help you there," he said. "Your mama has made it pretty clear that she wants no part of the show and she especially doesn't want you involved."

"She's being unfair, like she always is. She doesn't want me to date Eric. She doesn't want me to be on the show. I'm like a prisoner in this house. Why is she being so mean?"

Clint got up and came around the desk. "Denny is not

mean, honey. She loves you, a lot. We all do. And since we've all been out in the world, we kinda know what could happen to a pretty girl like you. You are not a prisoner but you do need to follow the house rules."

Trish's frown was full of pout. "But if you don't let me go out into that world, I'll never learn the way y'all did. How can that be fair?"

The girl had a point.

Clint grabbed her and hugged her in spite of her standoffish nature. "I'll talk to your mama about this party, honey, but you being on the show, that's nonnegotiable. She's already mad as a hornet because your aunt and I are on a reality show. She won't agree to let you pile in with us."

"Just ask her, please?" Trish gave him a quick hug and stepped back, her sequined brown boots tapping her retreat. "You know, if you'd just get her to agree to let me be on the episode that highlights your charity work, it could help raise money. I've worked with your organizations before—she approved that."

"Going on field trips to homeless shelters and working at the rummage sale at church are totally different from being seen by thousands of people on a television show," he said, already feeling the pressure of this battle. "But you have been a huge help with the Galloping Griffin Ranch. Maybe you can tag along on one of the Horse Therapy Ranch segments."

"So...you'll talk to her, right?"

"I said I'd see what I can do. If she doesn't agree to you being on the show, then we're done with this conversation."

Trish looked disappointed but she slowly nodded.

"Okay. Just think about it. I could get some of my friends to help with whatever projects you want to showcase."

"Go for it. Mighty generous of you." Clint grinned and shooed her toward the door.

"I'm going," she said, waving goodbye. "I have to clean my room and wash my clothes before I can even get on my phone."

"You have a horrible life," Clint quipped.

She frowned her way out the door.

Clint sat back down to take in the conversation. Trish was young, pretty and impulsive, three things that could either serve her well in life, or do her in much too quickly.

He should know. He'd been young and impulsive once himself.

And he had a lot of his own secrets to hide.

Victoria needed to create some drama for the second episode of the show. A nice hook and a cliff-hanger of an ending the way they'd used Susie coming on to the show as the first episode's cliff-hanger. So she went back over her notes and jotted down certain interviews to see if she could pluck out some juicy sound bites to foreshadow the coming weeks.

Because *Cowboys, Cadillacs and Cattle Drives* worked with different talents and changed things up every few weeks, the audience always expected a peek into the private lives of country singers, Southern-raised actors and high-profile Texans like Clint Griffin. She expected the first episode of life with Clint to be a ratings bonanza. The early buzz was already starting. Her viewers loved a train-wreck personality.

She'd believed Clint Griffin was that type of man.

Now she had to wonder why he put on such a good

act, even with no cameras around. The man loved this place and he seemed capable of taking care of things. She'd seen that in the first few days here.

So why was he trying to make the world think he was always on a perpetual party train?

"That's the question," she mumbled to herself. That's what she needed to find out. She only had a few weeks to drag the truth out for the finale. She also wanted to highlight his songwriting days and see if he'd play his guitar for the show.

Tonight was the bar scene. Glancing at her watch, Victoria decided it was time to head out to the nearby watering hole. She needed to round up the troops and get going. This would be a big, crazy take and with a huge crowd in a bar, inhibitions would go straight down the hatch with each drink. Anything could happen. Her job was to make sure they got the tension going without anybody getting hurt or going to jail.

But when she stepped outside, she found Clint standing there waiting for her. He looked good. A button-down Western dress shirt in stark white, jeans that looked worn in all the right places and sleek black boots that probably cost more than she made in a month. When he slipped off his beige cowboy hat and nodded a greeting, Victoria took a deep breath. A heated rush moved over her body and settled deep inside her soul.

"Hello, darlin'," he said. "Ready to rodeo?"

"I'm ready," she squeaked. "Should be an interesting night."

"Ain't it always?" he asked, knowing the answer.

Always, wherever he was concerned.

His stormy gaze swept over her. "Nice dress and killer boots."

She looked down at her turquoise-and-brown leather boots. "I've had these for a long time. They used to be my mama's."

"Vintage, as Susie would say."

"Old, as my mama would say."

"Does your mama still live around here?"

"She lives in Tyler now. We see each other every few months."

He nodded. "I was going to have you bring her out to the ranch."

"I can't do that," Victoria replied, touched. "I mean, I don't mix my mother with my job."

He smiled, tipped his hat then started walking away. "So I reckon I'm not the only one who has to follow that rule. See you on the set then."

Bracing herself for the torment of watching Clint work a roomful of cowgirls during ladies night at the Bar None, Victoria ticked off the many reasons she couldn't fall for this man.

He's a cowboy.

He's too hot to handle.

He's a player.

He kisses way better than anyone else.

He's the talent. You're the...

She stopped, wondering what exactly her title should be since she did just about everything.

You are single, self-sufficient and successful.

And she intended to keep it that way.

But seeing the look in those dove-gray eyes made her wonder what it would be like to let go and walk on the wild side with Clint Griffin. She'd get to see that tonight even if she couldn't be part of the fun. Which only made her job worse. She'd have to live vicariously through a group of high-society debutantes who didn't really get Clint at all.

Victoria stopped herself and thought about that. Did she get Clint? Did she finally see that he was just a human being who'd been through a lot? She'd been hesitant during this whole thing. But she'd chalked that up to her resentment of Clint.

Now that resentment had turned to a grudging respect and…a big attraction.

Dangerous territory.

Trouble.

But then, she'd expected trouble from the get-go.

But she hadn't expected to actually find herself on Clint's side.

Chapter 12

The tiny Bar None Grill was hopping. Victoria listened to the sounds of big pickup trucks slinging rocks as they either sped into the gravelly parking lot, or left with some-one mad behind the wheel. Each time the heavy wooden doors swung open the twang of a country song told the tale of love gone bad, usually involving a tractor or a pickup truck.

Her crew had parked off to the side to stay out of the fray, but it was ladies' night and all bets were off. Word had gotten out that Clint Griffin and the team from *Cowboys, Cadillacs and Cattle Drives* would be filming live tonight. Victoria wondered how many cute cowgirls that big iron-muscled bouncer would have to turn away. Maybe she was imagining things, but it looked like the women were outnumbering the men three to one.

"Natives are restless," Ethan said with a cheeky grin. He hefted his twenty-five-pound camera on one broad shoulder and did a scan of the parking lot. "Everyone accounted for?"

Victoria inched close enough to read the fine print on his faded One World T-shirt. "If you mean Susie, she's already inside. A friend picked her up earlier. A very muscular male friend."

Ethan looked guilty, but shrugged. "I wasn't talking

about anyone in particular." But his perturbed expression told Victoria something completely opposite of what he'd just said.

"Right."

Victoria knew the symptoms. She had a case of the same malady. She couldn't help but look for Clint as they made their way into the hole-in-the-wall cantina. She saw him holding court at the big planked bar that covered one side of the barnlike building. He'd tucked his hat back on his head and a few golden-brown bangs dipped over his brow like a question waiting to be answered.

Through the crunch of empty peanut shells on the painted concrete floor, Ethan shoved up close. "Right," he echoed in her ear. "I'm not the only one with a crush on the talent around here."

Victoria stood up straight and silently wiped the open-mouthed gape off her face. "I have no idea what you're talking about."

Ethan only winked and kept walking. "I'm on the clock," he called back as a sign for her to get it in gear.

Victoria managed to find a stool and table on the far side of the bar where she could check hot-sheets and interview prompts. And watch for signs of trouble. Clint knew what to do.

"Just be you," she'd told him on the ride over.

"And who exactly do you think I am?" he asked in that drawling, dangerous voice while he gave her that lazy, lingering look. Her insides were still doing a little tap dance.

"I don't know," Victoria admitted. "I'm still trying to figure that one out."

After that he'd stayed tight-lipped during the few miles to the bar, a rare thing for Clint Griffin.

Finally, unable to take the silence, she had prompted him with a few questions. "Are you close to both your sisters?"

He shrugged and made a face at her small video recorder. "Close to my sisters? I reckon. As close as anybody can be. We fight, we forget about it and we get on with things."

She liked that statement and was glad she'd caught it on tape. "That'll make a great sound bite."

Clint nodded and chuckled but she thought she'd seen a touch of disbelief in his eyes before he looked away. Was the rhinestone cowboy having second thoughts about his fun-filled life? Or was he tired of this night after night?

Her thoughts headed into forbidden territory as memories of their nights out by the pool moved like hot smoke through her mind. He'd seemed different on those nights. More relaxed, more real. A man she could admire. A man she enjoyed kissing.

Now that they were inside, she decided he was doing just fine. He had women surrounding him on one side and he had men asking him questions on the other side. The king was in his domain and all was right with his world. He hardly seemed to notice the cameras.

Victoria went about her business and made sure everyone who entered Bar None tonight understood their image might wind up on a reality show. If someone protested or didn't want to participate, they'd have to blur out that person's image.

But from the looks of this gussied-up crowd, everyone wanted in on this shoot with the infamous Clint Griffin. She motioned to Ethan and mouthed, "Get in tight."

Ethan muscled his way into the elbow-to-elbow crowd and did a sweep of the bevy of pretty women vying for

Clint's attention. It didn't take Clint long to get out on the dance floor and strut his stuff there, too. Soon he had a redhead on one arm and a brunette nipping at his boots. Well, that was refreshing.

While Victoria watched him doing the Texas two-step with about ten women behind him, she thought about his somber mood earlier. The man flashed hot and cold and that drove her nuts.

She could never get a bead on the real Clint Griffin. Remembering the conversation she'd overheard earlier that day between Clint and Denise, she figured he was in a bad mood because his sister disapproved of this whole thing.

And she disapproves of you, Victoria reminded herself. She'd passed Denise in the kitchen and the other woman had given her an irritated look and kept walking.

"Not my problem," Victoria mumbled while she searched for Ethan. She saw him doing a close-up on Susie and her date.

Thinking to stop Ethan before he went too far, she was headed onto the dance floor when a strong hand grabbed her and pulled her around. She whirled, ready to do battle.

And glanced up into the face of her ex-fiancé.

"I thought that was you," Aaron Hawkins said as he pulled her close in a bear hug. He hadn't changed a lot. He wore nicer clothes now, but he had on black boots and his hair still curled against his collar. His eyes, however, seemed darker than she remembered. Maybe because he'd been drinking.

Smelling beer on his breath, Victoria lifted away then took in his blue shirt and tight jeans. "I'm on the job, Aaron."

"You taping?" He did an elaborate eye roll. "Same old Victoria, still putting that job ahead of everything else."

That stung but she took the heat and tried to move on. Aaron looked a little worn around the edges. Obviously, he still liked to drink too much. "Yeah, same old me. And I see you still like hanging out in dives." But how had he wound up in this dive so far out from the city?

"Sure do. Heard there was a big party here tonight so…here I am." He tugged her back. "Hey, how 'bout one little dance, for old time's sake."

Victoria glanced around and saw Clint watching them. "I can't, Aaron. I have to—"

But Aaron wasn't listening. He yanked her so hard, she rammed into his chest and before she could push away, he had her in a tight embrace that turned to a slow dance.

"You're drunk," she said into his ear. Any lingering feelings she'd had for him in the years they'd been apart disappeared in a haze of anger.

"You are correct," Aaron replied on a slur. "You should lighten up and let go more often, Vic."

She'd never liked his nickname for her. And he'd never liked that she wasn't a party girl.

"Aaron, I have to go."

He ignored her and pulled her up against him again. "Not so fast. We've got a lot of catching up to do."

Victoria decided she'd have to end this dance the hard way, so she pulled back and stopped dancing. Aaron almost fell but he held tight. "What'sa matter? Used to love to dance."

"You need to let me go," she said on a shout.

"No."

She tried one more time, tugging her arm and twisting away.

Aaron laughed and forced her back into the dance.

When she turned again, Aaron suddenly disappeared and she was standing there wondering what had happened.

Then she heard a growing cheer of "Clint, Clint, Clint."

And realized what was going on. Clint now had Aaron by the collar and was heading toward the door with him. The crowd parted and the chant went up. Aaron was too drunk to see that he'd made a fatal mistake.

"I've got this," she said, running to catch up with Clint. "Let him go."

Victoria tried to get between them but Clint ignored her and kept guiding Aaron to the door. "I'll let him go, out in the dirt."

Not happy with that, Aaron shoved Clint away and started back toward her. "Victoria, why won't you dance with me? Don't you love me anymore?"

She shook her head, tried to get away, tried to warn Aaron to leave. "I can't—"

But too late. Clint pulled him around and lifted him off the floor with more force than he had the first time. "The lady doesn't want to dance. You need to leave. Now."

Then everything seemed to explode. Aaron tried to slug Clint. Clint came back with a right hook that sent Aaron sprawling. The bouncer came running inside to tug people apart. Women were screaming and men were shouting. Everyone was in on the fight.

Susie shrunk up into a corner behind her boyfriend, her eyes wide but a smirk on her face, all the same.

And Ethan was recording the whole thing with a wide grin on his face.

Two hours later Victoria sat in the kitchen with Denise and Clint. No one was talking much. Denise was busy shoving an ice pack at Clint's black eye. Clint was busy brooding over having his fun night cut short.

"Did you get that idiot on tape? Did you get the fight?" he said on a low growl. "'Cause that right there, darlin', was classic Clint Griffin."

Denise's dark frown chased Victoria. "I'm thinking Ms. Calhoun made sure the whole fiasco was filmed." Holding her gaze on Victoria, she added, "But you're right about one thing. My brother can't seem to stay out of bar-room brawls. Mother will be beside herself over this one." She stopped. "A record for you, Clint. One whole month without a public display of your temper."

"Enough," Clint retorted. He got up and dropped the ice pack on the counter. "The dude had it coming. Some drunk stranger messing with a woman who didn't want to be messed with. I had to step in."

Victoria didn't want to add to the confusion, but she had to be honest. "He wasn't exactly a stranger. I used to be engaged to him."

That sobered Clint up and brought Denise's chin up. Clint sat there staring at Victoria as if he'd never seen her before. "You don't say?"

Denise hissed a breath. "Did you invite him there to stir up trouble for the show?"

"Of course not," Victoria said. She stood, telling herself she didn't owe these people an explanation. The less she got involved, the better. Another rule she needed to remember.

"How'd he know you were there then?" Denise asked, accusation fairly steaming out her ears.

"Denny, cut that out," Clint retorted, but he looked at Victoria with his own brooding pout. "How did he know we were there?"

"I don't know how he found me," Victoria replied. But she had a sneaking suspicion that Aaron had seen the ads and teasers for the show and had decided to ambush her. That had brought one too many cowboys into the scene.

"If he's your ex, why would you want to even include that in the show footage?" Denise asked, hammering things home in a blunt way.

"I didn't plan this because I didn't know Aaron was going to be there," Victoria said, still standing. "But in the end, my producer and I will decide what goes in and what stays out."

"Right, anything to bring in ratings," Denise replied. Then she turned on Clint. "Are you happy now? Do you actually want people to see you duking it out with another man just because she didn't want to dance with him?"

"I said that's enough and I mean it," Clint shouted. He grabbed Victoria by the arm. "Let's get out of here."

"I need to get to my room," Victoria said, hoping he'd let her go. "I don't owe either of you any explanations."

"Good idea," Denise said. "I agree, the more you stay out of our lives, the better." Then she put a hand on her hip and gave Victoria a defiant stare. "Because, really, we don't owe you any explanations, either."

"Denny, hush up," Clint said, but his tone was gentle even if it did hold a backbone of steel. "Victoria, come with me. I'll walk you to your door."

Not wanting to escalate things, Victoria nodded and gave Denise an apologetic look. But she didn't say she was sorry, maybe because Denise had already turned away.

Clint made sure he got Victoria away from his well-meaning but bitter sister. Denise had a chip on her pretty shoulder but she also carried the weight of the world, too. He'd talk to her later and calm her down.

"She's not so bad," he said to Victoria as they strolled past the pool. "She just worries about Trish."

"I understand that," Victoria replied. "She's a mother who's trying to protect her daughter. We've disrupted her life and she's afraid for Trish's sake."

"Yep." He glanced out into the dark night. He could hear the cattle lowing in the moonlight, could hear the rustle of some nocturnal bird up in the big oaks. He wanted to explain things in a better way, but some things just couldn't become public knowledge. "She's always been overprotective. But she shouldn't take things out on you."

"It was my fault," Victoria said, her voice low, her tone full of regret. "I shouldn't have provoked Aaron."

"No," Clint said, angry coloring the protest. "You don't have to apologize for refusing a man, Victoria. You should know that."

"I do know that," she said, her head down. "But I was caught off guard. I haven't seen Aaron in over two years. The last time I talked to him I was wearing a wedding dress and we were standing in the hallway of my church. After telling me it wasn't me, it was him, he left me standing there."

Clint wished he'd gone ahead and strangled that arrogant nutcase. What could he say to that confession? "Wow."

"Yeah, wow." She clammed up like a catfish hooking a worm. "It's embarrassing enough and now he thinks he'll get to be in on taping this show. But he'll get cut because I can't be in the scenes."

"Do you think someone tipped him off that we'd be there tonight?"

"A good possibility," she replied. "We've already started the teasers. And he always was a ham. He used to come along with me to watch some of the tapings. I just can't imagine why he decided to crash tonight. Last I heard, he was dating a financial manager."

"I'm not talking about the show or him with another woman," Clint told her after they'd stopped at the little porch off the pool house. "I mean, did someone tip him off that you'd be there?"

"Who would even consider doing that?" she said. "Very few people even know him or that I was engaged to him. Just a couple of people at work—"

"Or how he hurt you? Does anyone know about that?"

She nodded, her head down again. "I don't like to talk about it but Samuel and my assistant, Nancy, both know."

Clint lifted her chin so he could look her in the eye. "You don't have to talk about it or explain it. For all the ground covered in the Metroplex and beyond, this area can really be more like a small town sometimes."

"You have a point," she said, her eyes turning warm. "Thank you, Clint, for…fighting for me. I can't remember anyone ever doing anything like that for me before."

He grinned, mostly to keep from kissing her. "Cowboy rule, ma'am. We don't cotton to innocent women being pressured by thick-skulled idiots."

She laughed, smiled, lit up the night. "You sound like a truly good person when you talk like that. A man with old-fashioned values."

"Hey, you can quote me on that," he said. "Now, you go in and get some rest. Tomorrow's another fun day on set, right?"

She managed another smile. "Right. We're going fishing at the pond. I haven't fished in a long time."

"You can always join right in."

She shook her head. "No, no. I can't join in. I'm better at standing back and watching. I think that's why I'm so good at my job."

"You're pretty good at other things, too," he replied, his gaze on her lips.

"Clint…"

He couldn't stop himself. He grabbed her and tugged her close. "Forget the rules. Right now it's just you and me and I want to kiss you."

He lifted her chin again, saw the fear and the need in her eyes, felt both inside his soul. Then he lowered his head and gave her a slow but firm kiss, with just enough demand to force her to relax against him and respond.

Then he lifted his mouth away from hers and smiled down at her. "You need to stop standing back, Victoria. You have a fire inside you that needs to get burning."

She swallowed, sighed. "And you think you can help me to burn, Clint?"

He nuzzled her clean, citrus-smelling hair. "I do believe I can."

In the simmering silence that followed, he felt the heat of that promise down to his boots. And he could tell she did, too.

But she pulled away and opened the door then turned to stare up at him. "Maybe I stand back because I don't want to get burned again."

Then she shut the door and left him there in the sweet wind of a hot summer night, wondering what it would be like to burn with her.

Chapter 13

Six a.m. fishing call?

Victoria decided she had to find another line of work. But this would be the last shoot of the week and they'd have a long Fourth of July weekend to rest and regroup.

She'd probably work throughout, but everyone else would get a chance to rest, at least. Right now she needed caffeine and a bagel. A knock at her bedroom door brought the smell of coffee.

Nancy stuck her red curls inside. "Hey, boss." She then stretched out her arm so Victoria could see the huge mug of black coffee with a bagel spread with strawberry jam and cream cheese balancing on top.

"Bless your heart," Victoria said on a low moan. "In the best way, of course."

"Of course," Nancy said through her own yawn. "Equipment's ready, boat's out on the pond. Talent is up and rearing to go."

"Even Susie?" She'd made it in around 3:00 a.m. with a very tired skeleton crew still taping her.

"Her Majesty has declined to participate in the fishing trip."

"Figures. I'll have to do some heavy edits on whatever Ethan and the crew got last night."

And she'd have to talk to him again and make sure

he hadn't gone over the line. Every time she'd caution him, the carefree cameraman would just laugh and tell her not to worry so much.

But she did worry. This whole shoot was becoming one big soap opera, crew included.

Why don't you give yourself that talk, too? she thought as she took a long drink of coffee. Just the memory of Clint's lips on hers burned her insides hotter than the scalding brew.

Deciding she needed to get back on task and provide a professional example for the rest of this wayward crew, Victoria made notes then checked her equipment and took a deep breath. She wanted to dig deep and encourage Clint to open up about why everyone around here seemed so protective of Trish. The fifteen-year-old seemed grounded and logical, or as grounded and logical as a teenager could be. If they didn't let up, Trish would rebel big-time and that could get nasty.

Right now, however, Victoria was going on another kind of expedition. She'd be following Clint around while he actually went fishing. Another opportunity to show his softer side. Soft? Hardly. Clint was a man's man. Nothing soft about him except maybe one little spot in his heart.

After they'd kissed again last night, she'd hurried inside the pool house and locked all the doors. He was too tempting. But she'd watched him out the window and he'd turned at the back door to the big house and glanced back at her. She'd seen his face in the security lights.

Fishing. It was just a little fishing expedition. Nothing to sweat over. He'd be surrounded by his people and she'd be protected by her people.

But when she got outside, the rising heat of the summer morning seared its way through her system with a hum of anticipation. She automatically searched the surrounding area for Clint and saw him down by the boathouse near the big pond. He waved then motioned for her.

Stalling long enough to look nonchalant, Victoria pretended to check her hot-sheets and did a slow stroll down to the water.

Everyone was gathered and ready, so she issued early morning orders.

"Ethan, let's follow the boat but stay back enough to get the full view of the lake. It's a beautiful day and Clint is having a little downtime." She turned to Clint and continued before she could look him in the eye. "And you will do your thing—fish, and I mean really fish. Catch us something. The audience will get a kick out of that."

Clint grinned. "There's this one old bass out here that I really want to catch. He's been a pain in my—" He caught himself and glared at the ever-present cameras. "He's been around for a long time. I'd love to catch him while I have enough witnesses to confirm that."

Victoria laughed and jotted notes. "If you catch him your fans will be thrilled. Our viewers love to cheer on the stars of the show."

"I always wanted to be the star of my own show," Clint retorted, his eyes warm on her. "Just never dreamed it would happen quite like this."

Victoria finally gave up on her notes and looked up at him.

Her breath caught in her throat like a hook caught in a net. Did he have to look that good in old jeans and a stark white T-shirt that fit him like a second skin? Even with that old straw hat, he still looked good enough to be very bad.

"Ready?"

She turned to find Ethan giving her a smirky smile.

"Yes," she said. "Ready to get this done and move on to the next step."

"And what is that exactly?" Clint asked, nudging Ethan out of the way.

Ethan's camera caught Clint moving toward Victoria. She made a face at Ethan, but he kept on taping. She decided to ignore him and do her job.

"The next step?" She thought about that. "I'm thinking a big, old-fashioned Fourth of July celebration. With as many of your friends you'd like to invite and fireworks and lots of good food and a big picnic—maybe out here near the pond."

"Have you talked to Denny and my mother about that?"

"I got the idea from Susie," Victoria replied. "She told me you have a tradition of holding a big barbecue on the Fourth. Will having us here be a problem?"

"I'll clear it," he said.

But he didn't look pleased. Susie had assured her he'd go for the idea. And Victoria should have suggested it to Clint before giving the go-ahead.

"We'll talk about it later," she said. "Right now we need to get you out on that water so you can show off your fishing skills."

"I got lots of fishing skills, darlin'," Clint said right into the nearest camera. "I like to hook 'em and reel 'em in."

He winked at the camera but Victoria felt his eyes moving over her. She didn't dare return that glance. Now that Ethan was on to her and Clint and their little flirtation, she had to be careful. Ethan would use what he knew to his advantage since he had the hots for Clint's baby sister.

But if Clint found that out, they'd both be in hot water. And she might be fired.

"Let's get rolling," she called, motioning for the crew to move into position. "I've got miles to go before I sleep."

Clint hopped on the sleek johnboat he used to get around the shallows and turned to glance over his shoulder. "I know where all the best fishing spots are located." Then he motioned to her. "I want you in the boat with me."

"Me?" Victoria jabbed a finger against her collarbone. "I can't get in the boat. I'm on the other side of the camera."

He gave her a hangdog scowl. "I don't want to fish by myself."

"Get someone else." She glanced back at the house. "Susie can be your sidekick."

"Susie is sleeping like a baby and besides, she hates fish and anything to do with catching them."

"I don't think—"

He stood steady on the floating, bobbing watercraft. "I'm waiting."

She stood unsteady on the solid, firm shore. "Clint, I can't get in the boat with you. I'd be in the take and I can't be a part of the show."

"You can do the shot," he replied. "Bring them in the follow-up boat, but I want you in the boat and I'll talk into your camera."

Ethan tittered on his own small rowboat. "Am I shooting or what, V.C.?"

"You're shooting," she replied, her eyes still on Clint. "And I'm staying on the shore."

Clint sat down. "I'm not going without you."

Since when had he turned into a diva? He couldn't make demands like this. Victoria glanced at her notes so she'd look like she was in charge of the situation. But she was way out of her element. None of the other "talents" she'd ever worked with had flirted with her the way Clint did. It was unnerving even while her backbone shivered in delight.

She put one hand on her hip. "Clint, this is not how it works. You don't get to boss us around and you don't get to make this kind of decision. It will work better if you just fish and talk into the camera. Or better yet, just talk to yourself."

He shook his head. "I need a person to talk with."

"I'll go, Uncle Clint."

Victoria turned around to find Trish running down to the water. "I love to fish. Let me go with you. You promised me about a month ago that you'd take me out on the pond."

Clint stood back up. "Tater, aren't you supposed to be working at the drugstore in town on weekends?"

"I don't have to go in until one. I want to go fishing."

Clint glanced from Victoria to Trish. "Not a good idea, honey."

Trish twisted a wad of her long hair in her fingers. "I don't understand why I can't be a part of the show. I live here, too."

Victoria felt a hissy fit in the air. She glanced at Ethan and gave a slight nod to keep shooting. They'd have to edit it down to Clint's reaction and his response, but this was becoming interesting. And it had distracted him away from insisting she get into that boat.

He sat down with a plunk of frustration. "I can't take you, Tater. Your mama doesn't want you on the show."

"But I want to go fishing. Just for today. You never take me fishing like you used to. You never do anything with me like you used to."

The old laying-on-the-guilt seemed to do the trick.

Clint shook his head and pulled out his cell phone.

Victoria heard him telling Denise that Trish really wanted to go fishing. "It's just us on the boat, out on the lake. Nothing to do with honky-tonks or wild women. Just me and the kid, okay?"

Apparently Denise didn't feel the same way. He held the phone away from his ear and shook his head again. "Denny, be reasonable. She's a part of the family and she wants to be on the show. We can limit her appearances to strictly being on the ranch and she'd only be a part of things during the day. No party shots, no drinking scenes."

He listened into the phone then clicked it off. "You can come, but your mama is fit to be tied."

Trish jumped up and down and hurried to the boat. "I'm gonna catch that big old bass you're always fussing about."

"Not if I can hook him first," Clint retorted. He grinned and helped Trish onto the seat. "You have to bait your own hook, too."

"I can do that. You taught me."

"I sure did."

Victoria noticed something she'd never seen before. Clint Griffin's face lit up whenever he was around Trish. He loved his family but he especially loved this young woman. Maybe because he was her only father figure and she was the nearest thing he had to a daughter.

Something caught against Victoria's throat and left a burning rawness. She swallowed, held herself in check. "Get the release forms ready," she said to Nancy. "Take them up to her mother."

"I'll sign the forms," Clint said, his eyes still on Trish. "Her mother won't mind."

"Are you sure?" Victoria asked. She liked to do things by

the book so she couldn't have a dispute later over who signed what forms. "This has to be right, Clint. She's a minor."

"I said I'd sign," he retorted on a cool, clipped tone.

"Okay, then," Nancy said. She climbed onto the boat and got her work done then scrambled out of the way.

Clint glanced up at Victoria. "I still want you in the boat."

"No."

"We'll talk about this later," he said, as if he thought he was the one in charge.

"We certainly will," she replied. "How about I get in the boat that follows you?"

He nodded but his expression remained hard-edged.

Taking that as a yes, she climbed into the equipment boat and prepared herself to follow him around the lake. She only wanted to get this day over with and have some downtime, away from Clint Griffin and his charming, conniving cowboy ways.

Or so her head told her.

But her heart was bobbing and weaving like the bright red cork on his fishing line. She sure felt sympathy for that old bass.

Clint watched as Trish took a squirming worm out of the bait box and slid it over the hook. She'd never been afraid of anything or anyone but now that she was growing up, he was afraid for her. The girl trusted way too much, but she could stand up for herself. Trish was fiercely loyal and loving and she didn't take any bunk from anyone.

Her mother was a lot like that, too. Denny was about ready to have him tarred and feathered. His sister liked her privacy and had guarded herself and Trish even more since her divorce.

Having camera crews around hadn't gone over well with Denise. But had he really expected her to accept this invasion of privacy with a smile and a nod? His sister had a lot at stake and here he'd gone and opened up their life to the world.

Putting his sister and her reasons for being so careful out of his mind, Clint reminded himself that he was doing this *for* Denny and Trish. This was easy money that he could put to good use without having to worry about bankers and lawyers trying to tie up his funds. She'd never have to worry about a thing and he could make sure her future was secure, no matter what happened to the ranch.

"You're too quiet," Victoria called out, her frustration evident. "Talk."

"I don't like to talk when I fish," he retorted. "I like it nice and quiet out here."

"But you wanted to talk before," Tater pointed out. She shot a curious glance toward Victoria. "You wanted to talk to her."

"I just needed someone to focus on," he said, careful that he didn't show any signs of interest in Victoria. "Now I have you so I guess we can get right into it. How's that whole party thing going?"

Tater lowered her voice. "Mom thinks I'm too young to go with Buster."

"Buster McGee? Are you kidding me? What happened to Eric?"

"Eric had to go on vacation with his parents as soon as school was out. We did go to that one party together but then he had to leave. He's bummed about it, but… Buster asked me to go to a party on the Fourth and I said yes. Eric wasn't honest with me. He kept letting me think we'd have all summer together when all the time he knew he had to leave town."

Clint winced on that one. "Sorry, doodle bug. But back to this Buster—"

"His real name is Tyson," Tater replied with conviction. "And yes, I want to go with him."

Clint couldn't let any of this conversation show up on the big screen. He kept his words low, too. "But your mama's right. With a nickname like Buster, he sure sounds too old for you. Don't you know any boys your own age?"

"He's only a year and a half older," she replied. "Why does everyone treat me like a baby? All the boys my age are so boring and lame." She shrugged. "They giggle and make jokes and I never get any of their stupid jokes anyway."

Clint was pretty sure what they were laughing and making jokes about. "Hey," he said to his pouting fishing buddy, "we all love you. It's our job to make sure you do the right thing. Maybe hanging out with the younger boys would work just fine right now."

Victoria stood up in her boat. "Clint, we can't hear you. Your mic-pack seems to be turned off."

"Really?" Clint looked shocked and pretended to be confused. He'd turned the darn thing off the minute Tater got in the boat. Then he shrugged. "Sorry."

"Clint?"

He glanced up at Victoria and did his finger across his throat to tell her this conversation would be cut if they recorded it. She frowned and sat back down.

Great. Now he had two females pouting at him.

Trish tugged at her line and made a groaning noise. "I'm doing the right thing. I'm finding a date to the biggest party of the year next to prom. Y'all made me go with a bunch of girls that night but I'm older now."

"By what? Two or three months. The prom was this spring."

She huffed another breath and copped an attitude that would cause water to sizzle. "I have to give him an answer soon or he'll ask that stupid Marcie Perkins."

"I thought you and Marcie were best friends."

"Not anymore. She sent out a not-so-nice tweet about me."

"What did it say?"

"I don't want to talk about it."

"And why not?"

Tater glanced at the cameras. "It's personal."

Clint wondered about that. "A rumor?"

Trish leaned in. "It was about Mom and Dad and the divorce."

"I see." He decided to change the subject so he turned on his mic again and motioned to Victoria. "How's school going? Won't be long before you'll be out for the summer."

"I hate school."

He was way behind on what was going on in her life. "You have to finish school so you might as well like it."

"I don't like it, but mom wants me to go to college."

"You will go to college. That's important, too."

"Did you like college?"

He thought about that, memories swirling with the flow of the water against the boat. But he wouldn't tell her he'd been distracted and confused his whole freshman year. "Yeah, I had a great time in college."

"Mom said you piddled away a lot of time and didn't learn a darn thing."

He laughed at that and caught Victoria watching them. "Your mama might just be right."

Next thing he knew, Tater was standing up in the boat. "I got one, Uncle Clint. I got a big fish."

Clint watched as she reeled in a nice bream. "Not that bass but a passable size, Tater. You might get a mess of fish for supper."

"I'm not gonna keep him," Tater said, her eyes wide. "I'll throw him back."

"Where's the fun in that?"

"He gets to live," she replied, her tone matter-of-fact and sweet.

"That's good enough for me, then," Clint said, content to watch her having a good time.

Why had he wasted so much time on drinking and tomcatting around when he could have had more days like this, out here on this quiet pond with Tater?

And why had it taken a reality television show and a woman who refused to fall for his bunk to make him see what he'd been missing?

He pegged Victoria with a long, hard stare and saw something there in her eyes he'd never noticed before. A longing, a look of resolve and understanding, seemed to pass between them.

Clint had the hots for her, no denying that.

And from the look on her face, she felt the same way.

But from the look on Tater's face, she wasn't too thrilled about them making goo-goo eyes at each other.

Problems with women all the way around. But then, that was nothing new.

Chapter 14

Victoria stood down by the big pond, a feeling of contentment centered in her soul. In spite of everything, today's shoot had gone pretty well. The fishing segments would show yet another side to the Cowboy Casanova. And fishing with his teenage niece would only add to his charm. Having Trish on the show would bring in a lot of younger audience members. And the more audience members they had, the bigger and better their sponsors would become. This could be a gold mine for the show. And a feather in her cap, too.

That was the goal, after all. Putting those warm and fuzzy feelings she'd experienced watching Clint with Trish earlier out of her mind, Victoria ticked off her list of reasons for being here. The most important being her job, of course. She needed to remember she liked her job and she liked to pay the rent. She also had a strong sense of ambition. She wanted to continue and move on up the producer ladder. So she shouldn't even be thinking about kissing the star of the show. But she couldn't get Clint's kisses out of her mind.

"That's certainly never happened before," she mumbled.

She turned to take one more look at the ranch before they called it a week and saw Tessa watching her from the edge of the patio. The older woman grinned and waved. Victoria lifted a hand in a tentative greeting. Tessa seemed to be everywhere at once. And she seemed to know that there was more than just her strong Columbia coffee brewing around here.

Once again trying to go over her schedule, Victoria started making her way toward the house. They'd be back late Monday afternoon to tape the Fourth of July segments and then the second episode would be complete. Two episodes down and three more to go. Then she'd move on to a safer subject.

She turned to leave and saw Denise marching toward her with a flashing fire in her eyes. Oh, boy. Not what Victoria wanted at the end of a long day. But she waited with an expectant burn hissing through her, too. Denise certainly liked to control things regarding her daughter. Victoria had been surprised that Denise had agreed to let Trish get in on the fishing segment.

"A word," Denise said without preamble.

"Sure." Since she had no way of getting around Clint's sister, Victoria dug in her heels and prepared to state her case. She'd handled worse than this one, but still she wondered if she could deal with an angry, protective mother.

Denise tossed her shaggy mane of hair and glared over at Victoria. "I thought we had an understanding regarding my daughter."

"We did," Victoria replied. "You didn't want her on the show."

"That's right," Denise retorted. "But somehow she managed to be featured in this morning's taping. And I just had a long talk with her. She thinks she'll be in every episode from here on out."

"That's not my call," Victoria said, trying to defuse

the situation. "I can't make that decision. Trish requested to be in the fishing segment and you gave her permission, then Clint was very careful in allowing what we got on tape. It's up to you if she shows up in any more segments."

"It should be my decision," Denise said. "But thanks to you and my brother, Trish is now all caught up in your show. I'll be the bad guy if I refuse to let her continue."

Treading lightly since Denise seemed to be waffling, Victoria nodded. "Look, I don't normally give advice to our talent, but... I understand your concerns. We rarely have minors on our show but when we do, we follow the laws and regulations and we make sure they aren't overworked or overexposed. We can work around anything too personal or embarrassing for Trish and for you."

Denise crinkled her brow in irritation. "I don't want you to work around things. I don't want my child involved in this show at all. Even if you protect her from the worst of this, she'll want to watch the shows because...this is her family. And she'll have to deal with what the other kids say about her. She's just been through so much already."

Victoria saw a solid fear in Denise's eyes. What was she afraid of besides the normal motherly stuff? Softening her stance, Victoria said, "Okay. I get it and that's your call, but you need to tell Clint and Trish how you feel. I can't forbid her to stay off the show, not if an adult signs for her to be on it."

"My brother signed for her today," Denise said, some of her steam running low. "He caught me off guard and in a weak moment because he knows how much she enjoys fishing, especially with him." She shrugged and looked out over the pond. "I hate to be the one who's always saying no to her, but that's my job."

Victoria felt sorry for Denise. Clint had obviously used his persuasive charms on her, too. "If it helps, the scenes we shot this morning were cute and sweet and I'll edit out anything too personal. Nothing that a teenaged girl couldn't handle. The viewers will get a kick out of it."

Denise pushed a hand through her hair. "I'm sure they will. I'm just not sure putting Trish on the show is a good idea."

Victoria knew to stay out of this but she couldn't resist asking. "Are you worried about her father?"

Denise's face went pale. "What about her father?"

"I mean, with the divorce and all," Victoria said, hoping she wasn't being too personal. "Are you afraid he'll object to her being on the show?"

A relieved expression washed over Denise's face. "Oh, I don't know. James was never in her life much when we were together so I doubt he'll care what she does now. But he might insist on having a cut of her salary or at least being in some of the scenes with her, though. He's so stuck on himself he can't see anyone else around him. And he doesn't think his actions have hurt his daughter at all."

"I'm sorry," Victoria said, meaning it. "Divorce is never easy. I've been through that myself and I was about the same age as Trish." She hesitated then added, "Maybe she wants to be involved in this because she needs some sort of connection with her family."

Denise's resentment flared up again. "You mean a connection with her flamboyant uncle. Yeah, she wants that. I'm just her boring old mother, but someone has to be the adult. If James does get wind of this, I'm sure he'll want a cut, too. I'm not sure Trish can handle him using her like that."

"We can handle your ex," Victoria said. "He has nothing to do with Clint and your family so he won't be asked to participate. And we can certainly tell him he's not part of our strategy."

"So what is your strategy?"

Victoria smiled. "Just to entertain people. Next, I want to have a big Fourth of July bash. Clint's approved that, but I'd really like to have the whole family involved. If you're willing to hang around, you can make sure Trish stays out of trouble."

Denise turned, angry again. "I've seen how my brother parties and I don't want Trish exposed to that. I'm sure there'll be drinking and dancing and no telling what else."

"In certain scenes, but not early on when it's just the family gathered for a picnic."

"And later?"

"Clint and his gang, doing their thing. Trish won't be allowed to participate at all."

"Right. I'm not sure I'll let Trish anywhere near that anyway. Maybe I can take her to a movie."

"We can tape them separately," Victoria offered. She was bending the rules way too much for this family but she'd never stooped to tricking people into being on the show and she wouldn't start now, especially with a minor involved. "And I'll edit these segments myself to make sure Trish is protected and only shown with Clint and Susie and the rest of the family—that is if you and your mother want to participate."

"Oh, I don't know about that," Denise said, shaking her head. "I'm too boring and our mother is a very private person."

What an interesting family, Trish thought. Two of the Griffin children were hams, but Denise and their mother were both a little more private and introverted. Trish must truly be conflicted with all these mixed messages.

"I'll work on getting her to do an interview after the taping, maybe add some of her comments about the traditions here on the Sunset Star. We need Miss Bitsy's perspective to complete the picture."

Denise turned toward the house. "I don't know. I'll talk to Trish and Clint again and maybe let Trish be in some of the family picnic scenes but I don't want to be on camera. And you're on your own with my mother."

Hmm, hostility there, too? Victoria wondered. This family was constantly shifting and surprising her. If she could get them all together in one big scene, she might get more than she'd bargained for. And her viewers would get a riveting and dramatic show to watch.

"I'll figure it out," she told Denise. "People need to see Clint Griffin as a strong family man so they can also see how complex his life really is. He runs deeper than people think. I never knew that about him before I put him on the show."

"Yeah, he's complicated," Denise said, her tone dripping with a cynical snark. "If only you knew."

Victoria lifted her eyebrows. "Care to fill me in?"

"No," Denise retorted. "I have to get back to dinner."

Victoria watched as Denise whirled and hurried back to the house. But she had to wonder what Clint's sister was holding back. This seemed to go beyond protecting a teenager. She was beginning to think the Griffin family might be hiding some sort of big secret.

Clint watched the exchange between Denise and Victoria, wondering what his sister had said to the producer. Victoria could hold her own with just about anyone from what he'd seen, but Denise was like a steamroller at times. He understood her reasons, but she needed to lighten up or Trish would start acting out in a big way.

"How'd that little discussion go?" he asked as his sister came through the French doors to the kitchen.

Denise turned up her perky nose as if she smelled something rotten. "Not so good. She's just out to make a buck and the more Griffins she gets on that show, the better. I'm not sure Trish should be a part of that, but then you know how I feel and you somehow managed to sneak her in this morning."

"Hey, she begged to go fishing and I did call you and talk to you first."

His sister moved to her usual spot behind the wide granite kitchen island. Honestly, she used that big counter as a shield between her and the rest of the world. "Yes, you called me—to tell me, not ask me, about Trish wanting to be on the show. You knew already I didn't want that, Clint. You put me in a bad position and now if I say no, she'll be mad at me. We already fight enough as it is."

"She's a teenager," Clint said, trying to be reasonable. "She stays mad all the time."

"I'm afraid she has your partying gene," Denise replied. "Or maybe worse, her father's need to always find outside entertainment."

"Is that what this is about?" Clint asked, his tone going soft. "That jerk ex-husband of yours has sucked the life right out of you, hasn't he?"

Denise lowered her eyes, but not before Clint saw the streak of humiliation in them. "James is the least of my concerns, but I do worry that Trish will inherit some of his bad habits. I mean, she was around him from birth."

"But she's not around him now and you and this family have been a big influence on her."

"So have you," Denise reminded him.

That ticked his hide since he'd tried to be on his best behavior around his niece. "Hey, I've never done anything in front of Trish that I'm ashamed of. I know she's heard and seen some things on television and in the tabloids, but I can't control everything that comes down the pike."

"But you should, for her, Clint."

The plea in his sister's eyes caught at Clint's heart. "Hey, I've tried to do right by her, haven't I?"

Denise stared over at him, her expression softening. "Yes, you have. And even this harebrained idea of putting aside your earnings on the show for her is noble if not misguided. Just…don't hurt her, Clint? Trish and I can't take any more hurt."

"I'd never intentionally hurt her. You know that."

Denise came around the counter and touched his arm on her way to the refrigerator. "No, not intentionally. But sometimes the best of intentions can lead to a whole lot of pain."

Victoria closed the door to the pool house and started toward her car. Everyone else had left for the day to begin their long weekend before they came back Monday to resume taping. But she'd lingered over the dailies, tweaking here and there to get the best possible fishing segment.

And to avoid going to her silent, empty apartment.

"I should have gotten a goldfish long ago," she mumbled.

Of course, Tessa was also headed to her car and naturally she'd heard Victoria grumbling. That woman had some sort of sixth sense when it came to pegging Victoria at her worst.

"Tan solo," Tessa mumbled, her smile charming as she waved good-night.

So lonely.

Victoria stopped at her car. Was she that pathetic? She lifted a hand to wave to Tessa, wondering if the colorful and observant housekeeper had her own family to go home to. Tessa stayed here at the ranch a lot, but she did take time off whenever she wanted it.

Tessa smiled and sped off in her little pickup truck.

Victoria let out a groan and scrolled down her take-out emergency numbers. She had her finger on the button of a favorite Chinese place when someone touched her on the arm.

"Let's go get a big ol' steak," Clint said, his grin even more reassuring than Tessa's.

Victoria glanced around. "Are you talking to me?"

"I don't see any other pretty girls standing around."

"What, you haven't called in the blond harem for the Fourth?"

"Funny. I do believe today was a blond-free day."

"And where is the elusive not-blond Susie?" His sister had never showed for the fishing segment.

"Off on an elusive date, I reckon."

Victoria leaned back against the warmth of her car, wishing her heart hadn't gone all shivery from his touch. "I was just leaving. I mean, I have things to do."

Clint leaned in, one hand bracing against the car door. His eyes were so gray, so stormy, so…interesting. And the way his gaze moved down her and back up to meet her eyes, well, that made Victoria forget all about Chinese food. In fact, she'd lost her appetite. Her mind zoomed in on his mouth.

"Look," he said, his words like a slow kiss, "it's Friday night, darlin'. I don't have anywhere else to go and from the looks of it, neither do you. I kinda wanted to take you on that boat ride—you know the one we didn't have this morning."

Victoria looked down at her sensible short boots and wished she was wearing stilettoes. But then, she'd probably just fall and break her neck if she did have on high heels. "A boat ride? What's that got to do with steak?"

He smiled again, zapping at her resolve. "I have the boat and I have the steaks, along with a salad that Tessa made and some good wine that I stole from the kitchen wine cellar."

She must have moaned, because he gave her a triumphant grin. "And I have chocolate for dessert. Tessa's famous spicy chocolate brownies."

"You are seriously killing me," Victoria said, thinking if she'd just gotten into this car five minutes earlier, she'd be on her way. On her way away from him and the hope of another kiss or two. Or maybe the threat of another kiss or two.

"I shouldn't—"

"Me, either, but we're alone and we might as well be alone together, don't you think?"

She didn't want to think. If she thought about this, she'd do the right thing and get into that car and haul buggy away from all that Clint Griffin charisma.

But she couldn't make herself do that. She wanted to go on a boat ride at sunset, with him. And frankly, she didn't care where that boat ride might take her.

"Victoria?"

She finally glanced up and into his eyes. He looked sincere, but he was a master at fooling people. She should remember that. But this was now and she wasn't some star-struck Plain Jane sitting in the corner of a bar.

But he's still a cowboy. A player. A Casanova.

"This is a big mistake," she said even as she tossed her stuff in the car and locked the door. "But I am hungry and I do love brownies."

"With wine," he reminded her. "Watching the sun set over the pond."

With him.

"Do you have a grill on that boat?"

He took her by the hand and pulled her back toward the house. "No, but I can build a campfire over on the back side of the pond. A private campfire."

"You're just full of surprises," she said to keep her knees steady. "How many women have been to this particular camp?"

He turned as they rounded the side of the house by the pool. "I've never taken anyone there before. You're the first, Victoria."

She didn't know what to say to that line. Was he telling her the truth or setting her up for yet another fall?

Chapter 15

"Can I go back into the pool house and freshen up?" Victoria asked. If they were going on a *date,* she sure didn't want to wear her grungy work clothes. On the other hand, she should just stay in her grungy clothes. And run into the house and lock the door. Hadn't she lectured herself about how being with Clint was a mistake?

"Sure, but don't be long. That sunset won't wait forever."

And neither would he. She hurried into the little house but didn't lock herself inside. Instead, she pulled out a denim dress she'd thrown into her overnight bag, and found a pair of low-heeled boots to go with it. Then she brushed her teeth and dabbed on some lip gloss and blush. Her hair was impossible so she just brushed it and let it go.

Taking a look at herself, Victoria stood still and realized she was about to step out into new territory. "You're crossing a big line."

She stood there, torn between going with Clint and sneaking out the back door. Would she ever be able to go back if she did cross that line? On the other hand, the more she got to know him the more she'd be able to make the show work. She could use the inside drama to pull out enough conflict to fuel the show.

But that would be sneaky and underhanded.

A knock scared her into action. "Coming."

She opened the door to find Clint waiting with an expectant smile. "Wow," he said, his gaze moving over her. "You sure clean up nice."

"Thanks." She wanted to tell him that she rarely got all dressed up and that this really wasn't dressed up. But she held back, thinking too much information might spoil the mood.

He took her by the hand and guided her out toward the pond. "I don't think I've ever seen you in a dress."

"My job requires serviceable clothes. I have to move around, do a lot of physical things."

"You do seem to be a jack-of-all-trades," he said. They walked toward the small dock and the waiting boat. "You sure work hard."

"Part of the job, being all things to all people, and yes, sometimes it's hard but it's what I do. I always wanted to work in television or the movies."

"But reality television seems a lot different than making a movie. Really hard at times."

"Yes."

Hard to give advice to a worried mother. Hard to avoid kissing a hunk of a cowboy. Hard to turn around and run from trouble.

To think her work used to be so easy. So uncomplicated.

Clint strolled along, his hands in the pockets of his jeans. "Don't look so worried and guilty, darlin'. So you need some downtime, same as your crew," he said, his tone sensible. "Tonight, we don't have to hurry. This is our time."

She let him help her down into the rocking boat, her

heart set adrift with each ripple of the water. "You understand we shouldn't be doing this, right?"

"Two adults, having some fun? Where's the rule in your guidebook for that?"

She sat down on the boat seat. "The rule being that I shouldn't be out here alone with our star talent."

"I love how y'all use that word *talent* to describe real people who happen to be on a reality show. I don't have a lick of talent—acting-wise."

She noticed that he skimmed right over the rules. "But you are the star of the show." And he was doing a pretty good job right now.

He laughed at that statement and picked up an oar.

She shifted on the boat. "What, no motor?"

His smile was smoking hot. "I told you this would be slow and easy."

Victoria swallowed her heart on that note, all sorts of images playing in her head. "Where's your mother?"

He frowned. "Don't be a buzzkill, darlin'."

"Just asking."

"She went out of town. She's so afraid y'all might get her on camera, she just stays away."

"Smart woman."

"We're alone, Victoria. Except for a few lonely bulls and a herd or two of cattle."

"Moo."

"You're funny. That's one of the first things I noticed about you."

She wondered what else he'd noticed, wondered why he'd noticed, wondered if she should tell him that he'd noticed her once before, long ago. No, that would definitely be a buzzkill.

"My sense of humor serves me well," she admitted.

"Don't I know it."

So did he hide things behind his bad reputation and his cool-as-a-cucumber attitude in the same way she used sarcasm and humor to hide her feelings?

She didn't ask. Instead she enjoyed the slow glide across the still water, the sound of croaking frogs merging with the soft "hoo-hoo" of an owl off in the woods. Nearby, a fish jumped. Victoria jumped right along with it.

"That ol' bass is watching out for us," Clint said, his smile soft and sure, his eyes matching the gloaming in shades of gray and midnight. He stopped rowing for a minute and centered his gaze on Victoria. "You know, you're not my type."

She clasped her hands together. "Wow, what a great pickup line."

He laughed, but his eyes stayed on her. "It's the truth. I haven't tried that with a woman in a long, long time. Going against type, I mean."

Struck by his honesty, Victoria put her hands together and stared back at him. "Why am I here, if I'm not your type?"

"I have no idea." He shook his head. "It's a mystery to me, why I can't seem to get you out of my head."

She wouldn't fall for that line just yet. "But you've had lots of women in that head, right?"

"I've been with lots of women, that's for sure. But not many of them have made it inside my head. Or my heart."

She tried to breathe. Tried to remind herself that this was Clint Griffin. The Clint Griffin. The man she'd come here to expose as the playboy he was. The man she'd had a love-hate one-sided relationship with for years now. The Cowboy Casanova. That Clint Griffin.

You've had a relationship with a memory. This is the real deal. And this time, she was a much wiser and more jaded woman, who'd kissed him two times too many already. A woman who still wanted to expose his secrets and get inside his head and heart.

But her reasons for wanting to do those things were fast changing from work-related to way too personal. This version of Clint Griffin was too raw, too real, for her to comprehend. And way too honest.

Unless he was playing her all over again.

"Did you run out of steam?" she asked, pointing to the still oars. She didn't know what else to say.

"Nope. I just wanted to get you in a place where you couldn't come up with some excuse for leaving."

She glanced down at the murky water. "Oh, a captive audience."

"I'd rather call it getting to know one another."

"Out in the middle of a pond, with the sun setting over the horizon. I never pegged you for a romantic."

"And how did you peg me?"

It was her turn to be honest. "As a player, a wild rodeo cowboy who moved from woman to woman without any qualms. A hard-drinking, partying man who was so focused on himself, he didn't have time for anyone else. You're known as the Cowboy Casanova."

"Wow."

She saw the stunned look in his eyes, saw the flare of pain followed by a look of resolve. "Tell me how you really feel, why don't you?"

"You asked," she said, sorry that she'd been so blunt.

"Yeah, I did. I reckon that's a pretty accurate observation, on the surface."

"But underneath the surface, I see a man who's torn

between duty and recklessness, a man who loves his family and wants to prove something to the world." She leaned forward. "That is the main reason you agreed to this gig, right? You wanted to show the world a little bit more than what's on the surface?"

He nodded, his smile tight against the hard edges of his expression. "I think so. A new challenge, a new slant. That and the money, of course."

"Of course."

She waited for him to say more, but he picked up the oars and started rowing again.

"Why is the money so important?" she asked, trying to sound casual.

He shook his head and laughed. "Haven't you heard— I've let the ranch run to ruin. I've gambled and lost. I've used up all the Griffin cash for parties and liquor and wild women."

"I don't believe that," she said. "Not after seeing the ranch and especially not after watching you at work on this ranch."

"And you got that all on tape, right?"

"Clint?"

"Hmm?"

"I didn't mean to be hurtful."

He gave her one of his famous deadpan glances. "And I didn't mean to be so honest."

They finished the boat ride in silence and when they reached the shore, he helped her out of the boat and turned her toward the west.

"Your sunset, darlin'."

Victoria watched as the bright orb colored in shades of bronzed gold and watercolor pink washed through the sky and dipped behind the tree line like a lost beach ball. But some of the brilliance had left the quiet night.

And she wondered if Clint had figured out why she wasn't his type.

Clint started the fire and pulled his supplies out of the ice chest he'd placed on the boat earlier. He'd decided to come out here, with or without Victoria. But he liked it better with her. She was way too blunt for his taste, but maybe he needed someone to be blunt with him. Most of the women he knew would say anything and lie through their teeth just to be seen with him. They wanted the fame and reputation that went with hanging around with a troublemaker.

Not this one, though.

He turned to glance at her. She was sitting on the old log he'd dragged up here years ago. Her dark gold hair tumbled over her shoulders in rich waves. The dress, faded denim and full-skirted, made her look young and carefree. The worn girlie boots made her look country but hip. She might be all of those things, but he knew that brain was on a constant whirl. She was always thinking, always planning, always going after the next segment, the next revelation, the next scoop. So darn good at her job she'd forgotten how to be good at life.

He should get in that boat and row as fast as he could. This woman was way out of his league.

"What is it?" she asked, her head lifting toward him. "What's going on inside your head?"

Clint came out of his stupor and walked over to sit down by her. "Nothing. Everything. How did you find me?"

She gave him a startled look. "What do you mean?

You're easy to find. Tabloids, newspapers, entertainment shows."

"I'm an easy target, is what you mean."

"Yes, that, too." She stopped and stared at the water. "Samuel came to me and asked if I knew you."

"And you said?"

Victoria looked almost panicked. Did she think he was giving her the third degree? "I said I knew you, yes. I knew of you, of course. I'd seen the tabloid articles and read the newspapers and heard the news."

"But you didn't really know me at all, right?"

"No." She lowered her head. "I didn't really know you at all."

"But you wanted me for the show, based on what you thought you knew?"

"Yes. We all thought you'd be good subject matter for our audience. They like to see their favorite people on the show."

"And I'm a favorite?"

"We think so. You're notorious, charming and photogenic, and…what we call a hot mess."

He leaned close, hiding the sinking feeling her words sent through him with a smile. "A hot mess, huh?"

"A little conflicted," she amended, her tone almost sympathetic. "But since I've been around you, I can see that you're not so much messed up as confused. Just like the rest of us."

Clint liked that assessment, but he hated that the world thought he couldn't walk a straight line and chew gum at the same time. "I'm sure confused right now," he said, his hand going up to her face. He rubbed two fingers down her cheekbone and was rewarded with a soft sigh. "I'd like to kiss you again but I'm afraid if I do that, we'll both be in a whole lot of trouble."

"An even hotter hot mess," she said on a whisper.

"Yes. Can you handle that?"

"No. I'm afraid I can't," she said, her breath warm against his hand. "I can't handle you and what you'll do to me."

"And what do you think I'll do?"

"Love me and leave me. Kiss me and abandon me. I can't afford to get involved with you, Clint."

"You think I'd do that to you?"

"You've done it to many other women."

He dropped his hand. "That's what you read in the gossip pages. But…there is always another side to any story. Those women—they weren't like you. They all wanted something I couldn't provide."

She lifted her head and gave him a direct stare. "What if I want something, too?"

He looked over at the fire. "I don't think you want what those other women wanted."

"Did they want to be with you?" she asked. "In a long-term relationship?"

"No. They wanted to be with the fantasy of me, or someone like me. They move from sport stars to movie stars to politicians, men of power. Then they get bored and come to me, and they expect me to give them some sort of cowboy fantasy. I think you want the real deal, don't you?"

She looked shocked and then she looked confused. Her eyes held his for a long, silent minute and finally she answered. "I never expected this. Since I broke up with Aaron a couple of years ago, I've sworn off of cowboys, playboys and men in general."

"Whoa. That covers a lot of heartache."

"Yes."

"Who broke your heart, Victoria? 'Cause I can't believe you fell for that jerk in the first place."

She glanced out at the water. "Who is not important. The why is, though. They all broke my heart because I let them, including that jerk." Dropping her head, she looked down. Her hair fell around her face like a cloak, hiding her expression.

He lifted her chin. "They? You've had more than one heartbreaker in your life? Besides the idiot in the bar the other night?"

"I've had one too many."

"Tell me what happened."

She twisted away and stood up. "Where's my steak? I'm starving."

He got it. She could pull every gut-wrenching memory out of the people she followed around, but she didn't want anyone to see her own pain. Maybe he should try a different tactic.

"I'll get right on that, ma'am," he said. Then he went about putting the steaks on a small wire grill over the fire while she paced by the shore.

Clint gave her some space while he prepared the meal. Once the steaks were medium rare, he opened the wine and poured her a glassful. "Here," he said, handing it over to her.

"Thanks."

She seemed pensive now, almost shy.

"Listen, you should understand something," he began, hoping he could say this in the right way. "I'm not such a mess that I can't be a good friend or a good listener."

She turned then, her eyes misty with moonlight. "I

believe that and I'm sorry I can't share the details of my past experiences. It's that old cliché—jilted and left alone. Once during high school—at the prom—and once in a wedding dress, on the day of my wedding. And once—"

She stopped, drank down her wine. "Once is one time too many. But strike three, and you're out. I'm out of chances, Clint."

Clint took her glass and set it down on the big log. Then he turned her to face him. "Let's try this—once is not enough when it comes to me kissing you."

She gasped, her eyes going wide. "But—"

"No more talking, darlin'," he said, his finger tracing her soft, warm bottom lip. "Put all that heartache out of your mind, just for now. Just for tonight."

He lowered his mouth to hers and drank in the fruity, sweet taste of wine and lipstick, drank in the wonderfully rich taste of her. He'd give her a kiss to remember, a kiss that would wash away all of her bad memories.

She seemed to understand. The way she fell into his arms and let out a little sigh only sweetened the heat between them. Victoria was kissing him back in an all-in way that drove him nuts while it made him smile. It also made him feel alive again and filled him with a hunger he'd forgotten.

She was giving him a kiss to remember, too.

A kiss that filled his head and his heart with hope and poured like hot rain over the emptiness he'd felt in his soul for so long.

Chapter 16

Victoria never made it back to her apartment in town. Clint woke her up on Saturday morning with a soft knock at her door and a breakfast tray waiting on the table out by the pool.

"How'd you sleep, sunshine?" he asked with a grin.

Victoria tightened the sash on her seersucker robe, memories of their evening by the pond still fresh in her mind. "Like a baby. I think it was the wine."

"Or maybe you finally relaxed a little last night."

Or maybe she'd had too much to drink and had kissed him one time too many. She'd broken her no-drinking-on-the-job rule, too. But the sweet thoughts moving through her head didn't seem to mind what she'd done last night. And technically, she hadn't been working. Amazing, how she could rationalize her actions in the light of day.

Too late to change things now. But she could still salvage the rest of her weekend by leaving. Right after breakfast.

She took the coffee he offered then sank down onto the nearest chair. Yeah, she'd relaxed enough last night to have a rather long make-out session with him. Taking a big gulp of the hot brew, she inhaled too quickly and started coughing.

Clint got up and took the mug from her. "Hey, slow down on the java. I got a whole pot ready and waiting."

Victoria recovered and sipped slower the second time. "Thanks. Tessa makes the best coffee."

He grinned again. "Tessa didn't make that, suga'. I did. Tessa has the weekend off."

Surprised, she sat up and gave him a big smile. "You make coffee?"

"And eggs and toast and I even cut up some fruit."

She looked at the tray with new eyes. He'd placed a pretty floral-patterned plate and fancy silverware on it, with a white linen napkin and her coffee. And he'd laid a bright sunflower across the napkin.

How did a tough-acting man like him know how to fix up a breakfast tray? Oh, right. He'd certainly done this many times over for a lot of women. At least she'd had the good sense to sleep in her own bed. Alone.

"The flower is so pretty," she said, unable to voice her real thoughts. Could this kind, romantic human be the same man she'd heard so much about? The man who loved women and left women? The man who had been called every bad word in the book, from scoundrel to hound dog to Casanova?

Remembering how he'd quizzed her last night about how they'd decided on him for the show, she took a deep breath. A moment of panic had hit her there by the fire. She'd wondered if he'd had her pegged after all, that maybe he'd remembered their one night long ago and had been playing her all along. But his curiosity had more to do with *why* they'd wanted him, rather than the who of it. And, she reminded herself, Samuel had come to her, asking about Clint.

"I stole that from my mama's garden," Clint said, referring to the sunflower. "She plants them every year along the side of the back porch. Loves to feed the seeds to the birds and squirrels."

Victoria glanced over at the old farmhouse. Sure enough, a row of bright yellow-and-brown sunflowers was just beginning to peek over the porch railing. "How old is that house, anyway?"

"Oh, I'd say close to a hundred and fifty years at least. Maybe older. I'll give you a tour later."

No, she thought. *No more tours or boat rides or distractions.*

"I have to go," she said, her hand holding a piece of toast. "I should have left last night."

He took the toast, took her hand, pulled her up. "Where do you need to be today, right now?"

She thought about that. The office would be on skeleton crew, but she could get a lot of work done if she got going right away. "I need to work. I have edits and dailies to go through. I have to do the hot-sheets for the barbecue segment and get the B-roll schedules ready—"

He shook his head. "You know it's a holiday weekend. And I got this whole place to myself until Monday."

"I thought your sister and Trish would be back today."

"I told them to take a shopping weekend, on me."

He'd sent Denise and Trish away? So he could be alone with her? Victoria glanced around and remembered even her kind-of ally—Tessa wasn't here. This had gone beyond a flirtation. He was gunning for her. Victoria didn't know whether to laugh or to cry. The thing she'd vowed to avoid had happened. She'd become a Clint Griffin conquest.

Giving in to the obvious, coupled with her lack of enough caffeine, made her cranky. "Is this how it starts?

You bribe your relatives to stay away and then you make your move?"

He blinked and drew his head back then sank back down on his own chair, his gaze hardening as he stared up at her. "I thought we'd gotten past your preconceived notions of me."

Victoria stared at the sunflower on her tray then picked it up. "I'm sorry, Clint. I never expected this, so I'm having a hard time accepting that you really want to be with me."

He gave her one of those cool looks that made her insides quiver. "From what I've seen, I think you have a hard time accepting anything and anybody, darlin'. You seem to be on this self-destructive, self-inflicted punishment that makes you stand back and observe instead of jumping in and rolling with the punches. Do you think all those other false starts were your fault? Is that why you're so standoffish?"

Stunned, Victoria tugged at her robe and sat back down. Did she really think that about herself, deep down inside? Did he really have that kind of insight on her feelings and her fears?

"I… I don't know." She sipped her coffee and nibbled on another piece of toast. "I mean, there must have been something wrong with me when my boyfriend broke up with me the night of the prom."

"Did he think that night would go way past the last dance?"

She nodded. "Yes, he did. I told him I wasn't ready for the next step and he didn't take it very well." She lowered her gaze, humiliation coloring her face. "He found a more willing partner for the rest of the night."

"Of course he did." Clint took her hand. "I should

know. I've done the same thing myself." He lifted his brow, surprise and what looked like regret filling his eyes. "More times than I can remember, now that I think about it."

She'd put him in that category, so she certainly could believe him. "Men who do that don't think past what they want. They're more into the instant gratification than a long-term relationship. I think I gave up because of that. I need long-term but I won't push for it, ever again." She tossed her tumbling hair. "I'm not a one-night-stand kind of girl, Clint."

He nodded, his stormy eyes going soft. "I kind of figured that out already."

And he hadn't pressured her last night. That had been another revelation. Victoria had chalked that up to her not being his type and him just having some fun because he was bored. Or maybe because he really wasn't all that attracted to her?

She lifted her chin, defiant against his usual mode of operation. "I like being single and on my own."

"But you were going to get married. You came close."

She nodded. "I did. I loved Aaron but I wanted a career of my own and he wanted me to stay on the ranch and raise his babies."

Clint frowned, another remorseful look moving like a shadow through his eyes. "You don't like babies?"

"I love children. I just wasn't ready to start having them right away. We argued about that constantly before the wedding and I guess he decided for both of us that it wouldn't work. He claimed I wanted a career more than I wanted a family." She shrugged. "Funny, but I thought I could have both."

Clint squeezed her fingers. "You should be able to do

that and if Aaron couldn't understand that concept, well, then good riddance to him."

"But he left me at the church. The church, with flowers and candles and a cake and our families. It was awful." She pushed at her hair. "I haven't felt...the same about anything long-term since." No, that wasn't true. A few months later, just for a few minutes during one long night on the town with her insistent friends, she'd felt pretty good again. One kiss from a cowboy had brought her to life. One kiss from this cowboy—this misguided, mis-understood cowboy.

No. Don't make excuses for him.

But she'd felt something that night with Clint. The way he'd kissed her had given her hope that she would find love again. But he'd only laughed and walked away. Another slap in her face.

Still, she'd been content since then, being single and free. Her life had moved on and her job had become her life. Up until now, that had been enough.

Hadn't it? Or had she just been fooling herself? Had she pushed to have him on the show to get even with him? Or had she lobbied for him to be the star because she wanted to explore her feelings and see what happened?

A little of both, she had to admit.

She couldn't let him do that to her again, even if it was a bit unfair to pin so much hope on one man and one kiss. All this time, she'd blamed Clint for being a player, when really, he hadn't played her at all. She'd been so caught up in the dream of what a perfect relationship should be she'd forgotten that one kiss didn't make for a lifetime commitment.

She needed to remember that now and let it be her mantra.

"I need to go," she said, determined to nip this in the bud before she got caught up in something she couldn't control. It wouldn't do to keep this going, whether he was serious or not. Clint was just having fun. She couldn't let herself believe anything else. She didn't want to believe anything else.

But she didn't move. Her feet didn't seem to hear what her head was telling her. Her heart pumped too fast for her to keep up with the message it was sending out.

"Stay awhile longer," Clint said in that sultry drawl, his gaze holding her there as if he could read her thoughts. "I like talking to you. I like being with you."

And she liked kissing him. Way too much.

"Besides," he said on a sheepish smile, "I have a surprise for you."

"What kind of surprise?" she asked, apprehensive and interested all at once.

"It won't be a surprise if I tell you."

"I really should get into town and get some work done."

"You can, right after the surprise."

Should she ignore that plea in his words or that plea in her heart?

But why leave in such a hurry? She had to work with him for a few more weeks so she might as well get used to his moves. She could handle this and then get on with her life when it was time to leave for good, couldn't she?

Clint didn't understand this need to have Victoria near him. He usually couldn't wait to get away from the clingy women who tried to rush him into everything from one-night stands to long-time commitments. He'd run for the hills after a couple of dates and never look back. Not fair to the women or him, but that was who he'd become. He didn't want to stop and analyze the myriad reasons he'd become gun-shy and unable to settle down. Didn't want to change, either. Changing was hard and he didn't have the courage or the inclination to start over now.

But Victoria wasn't asking anything of him. Maybe that was why he felt comfortable with her. She was strong and independent and stubborn and hardworking, traits he admired even if he couldn't claim them himself. Victoria Calhoun knew who she was and knew what she wanted out of life. She'd never once lied to him or tried to play games with him.

And she had the most kissable mouth. Each time Clint kissed her, he felt as if he'd known her forever. There was something there between them, some sort of chemistry that pulled them together. He couldn't explain it, and he'd never felt like this before so it both pleased him and confused him. New and interesting and challenging. Could that be it—this thing driving him toward her. Just a new challenge, a refreshing break from the mundane life he'd settled into? The life he was now bored with seemed tawdry and tarnished compared to the fresh-air feeling he got when he was with Victoria.

Would it hurt to try something new?

He looked at her now and decided to run with this, see where it took them. What could it matter if it didn't work out? They'd been honest with each other. They both knew the score.

But he hadn't told her everything and he didn't intend to tell her or a television audience his deepest, darkest secrets.

No one needed to know every detail of his past.

He remembered other times with other women and

how things hadn't quite worked out. But he'd put those harsh memories out of his mind, some of them buried so deep he couldn't bring them up. Not yet. Not now. Best to leave some things buried and done.

"Hey, cowboy, what are you thinking about?"

He glanced up to find Victoria staring at him with those big green eyes. "Nothing," he said, wishing he could tell her everything he wanted to say. "Just that I'm…entering new territory here—with you."

"Same here," she said, a look of relief washing over her features. "We need to take this slow. It could be happening because we've been forced together. When we're done taping, who knows?" She shrugged and her hair did that carefree tumbling thing around her shoulder. "No promises, okay?"

He should have been relieved, too, but instead he already felt that old emptiness, that old hunger eating at his insides. But he put on a good front. "Yeah, good rule. No promises. I've never been any good at keeping promises, anyway."

She shot him a shaky smile. "Okay, then. I'm going to change out of my pajamas."

"Will you stay?"

Doubt darkened her eyes to a deep green then something else flared and she perked up and smiled. "Sure. I can get some interviews with you before the picnic on Monday. Will your mom be back by then? I wanted to talk to her, too."

"My mama?" Surprised at that, Clint shook his head and hid his irritation. "I told you she's not interested. She'll probably stay away from the barbecue if she thinks she might be on camera."

Victoria looked disappointed but she nodded. "All

right. We won't force her." She turned and headed to the pool house but twisted back around. "I'll be back in a few minutes. I'd love to take that tour of the farmhouse. Maybe get some background shots for the show."

Clint stared after her, wondering if he'd underestimated Victoria Calhoun. The woman was good at her job, good at persuading camera-shy people to open up and put themselves out there for the world to see and hear. She'd won over both Susie and Tater and she almost had Denny convinced. Was his wary mother next?

He'd been so caught up in his attraction to Victoria he'd forgotten one very important possibility—she might be using him to get what she wanted. And this time, he might be the one left high and dry when it was all over.

Chapter 17

Victoria had only agreed to let him show her Mrs. Griffin's house because she'd realized something else about Clint. The man didn't want to be alone. Ever.

Excited now, she figured this would add a delicious component to the show's already growing conflict. If she could get Clint to open up on camera about why he had such a great need to be a social animal, they might get a breakthrough to ratings heaven. Getting to the heart of the matter always kept an audience riveted to the show. Her gut told her there was a lot more than a cattle ranch and oil wells to the Griffin family dynamic.

Grabbing her recorder and her notepad, she headed back out and found him waiting patiently on the small pool-house porch.

"That was fast," he said, his tone low and gravelly, his expression unusually somber.

"I'm low-maintenance," she said. "I hope you don't mind if I get some footage for exterior shots while we're walking."

"Not at all. That's your job."

His remark had tapered off on a hint of sarcasm. Did he resent her working during her alone time with him? What did it matter? She needed work to keep her mind off of him and she had to stay focused on the show. This

extra footage and a possible interview would be great
when she started editing the rough cuts. And this busy-
work would force her to keep her hands to herself and
her questions on business.

But he wants your mind on him and nothing else.

Was he the possessive type? He'd never acted that
way before. From what she'd seen and now had on tape,
Clint could walk away from any type of commitment at
the drop of a big cowboy hat.

He'd walked away from her once.

It was one stupid kiss, she told herself. *Get over it and
get on with your work.*

Ironic, how following him around for work only forced
her to get closer to him each day. But she put that out of
her mind and concentrated on getting the work done since
she'd already goofed off enough this weekend.

The morning had turned hot but a light breeze moved
over the pastures. The scent of magnolias and honeysuckle filled the air with fragrant lemony-sweet notes.
Up in the cloudless blue sky, a lone hawk soared in a
predatory circle.

"Should be a great holiday weekend in spite of the
heat," she said, hoping to engage him in conversation.

"Yep."

Okay. He wasn't the brooding, silent type. Clint always had something to say. They walked on, both quiet,
until they reached the farmhouse. Victoria turned on her
recorder and waited.

"So this is the old homestead," he said, smiling for
her camera. "My family settled here in the late eighteen
hundreds and we've been here since. A lot of history in
this house. Started out as a one-room cabin but through

the years, it's changed and grown and become pretty modern by country standards."

Victoria zoomed the camera's lens out for a wide shot that centered on the big white house. A deep wrap-around porch opened around the back and continued on one side to the whole front of the house. A second floor had a smaller porch. Lace curtains hung from several of the windows and white rocking chairs graced the gray-planked porches. Red geraniums and flowing ferns sat in colorful pots along the porches. She couldn't have asked for a more American home to showcase for the Fourth.

"It looks as if it came out of a Norman Rockwell painting," she said, snapping pictures with both her video and still camera. "It's so beautiful."

Clint glanced back at his house. "Yep. Kinda opposite of what my mama calls my monstrosity across the pond."

"I like your house," Victoria replied. "But I have to admit I love this one."

"Most folks who visit love the old house. They find it quaint and charming. They like how we all live here together." He shook his head. "Sometimes I wonder about that."

Victoria gave him a nod of approval. "It sure shocked me to find out you had family living here. The rumors—"

"Suggested that I only allowed a lot of women and party people into my humble home."

"Yes."

"The world will see a whole new Clint Griffin," he retorted. "As I said, there's a lot of history surrounding this land." He let out a sigh. "Maybe that's the real reason I decided to be on your show. I wanted to set the record straight. I do like to have fun and I love women—can't help that. But I also love my family and my home. My heritage means a lot to me so I've tried hard to protect it and do right by my family. I want you to work on what we talked about—showcasing one of the organizations my family founded and continues to support."

"I can do that," Victoria said, glad to see his eyes twinkling again. "What do you suggest?"

"Remember I mentioned the Griffin Horse Therapy Ranch? We call it the Galloping Griffin."

She nodded and she'd done her homework. "Sure. It's a small ranch near Mesquite that allows ill or traumatized children to learn to ride horses. Animal therapy, right?"

"Yes. That's it. We started that organization."

The man was just full of surprises. She'd read that *he* had started the therapy ranch. Him alone. "I've heard a lot of great things about the Griffin Horse Therapy Ranch," she said. "I'd love to include that in the show." She shook her head. "But you started it, and you don't seem to want to take credit."

"Why would I?" He glanced back at the farmhouse. "I brag enough as it is. Some things need to speak for themselves."

Victoria's heart got all soft and pudding-like. "I'd love to hear all about your work with the ranch and about the history of your family," she said, her mind and heart deep into what had made this house a home. "We can showcase your Texas roots here and then do a segment at the therapy ranch to add to what we have."

His expression changed to relaxed and relieved, but he didn't seem so hot on the idea. "You don't want too much of that boring stuff on the show, though. Where's the drama?"

"Drama is everywhere," she said, too caught up in the image of this house and the amazing organization he'd mentioned to listen to his sarcasm. "You can't tell me that your family history didn't have some drama."

"Yes, to hear my parents and grandparents talk. And that's sure still true around here." He looked up at the house. "I've seen enough chaos and drama to last me a lifetime."

Victoria itched to hear his true story. "Really now? You need to let your audience in on some of that, because trust me, it won't be boring at all."

He gave her a hard-edged stare. "I thought that's what I was already doing, but I reckon pool parties and bar fights aren't the only drama in Dallas."

Victoria decided not to push on that for now. If she kept him talking about the house maybe the conversation would organically turn to the stories behind the lace curtains.

She walked up to the house and sat on a step.

"Beautiful," she said, wishing she had time to really research the history of this place. Wishing she had time to hear about the real hard-won fortunes of this family—covered wagons, hostile natives, danger at every turn. Real cowboys, real men doing what they had to do to survive and real women doing what they had to do to keep up and find their place.

"My parents lived here together and raised us here. I built my house after I made it big in rodeo and sold a few songs to Nashville. But my folks loved this house. It'll always be part of the Sunset Star. I promised my daddy that before he died."

Victoria didn't miss the hint of regret and grief she'd heard in his words. Her pulse raced, giving her a buzz of awareness that she only got when she felt a big revelation about to hit the air. But she kept things light.

"It's a perfect backdrop for our viewers to see how you were raised. I'm sure they'd love to hear about your childhood."

"Yep, I guess they'll wonder where my parents went wrong," he quipped with a classic Clint Griffin grin.

Glad he was willing to talk about the house and his family, Victoria went on with her easy questions. "So tell me about the picnic. I know it's an annual thing but this year will be unique since we're here taping. How will that go with your family? Do you expect things to be any different?"

He shrugged, gave her a quick smile. "It's a big Texas-type affair with the usual—roasted meat, lots of side dishes, my mama's cream cheese pound cake with strawberries and homemade ice cream. Kind of tame, so don't get your hopes up on something scandalous happening there."

Scandal? She wanted his kind of scandals, didn't she? "But you did invite some of your partying friends, right?"

"They'll come later in the evening," he replied, his eyes on the farmhouse. "My mama doesn't allow such shenanigans when she's around. She has a strict policy against too much drinking and carousing that even my daddy had to honor and respect."

Victoria wanted to zoom in on his parents so she could understand him better, too. "You never talk about your dad much," she said. "What was he like?"

Clint turned from the porch and tossed Victoria a harsh glare. "Is this for the show? Or do you really want to know?"

So he *was* a tad upset that she'd combined work with play. Too bad. She had to put her work first to protect herself and she couldn't help that his mood had changed.

"I really want to know," she admitted. "But if you don't mind a few mentions of him on the show, that can't hurt."

A sharp chuckle rumbled in his throat. "Nah, can't hurt. Not at all." He lifted his hands to the sky then dropped them back down. "I reckon I might as well get it all out in the open."

Victoria heard the anger in his words. She'd obviously hit on a sore subject. She didn't say anything but sat there, hoping he'd tell her something she didn't already know.

Clint looked over at her and reached out a hand. "First, give me that video recorder."

"What? Why?" Victoria didn't want to let go of her crutch. That little machine kept an element of work in this intimate stroll. But Clint wasn't having any of that.

He took the handheld recorder away and placed it up on the porch, out of her reach. "Not everything I say to you has to go on the show, understand?"

She nodded, her hands itching to get her recorder back. She'd never seen this flare of anger in him, at least not to this extent. She wanted to get that emotion on the air. She also needed the protection of having her camera as a shield.

Right now, however, she wanted to know what had really made Clint Griffin the man he'd become. And she wanted to know for herself. She placed her notepad on the porch step. "Okay, so talk. No cameras and no notes."

Clint glanced down at her then sat next to her on one of the wooden steps. "What can I say about my daddy?"

Before Victoria could prod him, the back door opened and his mother stepped out, her regal expression sharpened with disdain. "You'd better not say a word about your daddy. I won't have my personal life spread across the universe because of some distasteful reality show."

Then she turned and went back into the house and slammed the door.

Clint glanced over at Victoria, his face stony. "I guess you won't be getting an interview with her after all." Then he leaned close and whispered, "And I'll have to save your surprise for later. I'm pretty sure our tour ends here, darlin'."

Clint walked Victoria back to the pool house, his mind on his mother's anger. Would she ever forgive him? Would any of them ever forgive him? How could he expect them to forgive him when he couldn't even get over the past himself.

"You've been kind of quiet all morning," Victoria said after they'd reached her door. "Is there something going on that you haven't clued me in on?"

He wanted to shout that some things had to remain private, but instead he grinned at her. "I never intended to clue you in on anything. I thought the whole point of this show was to have a little fun and make fools of ourselves doing it." Then he turned somber again. "And I guess y'all want to expose me for what I am."

"Fun is good," she said, a worried look clouding her eyes. "Drama, fun, unanswered questions, a little mystery and a strong conflict—those elements make a good reality show. It's not so much about exposing you as showing your everyday life."

Clint got how she'd glossed over the whole situation. They were here to expose him and everyone knew that. His family worried about that very thing.

He leaned close and enjoyed the fresh-air scent of her hair. "I told you we have a lot of drama around here, but we're not used to airing it on national television. So bear with us, darlin'. You'll get what you need for the show."

She turned to give him an eye-to-eye stare. "And what about me, Clint? Will I get the answers I need for me?"

"What other questions do you want answered?" he asked, wondering if he was already in too deep with this woman.

Victoria didn't know how to answer that question. Nor did she know how to ask the right questions to get him to really open up. And to get him to confide in her as a friend or maybe more.

"I guess I'm wondering if you're just messing with my head because I'm an easy target."

He gave her a surprised stare. "You, an easy target? Honey, you're harder to pin down than a scared calf. You shy away from talking about yourself but you thrive on getting the goods on everyone else."

Squirming underneath that condemning analogy, she shook her head. "That's my job—to make our talent talk, to get to what makes people tick."

He put a hand in her hair and gave her a heated gaze, his eyes going dark with some emotion she couldn't recognize. "You don't need to know what makes me tick, not when it's just you and me. And you won't get everything out of me for this show, either. A man's got his limits, Victoria."

Her own anger and frustration bubbled to the surface like thick, murky oil. "Is that a threat, Clint? Do you have a limit on how long you can string a woman along before she gives in to all that charm? Is that what you're trying to tell me?"

Before she could move, he grabbed her cameras and

her notes and tossed them on a chair, then pushed her back against the door and slammed his mouth down on hers.

The kiss took Victoria's breath right out of her body and replaced her need to breathe with a white-hot need to only breathe when she was in his arms. Her logical mind told her that would be impossible, but her heart hammered away at making it a reality. Her reality.

When he finally lifted his mouth away and stared down at her, she leaned her head against the door to gain some strength and take in air. "Clint—"

"I know, darlin'," he said, his hand moving down her cheek with a lingering touch, "we shouldn't be doing this. I shouldn't want you the way I want you. We're working together on this show and it's your job, your passion, to make this the best show possible. Me, I just signed up because I'm bored and because I want Tater to have a good future—"

He stopped, shock and realization filling his eyes. "I want my whole family to have a secure future."

Victoria didn't know what to say, what to do. "But you didn't have to be on the show. You told me you're okay, that the ranch is okay. Clint, what's going on?"

He backed up, his eyes holding hers. "Let's just stick to the plan," he finally said. "I need to do that."

"What do you mean?"

He gave her a look full of regret and resolve. "You're right. I shouldn't be messing with you like this. I know better. I'm sorry."

"But—"

Victoria couldn't breathe. She hadn't imagined that being without him would cut the very air out of her lungs, but just watching him walk away left her frozen and cold.

What just happened? she thought, her gaze following him as he stalked into the house. She'd been on the brink, on the cusp of giving in to her fierce need to open her heart to him. And now he was the one being all noble and logical and sanctimonious?

Had he planned it that way? Had he somehow inadvertently managed to do it again? To walk away from her without another thought? Or had his mother's harsh words caused him to back off?

No, she told herself as she hurried into the pool house and got into a long, hot shower. *No,* this man, the man she'd kissed last night and today, was different. He had a soul and he had a thing for her, no matter what or no matter who got in the way. Amazingly, she'd seen it there in his eyes, that hunger that she could feel inside her own heart. Or had she just imagined that he had this same overwhelming, consuming need?

What did it matter? She had a job to do and he had his reasons for backing off. He'd mentioned Tater. Victoria knew he loved the teenager and since he was the only male in this household, maybe he'd only meant that his sister and her daughter depended on him. He repeatedly told her that he wanted the money to go to his niece, so she'd have a secure future. But wouldn't he also want to share that with Susie and his mother?

Susie is getting her own salary, Victoria reminded herself. Much less than Clint, but nothing to sneeze at. Denny and his mother didn't want to be on the show. If he didn't need the money, maybe Trish was the obvious choice. Because something sure had him walking away instead of telling the truth.

Chapter 18

Victoria managed to get in her car and leave the premises without looking back. She should be relieved that Clint had finally seen the light and backed off. She'd wanted that the whole time.

Yeah, right.

She'd wanted the man to kiss her, hold her, whisper in her ear the way he'd done that night long ago. She'd wanted him to remember her, to be attracted to her, to care about her.

He does.

Yeah, he does, but now he's gone all gun-shy. Was that why he pushed women away, why he never made a commitment?

And even if he did feel something for her now, how long would that last once the show was wrapped up and done?

Based on his track record, not very long. He had an aversion to settling down. Or maybe to just settling. She wished she could figure him out, but right now she needed to figure out how the story arc for these episodes would pan out.

She didn't want to care about Clint but somehow after being around him for longer than a couple of hours, she'd seen so many different sides of the man she wasn't sure who the real Clint Griffin was anyway. Great for the subject of the show. Not so great for the woman who'd come here to capture him and have him skewered like a jackrabbit.

"You knew not to dabble where you shouldn't," she told herself as she headed into the city. The radio blasted a country song and the heat of midday blasted the battered leather seats of her tiny car. She'd never felt so exhausted and downtrodden.

But she could only blame herself. She'd fallen into the same old pattern of getting too involved with a man she shouldn't give a second glance. Working alone inside the cool, quiet studio building should soothe her nerves and get her back on track. So she moved through the quiet, empty hallways and let out a sigh of relief when she walked into her cluttered office. After reading two messages Nancy had left, and listening to several voice mails, she got herself a soda and rubbed her hands together. Time to make the magic happen.

But the minute she got settled in the dark production room, her cell phone rang.

Aaron.

Just what she needed. Only because she was bruised and battered, Victoria answered, ready to do battle. She could take out her frustrations on her ex-fiancé. "Hello?"

"Where are you?"

She glared at the phone. "None of your business."

"Look, we need to talk. I've heard rumors about you and Clint Griffin."

Shocked, Victoria rubbed her suddenly throbbing forehead. She would really have to be more careful. "What kind of rumors?"

"That you two are doing a lot more than just what's scripted on the daily hot-sheets."

Victoria gripped the desk in front of her. "I have no idea what you mean and again, what I do now is not any of your business."

"I care about you," he said on a long whine. "I made a bad mistake, letting you go."

"More than one?" she asked, memories now shouting out what her mind hadn't comprehended when they were together. He had never wanted to marry her anyway and he'd treated her horribly. Now he'd hit bottom on the playing-the-field game and so he thought he wanted her back. But he was still trying to control her. A good lesson for her to remember with Clint, too.

"I shouldn't have walked away," Aaron said. "Can we…maybe start over?"

"Are you kidding me?" Victoria wished she'd ignored his call. She wished she'd never gone out with him, but he'd been so sweet and considerate, until she'd fallen for him. Then he started changing. He'd fooled her once, but not again. "Aaron, we are over. We've been over for years now. Why this sudden change of heart?"

"I miss you."

The whine in his words was comical. Had he practiced that line all day? "You miss having someone to boss around."

"I didn't boss you. I tried to offer you advice. Is that so wrong?"

"It is when it turns into criticism and condemnation and you want me to give up my life so I can cater to your every whim." She pushed up out of her chair. "I'm doing okay now. I'm happy on my own. And I have a ton of work to do."

She hit the end button before he could respond. When her phone started ringing again, she put it on mute and went to work on the rough cuts of the first couple of shows. Soon she was immersed in edits and dailies, notes on the character arcs and the big picture of how this season of the show should end. Right now, she didn't have a clue, but she had a feeling she could find some more interesting tidbits from Clint's past if she pushed. They'd do the sweet and noble episode, showcasing the history of the Sunset Star, coupled with the philanthropic work at the Griffin Horse Therapy Ranch, too. And then they'd need to end with a big reveal of something no one knew about Clint Griffin. Something a bit scandalous but not too overpowering. Enough to close the season on a cliffhanger so the show might get picked up again in the fall. And Clint might continue to be the star.

But did she want to push that far, go that deep? She wasn't sure. In fact, the only thing she knew for sure right now was how things between Clint and her should end.

Sooner than later. Like right now. She was almost relieved that Clint had walked away. Almost.

But it had to be over before Aaron started snooping around where he didn't belong and caused her even more trouble.

Later that evening, Clint walked back over to his mother's house. They needed to have a talk. After he and Victoria had ended their tour and he'd told her to go on into town and get her work done, he'd thought about going into the city to find some entertainment and some willing arms for the night. But what had once worked to soothe all of his problems now seemed shallow and just a waste of time.

But then, he'd wasted so much time already.

He took the porch steps two at a time, his boots clicking a quick *tap, tap* as they hit the planks. Then he unceremoniously opened the kitchen door and marched in.

"Mama?"

"In the den."

And didn't she sound chipper?

Clint turned past the big, wide kitchen and headed across the multi-windowed dining room to the front of the house. His mother was sitting by a window, reading a thick hardback novel. Bitsy looked up with a serene smile, but her eyes, the same gray as Clint's, didn't look all that peaceful.

"I was wondering when you'd make it back over," she said, her tone cultured and as creamy as soft butter. "I needed to apologize for my impolite behavior earlier."

Clint let out a tight little chuckle. "Yes, I guess you were worried about saving face since you weren't exactly hospitable to Victoria this morning."

His mother put down the book and touched a hand to her fluffed and sprayed grayish-white hair. "I told you from the beginning I didn't think it was wise to open yourself up to such intimate scrutiny, Clint. But it all happened so fast, I didn't have time to make myself clear and well, after that I tried not to interfere with your latest project. You went ahead with that strange show anyway, knowing that your sister and I didn't approve."

When had she ever approved of anything he'd done?

"And I told you my reasons for doing it, Mama. It's not Victoria's fault that you don't agree with me. So if you want to be rude, be rude to me. I'm used to it."

His mother narrowed her gaze, her eyes moving over his face with a haunted look. "I happen to like Victoria but that doesn't mean I want her and that little camera lurking about our home. That young woman asks way too many questions."

Clint slapped his hands against his jeans. "That young woman is doing her job and I invited her to stay on the property so we could work together and get this over with. We'll only be filming a few episodes for the summer."

"You don't see it, do you?" his mother asked.

"Oh, I see that you and Denny have it in for me and the whole crew. I see that you disapprove of Susie being involved, too."

Bitsy gave him an indulgent smile then shook her head. "You wouldn't know the truth if it spit in your eye, son. You saw a pretty woman and you went after her. Other than being puzzled since she's not your usual flavor of the month, I'm not so old that *I* can't *see* that with my own eyes."

Clint paced in front of the sterile, empty fireplace. "I won't deny that I like Victoria. She's different and she's interesting, but I agreed to do the show for other reasons." Then he added for himself, more than his mother, "Besides, you're right. She's not my type."

Bitsy put her hands together over her skirt. "Of course."

Her jewel-encased fingers winked at him, mocking him with expensive, shining beams that made him feel like he was caught in a too-bright spotlight. "You say you want to make sure Denny and Trish are taken care of. Clint, you know full well that your daddy made preparations for that way before you had a worry."

"I have a worry now, Mother."

"Oh, you must be very angry with me. You only call me 'Mother' when you're mad."

"I am mad," he replied. Turning to the mantel, he placed his hands on the rich pine wood and looked down at the black hole where a roaring fire would burn later in the year. "I'm mad, frustrated, tired and wishing I'd had the good sense to do what was right long ago."

"So you're trying to make up for that now?"

"I will always try to make up for that, yes."

He turned, put his hands on his hips. "But I'll never be able to change the past and you will never be able to forgive me my trespasses, and we both know it."

"We don't discuss such things," his mother reminded him. "And you have no need to ask for my forgiveness. We handled the situation and that's that. I only worry because your friend seems to want to dig too deeply into our private affairs."

"No," Clint said, a steam-hot fog covering his brain, "you only worry because you have to put on that serene front you've managed to hide behind for so many years. Who's gonna give you forgiveness, Mama?"

Bitsy stiffened in her high-back chair but her expression was filled with regret. "This isn't about forgiveness. It's about doing what's right. You need to leave well enough alone, son."

Clint looked down at his slender, regal mother and wondered how many secrets she held in her heart. Besides his, of course.

"I've done that for years," he said. "And it just ain't working for me anymore."

"Isn't," Bitsy corrected. "You need to use your best grammar, even on a reality show."

Clint shook his head and smiled then walked over and leaned down to kiss his mother. "Wouldn't want to embarrass you by using bad language, Mama."

Then he turned and walked out.

Two hours later, Clint got in his sports car and headed for Dallas. His mother was off at a movie with a friend. Susie was off with her new boyfriend. Denny was home alone working on her scrapbook and Tater had been allowed to go the big party with Buster so she was enjoying the holiday weekend out on the Trinity River with her friends.

Clint was alone. Again.

After he'd given her what one might call a quick brush-off, Victoria had slipped away and probably wouldn't be back until the big picnic and barbecue Monday night.

He was bored. And spoiling for a fight.

So he put the top down and let the hot summer wind hit his face and wondered once again how his happy, empty home had now become progesterone central. Too many female hormones in one place could drive a man crazy.

Well, he'd invited them all to live with him, but why? What had he been thinking?

You felt guilty and lonely. Plain and simple.

Guilty that he'd never found a real job. Guilty that his daddy had expected more from him and had been disappointed until the day he died. Guilty that he'd done some things that he wasn't proud of. Guilty that his sister's husband had left her for another woman and she had no place to live. Guilty that his baby sister had lost her job and had to tuck tail and face their formidable mother.

Guilty as charged.

Lonely. Penance for feeling so guilty. And that, nosy audience, was why he kept people around him all the time.

Sure, he shouldn't feel that way, since most of those

things had been beyond his control and some of them hadn't been his fault at all, but he'd promised his daddy he'd take care of the family and he'd done a lousy job from the get-go.

He zoomed up the interstate and headed for his favorite honky-tonk on the outskirts of the city. The parking lot was packed with pickup trucks and convertibles, a sure sign that the holiday Saturday night was in full swing.

Clint rolled out of his low-riding car and headed inside, intent on losing himself in a bottle of tequila. After all, as the song went, he had a lot to drink about.

At around eleven that night, Victoria ran out of pretzels and chocolate after she'd foraged through both the snack room and several nearby desks. Time to go home and order either a pizza or Chinese. Or maybe just crash in front of the television with some ice cream. A sappy movie would suit her mood just fine.

She hurried through the dark parking garage and worried at the wisdom of being alone in this building on a weekend night. But the garage had security cameras and an adequate guard. She'd made it to her car when she heard footsteps behind her.

"Vic?"

She knew that voice. Aaron. Trying to stay calm, she hit the unlock button on her key and opened the door of her car. With her phone in her hand, she turned, ready to get in and lock the door if Aaron tried anything.

"Aaron, what are you doing here?"

"I wanted to talk to you. I need you to listen—"

Her phone buzzed, still in silent mode, and scared her so much she jumped. When she glanced down at the caller ID, she wanted to cry. Clint.

Should she answer and ask him for help? Or should she let it ring and try to get away from Aaron?

She didn't have time to decide. Aaron twisted the phone out of her hand and stared at the screen. "Clint Griffin." He sent her an accusing glare. "So, nothing's going on between you two, huh?"

"Give me my phone," she shouted, hoping the aging guard at the gate around the corner would hear. If she could get to her purse, she'd pepper-spray Aaron and get away from him.

The phone went to voice mail but Aaron held it away. "You lied to me."

"I did not," she said, anger overtaking her fear. "I told you what I do now is not any of your business. If you don't give me back my phone, I'll either scream for help or I'll kick you where the sun doesn't shine and get it back myself."

"Whoa, I'm scared," he said, his words slurring.

Her phone started buzzing again.

Aaron laughed and held it up. "I'll talk to him."

When he turned away, Victoria reached in her purse and found her pepper spray in the outside pocket. Then she honked the horn with the other hand.

Aaron pivoted and shouted, "Stop. I just want to talk to you and I don't need him calling you while I'm doing it. I want us to have another try, Victoria."

"Not anymore," she said, the spray aimed at his face.

He screamed and dropped down. The phone fell out of his hands and skittered against the concrete.

Victoria grabbed her phone, got in the car and peeled rubber to get away. At the gate, she reported him to the guard. "I don't know how he got in."

"You'll need to wait to talk to the police," the guard said. "Meantime, I'll alert security."

Later, as she drove home with shaking hands, Victoria wondered if someone had given Aaron access. But who would want to stir up trouble like that?

Someone who wants to keep this show up and running.

And that could include just about anyone who worked for the show...or someone who wanted to stay on the show.

Chapter 19

Still shaking when she got to her apartment, Victoria immediately hurried to her second shower of the day. She really wanted to wash away the remnants of this night, especially having to explain to the Dallas police why she'd felt threatened by her ex.

Aaron wouldn't be bothering her again anytime soon. She'd agreed not to press charges and he'd angrily agreed to quit pestering her. Victoria hoped the threat of jail time would calm him down.

After she ran the hot water until she'd steamed up the whole bathroom, she finally turned off the shower and toweled herself dry. Throwing on an old Lucille Ball T-shirt and some baggy shorts, she went to her take-out menu and ordered Chinese. Then she opened a bottle of wine.

"Home at last."

She sank down on the couch and stared at the silent television. Why did she even care about any of this? After working her tail off to make this show better, what thanks did she get? Her salary was pretty good, but could be better. Her boss loved her work to the point that he could sit back and let her have free reign over most of their projects, but he tiptoed around giving her a salary increase to go with that responsibility. Her personal life was a joke.

She used work to keep her busy and normally, that system suited her. But lately, not so much.

But tonight, sitting here remembering how Clint had kissed her and treated her like a real woman as compared to how she'd just had a scary run-in with her ex, she wished she could just go far away from *Cowboys, Cadillacs and Cattle Drives.* Forever. She had no business feeling this way about Clint. It was dangerous, going down this road.

Her thoughts went back to the old homestead. She'd love to do a straight historical document on that house and the history of the Sunset Star Ranch. But Bitsy Griffin didn't really seem ready to commit to any television, especially the documentary and tell-us-the-story-of-your-life kind. In spite of that, Victoria found herself making notes about the house with each sip of wine. Before her dinner had arrived, she'd mapped out several segments for the "feel-good" episode.

When her phone buzzed, she grabbed it to see if Aaron was calling her again—maybe from jail. Did she have to get a restraining order?

But she saw Clint's number.

Giving in to an aching need that was having a tug-of-war with her hurting heart, she answered on the third ring. "What?"

"Well, hello to you, too, darlin'."

Great, another drunk cowboy. "Clint, what do you want?"

"You," he replied then went silent.

In that moment of supreme silence, Victoria's breath hitched and left her body. But her brain came to the rescue with a glaring neon warning that said, "Don't do it, girl."

"We're done, remember? You told me that this morning."

"I lied. Was in a bad mood."

What was it with men who suddenly had a change of heart? Oh, wait, they didn't actually have a heart, but they were very fickle and wishy-washy and unable to make long-term commitments. They wanted to suddenly be with you, but they had stipulations that sucked the life right out of you.

She sat up, wishing she'd thrown her phone out the car window. "Where are you?"

He laughed. "Blue Spruce. I mean, Blue Goose. Or Cooked Goose." More husky laughter and some feminine giggling and shrills in the background.

Her heart doing a fast drop, Victoria stood and started pacing. "Why are you calling me?"

"Told you, I want to see you. Where do you live?"

"You can't come here," she said, her mind humming with regret. "Let me talk to the bartender."

"What? Why him? He's fifty and bald."

"Just let me talk to him, Clint."

After more chatter and some giggles and a fumbling sound, a sane person named Jasper came on the phone and promised her he wouldn't let Clint drive. "Hey, the man's bringing in the party crowd so we don't want him to leave. Even got some television cameras here."

Television cameras?

"Put Mr. Griffin back on the phone, please."

She waited for Clint's voice. He laughed his way to the phone. "Don't you just love Jasper?"

"Yeah, he's great. Listen, Clint. Can you hear me?"

"Sure, suga'. Hear you but want to see you."

"I'm coming there," she replied. "Don't leave, okay?"

"Won't leave you again, ever."

Victoria reminded herself that was the liquor talking. "Just stay there. I'll see you soon."

Hurrying, she pushed at memories of the first time she'd been in a bar with Clint. He'd been drunk that night, too. And he'd whispered sweet nothings in her ear. Sweet words but words meaning nothing.

So why was she so worried about him tonight? She knew why in her heart, but as always, work issues fueled her rational decision.

Because if Clint went down in his own fire, she wanted to get him on tape. She had to find out who had shown up with a camera and she'd have to find a way to get her hands on that footage and use it for the show.

She got her stuff and started toward the door. When she opened it, a redheaded delivery boy was standing there with her Chinese food. She paid him, grabbed the bag and set it on the kitchen counter.

She was starving but her food would have to wait.

Clint squinted and searched the big long room.

Had he just talked to Victoria, or had he only imagined that conversation? And who was that over in the corner with a camera? Ethan? With his sister Susie?

"Hey," Clint called, glad to see a familiar face from the show. But he didn't remember a taping tonight. And how did Ethan know he was here? And why was Susie hanging on Ethan's arm? He tried to make his way toward the camera, but the crowd was getting kind of rowdy and it was hard to breathe or get anywhere without stopping to dance. When a cute waitress brought him another beer and another tequila shot, he chuckled and gave her a nice tip and decided to dance his way toward the camera.

A few minutes later, he glanced back at Ethan and saw Victoria standing there, staring at him.

"Victoria," he called, pushing to get to her. Somebody elbowed him in the stomach and his full mug went up, spilling beer on the head of a big, brooding biker covered in mean-looking tattoos.

And after that, things got ugly.

The Tex-Mex cantina was packed to the rafters with pretty people having a very good time. Between the music and the crowd noise, Victoria found it hard to think, let alone find Clint.

But then, all she had to do was follow the noise toward the dance floor, where he seemed to be holding court. She was headed that way when she saw Ethan standing in a corner, his camera on his shoulder, a big grin on his face. Even more surprising, Susie Griffin was there, too, and dressed to impress. When she saw Victoria, she took off toward the ladies' room. What was going on? Victoria hurried to reach Ethan, saw Clint staring at her, then pivoted back toward Ethan.

"What are you doing?"

He pointed to the dance floor, his camera braced against his shoulder. Susie was nowhere to be found.

Victoria whirled around toward the ruckus on the dance floor and saw a giant of a man slam his fist into Clint's face. And Ethan was taping the whole fiasco.

And who, she wondered, had given him the go-ahead on that?

"Thanks for bailing me out," Clint said two hours later. "I don't know where my car is."

"Your car is still at the cantina," she replied, her mind

full of turmoil while she drove through dark streets. "We'll get it later."

Later, after he'd sobered up.

"So I reckon I'll make the morning news," he said. "Again."

"You're already streaming on all the social media networks." Any publicity was good publicity when it came to their show. People behaving badly always drew attention. She should be thrilled, but she felt sick to her stomach. Ethan had left right after recording the fight and the arrest. She really wanted to ask him why he'd been there with Susie and who had given him clearance to tape at that particular bar.

Glancing over at yet another shiner coloring Clint's left eye, she wondered what to do with him. "Do you want me to take you home?"

He sat back against the seat and closed his eyes. "No."

"Where do you want to go?"

He turned and stared over at her with his one good eye. "Your place."

Victoria hit a hand on the steering wheel and shook her head. "No. Not a good idea."

He nodded. "Best idea. I got too much trouble back home." Then he leaned close. "I need a place to lay low."

"And sleep it off?"

He nodded, closed his eyes. "Yeah, need to sleep off about fifteen years. Tired."

Victoria wanted to reach over and push his curling hair off his bruised brow, but her white-knuckled grip on the steering wheel kept her from doing that. She almost questioned him about those troubles but that would be taking advantage of his still-a-little-drunk state of mind.

Goodness, she had somehow grown a conscience.

She didn't dare touch him so the only thing she could do was go home and take him with her. She parked the car and took another minute to study him. The man was still good-looking, even with the fragments of a rough night and too much liquor coloring him in shades of amber and ash.

"Okay, you can do this," she whispered to herself. But she wasn't sure how to get him out of the car and into her apartment upstairs.

When he heard the passenger door open, he sat straight up and said, "Hey, I'm starving."

"I have Chinese takeout. I'll heat it up when we get upstairs," she told him as she urged him out of the car and set his battered hat down on his head.

Clint grinned, lifted his hat in a sloppy salute and leaned heavily on her arm all the way to the elevator. While he tried to nuzzle her neck, she managed to hold on to her tote and get the door open, but she had to keep him propped up with her lower body so she could block his fall. Clint took that as an invitation to get close.

When they slid inside, all bags and arms and legs, Clint kicked the door shut and gave her a lopsided grin. "I'm in Victoria Calhoun's apartment. And I smell Chinese food." He gave her a peck on the nose then spun around and headed toward the couch.

Where he dropped facedown and promptly fell asleep.

Clint woke up and opened one eye, the smell of stale Chinese food making his already roiling stomach protest with a recoiling velocity. The other eye didn't seem to be working. Every muscle in his face screamed in pain, so he lay there for a minute and prayed he'd just die and get it over with. The smell of coffee prompted him to lift his head and that's when the pounding started.

He wasn't sure where he was at first but when he saw Victoria moving around the tiny kitchen in a long sleeveless dress that looked floral and bohemian, he thought maybe he'd already died and gone to heaven.

She was barefoot, her hair tugged up in a loose kind of crazy bun. She looked so good, he shut his eyes to keep dreaming. But the sun was coming in through the big window over the kitchen sink.

This wasn't a dream.

"What's going on?" he said, but the question was low and husky and he wasn't sure she'd heard.

She turned, her face devoid of makeup, her eyebrows lifting in two graceful arches. "How's the brawler this morning?"

Clint squinted and made a slow effort to sit up straight. "Not so good. My head feels like a truck hit it."

"Not a truck," she said, bringing dry toast and steaming coffee. "It was a biker. A really big biker who didn't like having beer spilled on his Faith Hill T-shirt."

Glad he didn't have to stand, Clint had vague flashes of clarity from the night before. Music, dancing, girls everywhere and... Victoria. Victoria at the police station.

"What'd I do this time?" he said, reaching for the coffee.

She lifted a laptop off the coffee table and sat down beside him, the motion of her movements grating on his nerves like steel hitting steel. "Why don't you take a look yourself?"

Clint sipped the coffee while grainy, static images of him laughing and drinking and, ultimately, getting in a big brawl, flashed across the screen.

"Cell phones and online videos," he said wryly. "Gotta love 'em."

"Yes. Especially when people sell what they tape to the highest bidder." She closed the laptop and stared over at him with those expressive green eyes. "But hey, the first episode of the show featuring you has now been moved up by two weeks. It airs in a couple of weeks. My boss wants to have a premiere party in downtown Dallas to keep the momentum going."

Clint stared at her as the reality of his reality show hit him with all the force of that biker. "I guess this is finally happening, isn't it?"

"Yep. Get ready to rumble." She went back into the kitchen and grabbed her coffee mug then came back and sat down across from him, not on the sofa by him, where he wanted her. "We've got reporters camping outside and I've called the ranch. Your sister Denise is very upset because the press has been blocking the front gate all morning. And you made the morning news."

"I'm sorry," he said, the words coming too quickly for his messed-up system.

"Oh, don't apologize," she retorted. "Samuel gave Ethan a promotion on the spot when he saw the footage. This brawl far outshines the little scuffle you had with my ex way back, oh, about three days ago."

"A lifetime ago," he replied, wishing he could get things together. "So I guess me acting like a crazed bull is fodder for the show, right?"

"That's how it works in my world," she said, her eyes going blank.

He tried to stand but changed his mind. "Thanks for letting me sleep on the couch. I hope I wasn't too wasted. I mean, did I do something I need to apologize for?"

"You were a perfect drunk. Passed out and slept right here all night. I had to eat the egg rolls and stir-fried shrimp all by myself."

He tried to clear his head. "Did I snore?"

She smiled at that. "No."

Now that he was feeling almost human, Clint leaned back and glanced around. "A studio loft. Very nice. Lots of windows." He blinked at her. "Lots of you."

"It's my little spot of heaven."

He could tell she wasn't sure what to do about him so he ate a couple chunks of toast and drained the coffee. "I could use a shower."

She pointed to a folded silk screen. "Bathroom is that way. Clean towels in the basket by the shower."

He found the bathroom and the towels and took a quick shower then found some mouthwash and combed his hair with his fingers. Putting back on his jeans but deciding to burn the bloody T-shirt, he emerged a little later to find her tapping away on her laptop.

But when she looked up and saw him, her eyes flared hot and her fingers stopped moving. She dropped the laptop onto the table, a look of fear and anticipation coloring her eyes.

Clint took that little moment of immobility to cross the room and grab her and pull her into his arms. He kissed her with a pent-up need that made his head pound with a different kind of pain. But he couldn't stop to save himself.

She didn't try to stop him, either, to save herself.

He finally stood back and looked at her, his hand on her hair. "Victoria, I—"

Then something flashed outside the window. Groaning, he glanced around, the bright light hurting his already hurting head. "What was that?"

Victoria pulled away, a look of shock and dread in her eyes. "A camera," she said, rushing to the window.

He followed her and saw a photographer leaving the balcony of the apartment directly across from hers. "Busted," Clint said, turning to stare at her.

"Worse than busted," she replied. "More like...fired."

Chapter 20

"They can't fire you for kissing me," Clint said, his feet braced apart with battle intent.

"Yes, they can," Victoria replied. She went about grabbing things to stuff into her tote bag. "I have to go to the office to do damage control."

"I'll go with you."

She whirled back around. "No, you won't. And don't you have a shirt?"

He glanced down at his stomach. "It was all bloody and yes, I'm going with you."

She ran to her closet and pulled out an oversize T-shirt she'd won from a radio station and used as a sleep shirt. "Put this on and call a cab. I can't be seen with you anymore."

Clint stared down at the black shirt then tossed it over his head. "You have to be seen with me. Victoria, we're in this together and I don't care what anyone thinks—"

"That's the problem," she said, all of her pent-up doubts bubbling over like oil spewing out onto a dry field. "You don't care—about what people think, about how your family feels, about how I feel. You only care about Clint Griffin and this need to mess up everything in your life. And now you're dragging me into your problems."

"Whoa," he said, a shocked look on his face. "Where'd

that come from? I thought we'd gotten past me being a no-good, fun-loving jerk."

She stopped and took a long breath. "We have. I mean, I don't know. I can't be sure, Clint. I can't risk losing my job just because you're having a little dalliance with me."

"A dalliance? Is that what you think this is? A fling with the only available woman?"

She nodded, her worst fear now hanging out there between them. "I knew going into this that you might make a move on any one of the females on my crew. I never dreamed it would be me. I shouldn't have encouraged you."

He dropped his hands and stood there staring at her for a minute then opened his mouth to speak. But he didn't say a word. He just turned and marched to the door. "I'll see you at the picnic tomorrow." Stopping with his hand on the knob, he turned around. "And for the record, sweetheart, I didn't exactly drag you into this. I don't recall you kicking and screaming every time we've been together. You came willingly because you want your precious little show to be a big hit. And because you want me the same way I want you. But I guess you'll keep right on denying that until the show is done and over."

Appalled, Victoria stepped toward him. "Clint—"

He held up one hand. "Don't worry. I'll make sure I'm on my best behavior toward *you,* but from now on I'll give you a show you won't soon forget." His eyes shimmered with an angry gray and his expression hardened into a granite resolve. "And once we're done, Victoria, then we're finished. For good."

Victoria made her way into the studio, hoping against hope that Samuel hadn't seen that photo of her and Clint kissing. But when she walked by his door, he was there, waiting.

"V.C.," he called, his tone jovial, his expression measured. "What are you doing here on a Sunday morning?"

She halted, her head up. "Working, of course."

"C'mere," he called, waving her into his office with one hand in the air, his famous two-fingered crook motioning to her. "We need to talk."

Victoria swallowed her dread and decided to meet her fate head-on. At this point, she didn't care anymore. She'd messed up and she knew it and maybe deep down inside, she was trying to sabotage her job so she could make a clean break and just get out of Texas.

Get away from cowboys.

"Have a seat," Samuel said. "Want some coffee?"

"No." She sank down and stared over at him. "Just come out with it, Samuel."

He lifted a bushy brow and scratched his beard. "Out with what?"

Could it be that the man who knew everything about Dallas ten minutes before the world heard, did not actually know about her flirtation with the star of their show? Flirtation? Yeah, right. More like a scandalous interlude. Fodder for the show, but death for her career.

"V.C., you got something to tell me?"

"No, not really," she hedged. "What did you want with me?"

He hit his desk with his left hand and pulled out the *Dallas News*. "I see where our boy Clint got into a spot of trouble at one of the local bars last night."

Surprised, she nodded. "Ethan told me you were ecstatic. I hear he got a raise and a new title."

"Yeah, sure." Samuel grinned. "I heard you were there, too. How come you weren't the one calling this in to me?"

So he was mad at her for not doing that part of her job?

"I had to get Clint out of there," she said, not bothering to explain. "He and Susie both were there. It all happened so fast." Susie had the good sense to make herself scarce so she was certainly no help to anyone. Victoria would have a talk with her later.

"Good move." Samuel leaned back, his old chair squeaking in protest. "I tell you, this will be so good for our premiere event. Couldn't have happened at a better time."

Victoria waited for the other shoe to drop. "I'm glad you're so happy about Clint spending a night in jail," she said. And instantly regretted it.

Because Samuel was now staring at her like a hawk about to grab a june bug. "Not the whole night," he said, apparently very pleased with himself. Then he held up a picture.

The one of Clint bare-chested and kissing her in her apartment early this morning. Grainy and cheesy-looking, the photo showed worse than the truth. But then, pictures always did that and this one looked too true for her to face.

She almost blurted, "I can explain." But instead, she held her head high again and stared down her boss. "I took him to my place after I bailed him out of jail."

Samuel sat there, twiddling his thumbs for what seemed like an hour. But only a couple of seconds had passed.

"Good move, V.C.," he said, nodding his head, his eyes gleaming with that greediness she knew so well. "This is gonna make our ratings shoot sky-high. I mean, one of our story producers having a side-thing with Clint Griffin. You can't make this stuff up."

Stunned yet again, Victoria sat there staring at him. "You mean, you're not mad? I'm not fired? You...you're glad I took Clint to my place?"

"Not only that," Samuel said, getting up to come around and lean on a cluttered corner of his desk, "I'm glad we caught you kissing him. It's a gold mine of scandal and the best thing to happen since we signed the man on to the show."

"What do you mean 'we caught you kissing him'? Samuel, what do you mean?"

He laughed and clapped his hands together. "Suga', I didn't just fall off the turnip truck. Everyone on the set knows you and Clint have a thing going on. So I told them to work on playing that up, to keep tabs on you and see what developed. That Ethan, he's sure good at covert assignments."

Victoria stood up and glared at her boss. "What are you talking about? You had Ethan following me? Was that him with that camera this morning?"

"Nah," Samuel replied, still chuckling. "We got someone else to handle that since we wanted to get in real close."

"And Aaron?" She slapped a hand to her head. "You leaked this to Aaron, didn't you?"

Her boss didn't even blink. "It added to the drama. Got a buzz going."

"And brought Aaron here last night. He's stalking me now, Samuel."

Samuel made a face. "I'll take care of that, don't worry. Sorry about that."

Victoria could tell exactly how sorry he was. "And did you send Ethan to that bar? Was he also casing Clint?"

Samuel shook his head so fast his jowls bounced. "No, ma'am. Someone else called that one in. Ethan said Susan Griffin called him and told him her brother was there."

Of course she did. With a sister like that, who needed enemies? Victoria wouldn't share that little tidbit with Clint. Not yet. She didn't need him having it out with his misguided little sister. But it would serve both of them right if she provoked them on scene.

Her blood pumping too hard through her temples, Victoria sank back in her chair. "Did you release that photo to the press? Or maybe you can blame that on Susie, too." When he didn't answer, she got up again. "Did you release the photo, Samuel?"

"Of course," he said, giving her a hard-edged grin. "Why wouldn't I? This is the best thing that could happen for us, for the show. With all the exposure right before the premiere, we're bound to get a record-breaking audience for the first show. I tell you, this is gonna put us back on top. Right where we belong."

"Right where we belong," Victoria echoed. "I can't believe you did that to me."

"I didn't do anything to you, honey," he said, his tone going down an octave. "You did this to yourself and we took advantage of all the dynamics of you mixing business with pleasure."

Victoria wanted to throw something. "Business with pleasure? Are you kidding me? This whole shoot has been anything but pleasure. Torment, stress, messy, hard to deal with, you name it, I've had it and you decide in the middle of me fighting my feelings for Clint, that you'll take advantage of that and use it for the show? What about what's good for me, Samuel? I've been fighting my feelings so I could respect the boundaries we've always adhered to and you're sitting there laughing about that?"

He looked confused then he shook his head. "You need to lighten up, V.C. This isn't about you. It's about what's best for the show. You know how that works."

"Yes, I do," she said, her temperature rising with each word. "I've seen your tactics, I've learned those tactics and used them but I never liked doing it and I always knew where to draw the line and now you're telling me none of that matters as long as we bring in the ratings?"

"Oh, it matters," he retorted. "But we'll decide about that after the show."

"I get it," Victoria said, realization burning through her system. "If the show succeeds I get to keep my job. If it bombs, then I'm in trouble and I'll take the fall. Whatever it takes to save face with the network executives, right?"

"That about sums it up," Samuel admitted without batting an eye. "I didn't make that policy, but we all know it comes down to a good show with a large audience. After that, heads will roll."

"*My* head," she said, wishing she could walk away now. That would be the best thing to do but she wasn't a coward. She would finish this to the bitter end and give Samuel his ratings. And she'd make sure she brought out the worst in Clint Griffin then she'd turn in her resignation and be on her way.

"It will all work out, kid," Samuel told her. "I see a promotion in your future—more money, too. You should be happy. Your little side fling is going to save us."

Victoria went into her office and shut the door then turned to stare out at the Dallas skyline. How had her stable, boring life suddenly become a page in the gossip section of the newspaper?

And how had she managed to let her heart get stomped on yet again?

Clint didn't stomp on you.

No, he'd made his intentions pretty clear from the beginning. And she'd almost given in to his sweet whispers and his amazing kisses. Almost. But it was time to get back on track and get this show on the road.

She'd just have to find the courage to face the world… and Clint, too.

Clint glanced at the clock. Sunday evening and here he'd sat all day, going over paperwork. He loved keeping tabs on the ranch but today, he'd had a headache and a heartache.

The one woman he wanted in his life didn't want him in her life. Unless he was getting into trouble on a reality show.

Irony was a bitter pill. How many times had he walked away from someone who loved him? The first time he'd broken a woman's heart had been right out of high school. He'd been young and stupid and a coward so he followed the advice of his formidable parents and he'd given up. The consequences of his actions during that long, miserable year still haunted him today.

Then after he'd barely finished college, he'd rushed headlong into a marriage that should have never happened. Marissa Granger—socialite, accomplished horsewoman, cheerleader and all-around pain in the neck. Marissa could be a handful on a good day, but married…? She turned into a diva with demands he just couldn't meet. After three years of being wedded to her and her big, rowdy, equally demanding family, he'd once again walked away. And he'd been walking away since then. It was much easier to cut his losses and keep moving than to face what he'd lost and couldn't have back.

Would he walk away from Victoria after this fiasco was over? He couldn't decide in his head, but his heart was dead set on sticking around. Maybe because Victoria was different. She wasn't an innocent schoolgirl and she surely wasn't a rich, spoiled diva. She was just... Victoria. Pretty, fresh, honest and hardworking. Sensitive, knowing and proud, too proud to give in to the likes of him. And that's what he loved about her.

Not his average one-night stand. Not a one-night stand at all since she'd resisted that notion. But he knew she enjoyed being with him as much as he needed to be with her. Somehow, they'd have to get past the ugliness of this mess and find a way to be together. Somehow, he'd have to convince her that they should be together.

Remembering her harsh words to him earlier, he wondered why he'd let things get so crazy. She would leave as soon as she'd done her job. And that would probably be for the best. He stared out the window, the vast acreage of this land he loved spreading in front of him like a plush green blanket. He had to get his life together and get things back on track with this ranch.

Someone knocked on the office door and then Denny hurried in and glared at him. "You know you've done some low-down things, Clint. But this last one tops the cake."

His sister was mad. Nothing new there. "I got arrested last night but the other guy hit me first."

"I don't care if you rot in jail," Denise shouted, her finger shaking in his face. "But to carry on with that Victoria Calhoun and right under our noses, that's just low. Trish read all about it on some social media site and saw the picture of you two kissing. Now she wants to know if you and Victoria are in love."

"And that's a bad thing?" he asked before he could hold back the words.

"It is if my daughter sees it and thinks it's romantic," Denise replied. "You're dallying with a reality television producer and now the world knows that."

"What's so bad about me finding a decent woman?" he asked, his head pounding like a galloping horse.

Denny shut the door and glared at him. "This is just the beginning. If they keep digging—"

"They won't find anything," he said, trying to reassure his sister. "This isn't about my past. It's about right now and the future. Stop worrying."

"I've already lost enough," Denise said on a low plea. "I can't take anything else. I mean it, Clint."

He got up and came around the desk and put his arms on his sister's shoulders. "You aren't going to lose anything or anyone. I'll make sure of that. You hear me?"

She nodded, sniffed and pulled away. "You should have never agreed to do that show."

"I know that now," he said. "But I'm going to finish it and then it will be over."

"Not soon enough," Denny said as she headed out the door. "You might want to talk to Trish and reassure her that you're still a decent man."

That parting shot hit home.

Victoria thought he didn't care about anyone but himself and his sister sure thought that, too. Maybe the whole world thought that. But he couldn't take it if Tater thought ill of him. He'd have to explain things to her and try to make her see that no matter what, he'd always be around to help her and her mother. That he'd always love her, no matter what.

And one day, he'd have to explain to his whole family why he had this close bond with Victoria. But that would have to be off-camera. Way off-camera. And then, it would happen only if Victoria was still around.

Chapter 21

He found Tater in her room, headphones on and her feet tapping against the floral bedspread. When he knocked on the partially opened door, she didn't even move. So he walked into the room and waved a hand in front of her face.

She lifted the headphones away and grinned. "Hey, Uncle Clint. What's up?"

He glanced around the girlish room then sat on the edge of a ruffled cushion on a wicker chair and immediately felt too big and male to be there. He'd helped his sister and Tater decorate this room the week they'd moved in about a year ago. They'd repainted and prettied things up to suit her and he'd enjoyed every minute of it. Now he felt like a rogue stallion in a henhouse. He wanted to crash his way out of here.

But he stayed because Tater was looking up at him with that sweet smile. "So...did you need to talk to me?"

Obviously, she was as confused as him about this visit.

"Just wanted to see how you're doing. How's the boyfriend thing coming?"

She sat up and shook her head, her long hair falling like golden-brown silk over her shoulders. "I don't know. One day we're okay and the next Buster gets all moody and mad. One day Eric is calling me, mad because I went out with Buster and Buster is mad because Eric keeps calling. Why are boys so hard to understand?"

"You're asking me?" He laughed, his nerves jamming up on him. "I'm a boy. I mean, I was once a boy and I do know that men tend to think a lot differently than women."

"Mom says men don't have logical brains," she retorted on a pragmatic note. "But then, she's a tad bitter regarding men."

Clint swallowed back a reply and moved on. "Have you heard from your daddy lately?"

"No," she said, her hazel eyes changing from bright to blank. "I don't care anymore. I have Mom and you and Granny and Aunt Susie. That's all I need."

She needed a father, a real father. But Clint didn't tell her that. "You will always have us," he said. "Hey, your mom told me you saw something about me on the internet."

She grinned. "Yeah." Then she turned and scrolled down the page on her phone. "Here. It's kind of hard to see but you and Victoria were having a major make-out session."

"What do you know about making out?" he teased, his mind whirling with images of beating up scrawny high school boys.

"Enough," she replied honestly. "When I showed it to Mom, she got all bent out of shape and freaked out, of course. I don't see what the problem is. I like Victoria."

Surprised, he laughed and then glanced down at the photo on the screen. This image might be grainy and unclear but he could see the whole thing with glaring clarity in his mind. Remembering that kiss and how Victoria had felt in his arms only made him want her more.

"I like her, too, but I don't think anything will come of this. Just me, being me."

"So you're not really interested in her?"

Hearing the disappointment in Tater's voice, he shook his head. "I don't know. She has her job and I'm me and, well, we have fun but I don't have such a hot track record with women."

"But you could, with the right person, couldn't you?"

He wondered if that question was for him, or for him to answer so she could hold out hope for herself.

"I guess some people can find a love to last a lifetime. Your grandparents did." He wouldn't tell her of the heartache his mother had suffered because of his daddy. And he wouldn't tell her that his daddy was a hard, demanding man who made everyone miserable, especially his proud, spirited mother.

"They did, didn't they?" She got up and danced around the room. "I'm going to keep my options open for now," she said. "Since Buster and Eric probably don't even know what real love is, why should I get all stressed about either of them?"

"Good point." Clint marveled at her wisdom. "You're smart to play the field. You're young and you've got a lot of years ahead of you. You'll have heartache and you'll have fun and a few good laughs. And one day, you'll fall in love."

"And maybe get married, but that doesn't have to be the main focus. I don't intend to rush into marriage. I want to be sure."

He saw the pain behind that declaration. "You're so right about that, darlin'." He stood and she hugged him close. "Listen, don't worry about that picture you saw. Victoria is a nice woman and she only brought me home because I was too drunk to drive and since I was inebri-ated, I tried to kiss her. That's what you should be aware of—don't ever get drunk and drive and don't drink so much that you quit being a lady. Even more important, don't start drinking at all."

"I know. Mom tells me that all the time. I don't drink. And I don't plan to. I've seen what that does to people."

Clint wondered if she was talking about him, but then her father had a habit of getting intoxicated at family gatherings.

At least Clint kept his bad ways away from her. Or he'd tried. But having his image going viral without the real story to accompany it didn't help her, either.

"Smart girl, since you're underage. Even smarter when you come of age."

In typical Tater style, she moved on. "So you and Vic-toria aren't having a hot fling?"

He quirked an eyebrow. "I can't believe you just asked me that! We're just friends and it's complicated."

"That's adult speak for 'I don't want to explain this to you because I can't explain it to myself.'"

"You think so?"

"I know so. Mom tells me that all the time when I ask her about Dad." She made a mean-looking face and mim-icked his sister. "'It's complicated, Trish. It's hard to ex-plain, Trish. Wish I could make you understand, Trish.'"

Clint wanted to explain all of it to her but it wasn't his place to do that. His sister was very protective of her only child and the whole family followed that cue. He'd always maintained a safe, uncle-type distance, but maybe he should be more of a presence in Tater's life now that her father had pretty much abandoned her.

Clint would never abandon her or anyone in his family.

"You know I'm here if you ever need to talk, right?"

She nodded. "Mom says you're the worst person to give advice, but I know better."

He grabbed her and hugged her again. "Let's keep that our secret, okay?"

"Right." She laughed a bubbly little chuckle then turned serious. "Are you okay, Uncle Clint? I mean, you hardly ever come up to my room for a little girl chat."

"Is that what this is, a girl chat?"

She giggled. "It feels that way. I think you're trying to find your sensitive side. Maybe Victoria is good for you after all."

He kissed her on the forehead. "You are way too wise for your tender years, girl."

She grinned and went back to her headphones.

Clint was still smiling when he got downstairs. Susie was sitting in the kitchen, her fingers tapping on her laptop. Since he seemed to be making the rounds on visiting his family, he walked to the refrigerator and found a bottle of water then turned to smile at her. "And what in the world are you up to, Susie-Q?"

She glanced up and looked as guilty as a wolf trying to chase a lamb. "Me, nothing much. Just catching up on email." She closed the laptop and gave him a fake angelic smile. "So how was your weekend?"

"I think you know exactly how my weekend went," he replied, a vague memory of seeing her last night flashing through his mind. "Hey, were you at the Goose around midnight?"

Her smile didn't bend. "Maybe."

"Susie?"

"Okay, I was there. I saw the whole fight and watched them take you away. Impressive."

Clint stared across at her. "You are one piece of work, aren't you? What if the press had taken your picture, too? You have to be careful about this stuff."

"What would it have mattered?" she countered. "Isn't publicity good for the show? I should have rushed right into the fray and put up my dukes, too."

"Are you mad because you didn't get any media time?"

She shook her head. "Of course not. I left before anybody saw me," she said, as if that explained her obvious glee in seeing him being hauled away. "But it's the buzz online. You're streaming on all the hot spots."

"Streaming?" Didn't she care that their mother might see that mess? "You sound a lot like Victoria and her crew. Eager to get me behaving badly on tape."

Susie got up, her eyes wide, her expression animated enough to tell him she was happy for his suffering. "Isn't that the whole point of the show? I mean, I've been getting offers from all over the country and the shows haven't even aired yet."

Clint shook his head. "But I'm sure you somehow leaked a few scenes here and there, right?"

"I don't have to answer that."

"No, you don't. You've never had to answer to anything much. You managed to get yourself on the show and now you're taking advantage of that and my good graces to make sure the world sees your talents."

"Dang straight," she retorted. "Ethan thinks I have the 'it' factor."

"Ethan? What's he got to do with this? He's a cameraman."

"Head cameraman," she corrected with a toss of her hair.

"You need to stay away from him," Clint warned.

"The same way you need to stay away from Victoria?" she responded.

Clint stared her down until she turned away but he could see the triumph in her eyes. She'd sell her soul to advance in the show. Susie wanted to be a star and she'd stomp over all of them to make that dream come true. He stalked out of the house, anger and regret warring inside his still-pounding head.

"I can't wait for this show to be over," he said into the night wind.

Victoria had never wanted to wrap a show more than she did this one. She wanted it over and done with and through and finished. She wanted to find another job and start a new life as far away from Dallas as she possibly could.

But first, she had to find Ethan and see just how much spying and conniving he'd been doing behind her back. With little Susie by his side, at that.

Of course, he didn't answer his phone.

Tomorrow, she'd deal with both of them.

Tonight, she had work to do. So she poured herself into getting together the hot-sheets for the picnic shoot and hoped she'd be able to maintain a professional countenance in spite of the many variables of this subject matter. When her cell rang, she answered without checking the number.

"Victoria Calhoun?"

She didn't recognize the voice. "Yes."

"Could you verify your relationship with Clint Griffin? Are you two an item?"

"Who is this?"

"Are you denying that he spent the night at your apartment?"

Flustered, Victoria let out a gasp. "What? He did, but—"

"Thank you."

The phone went dead and she sat there, realizing she'd just messed up again. "No comment" would have been better, but the reporter would take that as a *yes,* too. It really didn't matter what she said, the press would take this and run with it and start all kinds of rumors.

Staring into space, she had a sick feeling this little scandal wasn't going away. She had to wonder why Samuel had set this into motion. She blamed it on Samuel and his need to keep the show alive, and Ethan and his need to impress both his boss and Susie. But shouldn't she blame someone else entirely?

Maybe it was you.

She'd deliberately gone after this assignment once Samuel had told her who he wanted for the show. She'd planned things down to the minute on getting Clint to sign up. She'd worked out all the kinks in order to show him in a bad light. She'd wanted to see him again and she wanted to control all the scenes and then watch him go down in flames.

Instead, she'd found out a few things about him she'd never considered before and she now was the one falling into the fire. He wasn't such a player after all. He was just a lonely, confused man who'd wasted a lot of time on frivolous adventures. But why? What was the real story behind Clint and his infamous acting out?

And how had she become *that* person? That person who went after others without regard for the damage it could do? She was the one who was suddenly burning out of control.

I need to find out the real story.

Her last hope in doing that would be when they taped the segments on the history of the farmhouse and took a crew out to the Griffin Horse Therapy Ranch. Clint's mother had grudgingly agreed to let them have a tour of the house. But she didn't want to be on screen.

"This house should be showcased," she'd told Victoria over the phone. "And if that means it has to be on your show, I suppose I'll jump on the bandwagon and go with my own agenda."

"I'll make sure the history is accurate," Victoria said. "I appreciate you allowing us to show off your home."

"Hopefully," Bitsy had responded in her high-handed tone, "this will steer you away from trying to figure out my son."

"I couldn't agree more," Victoria had replied.

But she wasn't so scared of Bitsy Griffin that she couldn't work around the woman's caustic remarks and haughty attitude. She would find what Clint didn't want the world to see, but it wouldn't be for the cameras.

It would be for herself. And for Clint. So she could understand the real man she'd fallen in love with.

Chapter 22

"I don't see how we can have a good Fourth of July get-together with cameras trailing you around."

Clint pinched his nose with his thumb and forefinger, Denny's displeasure grating on his nerves like a loose fence wire snapping against an old barn. His sister seriously needed to get out of the house more—with people who could change her sour outlook on life.

"I get it," he said, holding up his hand to stop her rant. "I get that you are not pleased with Susie and me being on the show. I get that you don't like Tater making cameo appearances on the show. But would you please just let me get on with today's episode. We'll have a few more and then it will all be over."

His sister put a hand on her hip and stared out the kitchen window. "It will never be over, really. We've all been exposed to your world, that world you keep around yourself to shield you from the real reality. The one where the rest of us have to clean up your messes."

Anger and lack of sleep poured through Clint's system. His sister had never seen his front as a way to take the heat off the rest of them. "Stop it, Denny. You haven't had to clean up any of my messes. You've never had to deal with the things I've dealt with and I'm tired of shouldering all the guilt you try to lay on me. If you don't like what I'm doing, then leave."

She looked so shocked, he regretted snapping at her, but there were things between them that needed to be said, that needed to be out in the open.

"Look," he began again, lowering his voice so the caterers couldn't hear, "I'm sorry and I know it's been hard for you, especially since James took off to parts unknown. But we're in this together. I told you the day you moved in that you and Tater have a home here."

The fear in her eyes made him flinch. "But you didn't tell me I'd have to deal with so many other issues, Clint. Do you know the real reason James left?"

Clint hung his head. He could guess but he didn't want to hurt his sister. "No. You never want to discuss him so I don't ask." But he had a pretty good idea.

Denny got closer, tears spilling down her face. "He couldn't accept the truth, Clint. He couldn't accept—"

"Good morning."

They parted and turned to find Victoria and her assistant standing in the dining room. Victoria took one look at Denny's face and motioned Nancy out of the room. "We'll be outside setting up. Just wanted to let you know we're here."

"Thanks." Clint stared after her, a million thoughts swirling like sagebrush through his mind. He really needed to sit her down and explain a few things.

But first, they had to get through this day.

He turned back to Denny and saw her wiping her face, a mask of grit and determination making her clam up again.

"Denny, we can talk later, okay?"

"No need to talk about this. You're in it to the end, but it's not going to end with this show. You've opened up a can of worms and we can't change that. You'd just better hope my daughter is protected. I won't have anyone hurting her, Clint. Not even you."

She walked off in a huff.

Clint whirled and headed outside, but Victoria was waiting just beyond the French doors. "Everything okay?"

"Define okay," he quipped, his tone full of a tiredness that zapped at his bones. "My sister can never relax and see what she's got in front of her."

Victoria's dark eyebrows arched in an upward interest. "And what does she have?"

Surprised at that probing question, Clint let the hot anger wash over him. "She's not part of the show, Victoria. Don't go looking for anything in her direction."

Victoria lifted her chin to stare him down. "I wasn't planning on doing that. I was asking you a question, as a friend. Off the record."

"Off the record, huh? The way Saturday night should have been off the record. But the cameras found us anyway, didn't they?"

Her eyes flared a deep green. "Are you suggesting I was involved in that?"

He didn't know. Susie had been coy but she'd practically admitted knowing he was at the bar and Ethan had found him and taped him with his little sister watching in the background. How many other people were involved in capturing that little scene?

Victoria dropped her clipboard down on the patio table. "You called me to that bar, remember?"

"I do, kinda. I was drunk."

"So you didn't really expect me to show up or you didn't really want me there? Or do you even remember why you called me?"

He was digging this hole too deep so he refused to tell

her he knew exactly why he'd called her. "I was drunk," he repeated to hide the scorch of needing her. "I do stupid things when I'm drunk."

She blinked back the hurt of that comment. "Yeah, and I do stupid things even when I'm sober. But you're right—we do have Saturday night on tape and we can use it." Then she picked up the pen she'd just dropped and tapped it on her clipboard. "I'm not the one who planned it out but I can't hide the facts. It'll come in handy for the rough cuts and then the premiere."

Clint wanted to fight, needed to pick a fight with somebody. Might as well be the one woman he couldn't figure out. "I can't say who got that ball rolling but it's turned into one big snowball, don't you think? A snowball in July at that. And I don't like it, not one bit."

"I'm sorry," she said, her eyes pooling into a deep green. "But this is what you signed up for and the stipulations of your contract are very clear. We can use what we taped if we choose to do so."

"Yep." He shook his head and laughed at himself for being such a complete fool. "Yep, you sure can. You can twist it and spin it and edit the whole thing to make me look even worse than bad. I hope you're happy. You've succeeded." He gave her a once-over then stared off into the pasture. "I'm the one who's been tricked."

Victoria didn't look so triumphant after all. "Let's just get this shoot over with, how about that?" She pivoted, grabbed her supplies and hurried off to boss someone around.

He'd hurt her and he hadn't meant to. But he was aggravated and confused and tired. He'd gone into this thing mostly because he'd felt an instant attraction to her and it sounded like a fun way to make some extra cash for two important things—his charitable organization and his young niece. Fun? Far from it. He'd get through this then get back to his life.

His wonderful, messed-up, mixed-up life.

Without Victoria calling the shots anymore.

Ethan sulked his way toward Victoria. "You know, it's hard to tape a family picnic when half the family refuses to be on camera."

"We're dealing with that," Victoria retorted, her mood going from dark to thunderous. And the skies looked the same way. "We pick up the thread with interviews and the scene cuts we'll use in the string-outs. I'll be depending on you to help me do the rough cuts on those this weekend."

"Got plans this weekend." His gaze shifted toward Susie.

Victoria glanced toward Clint's baby sister. She was with hair and makeup, issuing orders and creating frowns. But she looked as hot as the summer sun in her red swimsuit and sheer matching cover-up. "Ethan, let's call a truce here. You've got the hots for Susie and I acted inappropriately with Clint. Can you cool your jets until this is a wrap? After that, what you and Susie do is your business."

"And what about you and Clint?"

"What about us? It was never anything to begin with and it's definitely over after Saturday night."

"Right." He swung himself and his camera toward Susie.

Victoria whirled and found Clint right behind her. Had he heard that conversation?

His branding-iron-hot eyes told her he had.

"So we're over?" He moved closer but kept his tone low. "Before we ever got started?"

"You told me that the other morning," she reminded him. "But after Saturday night, I think you made a good call. We have no business together, whether we're working with each other or not."

"And by working, you mean as a couple? Or on the show?"

"Both."

He hissed a breath. "Well, it's all over the news that we're an item."

"We…were never an item, Clint," she said, thinking that was far from the truth. She should tell him the real truth. That her boss had been spying on them so he could get just such a shot to send to the media. "I knew the rules of this game and I broke all of them. Now I have to focus on getting this finished. After that, as you've already informed me, we're done. For good."

He nodded but the look he gave her was full of denial. "Got it." Then he turned and stomped off toward some of the people gathering for the cookout.

Nancy rushed up to Victoria. "We got trouble. The head of catering is having a major fight with Denise. She says they brought the wrong kind of fajitas. The man swears they didn't."

"I can't get that on tape," Victoria snapped. "Denise won't allow it."

"But the caterer will," Nancy replied with a smug smile. "In fact, he insists he'd like to be on air to promote his business."

"See what you can do with an on-the-fly interview," Victoria said. "Get a release and we'll see if we can use it in the string-out."

"Great." Nancy whirled to pursue this new thread.

Then Susie pranced over. "What is the matter with your crew today? I need some fruit water and I can't get anyone to bring me any."

"We don't wait on people," Victoria said. "You'll have to get your own water. We're in the middle of setting the scene."

"And if you want me in the scene," Susie replied, "you'll make sure I get my water."

Victoria was about to let the little diva have it when a shadow fell across the grass. Turning, she expected Clint to be behind her. But instead, she found Bitsy standing there with a look of disdain. Aimed toward her youngest child.

"Susan, for goodness sake, don't be a brat. Go into the kitchen and help Tessa make the water. You just have to cut up a few pieces of orange and lemon and add some sliced strawberries. I taught you that when you were eight years old. Now go."

Susie's bright red lips opened then closed. Her mother stood there, looking elegant in white linen and a matching red, white and blue scarf draped around her neck. Elegant and intimidating.

"Oh, all right!" Susie stomped off, teetering on her four-inch heels.

"That one has always been a lot like me," Bitsy said with a slight shake of her head.

"You?" Victoria stared toward the house. "I can't picture you throwing a diva tantrum."

Bitsy chuckled and touched a hand to her hair. "I was quite the pistol in my day."

Smiling, Victoria quirked her eyebrows up. "We'd love to see some of that in the show."

"Not a chance," Bitsy replied with a serene smile. "I'm a bit camera-shy these days as you well know. Let the kids work this out amongst themselves." She started to move on then stopped and gave Victoria a shrewd appraisal. "I don't mind helping you with the history, however. I don't want to live my life on camera, but I can certainly supply you with the facts. Maybe you could tape an interview of me doing that."

"Are you sure? I thought you disapproved of all of this."

"I did," Bitsy replied. "But this show might just be the incentive they all need to get on with their lives. And after sharing the history of our ancestors, maybe I can get on with mine, too."

Thinking that was an odd thing to say, Victoria wanted to probe a little more but backed away. Baby steps, she told herself. "That's the part I like about my job. It's all about watching people turn from broken and messed up to owning their mistakes and taking responsibility so they can move on."

"If only," Bitsy replied, her vivid eyes filling with doubt and sadness. "I don't like airing out our issues on a television show, but then I'm old-fashioned. I'm used to keeping secrets and carrying on with a smile. I only hope Susan won't be disappointed when things don't turn out the way she hopes."

"It's okay," Victoria said, not knowing how to handle this. "She has star quality."

"It's not okay but she's had the acting bug since she sang a solo in the kindergarten play. I find it distasteful but then, I used to want to be a country singer. Almost went to Nashville, but… I fell in love."

"With Clint's father?"

Bitsy nodded and turned to go.

"Miss Bitsy?"

The older woman turned back toward Victoria. "Yes?"

Victoria decided to plunge right in. "I do love your house. It would mean a lot if you're really interested in letting me interview you about the history of the Sunset Star."

"We'll talk. But as I've said, I don't want to be in on this show," Bitsy said, her voice tinged with the old haughty disapproval.

"No, ma'am. For me. For a documentary. I don't have any backers yet and I don't have a distributor. In fact, I don't even have enough money to be asking this. But I'm fascinated with you and your house and…the life you made with Clinton Henry Griffin."

"Why?" Bitsy asked.

Victoria squared her shoulders. "Because that's the real story behind all of this. And that's the story I'd love to show the world."

"We're rather boring, my dear," Bitsy said, but Victoria saw a trace of pride in her expression.

"I don't think so," Victoria said. "But you can think about it and we'll talk later."

Bitsy nodded, her hands folded over her billowing scarf. She turned to walk away and slowly pivoted back around. "You'll do right by my son, won't you, Ms. Calhoun?"

Astonished, Victoria took in a breath. "Of course. I try to keep my perspective with each story. I don't intend to lose it now. Not with this one, not with Clint."

Bitsy lifted her gaze and met Victoria head-on. "Good."

Nancy made her way through the maze of cords and electronic equipment. "What was that all about?"

"I'm not sure," Victoria replied. "But I think Bitsy Griffin might be warming to us."

"Well, that'll end after she hears what the caterer has to say," Nancy replied. "I got a great interview with him, hidden in the pantry closet."

"Hmm. Let me see," Victoria said. One part of her wanted to shout for joy, while the other part wanted to tell Nancy to erase whatever juicy tidbit the angry caterer had just revealed.

But the day took on a much more important tone in the next few minutes.

"Hello, darling," she heard a feminine voice shout.

Turning, she watched as Clint's face went pale and then crimson. He marched toward the stunning woman standing under the covered patio. "Marissa, what are you doing here?"

"I heard you were having a little backyard get-to-gether," the dark-haired woman said. "I thought I'd come on by and grab a Buffalo wing…or something."

Ethan nudged Victoria. "Tape or don't tape?"

"Tape. Definitely," she said, a sick feeling in the pit of her stomach. And she remembered that name from her research.

Clint's ex-wife was back in town.

Before anyone could react to that, Victoria heard a commotion from inside the house.

Denise followed a tall, good-looking man out into the yard. "James, you can't be here. Don't go out there."

"I can go anywhere I want," the man shouted. Tugging off his sunglasses, he scanned the yard until his angry gaze landed on Clint. "Where is my daughter? Where is Trish?"

And now, Denise's ex-husband was back on the ranch.

Ethan let out whoop of joy. "This is getting better and better."

Victoria would normally agree with him. But watching the shock and horror on everyone's faces, she thought things couldn't get any worse.

Only they did. It started raining.

Chapter 23

Everyone started running for cover underneath the large tiled patio. Victoria motioned to the crew to stop taping then told them to hold off until the rain stopped. The technicians covered their equipment but Ethan and the other camera people moved to safety and kept on roving around with one camera. She almost told them to stop, but this was too good to shut down. Of course, they'd have to edit heavily since most of the people involved didn't want to be seen on the show.

"Get as much as you can," she told Ethan. "We'll edit it down to insert into the rough cuts."

He nodded and discreetly went about his work. At least he was good at his job. All of her crew members knew how to handle anything from broken stilettoes to rogue Texas rainstorms.

She just wished she knew how to handle the red-hot cowboy who was the star of the show.

Clint's gaze moved from Marissa's triumphant smirk to James Singletary's glaring, anger-infused scowl. Being crammed on the patio with them was not his idea of good clean fun. And how was it they'd both managed to show up at the same time? He was beginning to think someone around here was leaking things to the press and to key people from his past.

"Well, ain't this a kick?" he said, giving in and giving up. He walked past Marissa and found the bar. "I'd like a beer and make it a long-neck."

One of Marissa's sleek brown eyebrows lifted. "I see you still like to solve all your problems with a bottle."

Clint grinned and saluted her then pushed a hand through his damp hair. "And I see you still know how to spend my money on fancy clothes."

His sexy ex-wife waltzed by him in her custom-made boots and leaned heavily on the bar then winked at the buff bartender. "I'll have a margarita on the rocks and put it on his tab, please."

The bartender grinned and handed Clint his bottle then went about making Marissa her drink. Everyone wanted a show so Clint decided he'd give them one. "Don't let a little rain scare you. Y'all come on in and let's get this party going. We got hamburgers, fajitas, barbecue and all the trimmings." He took a long swig of his cold beer then laughed and raised his bottle in a toast. "And later, y'all can skewer my liver on a spit and watch it fry."

"Clint, really," Bitsy said from her cushioned chair far away from the rain, a glass of white wine in her hand. "Don't be vulgar."

"Vulgar?" Clint moved toward his mother. "Vulgar? Is that what you think I am, Mama?" He glanced over at Denise and saw the fear and dread in her eyes. "Denise, how do you feel about me?" He finished the long-neck then motioned for another.

"Stop this," Denise said to Clint in a low plea. "And tell your friends to turn off those cameras. The last thing I need is James ranting on a television show."

Clint didn't care about the cameras anymore and he didn't care who heard him. He put a hand up in warning and said, "Oh, no. If you don't want him to be on camera, then you need to tell James to leave right now. This is my house and my rules."

Denise glared at him, a hurtful sheen in her eyes. "You're right, of course. That means you'll be the one to face the consequences then." She walked toward her ex-husband.

Marissa made an unladylike snort and took a long sip of her drink. "I can feel the love."

James Singletary advanced toward Clint. "Your rules? Since when have you followed any rules?"

Clint's temple throbbed with an angry pulse. This might be his biggest throw-down ever. But he was spoiling for a fight and he was tired of hiding behind a facade. Maybe it was time the entire world did find out the truth about him and his family, camera or no cameras. James Singletary would make a perfect punching bag since Clint had never liked the man in the first place.

He faced his ex-brother-in-law and grinned. "Nice to see you again, too, James. Where you been hiding your sorry self?"

"None of your concern," James said, advancing again. "I'm here to make sure you're not exploiting my daughter."

"Your daughter?" Clint tossed his empty beer bottle onto a nearby table. It fell and rolled but someone caught it before it hit the tile of the patio. "*Your daughter?* Are you serious? I mean, really?"

Denise moved between them. "Clint, please don't do this."

Clint looked past her at James. Wearing a suit in ninety-five-degree weather and now wiping the damp off that expensive suit. So typical of that phony, good-for-nothing player. "You are not welcome here so you need to leave. Now. Go on. You won't melt in that rain."

James stepped closer and took off his coat. "I'm not leaving until I talk to Trish. I heard on the radio about your so-called stint on some reality television show. This is low even for you, Clint."

Marissa bobbed her head. "Well, I heard about it on one of those local talk shows. Heard the warm-and-fuzzy Griffin family was throwing one of their famous barbecues—for the cameras. I thought it sounded like fun." She turned toward the cameras and beamed a smile. "I'd love to tell the world all about my years with Clint Griffin. Ask away."

Clint fisted his right hand. His knuckles were still swollen and cut from Saturday night's ruckus but he didn't care. He'd slug James and then he'd escort his ex-wife off the property.

"Marissa, I'm not sure why you're here but you can leave, too."

Marissa patted his cheek as she walked by. "Not a chance, darling. We're just getting to the good part." She found a spot off in a corner and curled up in a big, cushioned wicker chair, her smile more lethal than a cougar's.

Ignoring her, Clint turned back to his sister's ex-husband, who right now could do the most damage. "You don't need to worry about what I'm doing, James. You left my sister and your daughter high and dry. But they're here with me now and they're safe. So you need to either take yourself right back out of the gate you came through or—"

"Or what?"

Clint turned to find Trish standing just outside the French doors with a boy who obviously must be one of the on-again, off-again boyfriends, her face red with embarrassment, her eyes filling with tears. "What's going on? Daddy, what are you doing here?"

Denise pushed at Clint. "Stop this, please." She hurried to Trish. "Let's get you back inside, honey."

"No." Trish pushed away. "I'm not a baby and I want to talk to my daddy."

Clint looked at Denise again and saw the warning inside her scared gaze. Now he'd gone and messed up big-time. Facing Trish, he said, "I don't know if that's a good idea, Tater."

Trish rushed to James. "Daddy, what are you doing here?"

James held out his arms. "I came to see you, baby."

Trish hugged him tight. "I've missed you. Why haven't you called me?"

James looked uncomfortable and Clint longed to make him feel even worse. "I've been working hard, sweetie. Had some trips to make. You know how it is."

"Yeah, we do," Clint said, his nerves twitching like live wires. "We all know you're a busy, important man."

Thankfully, the rain let up and people started moving out of the stuffy confines of the patio. The awkward silence was soon followed by whispers and even more awkward laughter. Some party this was turning out to be.

Denise waited for the crowd to part and had a stare-down with Clint before turning to her upset daughter. "Trish, if you want to visit with your father, we should go inside. Remember, your uncle has a show to tape."

James laughed and smiled. "Yes, don't let us stop *your* work, Clint. I'm sure this is much more important than me visiting with my only child."

Clint had had enough. He pushed past Denise and

grabbed James by his loose silk tie. "Don't come into my house and act so high-and-mighty, Singletary. You know what you've done to this family."

"What I've done? Really?" James shook his head, his expression shadowed by disbelief.

Trish started crying. "What do you mean? What are you talking about? Let him go."

The fog of anger in Clint's head disappeared when he saw the look of terror on Trish's face. He dropped James's shirt collar and stepped back. Then he turned to Trish. "I'm sorry, honey."

Trish headed into her daddy's arms but the hurt on her face broke Clint's heart. He'd never seen disgust or disappointment toward him on that sweet face and seeing it aimed at him now nearly killed him.

"Trish?"

She ignored him and walked arm in arm into the house with James.

"This is on you," Denise said before she followed them.

Clint glanced around and saw the whole slew of friends and family and camera people and crew people staring at him. Of course he'd been the one to make a scene. Of course this was on him. He caught his mother's eye and expected to see disgust on her face, too. But instead, she lifted her chin in what could be mistaken for a gesture of encouragement. Or maybe she'd just given up on him, too.

He must have drunk that beer too fast. Heading back to the bar, he ordered another just to be sure.

And of course, Victoria and crew had captured yet another of his shining moments on tape.

Victoria didn't know what to say or what to do. She used to be good at her job, good in a pinch. But today, she felt as scattered and windblown as the tall pines bending in the wind on the other side of the pasture. Thunder rumbled a warning off toward the west but right now a steamy sun was determined to show its face on this dysfunctional get-together.

She scooted toward her assistant. Nancy loved the drama of their work so she was completely absorbed in the undercurrents moving through the crowd.

"So, I wonder how both of the exes managed to show up here at the same time," Victoria said on a quiet whisper.

Nancy cleared her throat. "I have no idea."

Victoria whirled to stare at her assistant. "Did Samuel have anything to do with this?"

Nancy giggled and covered her mouth with her hand. "What?"

"Right," Victoria replied. "You don't have to explain. I think I'm beginning to see the picture."

Nancy snatched at her spiked red hair and gulped. "I'm not sure what you mean." Then she jumped up and ran into the pool house.

Victoria didn't go after her. If Nancy had been told to leak information for the show, it wouldn't be the first time. He'd had Victoria do the same when she'd been a rookie. But for some reason, her boss seemed to be leaving her out of the loop on decisions that would affect the show. He was doing it because she'd been having off-the-record sessions with the star and because he needed to get everyone all pepped up for the premiere. He'd done the same before, but Victoria had never known him to go this far and to use her as a scapegoat.

She'd deal with Samuel later and it would be the last time she'd ever have a talk with him of any kind.

Clint's ex was still here and cozying up to the bartender. His mother was glaring at Marissa with a definite disapproving look. But she'd noticed Bitsy watching Clint with a new interest, as if she'd only just realized something about her son. What was that all about?

Clint was now having a water-gun fight with several "crashers" who'd heard about the party. Bitsy was sitting up in the shade with some friends she'd invited, whispering and exchanging knowing glances with the other ladies. Denise had taken Trish inside and refused to allow her to be in on the shoot. James was still with them, apparently berating his ex-wife regarding her parenting skills from what Victoria could glean from crew members who'd gone in and out of the house. And Susie was starring in her own sideshow, surrounded by several able-bodied young friends, a margarita in one hand and her blinged-up cell phone in the other.

Clint would glance over at Victoria every now and then, the expression on his face even more thunderous than the angry western sky. She pretended to be checking her notes but she could feel the heat of his scowl and hear the sarcasm of his flirtations.

Nancy finally ventured back out, a sheepish look on her face. "Samuel made me do it."

"So they didn't hear about today on the news?" Victoria asked.

"They might have, but they already knew." Nancy shrugged. "But no one coached them on how to make a scene."

"I've figured a few things out and Samuel knows I'm

not happy, but I'll talk to him again later," Victoria replied. "Let's just get this done and over."

Nancy looked relieved then glanced over the growing crowd. "At least we're getting some good footage."

"Is this their reality?" Victoria whispered.

"I guess so," her assistant said. "We've got enough footage here to put together two more episodes, but I'd suggest we save some of this for the website extras."

"Good idea," Victoria said, thinking the best thing for everyone would be for them to pack up and leave. "We need to get a release from Trish's father. I don't think he'll want to be involved in any of this."

"Don't be too sure," Nancy replied. "I heard him telling Denise he'd be glad to help expose Clint for what he really is."

"You amaze me," Victoria replied. Nancy was so good at subterfuge she could work for the CIA. And since Samuel had gotten things started, why not run with it? "Work on him but stay discreet. Denise is already upset with all of us."

Nancy nodded and leaned close. "Yes, and I'm getting these vibes about that."

"What vibes?"

Nancy put a hand over her mouth. "I think it has something to do with Trish."

"What did you hear?" Victoria asked, moving with Nancy underneath the shade of an old live oak away from the crowd.

Nancy wiped the water beads off a wooden chair and sat down. Victoria did the same on the chair across from her.

"James isn't happy that Trish is making appearances on the show, of course. But he said something about the truth. Something like, if this brings out the truth maybe we can all move on with our lives."

"Bitsy said almost the same thing to me." Victoria sure wondered what the big secret might be. "And what did Denise say to that?"

Nancy glanced toward the house. "She said everyone else would be able to move on, but Trish would be devastated."

"Trish? Devastated?"

Victoria had figured there was much more to this story, but her stomach twisted with a sensation that warned her of more to come. Why else would James put in an appearance? From what Clint had told her, the man had practically forgotten he'd had a wife and child. And what about Bitsy's odd remarks to her earlier. Did Clint's mother want something big to be exposed on the show? But why? And if so, why didn't she join in to uncover the truth?

She should be writing these questions down for a teaser commercial.

"Maybe they're using the show to do a big reveal," she said. "I mean, if something bad comes out on the show, the world will hear it and talk about it and then it'll be over. But that doesn't make sense, either. Denise wouldn't want that—she doesn't want Trish to go through that and Bitsy shouldn't want it but she seems to be shifting more in the direction of approving the show."

"We have a lot of variables going on here," Nancy replied. "I think James is here to get in on the action and gain a few fans for himself. He seems to have a real narcissistic attitude. But Denise is dead set against that notion."

Victoria thought back over the past few weeks. "Clint

wanted to do this show for a lot of reasons, but he kept going back to setting up a trust fund for Trish."

Nancy bobbed her head. "But they've got money, so why bother?"

"People with money always have a need to keep making more, but maybe Clint saw this as a way to make some easy money for a good cause?" At first, Victoria had figured Clint wanted to be on the show strictly because he was vain and self-centered, but after being around him and seeing him interacting with Trish, she believed he truly wanted to do this for his niece.

"And Susie just wants to be discovered," she added, watching Susie splashing with her friends at the shallow end of the pool. When she felt Clint's eyes on her, she turned back to Nancy. "They're all protecting Trish. Understandable, since she's a minor and things can get pretty wild on the show."

Nancy took the big plastic bow out of her hair and reworked her short spikes. "But we've kept things pretty calm even with the pool and bar scenes. The kid wasn't exposed to any of that. They won't even let her out of the house today."

"No." Victoria thought back over tidbits of conversations she'd heard, and in her mind pieced them together to form a streaming script in her head. Then her mind cleared and she looked up and saw Clint watching her, one arm around a blonde and the other holding his beer out of the water. Why did he have to keep giving her that bad-boy, I-dare-you-to-stop-me look?

"They're trying to protect Trish but I don't think they're worried so much about exposing her to the party life. They party all the time here but they do keep things pretty tame when she's around. However, they might be trying to protect her in another way."

"What's that?" Nancy asked on a dramatic whisper.

"Maybe they don't want the world to know *something* about Trish," Victoria replied. She thought about Denise's overly protective stance and how James had shown up because he was worried about Trish. Then she thought about Clint's need to set up a trust fund for the girl. "I have no idea what that something might be but I'm going to do my best to find out."

Nancy rubbed her hands together. "That will be perfect for the show's end-of-season cliff-hanger."

"I won't be doing it for the show," Victoria replied, her gaze on Clint. "Whatever it is, I want to know but I won't be the one to reveal it to the world."

And she hoped Samuel wouldn't reveal it, either.

Chapter 24

The rain came back and everyone either went inside or left for home. Bitsy was the first to go.

She got up and announced, "My son is upset and I can't tolerate his drinking. I've lost my appetite so I'm leaving."

Since her "just-family" Fourth of July celebration had been crashed by too many uninvited people and too much rain, Bitsy invited her friends over to her house for coffee and cake. Some accepted and grabbed umbrellas for the walk and some nodded goodbye and got into their cars. But everyone was discussing the new developments on the Sunset Star.

One of Bitsy's friends cornered Victoria. "I can't wait to watch the show. It's too good to miss anyway, but knowing what I do about this family—well, it's gonna be good is all I can say."

Victoria wanted the show to be good but that little twinge of guilt that had sprouted in her brain was now shouting at her to stop before someone really got hurt. It was for that reason that she didn't badger the excited woman with questions.

"I guess we won't be seeing any fireworks tonight," she said to Ethan as they watched the rain come down in gleeful gray sheets.

"The only fireworks going on here are inside," Ethan said, his ever-alert gaze scanning the yard from where they sat by the pool-house door. "Dullsville."

"And Susie left with her boyfriend an hour ago," Victoria pointed out. "At least you got them on tape arguing." She yawned and pushed at her hair. "What's the deal with you two?"

"We're done."

Victoria wondered about that. "A short romance."

Ethan lowered his head, his shaggy hair grazing his face. "Yeah, well, that little candle burned out once she started treating me like one of her lapdogs turned lackey. I think I see why she didn't make it in Hollywood."

"No talent?" Victoria asked, surprised that Ethan had admitted to failure.

"No, she can act," he said with wry grin. "But her attitude sure stinks."

They laughed and toasted each other with bottled water.

Then Victoria twisted toward him. "Did you know Clint's ex-wife would show up today? Or Trish's dad?"

He shook his head. "No. I was as shocked as you but I couldn't stop taping. You know, that train-wreck kind of thing."

Victoria believed him. "But you were tipped off Saturday night. By Susie?"

"Yeah." The guilt on his face told the tale. "She promised me she'd be there and that Clint would probably be in a really rowdy mood. Said it would make good television."

"And since when do you follow orders from one of the hired talents?"

His grin was sorrowful and swift. "I didn't follow or-

ders. But I did follow her. I wasn't thinking real straight."
He shrugged that confession away. "And when I got there,
I hated to miss such a good opportunity."

"Apparently, Samuel thought it was a brilliant move."

"So brilliant. I got a promotion but lost the girl."

"Welcome to my world," Victoria retorted. Then to
comfort him, she said, "So she left you hanging and did
a quick exit once the brawl started."

"She sure did. Didn't want her clothes or hair to get
messed up." He rolled his eyes. "Talk about spoiled brat."

Victoria snorted a reply to that. "I guess our little starlet only likes pool shoots."

"You got that right." Ethan stared out into the rainy
late-afternoon shadows. "Then when I called Samuel to
tell him what had happened, he asked about you."

Victoria could fill in the rest. "He wanted to know if
I'd shown up and if I'd left with Clint?"

Ethan nodded. "I told him you'd followed Clint downtown to bail him out. He wanted details."

Victoria looked down at her rhinestone-encrusted san-
dals. "Has Samuel known all along about Clint and me?"

Ethan stared off into the growing darkness.

"Look, it's okay," Victoria said. "I'm beginning to
piece things together. It's all happened as if right on cue
and since I used to do a lot of the extra research and all
kinds of spying, I can see why my little sideshow would
intrigue Samuel. But he should have come to me first."

"Would you have agreed to be part of the drama if
he had?"

"No." She let out a sigh. "No, and he knows that. From
what I can see, he probably knows a lot more."

Ethan got up and stretched. "Yeah, you might be right
there, too. Samuel's a smart man. Somehow, he saw the

tension between Clint and you just from watching the dailies. Have to wonder if he knows something we don't."

He turned, waved his right hand to her and headed for the production trailer. "I think I'll find someplace more fun to celebrate what's left of this holiday."

Which left Victoria wondering what in the world was going on around here. Had Samuel purposely shoved her right into Clint's arms? But how and why? She'd never talked about Clint to anyone at work.

Except Nancy.

She got up to find her assistant but before she could get two feet, Nancy came bouncing around the corner. "Oh, hi. We're all going out to find something to do. Wanna come?"

"No," Victoria replied, very aware of Nancy's evasive eyes. "But before you go, I need to ask you something."

"About the big secret?" Nancy asked, her tone gleeful and greedy. But her backward walk to get away told the truth. She knew she'd been busted.

"No," Victoria replied. "About our private conversation a few months ago—the one where I told you Clint had kissed me one night in a bar."

"Right. Okay. But I need to go and we might be way late."

Victoria sent her a direct-hit kind of glare. "I need to know the truth, Nancy? Did you tell Samuel about that night?"

Nancy clutched her purse and slowly walked back toward Victoria. The expression on her face showed remorse. "I let it slip one day when we saw Clint on the news. I thought it was sweet. I never dreamed he'd use it to lure you into bringing Clint on to the show."

Victoria's heart pierced and her pulse butted against her temple. "So Samuel knows everything?"

"Pretty much. He got all excited and brought you in right away." She shrugged. "But…it's all gonna work out, isn't it?"

Victoria let out a groan. "Work out? I've been accused of having an affair with the man. Samuel sent that photographer to spy on us. He's using me to create publicity for the show." She put her arms against her midsection. "I thought I could trust you."

"You can," Nancy said. "It just slipped out and I didn't think anything about it. I didn't even know Samuel was really listening."

"Oh, he was listening all right," Victoria replied. "Go on with the others. I'll figure this out."

"I'm sorry," Nancy said on a soft whisper. But she turned and came back to hug Victoria. "I think this is a good thing for you. The man can't stop looking at you."

Victoria stood silent as her friend walked away, but she had to wonder what good could come from her trying to expose Clint and having to dig deep in order to do it.

Her whole world was shifting right out from under her feet and she'd let it happen just so she could finally confront Clint Griffin one more time. And for what? Did she hope seeking revenge on a drunk cowboy would make her life better? Well, that hadn't worked out. She felt worse than ever about all of this. And now that Samuel had a pit-bull hold on this situation, it was too late to change any of it.

Clint's foul mood rumbled as dark and dangerous as the rain outside his office window. Marissa had finally left, but not until she'd told him in no uncertain terms that she should have been part of his big television debut. And not until he'd also told her in his terms that she would not be involved in the show in any way.

"I mean, I was your wife for three years," she'd said in the kitchen, her famous pout looking a bit tired and wrinkled in spite of the BOTOX he'd probably paid for.

"And you have not been my wife for three years." He couldn't help but add, "For which I am eternally grateful."

She gave him that look that begged him to just try and take her back. Only he didn't want her back.

"So why are you here, really?" he finally asked, as sure of her ulterior motives as he was sure of the sun rising tomorrow.

Marissa slinked her way around the counter. "Well, isn't it obvious? I've been waiting for you to come to your senses and since that apparently isn't going to happen, I decided, really and truly, that I wanted to get in on this reality-show stuff. You know I should be on this show with you." She puffed her big Texas bangs. "I love *Cowboys, Cadillacs and Cattle Drives.* Watch it every week. When I heard my own ex-husband would be featured on the summer episodes, I almost fell off my massage table. I could use a cut of that action."

And the "really, truly" speech had come out. It was all about the money with Marissa. "You weren't invited to this little shindig, sweetheart."

Her black eyes turned to a shining onyx. "But I could be. Think about how we used to fight and make up. The world would love to watch that."

Long ago, that line coupled with those come-hither eyes would have worked. But not today. Not ever again.

He thought about Victoria and her sweet lips.

"No," Clint told Marissa again. "Look, it's good see-

ing you again and all, but it's late and this party is over."
Then he escorted her to the door. "I gave you a big divorce settlement, thanks to your uptown lawyers. I'm not
giving you anything else."

Denise and her ex-husband came out of the front living room, where they'd been huddled talking for hours.
Tater had gone back upstairs with her boyfriend and her
door was shut and locked. She didn't want to talk to anyone about anything and she didn't care that she wasn't
allowed to have boys in her room.

"Fun times, discussing old times," Clint announced
to all of them. "Man, what a day." He thought of Victoria again and wondered where she'd gone. Probably as
far away from him as possible.

After a little more awkward chitchat and James threat-
ening all of them to back off of his daughter, Marissa had
left side by side with James Singletary. And they'd both
been making eyes at each other on the way out.

Perfect for each other, Clint decided.

When he turned back to Denise, she wasn't smiling.
She stalked away and then he heard yet another door
slam.

Victoria toweled off and got dressed in the most comfortable things she could find, a pair of black leggings
and an oversize baby-blue tunic. Barefoot and cocooned
in this temporary world by the soft dripping of a now-
gentle rain, she settled in to work.

But her mind kept going over the dynamics of this
family. Old money and eccentricities were common in
Texas. Everyone had secrets. But what kind of secret
would make Clint's family cringe in fear and fight against
any publicity?

Clint didn't seem like the secretive kind. His life was out there for the world to see and being on this show would only magnify that notion. So what was the big deal?

Trish seemed to be the big deal.

What are they trying to protect you from, Trish?

What are they trying to keep you from finding out?

She glanced back over her hot-sheets and studied her show notes and then went over the latest string-outs, the steady progression of the character arcs moving through her brain. Clint was the main character here and for the most part, he'd done what he'd promised. He'd shown himself in both bad and good lights. The audience would love Clint being himself. The man oozed cowboy charm and good-ol'-boy badness.

But in the moments they'd captured him sitting quietly in a corner, she was beginning to see what he was trying to hide. This was important because she'd have to find a way to bring it to the surface as the show progressed. This was the meat of Clint's conflict.

He didn't like being alone.

He didn't like the way his life had turned out.

He didn't want to settle down and yet he wanted to make sure his home and family were safe.

Especially his niece, Trish.

Trish.

It always came back to her.

Nancy had inadvertently mentioned Victoria's story about Clint and that kiss to their boss and had betrayed her trust, but Samuel had made the decision to use that information to bring Victoria and Clint together for the sake of a more juicy show.

Somehow, Victoria had to wrestle back some control over this situation. Now she wanted to delve into Trish's background because she needed answers for herself. Starting with Trish's parents. She didn't need Nancy for this, and considering her distrust of her assistant right now, Victoria decided she'd keep this research to herself.

She was about to do some online searches regarding James Singletary when she heard a knock at the pool-house door.

Maybe Nancy had forgotten the other key. Victoria thought about ignoring her. Let her stand out in the rain and stew. But she couldn't bring herself to be that mean.

When she opened the door, Clint stood there with a basket full of two beers and a leftover plate of hot dogs. "Hungry?"

She stared at the food and the drink, her mind warring with her growling stomach. "Uh, I guess."

He took that as his invitation to come in. "You all alone?"

Was that glee or dread she heard in his voice?

"Yes. The crew got restless so they went to your favorite bar to pass the rest of the holiday."

"You didn't want to go?" he asked, his gaze traveling up and down her, then moving all around the room.

"I thought I'd get some work done."

"You're always working."

She nodded, took the food and set it on the small round table near the big window. "Yes."

"Mind if I sit?"

"No." She motioned to the table. "We can eat."

He pulled out a chair for her then found his own. "Oh, I forgot this." He pulled a foil-wrapped bundle around from behind his back. "My mom's pound cake."

Victoria almost blurted "I think I love you." But she

caught herself and grabbed a hot dog before she could speak. "I'm starving."

"You always forget to eat."

Amazed that he noticed things most men wouldn't, she smiled. "You always manage to feed me."

"My pleasure," he said. Then he opened their beers. "So...are you still mad at me?"

"Mad?" She nibbled her hot dog and dug into the baked beans on the plate. "Why would I be mad?"

He took a swig of his beer. "I kind of told you we had to cool things."

"I've been telling you that since the beginning," she replied. "So no I'm not mad. I'm just confused and disillusioned and tired."

"I hear that. Same here."

Victoria didn't know how to handle a reflective Clint Griffin. "Look, I'm a big girl. I'll be okay. I've never had this happen before and...it can't happen again."

He leaned up and put both elbows on the table. "After the show is over—"

"I'll start work on the next one."

But that wasn't exactly true. She planned to turn in her resignation and maybe head to California.

"I mean," he continued, his eyes full of dark clouds, "can we finally see each other then?"

"I don't know." That was the truth. She didn't know at all.

"Not the answer I wanted to hear."

"I'm sorry." She pushed her plate away. "We've been forced here together and the situation gets intense sometimes. When this is done, you'll have other offers."

"From other women?"

"Well, yes, that, too. But, Clint, you'll be a household

name. You'll get endorsement offers and invitations to be on talk shows. People will want you to make guest appearances at their fund-raising events and at sporting events. You'll be so busy you won't even think about me."

"I could never be that busy," he said. Then he reached over and took her hand. "I don't care about all of that. I want you in my life."

"But for how long?" She pulled away and got up, her heart strumming like a guitar chord. "Thanks for the food but I think we need to leave things the way they should have been all along. Professional and friendly. We only have a couple of shows left to do and then the premiere. After that, you'll be switched over to the PR team and you'll be on your way."

He didn't move to leave. "Look, I know I've got a bad reputation but a man can change. I have changed. I didn't come here to talk about me and all that other stuff. I wanted to spend time with you, to hear about your childhood and your family."

Victoria's emotions bubbled toward an explosion but she took in a breath and counted to ten. "I grew up in a trailer park out from the city. My parents fought all the time, over money and everything else so they got a divorce. I don't have brothers or sisters to turn to. My mother lives in East Texas and I see her about twice a year. I have friends and a good job and I was content with that until—"

He stalked to her and pulled her close. "Until this."

The kiss was sweet and dependable and dangerous and dark. It was every memory she'd ever had of his kisses magnified into one big, booming need that rattled her far more than the distant thunder. She shouldn't need him this way.

But in her heart, she admitted and accepted that *this* was the real reason she'd come here. This was what had motivated her and driven her and held her. She'd worked hard to make sure she showcased his foibles and short-comings, but he'd surprised her by being a completely different man than the one she remembered.

None of that mattered anymore. She could see the truth. She'd wanted to be back in Clint Griffin's arms. But now that she had that dream conquered, it was destined to turn into a very bad reality. She couldn't tell him her true reasons for being here.

Victoria forced the rush of feelings away and stood back. "This has to end now, Clint. And we can't pick back up after the show. I'm sorry."

Chapter 25

A week later, Victoria sat with Bitsy Griffin going over the notes for their first interview about the history of the Sunset Star Ranch. After they'd talked for hours about the ranch and Victoria had pored over stacks of documents, old newspaper clippings and history books, Bitsy had called her to ask her about doing an interview for the next scheduled taping of *Cowboys, Cadillacs and Cattle Drives.* Victoria had readily agreed to the interview followed by a voice-over and a tour of the house. It would still be included with the Griffin Horse Therapy Ranch segment and together the two would make a nice bookend to showcase Clint's philanthropic and patriotic sides.

Victoria thought this episode would be the one she'd be the most proud of. She only hoped Samuel would see the value and agree. She wanted to bring the story arc full circle with the last episode, but she had yet to find anything tantalizing enough to end the show with the audience wanting more.

"I can't wait to have you on the show," Victoria said now, meaning it. "What made you change your mind?"

"You," Bitsy said with a serene smile.

Shocked, Victoria didn't say anything for a minute. She'd always liked Clint's mother, but Bitsy was forever amazing her and throwing her off course. "What do you mean?"

Bitsy poured Victoria another glass of iced mint tea and pushed a plate of finger sandwiches toward her. Then she sat back and gave Victoria an all-encompassing stare, her head high, pearls shimmering. "You really do seem interested in this old place. It's impressive and I believe it's genuine."

"Who wouldn't be," Victoria said between bites of pesto and smoked country ham. "It's amazing."

"You're one of the few to ever see that."

So she got points for liking the house, but Victoria had been around Bitsy long enough to know there had to be more. "I want to do a good job on this segment. We had a great time out at the Galloping Griffin Ranch the other day. When I put the two together, I think my boss is going to agree this shows a whole new side to the Griffin family."

She hoped Samuel would like this episode. Clint had taken Trish with him and they'd done a great job of meeting with the Griffin organization and taking the crew around the grounds. The few ill or disabled children who'd been going through therapy the day of taping had the choice of remaining off camera, but some of the workers and several of the parents and children had all vouched for the success of the program. She'd sent Samuel the preliminary dailies so she hoped he'd approve.

When this was all over, she planned to confront Samuel. She would wait until after the premiere to tell him she knew the truth about him going after Clint because she and Clint had a brief history. She'd turn in her resignation and after that, it was up to him how he handled that truth.

Meantime, she still had nothing to go on regarding whatever Clint and his family seemed to be hiding. Maybe she was imagining things. But if she was honest with herself, she'd have to admit she'd been stalling on finding this big secret. She couldn't hurt Clint or his family by exposing whatever they were trying to hide on national television.

And that was a new kind of thing for her.

"That's the other reason I decided to go out on this very big limb," Bitsy said, bringing Victoria back to the present and hitting the nail on the head. "I'm tired of all the negative publicity my son seems to generate." She placed some strawberries on Victoria's aged china plate. "My son is a good man but the world doesn't know that. He has a sweet but misguided habit of taking on the burdens of others. I'm hoping this show will show his good side, too."

"It will, if I have any say," Victoria replied. She'd seen that sweet but misguided side and she'd tried to capture it in bits and pieces to show the world. Scenes of Clint working with his ranch hands, herding cattle and cleaning out horse stalls would be interspersed with Clint playing as hard as he worked.

But right now she didn't want to talk about Clint or the publicity, good or bad, and especially with his mother. She and Clint had reached a silent truce of professionalism and polite courtesy that skirted around their feelings for each other. But the air between them sizzled like a live electric fence, making it hard to resist him. She had to get this done and get gone. It hurt too much to be around him because she couldn't be sure he'd be around for the long haul.

"I think people are going to be pleasantly surprised

about this show," she said, for lack of anything else to say. "Clint is so much more than a brawling cowboy in a bar."

"And that's the third reason," Bitsy said with a full-fledged smile.

Victoria giggled to hide her embarrassment. "I have to ask again. What do you mean?"

"I mean that you have changed my son," Bitsy replied, her fingers clutching her three-strand pearls. "I didn't see it at first since I was so against this whole thing. But the more I watched him with you and the more I saw how you seemed to calm him down, I knew you had some special way of getting to him. Maybe it's the interviews—mercy, we all need some sort of therapy and talking to, and you seem to soothe him in the same way our horse trainer soothes a stallion."

Victoria had to bite her tongue at that comparison, but her mind went back to the big black stallion in the stunning portrait she'd seen the first day she came here. Clint knew that stallion's restless spirit. Victoria only wished she could figure out what was making the man so restless. But Clint didn't trust her with his deep dark secrets and maybe that was the real reason she couldn't carry on with him after the wrap.

"He's relaxed and happy when you're around," Bitsy said with pinpoint precision.

So what was she now? A cowboy whisperer?

"I just listen," she said. "And I've been trained to ask the right questions."

Bitsy made a sound that came out like a dainty little snort. "You have, indeed. But it's more. Clint likes you. He's been in love with a lot of women, some good and some bad. But he's never liked any of them very much."

Shocked yet again, Victoria blushed and searched her

notes. "Well, thank you for saying that but Clint and I get along because we do like each other. It's a good *working* relationship." And she had to keep it that way. So she changed the subject. "Now, we've gone over the time when Fort Worth was just a mud-hole cattle town on the Trinity River."

Bitsy smiled but nodded. "Yes, as I said, my husband's great-grandfather Joseph Hoffman Griffin settled here and worked on another ranch until he could secure his own land and move his stock along the Chisholm Trail. Then of course there was the Mexican-American War and later the railroads and then the Civil War. Griffins were involved in all of those events." She tapped the stack of old documents and history books she'd suggested Victoria read. "I've told you most of it but you'll find details in there. A mess but I try to keep it all together. It's our life, good and bad."

"And full of life-changing events," Victoria replied, her notes crinkling the spiral notebook in front of her. A lot of life-changing things had happened to her on this ranch, too.

"This old place holds that kind of power," Bitsy said, her gaze moving over the pictures she'd displayed for the crew to capture on tape. "It's important to me that this is expressed thoroughly on the show. I didn't think I wanted it to be part of such nonsense, but it needs to be there. It's part of Clint's heritage, after all."

"It will be there," Victoria said on a promise. "I can't thank you enough for giving us clearance on this."

"A one-time deal," Bitsy replied, her sharp gaze brooking no discussion. "But I'll be happy to cooperate in any way."

"We'll schedule this for the next-to-the-last show,"

Victoria explained. "Then on the final episode, we'll probably do a montage of the two sides of Clint Griffin and end with some sort of cliff-hanger. In case the bigwigs want to bring Clint back for more in the fall."

Bitsy's serene expression disappeared in a mist of concern. "And what will ending with some sort of cliff-hanger entail?"

"I don't know," Victoria said, careful to watch what she divulged. "I shouldn't even be discussing this with anyone."

Bitsy took a sip of her hot tea. "You won't do anything to hurt Clint, right?"

Victoria swallowed her worries and shook her head, thinking that was an odd question. But then, Miss Bitsy always asked strange questions. "Oh, no. I don't intend to do anything like that." But she might have to fight to keep Samuel from doing anything too drastic. "It should happen organically from the segments we've already taped. We're done with the edits we've put together for the premiere episode next week. I hope you can come. The premiere party and private showing will be at the Reunion Tower."

"I might attend," Bitsy said, getting up to put away their dishes. "I'll try to convince Denise to drive me."

"Yes, the whole family is invited. It'll be a glamorous, exciting night."

"I'll have to search for the appropriate dress."

Victoria gathered her recording equipment and the papers and books and motioned for the nearby crew to wrap things up. "You'll look great no matter what you wear, Miss Bitsy."

Bitsy patted her hair. "Thank you, but I haven't gone to a fancy affair since before my husband died."

"I'm sure you miss him," Victoria said, unable to find any more words of comfort.

"Every day." Bitsy straightened the tablecloth. "A lot of memories in this place."

Victoria thought she saw a trace of anger cornering Bitsy's regret. Another secret?

She wondered if Clint's mother was lonely. Maybe getting involved in this history lesson had helped to alleviate some of Bitsy's grief and open up her eyes to the outside world.

Researching this history sure had opened up Victoria's eyes to the Sunset Star world.

Later that day, Victoria was back at the pool house going over some of the newspaper clippings Bitsy had loaned her. Most of them held articles about the Sunset Star, one of the largest working ranches in the Dallas–Fort Worth area. One of the first large spreads settled near the Trinity River. One of the first spots of land where oil was discovered.

The list went on and on. She wouldn't be able to use all of this for the show, but she could take notes and maybe come back on her own and expand her research into a documentary on Texas history.

She skimmed a couple more clippings then decided she'd go for a swim. It should be safe since she'd heard Clint's car driving off earlier. He must have decided to take the night to get away from the cameras. They'd resume production on the last episode in a couple of days.

When she picked up the pile of papers, a folded-up page fell out onto the desk. Victoria blinked after reading the cut-line: *Dallas dynasty to continue with the merging of two powerful families. Clint Griffin rumored to marry Heather Madison.* The article went on to explain that the happy couple had been dating for some time but planned to wait a couple of years to get married. Both planned to go to college, together if possible.

Victoria read the date then read the article again. Clint would have been nineteen and just barely out of high school. But he never mentioned being married before Marissa. He would have been in college the next fall. She stared down at the girl looking up at Clint and felt her heart bottom out.

The girl looked just like Trish.

Okay, it had to be the long light brown hair and the petite build. Nothing more.

She searched several more clippings but there was nothing about the actual marriage ceremony.

Had Clint been married before? Or had they broken up? Was this what they'd all been trying to hide?

She hurried to her laptop and started searching. She did a search of the Madison name and after going down a lot of rabbit holes, she finally got a hit from almost fifteen years earlier from the obit files of one of the local papers.

Heather Madison had died in a car wreck. It was dated almost a year after the wedding announcement.

Clint had lost his first love in a car accident.

How tragic, how horrible. Was that why he'd become so reckless and out of control?

She studied the picture again, the resemblance of this girl to his niece uncanny. He wanted to take care of Trish because she was his sister's daughter but maybe it went deeper than that. Maybe Trish unconsciously reminded him of another young girl who'd lost her life way too soon.

Victoria sat back down and started another search, trying to find any references to the wedding. Nothing came up but she might be looking in all the wrong places. Grasping at straws now, she did a search of Clint's entire family, each by name.

Denise's name came up. It was a birth announcement for Trish Madison Singletary. And the date was only three months before Heather Madison had died.

Denise had named her daughter after the girl Clint was supposed to marry.

Victoria sank down on the nearest chair. What was going on around here? Her mind was racing with the possible and the improbable. Her gut went with the improbable.

But before she started digging any deeper, she had to ask Clint. She owed him the chance to explain. Off the record.

Clint was in the den watching a Texas Rangers game on the big screen. The past few days had been a lot calmer than any time this summer. He'd had a great time with the kids and counselors at the Griffin Horse Therapy Ranch and the show's crew had followed him around enough to get some good material for the show. This was important to him and one of the reasons he'd agreed to do this.

That and Tater. She still wasn't speaking to anyone very much. Clint figured she was hurt by her father's rejection and the argument James and Clint had on the Fourth. His niece had never seen his bad side until that afternoon, when he'd almost slugged her father. He hated that but she had gone with him to the therapy ranch and after a few minutes with the kids and the horses, her mood had improved. Victoria told him things looked good for this segment of the show.

He watched the game, but his mind was whirling like that pitcher's arm. Fast and furious.

Only one more show and he'd be free and clear. It would be over. But according to Victoria, his life would change. He wondered if he'd be able to handle that bright spotlight that had been following him around for so long. Would the glare be too harsh now that he'd been through the show and all the emotions and angst that had bubbled to the surface?

Time would tell. He only wanted to get this done and get on with finding a way to have Victoria in his life, no spotlights or camera included.

"Hi."

He turned to find her standing there in the archway from the wide hall, her hair caught up but falling around her face, her T-shirt and jeans wrinkled in all the right places. "Well, hello there. I figured you'd be either asleep or out there swimming in the pool."

She looked sheepish. "I thought about swimming but I saw your Corvette out near the garage and knew you were home."

"So you only swim when I'm not around?"

"I don't want to be intrusive so I only swim when I think no one is around."

He got up and strolled over to stand in front of her. "Right." Then he lifted his hand toward the big leather sofa. "C'mon in. The Rangers are losing and I'm about to fall asleep."

"This can wait…."

But the look in her eyes told him it couldn't wait.

"How 'bout we take a stroll out toward the back forty. It's a nice night and the moon is shining so big you can see it grinning."

She nodded and waited for him to turn off the television.

After they'd walked through the quiet house, she asked, "Are you all alone tonight?"

Not with you here, he thought.

"Not really. Denise went up to her suite a while ago and Tater is still steamed about the brouhaha on the Fourth. I've tried to apologize but she's still being close-mouthed about it. I'm glad she went with us the other day, though. She'd so good with those kids."

"You and she are close," Victoria said in a statement.

"I think that's a given, yes."

"Why?"

Clint cut his gaze toward Victoria. "Why? Well, she's my only niece." His gut burned with a secret yearning to tell her the truth but...he couldn't do that.

When they were away from the house and out underneath the spotlight of that moon, Victoria leaned on the fence and turned to face him.

"You lost someone you loved long ago, didn't you?"

And then he knew she'd probably pieced it all together. But he couldn't be sure. Did he stalk back to the house and leave her hanging or did he trust her enough to tell her the truth?

She waited, her eyes wide and dark with hope. "Clint?"

"Yes, I lost someone I loved but... I gained someone else I love even more."

"Trish?" she asked, her question low and sure.

He didn't speak. Instead, he turned and gripped the nearest fence post and accepted that at long last he'd be able to talk about the things he'd held so tightly guarded in his heart.

"Yes. Trish."

Chapter 26

"You were so young," Victoria said, her eyes pooling a deep green. "I never found anything about the wedding, just a picture of you two at a party. It was in with some of your mother's papers. The caption hinted at a wedding one day. Were you ever married?"

"Bitsy kept that?" Clint closed his eyes as the memories swept over him like a dust storm, dry and piercing. "We'd planned to get married after college. A big church wedding with all the bells and whistles. Heather used to talk about it all the time. But when we did get married, we had a private wedding. Just the judge and our parents."

"Oh."

He looked down at Victoria's pretty face and accepted that she was exactly the one person he owed an explanation. And it had nothing to do with the show, or her job. He'd gotten himself into this fix but she could be the one to help him out.

"I need to explain," he said. "I need you to understand that what I'm about to tell you can't be repeated. I mean that, Victoria."

She nodded, her eyes big and bold and sincere. "I won't say anything to anyone."

"We were in love," he began, his breath hitching because he wanted her to know the truth. Not used to talking about this, he hesitated to even speak it out loud. "But we had promised our parents we'd wait till after college to get married."

Victoria stared up at him with that clicking, swirling mind of hers and then she let out a sigh. "But Heather got pregnant."

The memories he'd held hidden away for so long came pouring over Clint like a hard rain. How had he let it get this far?

"Yes. Right after we graduated high school. We told our parents we were going with some friends to a concert and we'd be gone for the weekend. They had no reason to doubt us, but we weren't with our friends. We got a room at a cheap motel and…well…it happened. We wanted to be together. Two months later, she told me she was pregnant." He shook his head, hung his hands over the fence railing. "I went to my parents and told them—one of the hardest things I've ever done—and they were furious, of course." He breathed in the warm night air, listened to the cows lowing off in the distance. "My mama was more accepting than Daddy. She tried to make the best of things, but it wasn't good."

"That's a lot to deal with when you're that young."

"It's still a lot to deal with," he said, wishing he could have a second chance. "They made us tell her parents and the next thing we know, we had some judge that my dad paid off to keep quiet, here at the house marrying us."

"But you never told anyone?"

"We never announced it but I think a lot of our closest friends figured it out," he said. "We moved into one of the rental houses near the back of the property that Mama and Denise fixed up for us and she stayed hidden for the most part. Heather had dreamed of this big

fancy wedding so she was sad and miserable and I felt
trapped and we didn't handle things very well. She went
back to her parents a couple of times early on but they
didn't want her there. Her mama told her she'd done this
to herself so she had to deal with it."

"But she didn't deal with it?"

"Neither of us handled it. We were in shock, I think."
He remembered the fights, the throwing blame at each
other, the feeling of failure every time he looked into his
daddy's eyes and the horrible regret each time he looked
at his new wife. "I started acting out by drinking and
hanging out all night with the bunk hands. That didn't
go over very well with anybody."

Victoria touched a hand to his arm. "What really happened? When she died?"

He turned, so glad to have this burden out in the open
he had to remind himself to breathe. "She left me but not
before she told me she didn't want the baby. Said she'd
give it up for adoption and we'd get a divorce." He lowered his head, stared at his boots. "I loved Heather, but
it was just too much. I tried to man-up, but at that time
I couldn't give her the life she wanted, the kind of life
she was used to already. My dad certainly didn't plan to
foot the bill so I had to work odd jobs to bring in some
money. Since her parents had practically disowned her,
she was in a bad way all around. I think she expected our
parents to support us or something like that and when
they didn't, she lost interest in being married and being
a mom. I didn't want to give up our baby. I didn't know
what to do because I didn't want a child of mine to be
raised by someone else. I figured I'd be okay. I'd keep
the baby and raise it myself. But my daddy had other
notions."

Victoria waited while he tried to form the words. "A perfect solution, he kept telling us. My sister couldn't get pregnant and the doctors had told her she never would."

"So you both agreed to let Denise and James adopt the baby?"

He nodded. "My daddy arranged the whole thing and Denise agreed. She couldn't wait for the baby to be born. They took Heather into their home so they could make sure she had a good pregnancy. James wasn't so happy about it, but he never really had a say. He did what my daddy and Denise wanted because he liked being married to a Griffin."

"What about Heather's parents?"

"They readily agreed to it. Nobody knew we were married or that she was pregnant. They told everybody she'd gone to Europe for a foreign study program and Denise was careful to keep her under wraps. Heather loved living with them and I'd go to visit, but it was never the same with us after she agreed to give up the baby. I went on to college and waited for my baby to be born. We'd have been better off if we had left for good but it would have never worked. Her parents have tried to reach out to us since…since Heather died, but my daddy made sure they'll never get close to Trish. They signed away that right in the same way they wrote off their only daughter. Never."

"So Heather gave birth and Denise and James took the baby?"

"Yep. Took my sweet little girl right out of my arms and walked away." He held Victoria's hand in his. "That was the worst kind of pain, promising them that I'd never tell her the truth." He put a hand to his heart. "It's a pain that has stayed with me, right here, for over fifteen years."

He thought about Heather and mourned her all over again. But when he thought about Trish, his little Tater, he lowered his head and thanked God she was nearby.

"Heather realized after we'd signed the papers that she'd made a horrible mistake. She couldn't forgive her parents or any of us for letting her give up her baby. She left me and went to live with some of her old friends in downtown Dallas. She tried to work at a couple of part-time jobs. She was taking all these pills and one night she just went out for a drive and never came back."

Victoria pulled him into her arms and hugged him close. "And you've had to live with that pain and having to watch Trish grow up, watching her deal with her parents' divorce and now, you're trying so hard to protect her. Clint, I'm sorry. So sorry."

Clint pulled back and touched a finger to her cheek. "I wanted to tell you. Wanted to explain why I held off on doing the show. But then, I thought maybe if I pledged the money to the two things I love more than anything else—my daughter and the organization she's been so involved with—then maybe I'd feel some sort of peace." He shrugged. "Who knows? Maybe deep down inside, I wanted the truth to come out. Only I never imagined Trish would want to be on the show."

"You took a risk."

"Yes, a big risk. And for what? More money? I rationalized that this would be money I earned on my own. The rodeo—set up by my daddy, of course. He didn't like me dabbling in songwriting, thought that wasn't tough enough for a Griffin. Even years later when I sold a couple of songs, he frowned and huffed. He'd pushed me and shoved me and forced me to give up my daughter and lose my sweet, terrified wife." He shrugged. "So I just went with it and drank myself to sleep every night. Then I got to hear his lectures every day until the day he died." He looked into Victoria's eyes and held on with all his might. "I'm still caught up in that loop. Can't seem to break loose."

"And you've had to hold back with Trish living in your home. Or is that the reason you brought Denise and Trish here?"

"I wanted her close by. I was so mad at James for his cheating ways and his callous attitude, but the man's had to carry my secret since the day he agreed to raise her. Can't blame him for hating that and the way our family held it over his head."

Victoria held him there, her eyes on him, her hand on his heart. "The world sure has the wrong idea about you, Clint."

"I don't care what the world thinks," he said. "I've let the world pick on me for years now to keep the focus off of them. I only care about...my...daughter. You can't let any of this come out in the wash, darlin'. I can't tell Trish the truth. Ever."

Still reeling, Victoria said good-night to Clint a little while later and went back inside the pool house. What should she do now? She was sitting on the type of scandal that could rock the whole state of Texas, but she couldn't tell anyone what Clint had just revealed to her.

Which meant she didn't have squat for a cliff-hanger that would draw viewers back for another season of *Cowboys, Cadillacs and Cattle Drives,* featuring Clint Griffin.

She couldn't tell anyone this even if she wanted to. This would hurt a sweet young girl and ruin her life. This would destroy a whole family.

And send your career skyrocketing.

She couldn't do it, no matter what.

But did Clint believe that?

He'd finally trusted her enough to tell her the truth so that meant he expected her to keep his secret. What else could she do?

Victoria poured herself a glass of ice water with lemon and sat down to go back over everything. She could beef up the conflict by editing down some of the interviews and B-roll materials. She could hint at some of the undercurrent in this family by pulling some of Susie's interviews and editing them to show Susie knew a lot more than she let on. That would bring viewers back, but that didn't mean Victoria and the production team would have to give them any big revelations if the show returned in the fall. They could come up with a new drama to throw in the mix.

And what about you? Are you returning in the fall?

She hadn't considered that. If she left the show, Clint might not want to continue. Or maybe he would and maybe they could finally explore the possibility of being together. But no matter what, she couldn't let Samuel get his hands on this information.

So she went back over everything again, searching for a tiny grain of intrigue that might hold the show together for another season. And then, it hit her with such clarity she let out a whoop of joy.

She'd found a way to salvage the show and save Clint's family from any more grief and public scrutiny.

Clint picked up the phone and stared at the caller ID. Victoria? At midnight? Didn't she ever sleep?

"Hello?" He'd left her two hours earlier, a sense of relief flooding through him since he'd told her that he was Trish's biological father. And she'd promised him she wouldn't use what he'd told her on the show. She'd also promised she'd never tell anyone what they'd discussed.

"I can't use it since you only told me," she'd explained. "It would have to come out organically on the show in order for it to even work. But I wouldn't allow that. I won't do anything to hurt your family or Trish."

He believed her.

"I've figured it out, Clint," she said now, her voice skipping excitedly over the wireless phone. "I've found a way to beef up the cliff-hanger without involving your family or…anything else from your past. Except this one thing, but it's a good thing."

"I'm all ears, sweetheart."

"Your songwriting career," she said, obviously very pleased with herself.

"What about it?"

"We can revive it. I know people who can help you, maybe get you a ticket to Nashville. The show can end with you announcing you want to write country-and-Western songs again." She let out a pleased sigh. "You'll have recording companies lining up to see what you've got."

Clint smiled at that, but his heart swung like a church bell ringing a warning. "That's mighty iffy, isn't it?"

"Yes," she said, "absolutely. And that's why it'll work so well on the show. Everyone will want to find out what happens to you in Nashville." She paused for a breath. "Everyone loves an underdog, Clint."

"We need to talk about this some more," Clint said, too tired to argue with her. Besides, she did have a point.

"I have one song I've been fiddling with lately," he said, admitting yet another secret. "I think it's almost ready."

"That's great. Perfect." She giggled into the phone. "I'll work on pulling up the interviews where you mention your songwriting and how you'd like to get back into that one day. Just enough to tease the audience here and there. In the meantime, you need to finish that song."

"Yes, ma'am," Clint replied, a feeling of hope coloring his world. "I can do that."

"We'll get together first thing tomorrow and go over what needs to be done for the last show," she explained. "I'll get the hot-sheets and scene notes all ironed out so you'll know exactly what to expect."

Clint hung up with a smile on his face. But this was a bittersweet victory. This was the surprise he'd been holding on to. He hadn't told Victoria that he'd written the song for his daughter.

Chapter 27

Victoria felt more positive than she had in a long time. She just might be able to pull this off and please everyone in the process. Samuel would love how she'd managed to set up the cliff-hanger by bringing in a record producer to surprise Clint and leave the question open on whether he'd make it in Nashville or not. Clint would be in a better place, knowing she hadn't ratted him out, and he'd get to go back to doing something he was good at and could be proud of—songwriting.

"I can't wait to hear Clint's song," she told Nancy while they finished up plans to tape the last episode. Everything was in place and Samuel had grudgingly approved it.

"I guess it's a plan at least, but we usually have something meatier on the season finale."

"It will be good," she'd assured her boss. "I'll drag out the drama. Country music is hot right now, Samuel. The fans will love that Clint has this dream. It makes him vulnerable and they can identify with that." She beamed a smile. "I can see trips to Nashville and the rise of a new star."

"Go for it," Samuel had finally agreed. "But make it work, V.C. We're counting on these episodes."

Victoria had worked double time to make this last episode cohesive and interesting. She and Clint had worked together but he refused to let her listen to the song. "I want it to be a surprise," he'd insisted. "The surprise I never got to show you before."

"A song?" She'd been floored by that confession. "You'd written this song already?"

"Yeah, but we kept getting off track. I wanted you to be the first to hear it since you encouraged me to take up songwriting again."

Victoria had been so touched, she'd almost cried. But they still had a lot to wade through before they could work on this thing brewing between them.

Right now, she'd settle for their late-night talks by the pool and him walking her to her door with a chaste kiss and a big smile. "I'm gonna miss you, Victoria," he'd said last night. "And as soon as this last show is a wrap, I'm going to ask you on a real date. Just us."

"But we both agreed it will be over then."

"First and only time I've ever lied to you." He kissed her again. "I hope you didn't mean what you said, either."

"I don't know what I meant. But I can be persuaded."

"And I'm so good at persuading."

She'd hold him to that.

"Let's go get started," she told Nancy now, her mood upbeat and hopeful.

They gathered their things and headed out of the pool house. Susie whizzed by with a secretive gleam in her eyes, causing Victoria to wonder what the starlet was up to now.

"Does she know her part of the script?" Victoria asked Nancy. She'd gladly turned Susie and her drama over to Nancy.

"She sure does," Nancy replied, waving to Susie. "That girl's a natural. Samuel wants to keep her around."

"I hope he wants to keep both Clint and Susie around," Victoria replied. "He does brag on both of them."

"Best season ever," Nancy said as they stepped around boom mics and equipment cords. "Last day for taping, too. It's been a long, hot summer."

"You can say that again." Victoria glanced over at the food table and saw Clint talking quietly with Susie. His little sister frowned but nodded her head. Victoria wondered what that was all about. Susie was as unpredictable as a Texas sky.

And that worried Victoria more than she wanted to admit. But Susie was already popular with their core fan base and that was just from the teases and commercials for the first episode.

Her unpredictable nature was born for reality television.

"You look way too serious," Clint said as he moseyed over to where Victoria was standing with Nancy. "Something up?"

"You tell me," she said, keeping her tone light. "Your sister didn't look too happy."

"She wants to bring a new boyfriend to the premiere Saturday night, but he hasn't confirmed the invitation. I told her to chill. She'll be the belle of the ball and I'm sure she'll be in love with someone else by the end of the night."

"You deal with more drama than you ever let on," Victoria said, proud of how far he'd come. "It's almost over, though, and you can go back to real life."

"And there's certainly no drama there." He winked at

her and got on his stool for what would be one of his last interviews. "Let's get this going," he said. "I'm ready."

But his eyes were on Victoria when he said that.

"I know the feeling," she mumbled. And of course, Tessa walked by and gave her a wide grin.

"We did it," Clint said later that afternoon. "Are we really finished?"

"That's a wrap." Victoria glanced around the patio and pool area where they'd filmed so many scenes. "We got your mother on tape for the historical segment and merged that with your Griffin Horse Therapy Ranch scenes." She touched him on the arm. "The scenes you did there with Trish are priceless. I can tell you love her a lot."

"I do," he said, glancing around. "And speaking of that, she's still kinda mad at me about last week. I need to talk to her."

Victoria nodded. "Okay." She turned away but Clint called after her. "Hey, don't forget we have a date. I know we have the premiere this weekend, but next week you and me—we're getting away from it all for a few hours. Are you up to it?"

Victoria remembered how adamant she'd been about ending things with him, but they had no secrets now. She wanted to be with him, to help him through all the things he'd held so close to his chest. And maybe she'd confess that he'd kissed her once, long ago. "Of course." She walked back and leaned close. "Let's just see how it goes after we're done here, okay."

"No promises?" he asked, his eyes warm with something that made her tingle inside.

"No promises, just…time together."

"I can live with that. For now."

He winked at her and went to find Trish.

She wasn't in her room, so he went over to Denise's suite. "Hey, you in there."

Denise opened the door, her eyes red-rimmed and wet.

"What's wrong?" Clint glanced around, looking for Trish.

"She's not here," Denise said. "We had a fight."

"About what?"

"She wants to invite James to the premiere. I think that's a bad idea. I don't even want to go, but she says they're gonna preview some of the other episodes and she wants me to see the scenes she's in. She wants both of her parents there."

Clint had to swallow a retort. "Let him come," he finally said. "He's the man who raised her, Denny."

Denise stared up at him with a frown but finally she let out a long sigh. "I guess he is. And it's nice of you to finally acknowledge that."

"I didn't have any other options," Clint reminded her, "but I'm glad she's always been close by."

"I'll let him know about the premiere," Denise said. "And, Clint, I'm glad you've been around, too. I know it's been hard on you, dealing with this. You might find Trish out in the stables."

He did. She was with the horse he'd given her for her thirteenth birthday. Peppermint. The little roan mare whinnied when she saw Clint coming. Tater stroked the horse's white nose and whispered into her ear.

"What you two doing?" Clint asked, so many things he wanted to say moving through his system.

"Nothing." Trish gave him a frown that looked a lot like her mother's. "Mom's mean."

"Your mom loves you," Clint replied. "We all do." It was his standard response to her petulant moods. And to cheer her up, he nudged her on the shoulder. "You can ask your dad to come to the premiere," he said. "I cleared it with your mama."

Trish's face beamed a bright smile. Then she rushed into Clint's arms and hugged him tight. He closed his eyes and took in the scent of sweet perfume and bubble gum. "You're welcome."

Trish lifted away to stare up at him. "I was mad at you, you know."

"I do know and I told you I'm sorry I jumped on your dad the other day."

"Why do you two hate each other so much?"

Clint had learned a lot taping the show over the summer. One thing being that he couldn't ever change the past. But he could try to change the future. "Because we are so alike," he said. "Your daddy and me, we make mistakes, but we both love you a lot."

Trish's dark eyes glistened. "Sometimes I just wish Mom and I could go home and we could all be together again."

"I know you do," Clint said, his heart cracking with that old wound. "I know you do."

"But I love you and Grandma, too," Trish replied. "Even Aunt Susie, sometimes."

Clint had to laugh at that. "I love her, too. Sometimes."

Victoria ran her hand over the long red dress she'd chosen to wear to the premiere of the first episode of *Cowboys, Cadillacs and Cattle Drives,* featuring Clint Griffin.

She'd gone to a lot of trouble to look nice tonight because she wanted Clint to be proud of her. She was very proud of him.

They'd talked on the phone most of the week.

"Can't wait to see you," he told her over and over. "I don't like postproduction if it keeps you in town."

"You'll see me Saturday night," she'd assured him. "And you won't believe how good the show's turned out, Clint. I've seen the first finished episodes and well, it's pretty good."

"I'm sure," he said on a laugh. "Since the hotshot all-around producer, editor and writer is the smartest woman I've ever known."

"It wasn't me," she told him. "It was all you."

Now she waited in the anteroom of the big hotel ballroom where they'd be showing the final product, hoping to see him before they went inside. All of the Dallas–Fort Worth elite, along with the lesser elite fans of the show, had come out to see the premiere. Or catch a glimpse of Clint and Susie.

Victoria nodded and greeted some network executives and then heard a commotion by the front doors.

Clint had arrived. Alone. But his mother and Denise followed him in. Then Trish with a somber James Singletary.

She breathed a sigh of relief. She'd expected some of Clint's socialite costars to insist on being his date. Apparently, he'd managed to squelch those requests and had instead brought his whole family. Susie sauntered in, wearing a white sequined gown, a new man on her slender arm.

But Victoria didn't give Susie Griffin a second thought.

She waited, her heart pounding along with the theme song of the show, and took in the sight of Clint in a tuxedo and crisp black cowboy hat with shiny matching dress boots. He'd never looked better.

When he glanced around and landed his eyes on her, Victoria knew she would love this man for the rest of her life. And tonight, after the show's premiere, she planned to tell him that.

"You look amazing," Clint whispered in Victoria's ear. "Let's sit together so I can hold your hand."

"No. I mean, we can sit near each other but you can't hold my hand."

"After this, you and me," he said, winking at her, his eyes doing that predatory sweep. "You and me, Victoria."

She couldn't wait. Everyone settled down to watch the premiere and as the show progressed, she breathed a sigh of relief. Everyone laughed in the right places and sighed in other places. The show that had started out as a close-up exposure of a burned-out cowboy had become a window into the life of a good man who'd had to deal with a lot in life. She was proud of her work and she couldn't wait to see the other episodes.

At the end of the first installment, Clint turned to smile at her. Then they went into the promos of all the upcoming episodes. She hadn't seen all of these since she'd been working so hard on getting this episode the way she wanted it.

But she waited for the teaser that would set up the very last show. She'd worked with production to hint at the big surprise Clint would share with the world.

But when the clip started to play, she realized something was wrong. Someone else had edited the clip.

Susie popped up on the screen with a grin and in a sultry voice announced, "This family is known for being rowdy and bothersome but what the world doesn't know—well, that's something no one will see coming." She did a mock survey, her hand over her eyes. "I predict lots of issues for the Griffin family on the horizon. And it involves a secret that my parents made us keep for over fifteen years." The scenes that followed included outtakes of the entire family but they'd all be taken out of context. Bitsy, Trish, Susie and even Clint were all in the strung-together outtakes. And it had been set up to look as if they were all keeping a big secret.

The voice-over encouraged audience members to stay tuned. And then the credits started rolling.

But Victoria didn't see the credits. She only saw Clint stand up, glare at her and exit the building.

Terrified, her heart pumping so fast she felt dizzy, Victoria worked her way to where Samuel was standing with some bigwigs.

"I need to talk to you," she said, her eyes scanning the lobby for Clint. He was supposed to be doing some interviews with the press.

Samuel gave her a big smile. "What a show. V.C., you have outdone yourself this time. Prime viewing. Prime."

"Who did that promo edit, Samuel?"

Samuel's smug expression didn't bulge. "We all pitched in. Had a lot of help from Nancy and Ethan and... Susie did a few extra interviews just to spice it up a bit."

"You shouldn't have let that last one make the cut. She's implying there's a big secret."

"There is a big secret," Samuel replied as he rocked back on the heels of his dress shoes. "One you neglected to include in the show."

"You can't do this," Victoria replied. "You can't. I promised Clint—"

"I don't care what you promised Clint. You work for me and you should have told me the truth."

"You'll ruin the whole family," she said. "You can't do this. You've tricked me, withheld things from me, used me—"

"No more than you've done to me, suga'. Now, I got to go. We've got a hit on our hands. Good job."

Victoria pulled away from his touch, disgusted that he'd done this without even warning her. When she looked up, she saw Bitsy and Denise leaving. Denise tugged Trish behind her and James followed close by.

Denise saw Victoria and gently pushed Trish toward Bitsy before she marched over to Victoria. "I will never forgive you for this. And I won't forgive my brother, either. I warned him over and over—"

"They don't know the truth," Victoria said. "They were just teasing the audience. It's not what you think."

"It's worse than what I think," Denise said on a low whisper. "And the very worst of it? You've hurt my brother. I'm not sure how he'll ever get over this if they do reveal what they've implied. I hope you're satisfied."

Victoria was far from satisfied.

Susie had betrayed her brother just to get ahead on television. But Victoria would be blamed.

She had to find Clint and make him see that she'd been the biggest fool of all.

Chapter 28

"Clint, wait."

He kept walking, the sound of his boots hitting the payment echoing as Victoria called his name again.

"Clint, please."

He turned, but only because he wanted her to know that he was done. Finished. Over. Because if Trish found out the truth, his life would be over. He'd lose the daughter he'd tried to protect and he'd blame himself above everyone else.

Victoria ran up the street. "We have to talk. I... I didn't know about Susie's promo piece."

"Do not lie to me," he said, jabbing his finger in the air. "I knew better. I knew I shouldn't have told you that but I trusted you. Trusted you, Victoria. I haven't trusted a woman since—"

"Since Heather," she said, her breath coming in gulps. "I didn't betray that trust. Your sister and my boss did that all on their own." She gathered a breath. "Clint, my boss knew I had a crush on you—from a few years ago when we met in a bar and you kissed me. He took that information and used it to get me to go after you for the show. And he's had spies all around the whole time. He set up the shot of us in my apartment. And there's more—Susie's been in on some of it."

He shook his head, amazed that she'd blame everyone else. "I don't believe you. Somebody tricked Susie."

"It wasn't me. He even got Aaron involved to the point that I almost had Aaron arrested."

Clint shook his head. "I don't care. If this gets out, I'm ruined. My family will be destroyed. And it's my fault. Me, Victoria. I did this, against my better judgment, against my sister's wishes. I did this. But I intend to get a good lawyer to get me out of that contract. It's over and I don't want to see you ever again. I'm done with the show and I'm done with you."

With that he turned and headed to the parking garage to find his car. But he couldn't help but hear the whispered sob echoing down the street.

"Clint, it wasn't me. You have to believe I wouldn't do that to you."

Victoria walked into Samuel's office the next Monday and gave him her resignation letter. "I'm leaving," she said. "I don't owe you two weeks' notice. I'll be out of my office by the end of the day."

Samuel took the letter and tossed it on his desk. "Is he really worth all of this, V.C.?"

"Yes," she said. "But that doesn't matter now. You and his conniving little sister and whoever else helped, you made sure Clint will never forgive me. He thinks I had something to do with that little promo trick."

"You did," Samuel said, his tone so sanctimonious she wanted to scream. "You wanted to do the man in and you had the perfect chance, but you choked. You got too close to the subject matter, V.C. So this whole blame game is wrong. You started this. You should finish it."

"Oh, I will," she said, his words smarting since they

rang true. "But I'll finish it my way, on my terms. Because I'm done with you and this show."

"You don't mean that."

She leaned over the desk and stared him down. "Look at me, Samuel." Then she turned to walk to the door. "This is me, leaving. For good." But she pivoted and held one hand on the facing. "Oh, you might want to consider this. If you go through with revealing anything other than what we've already taped about Clint going to Nashville, he will come after you with every lawyer in Dallas. Every big-ticket lawyer. And you know what that means. Our sponsors don't like the suits getting involved. Just something for you to consider."

Samuel didn't say anything but she took comfort in the streak of fear she saw in his aging eyes. Then he blurted, "He signed a contract. Iron-clad."

"And you think that'll stop a Griffin? Think again, Samuel. You won't win."

With that, she walked back to her office but turned at the door. "Ethan, Nancy, you can come out now. And you can fight over this office. I'm about to vacate it. Good luck to both of you. You're perfect for this job."

The whole floor of workers went quiet. Some people looked at her with awe and admiration but Ethan just shook his head and walked away. Nancy didn't even show her face. She couldn't blame them. Samuel probably threatened them or bribed them. Either way, it would have been hard to say no. She should understand that. He'd certainly persuaded her so many times before.

But she was done with that now.

She would find another job and she'd be all the more better because of it. Except for Clint.

She'd never get over Clint.

* * *

He'd never get over her.

Clint stalked across the pasture to talk to his mother. She'd been awfully quiet since that fiasco of an ending two weeks earlier at the premiere. But she'd summoned him. Probably to let him know how disappointed she was in him and this whole affair.

But his mind was on Victoria. He'd had such silly notions for her. He'd wanted her in his life. Had considered her as being the one who could heal his ripped heart.

Instead, she'd ripped his heart again. Old scars, new wounds. After he talked to his mama, he intended to get drunk. Alone. In his room.

Bitsy was waiting for him on the porch. "Clint. It's good to see you, son."

Clint wasn't in the mood. "Just cut to the chase, Mother."

"Oh, all right. Can you please come into the den? I need to show you something."

Thinking he'd get this over with, Clint abided. "Make it fast. I've got plans."

"I'm sure you do."

His mother. Ever the cool, calm matriarch. He followed her with a low grunt of impatience.

When she turned on the DVD player and he saw the credits for *Cowboys, Cadillacs and Cattle Drives,* he got up. "No, ma'am. I'm not interested in watching this."

"Sit down, son," his mother commanded. "This is important."

"Where did you get that?" he asked, steam rising in front of his eyes.

"Victoria sent it. It's the episode about the Galloping Ranch and our history." She motioned to a chair. "We're going to watch it without comment until it's finished."

Clint plopped down and glared at the screen. This was ridiculous. But he soon found himself engrossed in what he was seeing. The segments at the Griffin Horse Therapy Ranch were filled with hopeful parents, praising the wonderful care their children had received. There were bits with just Trish and him, talking and laughing and petting the animals. Quiet beautiful times with soft, muted shots of a man and a young girl, both involved in something they loved.

The history of the Sunset Star was thorough and poignant, with his mother doing voice-over and answering interview questions like a pro. He heard things he'd never heard before about his own home. And he saw things he'd been too blind to see.

"This ranch had withstood so many things," Bitsy said into the camera. "But love has held it together. The kind of love that doesn't keep count, that doesn't question or condemn. I don't always say it or act in loving ways, but I'm proud of my home and my children. My son, Clint, has been at the helm since his father died and I couldn't have asked for a better man."

When the piece ended and the room went silent, his mother turned to him. "Victoria didn't betray you, Clint. Your sister Susie wanted a bigger cut of the profits and she wanted more airtime. She's already managed to get a new contract for her own show next season. *Susie's Sunset Star,* I believe it's being called. She won't tell you the truth, but I saw it the night of the premiere. My own daughter, greedy to the point of selling out not only us, but her own soul."

Clint shook his head. "How do you know Victoria wasn't in on it?"

Bitsy gave him that disappointed look he knew so

well. "No woman could make such a dramatic observation on the good around here as what we've just watched and then turn around and send it all crashing down. She loves you. She didn't betray you."

He closed his eyes and let out a long sigh and remembered Victoria telling him she'd had a crush on him for years. He'd been so angry the other night, he'd put it out of his mind. Had he kissed her once long ago? Had he been too drunk to remember? He didn't know. He only worried about Trish these days.

"Did Susie tell them everything?"

"No, she didn't tell them anything but she hinted enough to string them along. I think that distasteful man Samuel has figured things out, but I don't think he'll make anything of it."

"He won't," Clint said. "And I have a whole team of lawyers who'll make sure of that."

"Of course." Bitsy got up and turned off the DVD machine. "I just wanted you to have the facts. Trish doesn't know what's going on and Denny will keep it that way. You need to do your part."

"And what is my part, Mother?"

"First, go and find Victoria and tell her you're sorry and you love her." She walked to him and put her hands on his arms. "And then, one day soon, tell your daughter the truth and let her show you that she's from good Griffin stock. Trish will be okay because we'll make sure of it. But I think it's time she hears the truth, but not from a television show. She needs to hear it from us. All of us."

Victoria was packing to go to Atlanta. She'd heard a documentary team there was looking for an associate producer. She'd applied for the position and had been called for an interview. Her flight left early tomorrow morning.

And not a minute too soon. She missed the Sunset Star, missed Tessa and Miss Bitsy and Trish and even Denise. She'd never speak to Susie again, but she missed Clint with each breath she took. To the point that she'd gone and sent his mother a DVD of the history episode. Would Bitsy show it to him? What did it matter now anyway?

A knock at her door startled her. It was close to eleven at night. But she headed to the big industrial door and stared through the peephole. At least she knew it wouldn't be Aaron. In the one kind gesture he'd done since she'd worked for him, Samuel had found Aaron a job down in Houston. He'd left Dallas.

No, it wasn't Aaron.

Clint!

She hadn't heard a word from him in the two weeks since the premiere. The first two episodes of the show had aired to good reviews and she had to admit, she'd done a good job of setting up the tension and Clint's character arc. She could see the subtle changes he had begun to make in the early episodes.

She could see through her tears that she'd been so wrong about him from the very beginning. But her heart was broken and wounded. Maybe beyond repair. Clint didn't believe in her the way she'd believed in him.

Did she dare open that door?

He knocked again. "Victoria, let me in. I know you're in there. We need to talk."

About what? He had accused her of the worst.

"Look, I went to your office and talked to Ethan. He admitted everything. It was all Susie's doing—her and

Samuel cut a deal. I'll get even with her later, but right now I need to talk to you. Ethan said you walked out, quit. Whatever. Just…let me in so we can talk?" Silence. And then he said, "Let me in or I'll kick this door down."

She clicked open the lock. "It's steel and heavy wood. You can't kick it in."

He pushed his way in and at least kicked it shut. "Then I'll die trying."

Victoria backed up but he stalked her until he had her in his arms. "I'm an idiot."

"Yes, you are. You believed—"

"I wanted to blame someone and you were right there."

"I'd never do that to you. You had to know that."

He leaned in, tugged her tightly against him. "I couldn't think straight. No, you'd never do that. And my sister won't get away with it, either. If Tater finds out the truth, it will be from me. Not up on a big screen."

"Good." Victoria stared up at him, looking for signs of alcohol. "You're sober."

"As a church deacon."

She had to smile at that. "Clint, I'm so sorry."

He wiped at a tear that escaped down her cheek. "Me, too. I rushed to judge you when it was my own kin doing the dirty deeds."

"She had a lot of help, a lot of persuasive tactics from my masterful boss. Cut her some slack."

"It'll take a long time to forgive her, but I'll make sure Trish knows the truth before Susie gets her way. If she thinks she'll be filming her new show on the Sunset, she's in for a big surprise."

"Good point."

He nodded then looked around. "Going somewhere, darling?"

Victoria wouldn't lie to him. "Atlanta. For a job interview."

"Oh, and when are you leaving?"

"Tomorrow." And she would go. She would. With or without him.

He nuzzled her ear. "Really now? I'm headed to Nashville tomorrow. What a coincidence. I have a lay-over in Atlanta."

Victoria's heart started doing a dance. A slow country dance. "Your song? You're going to meet with someone about your song?"

"Yep. I wanted to write you a song, but as it turned out I was really writing it for Tater. It's called 'Things I Can Never Tell You.'" He shrugged. "That's the big surprise I kept mentioning. It was supposed to be included in the last episode of the show…but it got edited out until the premiere for next season. Too bad they won't get their grimy hands on me or my song now."

Victoria's eyes grew misty. "I can't wait to hear it."

He grinned, pulled a hand through her hair. "Atlanta and Nashville aren't that far apart, you know. I can change my flight to go with you and then you can come with me. That is, if you want to do it that way."

She laid her head on his shoulder. "I'll see what I can do, but yes, that might work."

Then he lifted her head, a thumb on her chin. "I really need to kiss you. Have I ever told you how much I love your lips?"

Victoria laughed and shook her head. "Yes, once a long time ago. But you were drunk and I was young and stupid—"

"What on earth are you talking about? You really need to explain that to me again."

She tugged him by the hand. "C'mon in and I'll order Chinese and tell you the whole story."

He halted, stared over at her. "Is this the last of our secrets?"

"Yes," she said. Then she pulled him into her arms and kissed him over and over. "But just the beginning of this, cowboy."

And she remembered kissing him once before, remembered how that kiss had shaped her life because of what she thought he was. Victoria gave in to the love she felt for the man he'd now become. And she finally shut the door on the Cowboy Casanova and welcomed the real cowboy she loved into her heart.

* * * * *

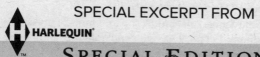
"Sorry," she said. "I just feel so helpless. Talk away. I'll keep my mouth shut."

"I don't want that." Then he caused her to catch her breath by sliding down the couch until he was right beside her. He slipped his arm around her shoulders, and despite her surprise, it seemed the most natural thing in the world to lean into him and finally let her head come to rest on his shoulder.

"Holding you is nice," he said quietly. "You quiet the rat race in my head. Does that sound awful?"

How could it? she wondered, when she'd been amazed at the way he had caused her to melt, as if everything else went away and she was in a warm, soft, safe space. If she could offer him any part of that, she would, gladly.

"If that sounds like I'm using you…"

"Man, don't you ever stop? Do you ever just go with the flow?" Turning and tilting her head a bit, she pressed a quick kiss on his lips.

"What the…" He sounded surprised.

"You're analyzing constantly," she told him. "This isn't a mission. Let it go. Let go. Just relax and hold me, and I hope you're enjoying it as much as I am."

Because she was. That wonderful melting filled her again, leaving her soft and very, very content. Maybe even happy.

"You are?" he murmured.

"I am. More than I've ever enjoyed a hug." God, had she ever been this blunt with a man before? But this guy was so bound up behind his walls and drawbridges, she wondered if she'd need a sledgehammer to get through.

But then she remembered Al and the distance she'd sensed in him during his visits. Not exactly alone, but alone among family. These guys had been deeply changed by their training and experience. Where did they find comfort now? Real comfort?

Her thoughts were slipping away in response to a growing anticipation and anxiety. She was close, so close to him, and his strength drew her like a bee to nectar. He even smelled good, still carrying the scents from the storm outside and his earlier shower, but beneath that the aroma of male.

Everything inside her became focused on one trembling hope, that he'd take this hug further, that he'd draw her closer and begin to explore her with his hands and mouth.

Don't miss
A SOLDIER IN CONARD COUNTY by Rachel Lee,
available February 2018 wherever
Harlequin® Special Edition books and ebooks are sold.

www.Harlequin.com

Looking for more satisfying love stories
with community and family at their core?

Check out **Harlequin® Special Edition**
and **Harlequin® Western Romance** books!

New books available every month!

CONNECT WITH US AT:

Harlequin.com/Community

 Facebook.com/HarlequinBooks

 Twitter.com/HarlequinBooks

 Instagram.com/HarlequinBooks

 Pinterest.com/HarlequinBooks

ReaderService.com

**ROMANCE WHEN
YOU NEED IT**

HFGENRE2017R

LOVE
Harlequin
romance?

Join our Harlequin community to share your thoughts and connect with other romance readers!

Be the first to find out about promotions, news, and exclusive content!

Sign up for the Harlequin e-newsletter and download a free book from any series at

www.TryHarlequin.com

CONNECT WITH US AT:

Harlequin.com/Community

 Facebook.com/HarlequinBooks

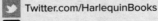 Twitter.com/HarlequinBooks

 Instagram.com/HarlequinBooks

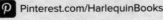 Pinterest.com/HarlequinBooks

ReaderService.com

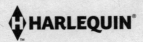 **HARLEQUIN**®

**ROMANCE WHEN
YOU NEED IT**

HSOCIAL2017

Reward the book lover in you!

Earn points from all your Harlequin book purchases from wherever you shop.

Turn your points into *FREE BOOKS* of your choice
OR
EXCLUSIVE GIFTS from your favorite authors or series.

Join for FREE today at
www.HarlequinMyRewards.com.

Harlequin My Rewards is a free program (no fees) without any commitments or obligations.

MYR17